THEN SHE
WAS BORN

CRISTIANO GENTILI

Translated by Lori Hetherington

This novel was originally published in Italian as *Ombra Bianca* by Ota Benga Editore.

This is a work of fiction based on true events.

A girl named Adimu, the protagonist of this novel, does not exist. Both Adimu and the succession of events narrated in the story are fruit of the author's imagination. However, every individual among the thousands of individuals with albinism living in sub-Saharan Africa—and this is a fact— has experienced at least some of the episodes the character Adimu faces. In this sense, and only in this sense, are the events in this novel absolutely and incredibly true.

Visit HelpAfricanAlbinos.com/en to be part of the first-ever Social Audiobook® project by lending your voice and spreading the initiative through #HelpAfricanAlbinos.

Eleven Nobel Peace-Prize laureates, including the Dalai Lama and Pope Francis, have lent their voices and support. Follow their example. It's free, it's simple, and it only takes a moment. **It is for a just cause**. The more who participate, the louder our voices will be heard!

Honest reviews of this book are necessary for our campaign. We genuinely believe that word-of-mouth is the best tool we have to get this story known and advance the success of this campaign.

We thank you for your support and cooperation!

THIS BOOK IS DEDICATED TO INVISIBLE PEOPLE

I fear you because you are different.

I hunt you because I fear you.

You are different, you are few, you are unearthly.

Suspended between two worlds, you are out of my control, and, just like the gods, you may be our blackest disgrace or the gold of our fortune.

And yet you cry and laugh as I do.

Are you, or are you not, human?

This is what I want to know. But…who am I to ask?

PART ONE

1.

The mother's body broke open to make way for the baby's entry into the world. Wild cries traveled beyond the sheet-metal door of the mud hut and into the crowded courtyard on Tanzania's flat scrap of an island. Ukerewe was a jubilant explosion of greens—from apple to emerald—framed by the rich blue of Lake Victoria.

Sefu—the father of the newborn—looked beyond the virile, though softening, sun. He considered the great bounty, the brawny progeny it had produced. That sun, too, would rest for the night. He imagined his son being born before the Spirits' sun sunk into the vast water. He thought of how everything was as it should be. It was almost sunset, and the cool air soaked in reddish light from the day's final rays. *Soon, too, our golden crown will shine, our own sliver of the starry canopy*, thought Sefu as he waited outside the hut.

More time had passed and the sheet-metal door remained firmly shut. It was the beginning of the rainy season so the weather was unstable and capricious. Sefu smelled the unmistakable scent of rain. He sensed that the darkness of night's first hours, assisted by monsoon winds, would coax heavy clusters of cloud that had been formed from the Indian Ocean. *Water will be dumped onto the land by the rise of the next sun*, he thought.

At last, the door to the hut opened. A woman gestured to Sefu. He could now enter. The courtyard grew quiet. He crossed the threshold, and the smile he'd worn since hearing the child's birth cries vanished.

He saw his newborn asleep on a bundle of rags in the corner of the room. His eyes opened wide, and he grabbed his hair with both hands. *This cannot be,* he told himself. His body stiffened as the tiny creature hypnotized him. He attempted to summon his finger to touch its belly, hoping this *thing* before him was but a figment of his imagination. Then, with its subhuman powers, it turned him to stone. She was a curse, a judgment. He repeated to himself the name of what she was, denying it at the same time.

The air in the hut was drenched in deadly silence. Only Sefu's breathing could be heard, and its rasp increased as rage filled him.

How could I have begot such a thing? he asked himself. He wondered if evil spirits possessed him while he had coupled with Juma. *Or maybe this demonic being is the fruit of another man's seed? That must be it,* he affirmed to himself. His wife had to have betrayed him and unleashed a curse by the Spirits of the Lake. His body could not have made *that.*

"It has to die," declared Sefu. Without so much as a glance at Juma, the mother of the phantom, he turned and left the hut.

LYING ON HER pallet, covered in brilliant-colored fabrics, her howls numbed by the murmurs of surrounding women, Juma registered this birth and her death as one and the same. She thought of how, in past seasons, she had miscarried two times, followed by boundless hemorrhaging that seemed to drain her soul and body. When she was with child this time, in her mind's eye, Juma had seen the fetus gripping her womb with its tiny fingers, stubborn and determined.

She remembered when news of the conception had spread across the island like wildfire over dry grass. She saw the streams and lake rejoicing and swelling beyond their banks. The trees had generated hearty sprouts, giving shape to longer shadows. The sun's light was clear and golden across the crimson earth. As her belly burgeoned, she trod the grass that grew greener and denser. She'd heard birds sing and caw louder than ever. The rain fell with the violence of gunshots. All of nature rejoiced with her, celebrating her baby's tenacity and perseverance. Her child would live. Juma knew that this time she would hold a crying infant in her aching arms.

And so she had. Though as she looked at what her body produced, she felt only scorn and disgust.

Juma was unable to explain what had gone wrong. She had diligently followed every directive given to her by the women of the clan. To ingratiate herself with the Spirits of the Lake, she had avoided arguments and malicious gossip. She had refrained from having relations with her husband during the last months of the pregnancy. She had avoided carrying water from the spring so that her child would not be born with water on its brain. And she had been faithful to Sefu—in body and spirit—a loving and devoted wife.

Yet she had borne this monstrosity.

If Juma had not felt it emerge from her own body—seen with her own eyes—she would have believed it came from another woman, from another clan, a wicked woman who deserved such a thing.

She seized the newborn with both hands and held it out to the midwife to calm its cries. The older woman shook her head; she would not touch this cursed *nobody*. Juma squinted at Nkamba—her mother-in-law, more ancient than even the midwife and shaped as a crooked shrub. She saw Nkamba's fear, and Juma wanted even more to annihilate the voice of that which came from her own flesh. In a fit of fury, she pressed the end of the swaddling cloth against its face. No one would blame her. She felt silent support from the ring of women encircling her and her offspring. However, the maternal instinct was stronger than Juma and—even though reason prodded her and she did want the child gone—she felt the cloth slip from her grip. She could not kill her own, however wretched it was. She drew the child to her left breast and felt it latch on and suckle with vigor. She recognized the lusty will of the thing that had inhabited her womb. Juma winced at the contact. From the corner of her eye, she scrutinized the tiny creature on her nipple, its pale skin against the dark flesh of her breast. *It has happened again*, she thought. *I've given birth to death. A white thing. If it lives, my husband will leave me.*

Juma pried the infant from her breast and set it on a bundle of rags in the corner of the room, farthest from the bed. A sweet scent radiated from the child, and it bayed like a homely pup. Overcome by fatigue and pain, Juma collapsed onto her palm-leaf bed, embraced by despair. Finally, she burst into a convulsive cry, clutching the bedding in her fists. That distant corner of the room was, for her, *the forest* where it, the nobody, would evanesce. The women surrounded her as Nkamba moved closer to the newborn, and one of them cradled Juma's clutched hands, murmuring soothing words as a woman had when she had miscarried.

Then Yunis, her dearest friend and cousin of Sefu said, "Juma, it is time to bring in your husband."

OUT OF THE stillness that followed Sefu's pronouncement and departure, Nkamba watched a stream of women trickle into the hut. Their voices trampled each other, echoing like the squawks of hungry crows in the cramped space.

"It'll have red eyes like the devil."

"It's a *zeru zeru*[1] with witchy, magical powers."

---

[1] Swahili for a person with albinism, meaning "phantom."

"Disaster will move into our village."

"Contagious hardship will follow in its wake."

"Listen: Before it's too late, leave it in the forest."

Juma, in a stupor, stared at the emptiness in front of her as the baby bellowed by the mud wall.

Nkamba observed the scene and her forsaken *mjukuu*[2]. From the moment she helped deliver her granddaughter, she had closed herself inside a remnant of silence, hypnotized with awe by the baby's indomitable spirit. Little by little, nevertheless, the comments of the women wormed their way into her heart like black mamba venom, reawakening a poisonous memory from tens of rainy seasons before. Nkamba's vision blurred; she lost her balance and dropped onto a stool.

Two women noticed her collapse and hastened to help her, flapping the hems of their skirts to yield a breeze on her brow, to give her much-needed air. When Nkamba revived, she went straight to her granddaughter and nestled her against her bosom. The others watched in shocked silence.

Nkamba understood what the clanswomen wanted her to do, expected her to do. She stared at the infant whose face softened and cheeks puffed as she rocked her to the rhythm of her heart. She thought of what had happened so long ago when she was a woman as young as Juma, and Nkamba decided the exact opposite would be this baby's destiny. She was disappointed by her son's cruelty toward one so helpless. She wondered how he would have treated his older sister. Nkamba slowly wrapped her *mjukuu* in a soft rag, which had been submerged in sweet grass to protect the baby's delicate skin.

Sefu hadn't yet been born when the event occurred that would change Nkamba's life forever; thus, he was unaware of her secret. And he was unaware of her oath to the Spirits when her only daughter was taken from her. One of her callous hands covered her belly; a rush of shame surged, and, immediately thereafter, an incredible strength purified her mind and heart. The Spirits of the Lake were bestowing Nkamba with the courage she needed to ask her son to spare the child. Or, at least, to convince him to call on the herd to spare her. With the tiny thing pressed to her chest, protected by a soft cloth, she left the hut under the gaze of the women, their necks craning to follow her movements.

---

[2] Swahili for granddaughter.

A BIRTH IS an event that brings together the entire community. Villagers, clan members, and strangers alike congregated singly and in clusters around the edges of the giant baobab, not far from Sefu's hut. A thick layer of cloud cover shrouded any hint of star or moonlight, and a deep, dead cavernous darkness hid the agitation that spread across the community from the affliction that had been brought into their sphere.

Nkamba spotted Sefu speaking with Kondo, the village chief, who had been Nkamba's friend from when she was a girl and belonged to the same clan as her husband, Kheri. If only Kheri had been home at the birth of their daughter, Nkamba's life would have been different. All of their lives would have been very different, she was certain, and Sefu would have an unshakable love for his newborn. Zuberi, the shaman or, rather, the witch doctor, with his darting teeny eyes, sidled up to Sefu and Kondo, adding a poisonous word, Nkamba was sure. He seemed to be always collecting information that he might store in sundry glass jars with acrid solutions or in wooden boxes. With her head held high, the old woman—baby soundly asleep and hidden from curious and hateful eyes—foisted herself near the triumvirate. Behind her son's shoulder, she touched his arm as she would have, so long ago, when she had been taller than he who was now such a colossal figure.

"Turn to face me, Sefu," she said.

Her son spun around, embarrassed by her public boldness.

"Give her one chance," said the old woman in a stoic whisper. "If you are the man who Kheri and I raised, the man who lovingly lowered his father into the earth and led him to his afterlife, you will not abandon this innocent baby girl in the forest." Nkamba felt the Spirits rise up her spine as she spoke.

Sefu was silent, examining his mother's tired yet animated face.

"Follow the example of our neighbors, the Masai," she continued, holding his gaze. "Tomorrow, at dawn, place the baby on the ground in front of the gate where the community herd is kept. Let the beasts decide her fate. If the cattle trample her to death as they leave their pen, that is her destiny; if she survives, I will raise her."

Sefu took his eyes off his mother. He let them travel toward the treetops. Then they veered down to Kondo and Zuberi, who were silent during Nkamba's appeal. Finally, he gazed into the crowd that had gathered and were meandering all the way from the hut to the sprawling tree. Sefu looked to the elders of the clan—Kondo and Zuberi—as though for a solution. Kondo's placid expression was one quite familiar to Nkamba, while

Zuberi appeared anything but serene. The deep crease between Zuberi's eyes twitched as though, Nkamba thought, in his mind he was concocting a muddy potion from the chaos of the situation.

Finally Sefu spoke: "This evil spirit cannot be my daughter." He turned his back to his mother and continued his conversation with the elders of the clan.

"But she is." Nkamba held up the child in front of him, forcing him to look at her. The baby hiccupped, inhaling too much air. "First she is the daughter of God and the Spirits of the Lake. Like every child is. And after that, she is your daughter."

The elderly woman had doubts about allowing a herd of cattle to decide the fate of the newborn, but that custom was her granddaughter's only alternative to imminent death in the forest, so Nkamba grabbed it. Like everyone in her tribe, she believed in the Spirits of the Lake. Those Spirits asserted that a *zeru zeru* be left to perish in the heart of the forest. She also believed, though, in the words of Father Andrew who, during Sunday Mass, spoke of a God who loved all living things indiscriminately. Nkamba saw God's love flow through this angelic soul that she cradled in her arms, and Father Andrew's God wanted the baby to live.

"I will consider it," concluded Sefu.

A murmur of incredulity snaked its way among the villagers. Each of them had something to say, and soon voices rose, not in conversation but as individual threads that wove into the voice of the land.

"The birth of a white shadow is a bad sign," declared a young fisherman on the fringes of the crowd.

"*Zeru zerus* must be left in the forest from the moment of birth as an offering to the Spirits."

"That is how it has always been. She has to die alone, far from the community."

"The entire population benefits when she is sacrificed to the Spirits—wealth and riches," added an elderly man, waving his staff in the air.

"Why is she so different?" asked a boy whose legs were so long and thin he looked like a gazelle. He was in that in-between age when childhood gives way to adolescence.

"It's obvious," said one adult. "So that she who is sacrificed for the well-being of the community can be easily recognized among the newborns. Though traditional sacrifice should be avoided. If the police find out, they'll arrest us."

"Well, then, what do we do?" asked the boy.

"We protect the father who allows the *zeru zeru* to die in the forest or who poisons it."

The boy nodded with gravity.

"We have a lot of problems," muttered a snaggletooth fisherman in an I ♥ NY T-shirt. "We haven't caught many fish lately, and the rice and cassava harvests are increasingly scarce. A limb of a *zeru zeru* woven into a net will make it impossible for fish to hide." Nkamba was aware that the fisherman had many worries of late. His fifth child had been recently born, and the family was always short of food, keeping him awake with worry at night, his wife had told her.

"If that thing is allowed to live, we'll have even worse luck. Let's get it the second it's dead so we can make amulets."

"While it's still alive!" cried one of the elders. "Everyone knows an *embulamaro*[3] vanishes at death."

A tall man, thin like a brittle branch and with pinhole eyes, approached the group. He had been standing on the sidelines up until then, silent and preoccupied.

"Listen to me!" he said, loud enough for everyone to hear. "You know if we can recover it while it's still living, the disgrace of its birth will transform into bounty, bringing us wealth and good fortune. Through its body, gold will rise! And when it's old enough, our village will have our own cure for AIDS."

Several of the men nodded, others whispered, and a growing hum emanated around the baobab.

Sefu gazed at the ground, his left eye dominated by a nervous twitch. Though Sefu was of large stature, some part of him was always moving, like a boat being bounced on the lake when the waters were choppy.

Zuberi seemed to take in that the new father had lost his bearings. He looked to the village chief and capitalized on Kondo's inertia by grasping Sefu's hands, snaring his eyes and attention. Like the tall thin man, Zuberi saw an opportunity staring him in the face. "Let the Spirits of the Lake decide through the beasts."

The baby's father inhaled with resignation. After the shaman had spoken, he had to obey.

One of the clansmen crowding around the tree also let out an expression

---

[3] Another Swahili term used to indicate a person with albinism, the prefix *embu-* is used to indicate animals.

of irritation when he heard Zuberi had decided to abide by the old woman's request.

Nkamba was amazed that Zuberi, not Kondo, had taken her side. *One never knows through whom the Spirits will speak*, she thought, *and that the words came from Zuberi, a self-important dolt, only reinforces that the Spirits of the Lake are protecting my mjukuu.* Swaddling the baby, Nkamba quickly withdrew from the crowd and returned to the hut.

As she opened the sheet-metal door, Nkamba ordered the loiterers out, protecting the babe in her arms.

The stream of women left without saying a word. One of them, however, the daughter of Nkamba's sister and a longtime friend of Juma, stayed behind.

2.

Since Yunis was of childbearing age, it was possible the taint of the birth would cling to her, curse her own future children. To protect her progeny, she knew she had to follow tradition. Yet, since the time she and Juma were children, the two had been inseparable, together taking the sheep and goats to graze. Not having a sister, Yunis took Juma as hers. Though they were born in different rainy seasons, they seemed to have a common destiny, at least until nine months before. As girls, they learned from Yunis's mother—side by side—how to sew and mend clothing. They both grew to be tailors. When they married, they shared the dream of having a home full of children. Then Juma had conceived but Yunis had not. When Juma's first pains came and she was certain this one would be born, Yunis felt like a dry stream. *Why can't I have children?* she had cried as she watched her friend's belly grow, repeating the whine to herself while attending the birth.

When she saw that the creature was not a baby but a *zeru zeru*, Yunis felt dismay and relief. Certainly it was better to wait many rainy seasons before conceiving, she told herself, than to give birth to a disgrace.

As a young woman of the clan, she had to follow the custom to ward off a similar disaster from striking her. However, a sense of guilt and fear of offending Juma and harming their friendship made her hesitant to go through with it.

The last of her qualms were brushed aside when one of the old women of the clan said before stepping out of the hut, "You have to do it. You belong to Sefu's clan. The spell will latch onto you all the more."

Juma will understand, Yunis told herself. This is how it's always been done. *Juma would not want me to suffer the same disgrace.*

She stared at her friend's belly in silence. Then she sipped some water to rinse her mouth, and she began: "Wretched *zeru zeru*." She spat with force at Juma, aiming directly for her navel with the intent of poisoning the root of the evil. She tilted back her head and spat a second time and then a third, as though she were releasing a scream of pain. And she continued to spit until she had no more saliva. Then she left the room.

NKAMBA SPENT THE night praying to the Spirits of the Lake and to Father Andrew's God—the God known as both the beginning and the end, the God with power over every human being.

"You give and take away, You create and destroy. Mungu, Mulungu, Ruwa, and Ishwaga,[4] Creator of the universe, of man, of woman, of the trees, the mountains, rivers, lakes, and animals, the rain and the dawn, Jesus Christ our savior. Every element is Your representative on Earth and reflects Your face. If something does not go well, it is because You are angry with man; every event occurs because You—Mungu—desire it. You were yesterday, You are today, and You will be tomorrow. You are pure, infallible, and wise."

Thus, Nkamba prayed. Thus, Nkamba reminded the Spirits of the Lake of her long-ago oath. The baby, however, cried and cried in her grandmother's arms before finally falling asleep, exhausted and hungry.

In the dark of night the old woman, crept to the pen where the cattle were kept, each one known to her by name. She stayed there only long enough to collect some urine from a cow to dampen a rag.

"This way you will recognize her as one of your own and do her no harm," Nkamba whispered, perhaps to convince herself.

THE SUN SHIMMERED pink on the eastern horizon the next morning. Nkamba, in her house, pinched the baby's arm fiercely and released the flesh just before damaging it. She wanted to make her scream. The infant needed to be heard—and heard well—by the animals in the pen. Nkamba said another prayer, and then wrapped the baby in the damp rag and left to take her granddaughter to the ritual that would determine all of their fates.

---

[4] Some names used in Swahili to indicate God.

3.

In the presence of the head of the village, along with the witch doctor, members of the tribe, and others who had gathered to witness the event, Nkamba set the yelling bundle on the ground, right in front of the pen's gate. She asked her son if she could be the one to open it. After a nod, Sefu waited, a motionless ebony statue against a gray sky that threatened rain. Most of the villagers hoped to see the hooves of the milk cows trample the newborn and, thus, ward off the curse that risked destroying their island world.

Nkamba observed her son out of the corner of her eye. If the baby was trampled, she would mourn for Sefu as well as for her grandchild. The evil that lived in her boy and allowed him to let his daughter die would condemn him to the same destiny that Nkamba had suffered. *Kheri would have behaved differently,* she told herself. She remembered the day he returned from Mwanza at the beginning of the long rains, all those years ago. When he had heard what had happened in his absence, he held Nkamba all night long, and together they cried and mourned and prayed.

She opened the gate.

The beasts bellowed and moaned and crowded the pen's entryway. They were restless and impatient to free themselves from the enclosure.

The first cow trod forward with uncertain steps. The animal lowered its muzzle toward the infant, obstructing the others behind it. It sniffed at the bundle and stepped over it. The second and then the third cow distinguished the presence of a living thing on the ground and sidestepped it too.

The pressure of the herd behind the few beasts that were loose began to build. They bellowed more and bucked, causing a frenzy as they jostled through the gate. The stench and the dust generated by the herd obscured the infant. Many hooves pounded the earth, one landing violently on the bundle. Nkamba held her breath; she had done all she could. The rest of the villagers were straining to see signs of life in the small bundle that the cattle had now passed. The din of the cows receded. In the distance, a crack of thunder sounded. A silence from the crowd of spectators could be felt by Nkamba.

Then, out of the hush, an acute and distressing cry from the tiny creature issued forth. A small white arm broke free and waved in the air.

Nkamba felt her heart do a flip. She was alive! Her granddaughter had survived certain death on her first day of life. The old woman looked at Sefu. Her son nodded, and she rushed to pick up her grandchild.

The baby cried and thrashed about. Nkamba held her tight, rocking her in the way a shell and its mollusk are moved by the rhythm of waves on the lake. The newborn had escaped her first threat, though Nkamba knew the dangers of life would never be over for her.

"What will become of you when I go to your grandfather?" she whispered.

The baby quieted. The older woman extended her *mjukuu* toward her son, presenting him with the gift of a small white body with its sparse, curly blond hair. Nkamba's tight-lipped smile transformed her eyes into two slits while her arthritic hands trembled under the slight weight of her naked granddaughter wrapped in a rag. It began to rain, and the raindrops released the sour smell of urine from the swaddling cloth. The sound of boughs and branches shaking in the wind shrouded the buzz of the villagers' pronouncements. The restless herd moved on, moaning, oblivious to their part in the drama.

Sefu looked to the side, in search of the head of the community who, in turn, locked eyes with the witch doctor.

Under the pounding raindrops, the baby had begun to whine again. The newborn's father waited for the pronouncement of the leaders of the clan. Kondo and Zuberi took their time. Finally the shaman tilted his head forward, ever so slightly, and the head of the village responded in kind. Nkamba inhaled deeply. For the shaman it was clear the Spirits of the Lake had spoken through the beasts. Sefu understood that it was their will that the *zeru zeru* live.

Looking at his mother, without so much as grazing the baby with his eyes, Sefu said, "May your will, as well as that of the Spirits of the Lake, and my word be done. It lives. However, it will remain unnamed and will not belong to my clan, and from this day forward, it shall live with you. As for me, I leave this house and shall return to live with my first wife and children."

Juma stared at the ground as her husband spoke. He had made it clear to her that he would never forgive what he considered her impure betrayal that led to the birth of the curse.

The racket of rain on sheet-metal roofs echoed the downpour of words from the villagers. Mindful that disgrace from the birth would affect them all—from the young to the old—they wanted to express opinions and participate in deciding the fate of the *zeru zeru* whose destiny was tied to theirs with a double thread.

Nkamba answered her son with a smile, pulling the child toward her bosom, and then she took two small steps to the side until she was standing in front of Kondo and Zuberi. Sefu understood that his mother wanted to receive their consent, face to face. She was looking for a single nod that would spread across the entire island, like a ripple of a wave to the water's edge. She had always been hardheaded.

The two men were stoic. Kondo broke the impasse when he commanded, "Go, Nkamba," accompanying his words with a gesture of his hand. The old woman shuffled in retreat without turning her back to them. Sefu and those gathered watched Nkamba until she disappeared inside the hut with the newborn, fully aware that until she was out of sight, the decision could be changed with the rapidity of clouds that clear for a beam of golden sunlight.

Sefu left with the elders of his clan. He promised himself that he would never so much as glance in the direction of the hut where he had lived with the mother of the *zeru zeru*. The crowd dissipated behind the leaders' slow steps; the two men were absorbed in a discussion that no one could hear.

JUMA, ALL ALONE, stared at the door of her hut. Crossing that threshold meant entering a prison without bars.

Your life as a shunned bride begins today, she said to herself. She looked at the room full of ritual objects for a propitious birth—libations, semiprecious stones, bones for divination. She thought about her joy during the previous months of pregnancy, before the skin of her daughter became whiter than the cloth in which she was swaddled. For an instant, Juma felt the creature move again inside her, recalling the vital force that filled her from the first moment she knew her womb was inhabited. Hate for this *zeru zeru* replaced her love for her real daughter, and the mother cried out for mercy, imagining her husband there with her. She thought of Afua, his first wife, many rainy seasons older than Juma and a big gossip. Juma had been so proud to have a husband who could afford two wives, and she had been convinced that she would always remain the favored wife. Rain began to fall again, and the fat drops pattered on the straw roof like twigs shaken by the wind. Then Juma heard a cry, and her breasts began to lactate.

Nkamba had been inside the hut, waiting for her. She walked in her daughter-in-law's direction, holding the baby out toward her.

Juma's body stiffened.

"My dear," Nkamba said with a smile, "you must feed your child."

Juma did not react, except to turn her face to the tiny window near the door. *The sun will come out soon*, she thought.

The baby wiggled in her grandmother's arms. Nkamba went to her daughter-in-law and unveiled the young woman's breast. Juma did not resist, and the baby latched onto her nipple. The new mother watched, her arms down by her sides. Nkamba held her granddaughter to Juma's breast, her hand supporting the baby's back. Then, with a surge of affection, she passed her other arm around Juma's neck and pulled her close. The tiny creature, who was between them, drank greedily from her mother. Juma wished a real baby was suckling, not a *zeru zeru*.

"I need to confide something, but I must be certain you will keep the secret," Nkamba said quietly in Juma's ear.

Juma shifted. Her mother-in-law might have knowledge about her condition. "My tongue shall fall in the lake and be eaten by crabs if I speak of it."

"My husband had gone to Mwanza. We did not have a field to plow nor a boat from which to fish; he was forced to look for work elsewhere. Otherwise, he would never have left me alone while I carried our first child. He would never have allowed her to disappear."

"Continue."

"The time of the birth came. I was happy, just as you were yesterday. My husband was far away, but I was surrounded by the affection of our families. I did not suffer pain and gave birth as quickly as a hen lays an egg. I offered the infant my breast, and the sensation gave me wings upon which to fly beyond the shores of the lake. Watching her latched to my breast, sucking my heart into her…It was the first and last time I nursed a child. Did you know that Sefu took milk from Arafa?"

"What do you mean, the first and last time?" asked Juma. "And who is this girl if my husband has no sisters?"

"Shortly after the birth of my firstborn, she, too, became *zeru zeru*, as my grandchild has. *They* used the same words with me as they have with you. They insisted the *zeru zeru* belonged to the Spirits of the Lake and it was to our gods she had to return. I believed and trusted them, that it was the best solution for the child and for me and my husband. Had Kheri been present, destiny would have led my daughter along the path to our home. Instead, I placed her in the arms of another woman, knowing she would be left in the forest." Nkamba shook her head and looked out the window. "Time passed, and I had another baby, but I was unable to nourish him. My breasts remained forever empty. The moment I gave up my daughter, I was cursed."

Juma could feel her mother-in-law's labored breath on her cheek and the mouth of the infant on her breast. Still, she remained frozen.

After a pause, Nkamba spoke again. "I do not want you to live with the remorse that has imprisoned me. We have saved her. Help me so that she grows and leads a rich life. I am old. How many more rainy seasons will I live?"

Juma twisted free from Nkamba's determined embrace and wrenched her breast from the baby's mouth. "I will not help it live!" she shouted. "I want to live with my husband! I want my previous life, not this *zeru zeru* that has destroyed my family!"

"I understand your pain," Nkamba replied, "but if you nurse the infant, I promise I will convince my son to return to you."

Juma's breath came in gasps. Sefu had always been deferential to his mother. Her only hope was her mother-in-law's influence over her husband.

"As long as I have milk, I will nurse it. After that, for me it is dead."

4.

Nkamba had prepared meat soup and had brought it to Juma, a delicacy to help the new mother recover from fatigue and produce good milk. The dish sat on the table. Juma ignored it. She went to the mirror, searching her reflection. What she saw disturbed her, and she turned the looking glass toward the wall.

The sun was setting. The last ray of light made its way through crevices in the roof and fell on Juma's drawn face. She felt as though she had aged ten rainy seasons since the previous sunset. She undressed. Naked and confused, she searched the hut with her eyes. She saw an unused cloth, left from the birth, lying in a corner, a long, narrow piece of white linen. She seized the bandage and began to wind it around her chest, tight and then tighter, promising herself to do so until her breasts went dry. She lay on her bed of palm leaves and held her husband's pillow close. His scent of nut and mango made her weep.

THE BABY ALWAYS took her mother's milk under Nkamba's vigilant gaze. Sometimes Juma, while nursing, would fall asleep with her daughter. The grandmother, noticing the serenity of the young mother's sleep, shook her head. *If only Juma had the courage to confess to herself the peace she found having the baby near!*

Only once did Nkamba trust her daughter-in-law to be alone with the infant. She was so happy seeing them close; Juma's long tapered fingers patted the little one's gold hair. Nkamba felt the need to share her joy with her husband. She went to his burial site, closed her eyes, and murmured, "Kheri, our baby has returned and is stronger than ever. This time she will live!"

Going back toward Juma's hut, the old woman quickened her step until she was running as quickly as her arthritic body would allow. Her granddaughter was screaming, desperation inflaming her voice. Naked under the cruel sun, the newborn lay on the yellow earth in front of the sheet-metal door. Nkamba threw herself on the tiny creature, snatching her from the jaws of the sun's rays, and carried her into the shade of a tree. She railed against her daughter-in-law, who stared at her—dully, lifelessly—from the doorway.

"I thought the sun might change her color," said Juma.

Nkamba gathered the baby's few things and walked away with short, rapid steps.

"You told me you would convince Sefu to come back to me if I fed the *zeru zeru*!" Juma shouted, running after them.

Nkamba wanted to yell back, "No, I will never keep my promise," that she would prefer to see Juma drown in the lake and be eaten by fish than meet her again in the market. However, she knew that keeping her word would be beneficial for the baby's future. If her son took back his second wife, perhaps he would also accept his daughter into his home.

"It is more in my interest than in yours," Nkamba said, turning away with the baby in her arms.

NIGHT AFTER NIGHT, Juma bound her chest before going to bed. As she slept she was haunted by nightmares and stabbing pain. Her breasts felt like blazing embers. One evening, she decided she would rid herself once and for all of the cursed milk that insisted on flowing from her breasts. She took a long strip of fine cloth, dampened it, and tied one end to a pole in the hut. From the farthest side of the room she began to turn in circles, winding the wet cloth around her chest so tight that she could barely breathe. Juma could have saved herself such suffering; Nkamba had already decided that would be the last day the baby would suckle from her mother. Starting the next morning, she would give the child goat's milk.

5.

Mosi—Father Andrew—was born on Ukerewe and lived there until he was fourteen years old. He was a solitary boy who did not like to participate in the diversions of other youngsters. By age eight, he was certain he would leave the island.

It happened on an afternoon when the houses assumed the color of the sun and the air seemed to shine with its own light; Mosi passed under the great baobab and spotted an unusual gathering. He squirmed his way to the front of the crowd. Two men, dressed in long black tunics, were talking about the life of a man with a foreign name.

"His eyes shone like rays of light, and his gaze was so blinding no one could look directly at his face," one of them said.

Slowly, as the news of the strangers' presence spread across the fields and among the village dwellings, the number of people under the great tree grew. The villagers listened with fascination to stories about this special man who spoke of justice and refuge and who defended the weak and oppressed. They were surprised to hear he had cured illnesses and deformities and that he was awaiting good, deserving men in a kingdom of light beyond this earthly life. Mosi was lucky enough to claim one of the books the men were distributing. "Here is salvation, justice, and eternal life," the Jesuit said as he handed the boy the leather-bound pages.

"I'll never sell it or feed it to the fire, I promise," said Mosi, who ran home, clutching the volume in his hands.

He often went to listen to the priests talk about Jesus of Nazareth. Gradually, Mosi fell in love with He who dispensed justice and love, and every day he read a part of the book that told the story of Jesus's life.

One evening, after he had stayed too long at the shore, tossing stones into the lake, he arrived home for supper only to find the table bare. His mother was waiting, furious, and his apologies were useless. He would be punished: his kerosene lamp would be taken from him, the one he kept next to his bed. Thus, he spent the night in darkness, unable to read the Gospel.

At dawn, he extracted the book from under his blanket and read the story of Jesus receiving a group of children whom adults had tried to keep at bay so as not to disturb Him. Mosi was such a child, and he was certain that Jesus wanted to receive him. It was then Mosi decided to follow His example: to help others. That would be his work. To spend his life without Him would be like living in a darkened room without the light of a lantern to dispel the gloom.

So it was that at the age of fourteen, Mosi went to Mwanza to enter the seminary. It was a challenge to convince his father he didn't want to marry. In the end, his mother's intervention and his own stubbornness prevailed. After long years of study and finally ordination, he began to travel among the villages in his service. Every Sunday he returned to his island to lead Mass. The day his aged father saw him for the first time after many rainy seasons—tall, well fed, and dressed in a black tunic—he was in awe and bowed his head. Father Andrew wrapped him in his arms, blessing him in the name of the one who had become his only God.

IT WAS SEVERAL months after her granddaughter's birth that Nkamba waited until the end of Mass to approach Father Andrew. She tired of her son's persistent eschewal of Juma. She had given up hope of his ever accepting his second wife and their daughter and had been trying to, at the very least, convince Sefu to agree to name the child. She decided to ask Father Andrew for his help on persuading her son. He was a learned man and came from a respected local clan. If anyone could help her, it was he. *He is a representative on Earth of the One who embraces the excluded, isn't he?* she asked herself. That was what Mosi always said.

The infant was sleeping, wrapped in a sling on her grandmother's back. Nkamba waited for the others to leave the priest's side. Once he was alone, she shifted the sling so the baby was in her arms, and she walked with determination toward him.

"My *mjukuu* does not have a name," she said, revealing the baby's face. "No one wants to give her one, neither her father nor Zuberi. Please, try to convince them; perhaps they'll listen to you."

The priest seemed to stifle a grimace. "Certainly they will listen to me. Only I—God's representative—can give a name to the child. Or rather," he pointed his index finger skyward, "only He can."

Nkamba looked at the sky, her granddaughter, and then at the young man who appeared annoyed. Her wrinkled face revealed contrasting emotions. For her, any god would do as long as the babe in her arms was given a name, and she imagined Father Andrew knew what she was thinking.

"You are a priest," she said finally, "but you are also the son of a farmer. Zuberi will not want you to give the baby a name."

"She will have a name and will be baptized in the open before the community," he said, smiling. "Return to me in a week."

6.

Zuberi, bent over his mortar, ground the pharmaceutical tablets to powder. With each strike of the pestle, he imagined his fame growing, stretching outside the limits of the island, reaching throughout the country and, perhaps, beyond. People would come from far away to request his services. One day even white men would appear. He puffed out his chest as he reminded himself that his family had been healers for twenty generations, and when future shamans spoke of Zuberi, the stories of his magic would be shared and swapped—they'd say he defined the Golden Age of the divinatory arts.

Jane, Zuberi's vervet, was sitting on the table watching her master, captivated by the sound of the pestle in the mortar. Her bright eyes—black like roasted coffee beans, white fur framing her thick-skinned face—skipped from Zuberi to the row of colored tablets.

"Lucky little monkey, how proud you must be to belong to the best healer in Tanzania. One day my name will be on everyone's lips!" he said, transferring the powder from the mortar into a wooden bowl.

There was a knock on his workroom door, and his daughter announced the visitors. Zuberi hurried to put the tablets back into their plastic vials, hiding them in a large drawer under his worktable. Drying the sweat from his brow, he opened the door.

Father Andrew entered, followed by his elderly father, Idi. Even though Idi was a humble farmer, he was considered one of the wisest of village elders and could not be ignored.

"Idi, welcome to my home. And I welcome your son too," Zuberi said with condescension. *What can this priest want from me?* he wondered.

"Thank you for receiving us," replied Idi. "I hope you and your family are in good health."

"I wish the same for you and your family."

After exhausting the required pleasantries and inquiries about the health of members of their respective clans, Father Andrew said, "I am here about Sefu's child. Don't you believe it's time to give her a name? Soon I will baptize her, though I'd like your approval."

Abruptly, the smile disappeared from Zuberi's lips, leaving in its place an indignant grimace.

"Never," he replied with irritation. "An *embulamaro* is without name. We must abide the Spirits of the Lake."

Father Andrew struggled with the temptation to leave the house and slam the door behind him. He remained silent for several moments as he considered how to reply. "Think, Zuberi. In our village every lamb, every cow, every goat has its name. Even your monkey has one! What could be wrong if we give one to the child?"

"It is simple. A *zeru zeru* is not a person, not even an animal," he replied, petting Jane, who obediently rubbed herself against the witch doctor's incongruous Western-style button-down shirt, a red cloth tied over his right shoulder to identify his tribe.

"What is a *zeru zeru* in your opinion? Do they not eat our same food? Do they not speak our same language?"

Zuberi shook his head and huffed, striding toward the door. Vexed, he opened it. "*Zeru zerus* have never had names. Why should that change now? Excuse me, but I have important things to attend to."

Alone once more, Zuberi considered why he chose to let the *zeru zeru* live. *Money is power and magic*, he thought to himself, *and let's never forget the riches that a* zeru zeru *can bring. I must hatch a plan to wrest from it all I can. It will be the centerpiece of my Golden Age.*

ALTHOUGH FATHER ANDREW had studied and led a life very different from that of his family, he had not forgotten his origins and held deep respect for his father. When he had requested Idi's advice after Nkamba approached him about naming her granddaughter, the old man had reminded his son of the importance of precise, unwritten rules that had to be followed and that it would be most advantageous to appeal to the clan's elders rather than to act discretely. "Your one God may be stronger than the Spirits of the Lake," the old man had said to his son, "yet it is here where the *zeru zeru* must live, and to give it a name behind Kondo's and Zuberi's backs would be a grave offense. Try to convince them to collaborate with you. Be kind and respectful so they will want to indulge you. Then you may act according to the wishes of your God."

Standing before Zuberi, Father Andrew had felt as if he were taking an examination given by a man who he held in disesteem; however, he had been aware that he needed to ingratiate himself, and he had prayed for strength to hold his tongue, which, with the help of God he had, until he was outside the hut. "Who does that charlatan think he is? God will punish him for his arrogance!"

Idi walked alongside his son. "Your God is powerless against our traditions. Changes need time, not threats. Forget about Zuberi for now, and let's pay a visit to Kondo," he said, placing his hand on his son's shoulder. "He knows the secret of balance. Plus, he has always been especially fond of Nkamba and might be inclined to extend her the favor."

KONDO'S HOUSE SAT in the central part of the village, protected by mango and acacia trees. The chief was expecting Father Andrew's visit. He remembered well Nkamba's countenance on the day of her granddaughter's escape from death—the expression of a suffering mother. He had seen her attend Mass and imagined her solitude. He knew that sooner or later, she would go to the priest and his God. It was for this reason that he had deferred the decision on whether the *zeru zeru* should live—any request she brought to him would be difficult to deny.

"And, so, Zuberi sent you away from his house," said Kondo. "He is ill-mannered, but do you want him as your enemy?"

Idi hastened to respond on his son's behalf. "No, the shaman was preoccupied when we intruded on him. We are ready to forget his offensive behavior so long as my son can give a name to the child, according to the will of his God."

Kondo rubbed his eyes and took a deep breath. "I speak to you, Idi, with an empty mouth. As a village elder, I trust you understand how difficult this situation is." Kondo paused.

The only sound in the room came from a fly that lifted in flight.

"Idi, if I follow the will of your son's God, I will disappoint many people. If I listen to the Spirits of the Lake, I will disappoint fewer, yet other problems will remain." Kondo drank some tea and filled cups for his guests. "...The most important one has to do precisely with a name for the *zeru zeru*," he added, as if he were talking to himself. "Never mind that the father made a public pronouncement that the baby would have no name."

Idi nodded. Father Andrew shifted nervously on the mat where he was sitting.

"Allow me time to think of a solution. When I have decided, I will let you know," said Kondo.

That evening Kondo refused the supper his wife had prepared. In the depths of the night, he stepped out of his hut and withdrew to a place under the great baobab. He needed solitude in order to reflect. Although for many, many rainy seasons, he had mediated the relations among inhabitants of the village, his old soul told him that this time too many forces conflicted, and the traditions of his people were like leaves on the winds. Idi was a good man. He came with respect to ask for justice from the head of his village, and he deserved to be satisfied. A slight breeze uncovered the full moon from behind wisps of sheetlike clouds. Yes, Idi's request deserved to be granted. As for Zuberi, he had the manners of a wild buffalo. His ambition made him blind, and his wisdom was barely as deep as a rice bowl. Many of the villagers—too many—were enchanted by his authoritative ways and his inflated promises. *People follow those who speak loudest without paying attention to the meaning of their words*, he thought with a touch of bitterness. Allowing Idi's son to give a name to the *zeru zeru* could be the perfect opportunity to establish a new equilibrium. It might reduce Zuberi's influence in the community, even if, in doing so, he would give greater credit to Father Andrew's God. Hadn't the Spirits of the Lake already decided that the child should live? Almost certainly, in this circumstance, the gods of Ukerewe and Father Andrew were in agreement. *And how relieved Nkamba will be. In consensus, there is peace*, asserted Kondo, *and if the Greater Spirits are in harmony, there is no reason why men should not be so as well.* He leaned his head against the trunk of the tree and looked up. The baobab was in flower; it was the blooming season. The large white hairy blossoms that hung among the leaves would bloom for this one night. It could only be a good sign.

It was decided. He would go personally to Zuberi. Dawn appeared in the indigo sky. On Kondo's way home, red beams—streaking through the chill and the sun, seeming so close to Earth as to threaten it—rose with haste above the horizon.

7.

Zuberi did not expect the visit from the village chief, nor did he imagine Kondo would take Father Andrew's request seriously. Just the same, the leader had come to his home in person to raise the question, a sign of respect and consideration of his position. They shared *ugali*[5] and fish, and Kondo spoke with him as if they were equals.

"There cannot be any harm if the *zeru zeru* receives a name," he said. "The Spirits of the Lake have already spoken through the animals, choosing life over death. Am I wrong?"

"Yes, so true. If, however, Sefu refuses to give a name to that creature, we have to respect him," declared Zuberi, his face solemn.

Kondo was quick to explain that neither he nor Sefu would be burdened with that inconvenience. "The priest and his God will give a name to the *embulamaro*."

A shadow of doubt crossed Zuberi's mind. What sort of power did Kondo attribute to the priest? he wondered. Who gave Mosi the right to decide the name for a member of the community? He considered if Kondo was plotting to depose him and replace him with the one-god priest! Ah, he forgot, they were speaking about a *zeru zeru,* a *nobody* that would never be accepted as a living being. Mosi could do what he wanted. Zuberi took three black cowrie-shell amulets from his pocket, threw them to the ground, pronounced magic words, and declared, "Nkamba shall choose the name, not the young charlatan. On this Earth, people follow the will of the Spirits of the Lake, not the futile desires of a foreign god."

Kondo nodded in silence.

"Although he is called 'Father Andrew' now, to us, he is always Mosi, the son of a poor farmer," added Zuberi, his eyebrows pulling down tight.

The head of the village left Zuberi's hut to complete his final task: to

---

[5] A dish similar to Italian polenta made of cassava flour and generally served with meat, fish, or vegetables.

speak with Sefu so that he would feel included in the decision. He set out for the father's house as soon as the sun was beginning to set and a breeze cooled the way.

SEFU SAT OUTSIDE his hut, resting. He listened to Kondo without commenting, his eyes locked on the fire below the lamb that was cooking for the evening meal. Though the sun had vanished beyond the horizon, darkness had not yet come, and the earth radiated the heat it had absorbed during the day. The sheet-metal door was ajar, and the sound of female chatter hovered in the air along with the scent of the searing meat. Kondo could hear children laughing in the distance and a woman's sharp voice, Sefu's first wife's, Kondo imagined.

"You have the final word, Sefu," said the old man after having set out the matter.

"Why ask my opinion on something I am completely indifferent to?" said Sefu. "You decide. You'll make my mother happy. She will be the only one to use the name. I, surely, shall never utter it."

Though Kondo was able to quash the conflict around the *zeru zeru* this time, he anticipated that future battles would arise that would cause casualties. He prayed to the Spirits of the Lake that they not tear his village apart.

ON THE SUNDAY of the baptism, as Nkamba sang a soft tune, she bathed the baby, rubbing her with a cloth soaked in warm water and soap. She wrapped the child in bright-colored fabric she'd bought the day before. At the service, no one from Nkamba's family was present, nor was the baby's mother. Nevertheless, standing before Father Andrew, cradling her granddaughter, the woman was happier than she had been for many rainy seasons.

"What would you like to call her?" asked Father Andrew.

"I believed you'd give her a name," she replied.

"I told you I would baptize her. You must choose the name."

Nkamba thought for several moments and then looked at her child's serious countenance. "She will be called Adimu[6]."

Father Andrew nodded. "What could be more fitting."

Yes, she is special, just like my own first child, Nkamba thought.

At that joyous moment, the old woman couldn't have imagined that before too long her beloved granddaughter would be taken from her as her own unnamed daughter had been.

---

[6] Adimu means "rare" or "special" in Swahili.

8.

The night Adimu was conceived, as well as on the day of her disappearance one year after her birth, Charles Fielding was on Ukerewe Island near the village of Murutanga. Mr. Fielding, a white African and owner of a gold mine in Mwanza—on Tanzania's mainland—was born and raised in Rhodesia, now called Zimbabwe, as were his parents and grandparents, descendants of the first English colonists who landed in the Empire's possessions shortly after the colonization of the southern hemisphere.

From the time of his birth, Charles had been away from Africa only for three interminable years. That period spent in England had been the worst of his life. The doctors called what he suffered "depression." He knew, though, the diagnosis was incorrect. What was destroying his very soul and body was "homesickness." His one desire was to return to the African continent. The specialists who had examined him had never set foot in Africa. They had no notion of how the land entered one's blood or of the true color values behind the words "green," "orange," "yellow," "blue." *No, not the shades one glimpses in this chilly urban penitentiary with the odor of combustion and exhaust but the tones of my homeland*, he thought, *with not the slightest trace of England's epithet gray. The colors in Africa, so pure, so alive, drenched in the scents of the flower, fruit, and plant that lend their names.*

Homesickness it surely was, and to simply survive, he basked in memories of his experiences on the golden continent. When he gazed at his good luck charm, he felt less alone. The small gold nugget had been mined by his father who had given it to him for his fourteenth birthday. The stone was the size of a walnut—rough and bright yellow like a canary with ochre bands—embedded in a cage-like setting and attached to a chain. Rather than set it on his desk, he hid it in his pocket. He would always keep it with him, he had assured his father.

At Oxford, where he studied economics, he'd met Sarah, the woman who would become his wife. From the day they first kissed, they were inseparable. Charles proposed on one knee, slipping on the ring that had belonged to his grandmother, which had arrived, via his mother, from Zimbabwe. The two lovebirds blushed when, awkward young man that he was, he placed the ring on his beloved's index finger, and Sarah gently guided him to her ring finger. The three-carat white pure Asscher diamond was the most beautiful gift Sarah had ever received and the only jewelry she would ever wear. She promised him she would not remove it until the day they gave it to their daughter.

Once he obtained the piece of paper that attested to his university degree, Charles convinced his wife to abandon her studies, and, saying goodbye to Europe forever, Charles returned to his Africa with his Sarah by his side. Although he was unable to live away from the land he considered home, Charles, like his parents and his grandparents, felt "European"— English, to be exact. He would come to realize, eventually, just how much his perception was distorted.

From the time he was a child, Charles was attracted to any object that captured light. As an adult, he developed a proclivity for small shiny things with a value of tens of dollars or more per gram.

It was during his early years that his father taught him the power of wealth. Mr. Finley Fielding was forever traveling, either for business or between bed partners. Once Charles learned how money made the man, he could not do without it.

One hot day, when Charles was playing alone in his room with a couple of gold nuggets, he heard his father's car being parked in the courtyard, and he saw the man enter the house. Finley had been away for quite some time on a business trip, and, overcome with anticipation, the son ran down the long staircase to the ground floor, threw open the door of his father's study, and lunged toward the man, hugging him about the hips.

"What are you doing? Stop behaving like a dog," Finley said, shaking his son and holding onto his arm. "Don't you see I'm speaking with your mother?"

Charles, excited, waved the piece of paper he was holding in his hand. "Now you're up to ten nuggets all together!" he shouted.

"Never a request for a horse or toys suitable for your age," the father said with good humor as he looked at his son while digging into his jacket pocket to extract a silk pouch, embroidered with his initials. "However, I believe your calculations are incorrect. Ten nuggets are too many."

The boy read from the piece of paper in his hand. "Two because you forgot to come to my end-of-year recital, two more because last year you were away."

The woman looked at her husband, an expression of reproach in her eyes.

"Two because Mama and I always dine alone," continued the boy. "And two more because you've never taken me riding. And the last two because you forgot to come see me play cricket, even though you had promised. All together that makes ten. Nuggets or gold coins!"

The father gave the pouch to his son. "Count them carefully," the man said.

Charles counted eight small gold nuggets and seven coins. "Yes, I have what I need."

"Are you sure? Did you take *exactly* ten?" insisted Mr. Fielding, jerking the bag from his son's hands. "Now we'll count them together, and if you took more than ten, I'll keep everything because you lied," he warned.

Charles became hysterical, thrashing his fists at his father's chest. "I didn't think you'd count! Give them to me; they're mine! You're never home, and I deserve them."

The telephone rang, and Charles's mother ran to answer it. "Finley, the minister is on the phone. He says it's urgent."

"Here, take them and stop whining," Mr. Fielding said, handing the pouch to his ornery son. "We'll talk about this later. Now Daddy has important things to do."

That evening, the boy cried himself to sleep, clutching his treasured gold.

As an adult, Charles would awaken at six. Though he had stopped smoking ten years earlier, every morning he would light a cigarette without touching it to his lips. He'd set it on the ashtray and let it burn. It was his way of testing his volition. Once his cigarette ritual was performed, he checked prices quoted for precious metals and the official exchange rate for principal currencies. He read the first page of the *Times* and the *Sunday Mail* that his faithful assistant, Jackob, set on his desk before 6:45 a.m. and, after completing his morning rites, he went into the kitchen where his wife prepared his breakfast.

Sarah had followed Charles to Africa without a moment's hesitation. He had been her one true love. Less than half a step behind him at all times, she saw herself as his shadow. Nevertheless, before he had entered her life, she had been popular and formidable, a spirited young woman who was the sun to many satellites. She contained a powerful magnetism that she never acknowledged, and it was that which attracted Charles. Although Charles was drawn to her strength, she was drawn to his vulnerability. When it came to business he was a bull, and she loved his confident, commanding presence, but she sensed something tender behind his bluster. She heard a harmonic minor scale reverberating from his spirit and that reminded her of her father.

She had dreamed of having a conventional marriage and desired children—something they hadn't discussed until after they were wed, though she had mentioned a daughter when Charles first proposed. As it turned out, she couldn't conceive, and he didn't wish to adopt, a frequent topic of conversation in their first years as husband and wife. In the end, she gave in. *We'll be together forever, and we'll have our own type of happiness, even without children,* Sarah repeated to herself every time the yearning for motherhood eclipsed her need to be a good helpmate.

On the day of Adimu's birth, Sarah was with Charles on Ukerewe. They had bought the only building on the island that could be called a *house* in the Western sense of the word. It was a rectangular two-story brick structure with ten brick columns fronting it, creating a spacious veranda. That the home was white resulted in a striking contrast to that dusty place where the lightest color was the ochre soil. The doors—heavy, engraved wood—and the low walls of the patio, constructed with perforated brick, made it appear extravagant compared to the rest of the landscape. The natives of the island believed it had fallen out of the sky during a windy storm. Surrounding the house was a yard, bordered by centuries-old trees—so tall they created constant shade—that towered over the house itself.

"Finally a real home," said Sarah with relief. For five years, since arriving in Africa, she had lived in houses with perimeter walls; this house, without a fence, gave her a reassuring sense of freedom. "Who was the previous owner?"

"It was built by the last king on the island, before Tanzania received its independence from the United Kingdom[7]," he said proudly. "I bought it from the heirs of a businessman who died when he was only thirty-three years old." Her husband's face became sad. Then his amused expression returned. "The homeowner's stomach exploded because he disobeyed an inviolable law of this residence. One that will affect us, too, that is, if we

---

[7] Tanzania gained independence in the years 1961-1963.

don't behave accordingly!" Charles snickered. "Jackob assured me. You trust Jackob, don't you?"

His wife giggled.

"Ah, yes, no one but the king may have sexual relations inside the house."

"Ours are not only sexual," she said with an air of false reproach.

Charles recalled how amused he was when he had heard the legend.

"It's a matter of witchcraft, sir," his assistant told him. "And it is not a good idea to go against witchcraft."

He had set his hand on Jackob's shoulder and said, "But now *I'm* the king of the island."

Charles left Jackob to his anxieties. Though he loved this land, he was glad, he said to himself as his hand felt in his pocket for his lucky gold nugget, that his English upbringing caused him not to believe in these silly superstitions.

After a few connubial squabbles about the name, they decided to call it "White House." Charles held that he had suggested it for its color, even if the high-sounding appellation offered association with another residence. The house was certainly worthy of an important man. *The most important man. A king among the most important*, he reminded himself.

Once refurbishments to the interior were complete, Charles and Sarah turned their attention to the garden and veranda. Shrubs and flowers were planted, arches and statues were ordered from grand department stores to embellish the open spaces, and heavy wrought-iron benches were imported from England, as were garden furniture from the colonial forge. After a long wait, every nook was ready to accommodate the Fieldings. Charles joked to his wife that at White House, they would rule over man and beast, and though Sarah laughed along with her husband, the statement couldn't help but make her flinch.

9.

Two coal black eyes were spying the house where Nkamba and Adimu lived, a single, rectangular room built from mud and sand brought from the shore of the lake and supported by an inner framework of woven tree branches. Season after season, rain eroded the outer layers, and near ground level, the roots of the plants used as foundation began to show. The home looked like an extravagantly shaped tree trunk, one of those oddities that nature seems to invent for no reason other than to startle humans. The roof was made of branches, held together with hemp cords and strips of palm leaves that were wrapped around a thick plastic tarp covered by a heavy mantle of long dry grass. It slanted steeply on all four sides of the hut to facilitate runoff during the rainy season. The door was made of sheet metal, rusted and reinforced by branches that Nkamba had added during Adimu's first weeks of life. From the outside, one barely noticed the holes Nkamba had drilled next to the entrance so she could look out at night without being seen. The inside of the hut was darkened by soot from the cooking fire in a corner on the packed earth floor. On the other side of the hut were the palm mats used for sleeping. Her furnishings consisted of a small table and two plastic chairs, a container for water, a few cooking utensils, a pile of wood and charcoal. The bathroom was outside, a hole in the ground about six feet deep, partially covered by planks of wood. Behind the hut was a spacious yard, marked off by a fence made of dry, thorny branches. Originally the fence had kept grazing animals away from the house, but after Adimu's birth, instead of a barrier to protect from intruding creatures, it had become a border established by others to isolate the old lady and the *zeru zeru*. Inside the fence grew three large papaya and two imposing mango trees. Under one of these lay the body of Kheri, Nkamba's husband.

DARKNESS TERRIFIED NKAMBA, and she cursed the moon and the stars. From the first night of her granddaughter's arrival, the slightest sound woke

Nkamba. She imagined a criminal hidden in the shadows might attack or kidnap Adimu. Nkamba developed an obsession with danger. She knew that only her rough and caring hands guaranteed the girl's safety.

In order to confuse the neighbors, she'd spend several nights each week sleeping in the forest. She feared those with evil intentions might hide in plain sight: moving locations would trick them. With Adimu fastened securely to her back, she ventured into the woodlands directly from the fields, always seeking new, well-hidden places. Under the green forest arches, cloaked in blackness, Nkamba kept vigil, her eyes and instincts alert in the gloom, ready to sense a threatening presence. Thus, she held the child in the hollow formed by her bony legs.

Nights spent in the hut were marked by agitation. The grandmother was afraid of dogs though always saved leftovers for them with the hope of keeping some feral ones nearby. They would be a deterrent for troublemakers and act as an alarm if someone came near. She reinforced the door with green branches—the most robust—and made arrangements for her bodily needs during the night.

Although her life had been upended by the arrival of her granddaughter, Nkamba did not neglect her husband. Upon returning from the fields of cassava and corn, she often sat under the mango tree and prayed at his tomb. Immobile, eyes half-closed, she'd whisper confidences while the baby sat on a straw mat in the shadiest spot under the thick, oblong leaves.

Most Sundays, grandmother and grandchild went to Mass. Nkamba believed there were never enough blessings for her little treasure. Surely some god would take her under his protection. For this reason, she prayed to them all, in particular to Mosi's one and only—the one that procured Adimu a name—known to have special regard for the weak and defenseless.

However, on one particular Sunday, after Adimu had completed a cycle of seasons, the child's restlessness prevented church attendance and an unexpected event occurred. On that Sunday, Adimu fidgeted on the mat and refused her *manioc* mush. Nkamba would get some milk for the baby, leaving her inside rather than exposing her to the sun, the child's true enemy. Most of the village was at Mass, at home, or at the lake. The old woman peered through the peepholes before leaving her hut. No one around. Nkamba slipped out. In her hands she held a bowl to collect milk from her small herd.

TWO COAL BLACK eyes, belonging to a young woman who was concealed behind a pile of stones and bushes, watched Nkamba leave the hut. As soon as Nkamba disappeared behind the first curve of the path, the clandestine woman, her face wrapped in blue fabric, came out of hiding and, with quick steps, approached the house. Adimu was lying on the mat, her white arms by the sides of her small body. The woman in blue lifted the baby, careful not to upset her, and she withdrew into the forest.

10.

Charles and Sarah spent the following morning preparing a list of things they needed for their domestic milieu. Jackob, who understood how to satisfy Mr. Fielding from years of close contact with his employer, took note of each request. The assistant had worked for white men since he was a boy and knew from experience how exacting they could be. Mr. Fielding, though, was distinct from other bosses. He was white and *African*, and Jackob considered him a great man, through and through.

Midday, Jackob languished as he read the things left to do on the list: call, buy, invite, extend condolences, order, arrange, reserve, inform about changes and preferences. He was nearly prostrate with fatigue; nevertheless, he stayed at work until every detail was crossed off the list with a straight line of his pen.

Jackob kept an efficient agenda and carefully set reminders to eliminate any oversights. He would not forget anything, ever.

He knew Charles inside out: his mania for details and his perfectionism, the satisfaction he got from jobs well done. Jackob labored to provide his boss with what he wanted and needed, intuiting, at times, his boss's desires, even before the man himself was aware of them. Jackob understood him at a glance and wanted little more than his boss's approval. Charles was much more than an employer: for him, Charles was a mentor, a man he looked up to and modeled himself on. Jackob had everything he had ever wanted. His salary was the envy of his peers. He had a car, landline phone, and the opportunity to work for a tycoon.

As soon as Jackob had received confirmation that the purchase of the house had been concluded, he notified a friend from university, the director of one of the most exclusive resorts in Zanzibar, to start training cooks and service staff for White House. Jackob personally selected the six guards for the residence and the gardeners and driver. He hired his cousin as staff supervisor and house manager. It was Jackob's wish that every detail would delight Charles and Mrs. Fielding, that even their most frivolous whim would be satisfied.

It was Jackob himself who took care of lunch on that Sunday. He had the table set in the garden in the shade of the enormous trees, dressed the table with bright cultivated flowers and fruits—a cluster of bananas, mangoes, and pineapple. He ordered an abundant meal of fried mandazi, stuffed zucchini, and sweet sausages from the kitchen, and he saw to it that a bottle of chilled wine was in a bucket.

Lunch was ready. The Fieldings were seated, admiring the well-laid table and anticipating the meal. Jackob waited until the couple was settled and then drove home in his old Toyota sedan to spend his free afternoon with his wife and newborn daughter.

THE YOUNG WOMAN'S steps were uncertain. She fought the temptation to look at the child as she tried to hurry. Adimu had awakened, and she fidgeted under the batik cloth she was wrapped in, chattering and emitting baby sounds. The woman kept repeating to herself that it was not a baby but a *zeru zeru*, that *it* was nothing. It could not be admired; there was nothing to love. In any case, the woman was struggling to not think about the small body hidden by the fabric. To fight the seduction of the tiny thing, she held it out in front of her and away from her body. When the breeze would drift toward her, she'd catch a hint of fresh milky baby scent.

In the clearing, where the vegetation was thinner, the young woman looked around with anxiety, turning right and left to be certain no one followed her. The forest shouted, became dense, and the paths before her grew confusing, hostile. Rustling. Animal sounds. Penetrating odors. The vegetation pervaded—opulent, intertwining, snaking so as to fill every space. The woman tried to concentrate on the correct path to follow, holding at a distance the tangle of sensations that were moving from her gut to her head. A corner of fabric slid to the side, and the baby's gaze met hers. With a toothless smile, Adimu put her chubby hand in her mouth. For a moment, they looked into each other's eyes. The little one smiled at her. The young woman shook herself, covering the tiny face to protect her body from the baby's charms, and she walked as quickly as possible.

Light from the midday sun worked its way between the weave of branches and bush. Though the woman felt hot, she hastened her steps, tripping on a clump of exposed roots. Right before the moment of impact with the earth, she used one arm to break her fall, protecting the baby with the other. Adimu cried. The young woman stood and, without hesitation, continued walking. She reproached herself for her behavior. She should have let the *zeru zeru* fall to the ground, even if she risked crushing it with her body. She reminded herself that she had taken it to keep away bad luck. Was she not crossing the forest to reach the place where it could be abandoned to the will of the Spirits of the Lake? A place known to few, though well-known to the rain that falls from the sky and courses along the trunks of trees.

When the creature cried, the woman's inner turmoil deepened. She tried to calm the *zeru zeru* by holding it close to her chest. The small body trembled under the batik cloth, and she lifted the covering to look at it. Adimu was still crying, large teardrops sliding down her pink cheeks. The woman felt cold, and her throat tightened into a painful knot. She looked around as if to search for help. She was alone. She set the bundle on the ground and examined the small body for injuries. Although there were none, she saw the infant was helpless. A small flame appeared to be lit inside the baby, directly under its white flesh. The young woman caressed the little thing, but the touch of her large hands seemed to agitate the child even more. She looked at her own chest, and after a moment's hesitation, she exposed a breast. Adimu sucked hungrily on the woman's indulgent yet empty bosom. The maternal contact must have calmed the child.

The woman leaned her back against the trunk of a tree. She closed her eyes. The melodic whispers of the forest and the contact with a burgeoning life hushed her solitude. She wouldn't be able to see her plan through. Impossible. The secret place she intended to take Adimu vanished from the paths in her mind, and a different road opened before her.

She stood and walked with determination in the new direction without lingering any longer before the muddle of branches. The woman whose face was hidden by a blue veil knew exactly where to go.

11.

"Listen to this story that has become legend. They told it to me the first time I set foot on the island," said Charles to his wife, eyeing a bunch of bananas that decorated the table along with other fruits. "Have you noticed there are no banana trees on the island?" He picked up the chilled bottle of wine, looked at the label, and poured some for them both.

Sarah searched the horizon, looking for a point of reference. "No…"

"Imagine. They say there was once a banana tree for every inhabitant."

"It's strange there are none now…Why is it?"

"It's because of their stupidity," the man said sarcastically. "In the eighties, a politician maintained that because of mosquitoes in banana trees, people were dying from malaria."

Sarah placed her fork on the table and leaned back in her chair. "And so?"

"And so…he convinced the inhabitants to cut them down. But the myth of mosquitoes in banana trees was one of many folk beliefs. The mistake was discovered too late." Charles took a sip of his Sauvignon Blanc, laughed, and then started coughing for having inhaled the alcohol.

THE WOMAN WITH coal black eyes ran through the thinning forest. As there was no filter of vegetation, the heat became unbearable. She finally reached the outer limits of White House's garden. The *wazungu*[8] were dining outside. She set the child on the ground with care, making sure the fabric covered the baby's flesh. Adimu was drowsy. She would soon fall asleep. The woman turned away, forcing herself to avoid a final glance at the bundle lying among the bushes. She took a few steps yet couldn't help herself from turning around, overcome by guilt. The child could be attacked and devoured by an animal before the white people noticed her. She veiled her face and picked up Adimu who wiggled under the cloth

---

[8] White men in Swahili (plural form of the word *mzungu*).

and began to whimper. Calling on her reserve of courage and considering how this bundle was the product of her best friend and cousin, the young woman walked toward the Fieldings's table, cradling it against her breasts.

CHARLES AND SARAH were raising glasses in a toast to their new house when they heard, from the green depths of the forest, the cry of an infant drawing near. They saw the vibrant blue of a woman's traditional dress emerge from the vegetation. Sarah searched her husband's reassuring face.

Charles noted a flash of anxiety in his wife's eyes. "Don't worry, dear. It's only a beggar with a child."

When the young woman reached them, she placed the sobbing bundle on Charles's lap. He looked down at the child, scowling, and was greeted with the light of small blue eyes and pouting lips that immediately grinned.

What kind of child is this? he asked himself. *A white Negro?* His mind lingered on the word "Negro."

Charles shifted his attention from his knees, compelling himself not to caress the baby or look at the woman who was standing in front of him.

"It is Adimu. I return her," said the young woman before she ran away in the direction from which she came.

Charles felt contrasting instincts—one was, shockingly, to protect the baby and the other was to flick it from him as if it were a scorpion that had fallen from the ceiling. His instinct to purge himself of the encumbrance won out. Unable to toss it onto the ground, he jumped up and ran after the woman, clutching the child in his arms. The woman, who was younger, lighter, and much faster than him, had disappeared into the dense forest. Charles faltered, then went as far as the edge of the property and set the child on the ground. He walked back to the table, took his place, and re-sumed eating his sausage, his eyes fixed on his plate. He knew that beggar women often left their children with whites for handouts and sympathy, a trick well recorded.

ADIMU WAILED. SARAH was petrified, her eyes drawn like magnets to the infant from the moment it curled up in her husband's arms. After she could no longer contain herself, she ran to the baby, lifted her from the ground, and hugged her, rocking her in an attempt to calm her cries. Sarah called the maids. Although at first the domestics were fearful of the *zeru zeru*, they followed Sarah's lead, and together they attempted to comfort the child, cooing at it and giggling endearments.

Charles phoned his assistant. "Get over here and help us," he growled at Jackob. "Someone has left a baby. A white Negro." He emphasized the last words.

Jackob told his boss he'd drop everything and be there in five minutes.

Sarah paced with Adimu in her arms. The baby's cries tormented her more than her husband's indifference. It seemed that nothing could console the sweet bundle. She walked over to Charles.

"You hold her," said Sarah, offering him the baby.

Charles remained still as his wife placed the baby carefully on his lap. He looked at it, balancing her on his knees to minimize the contact between them. Adimu stopped crying.

A titter escaped from Sarah's lips. "You look good with a baby on your lap. And she feels safe with you; she trusts you."

"You've got to be kidding. Get her off me immediately," said Charles, relieved to see Jackob's Toyota driving toward the house. The car pulled to a stop in a cloud of dust, and Jackob got out, slamming the door. As soon as Charles saw his assistant, he lifted Adimu and handed her to him. The baby started screeching again. Jackob, unperturbed, held the baby gingerly as he asked the cook, Adamma, for help.

"Take her away," urged Charles. "She's given me a headache." Charles thought of how his own father, Finley, wanted nothing to do with him when he showed any emotion. It was how he learned to be stoic, his most serviceable quality, he thought.

ADAMMA REACHED FOR the baby and hurried into the house, followed by the maids. Sarah would have liked to go with them but chose to stay and listen to what the men had to say.

"I want her taken back to where she came from, immediately. How can we find out who her parents are?" thundered Charles.

Perspiring, his assistant said, "I'll take care of it. No problem, sir, I know where she's from."

"Praise God," mumbled Charles, pouring himself another glass of white wine.

Sarah studied her husband. For a moment he seemed like a stranger. Although he had made it perfectly clear he didn't want to be a father, the man she knew had a sensitive soul and would be loving to a defenseless creature. *How could he place a human being on the dirt where there are snakes and insects that could harm her?* she wondered. *What kind of a person does that?* Then the young woman who placed the baby in Charles's lap flashed through Sarah's mind, and Sarah considered why, in the first place, the mother might have brought the baby to her and Charles. "Maybe the baby's been rejected by her family. If so…we can keep her." The words tumbled out of Sarah's mouth before she had time to reflect.

Charles froze. "What in the world?" He put his hand in his pocket to touch his gold nugget, his face a mask of shock. "Don't even think it. We have gotten this far without problems…Why change now?"

"She must be returned to her family," intervened Jackob. "She is part of a clan. You cannot keep her, madam, not even if sir agreed. Besides," he added *sotto voce*, "it is a *zeru zeru*. It is imprudent to have anything to do with her. Bad luck!"

"How is it possible to trust a child to a mother who abandoned her?" asked Sarah. Her voice trembled through the lump in her throat.

"Well, with all the little snotty, needy children on this continent, why should I take care of her?" her husband asked.

"Madam," interjected Jackob, "the family probably believes the child is your husband's because of the color of her skin. Let me take care of this matter. I shall take her back to the village myself."

Charles nodded and squeezed his wife's arm.

"No, we're coming," she said. "She was left in our hands, and we will take her back to her parents."

"Why on earth should we waste our time if he can do it?"

"For God's sake, Charles. Is she an object or a human being? The child will be returned on the condition that the family promises to care for her," she declared.

Jackob shook his head. "Your request could be interpreted as interfering with the traditions of the island," he said. "I believe it's imprudent."

"Who cares about prudence!" Sarah snapped. She got up and went inside. It was cool in the house. She stopped in the entry and brushed her fingers over a bouquet of red and orange flowers arranged in a crystal vase. The sensation that Charles was a stranger passed through her again.

"Madam, what does Mr. Jackob suggest?" The voice of the cook startled Sarah and returned her to the present moment.

"He echoes my husband's sentiments, like always," said Sarah, shaking her head.

In the garden, Charles and Jackob lingered, immersed in discussion.

"Your wife seems very convinced, sir."

"She is a stubborn woman. It will be difficult to make her change her mind," said Charles with a touch of pride. He had always admired his wife's decisive character, even if in that moment he would have preferred docility.

"I want this matter resolved as soon as possible. Go to the child's family and tell them to take her back and care for her." Charles paused and sipped some wine. "I want to make my wife happy."

"It could be difficult, sir," said Jackob. "*Zeru zerus* are repudiated by the community and by their families. They are magical, malevolent beings. People are afraid of them."

"Nonsense. I shall pay them well so long as they do as I say. With a handful of money, fear will magically go bye-bye. Let me know if this speaks the family's language," he said, handing Jackob a stack of bills.

JACKOB LEFT IN the golden afternoon light. Although the sun's rays stretched across the land, the heat persisted, unbroken. While he drove toward the village, Mr. Fielding's assistant concentrated on how he could best resolve the problem. He had no intention of going to Zuberi. And he couldn't simply show up at Sefu's home as he knew Sefu had denied the *zeru zeru* was his. Be that as it may, Jackob had to indulge his boss. The solution of how to handle the delicate matter of the *zeru zeru*, he knew, would be found with help from the village chief.

12.

Kondo sighed when Jackob explained the situation. The white shadow was causing much trouble. First the name, now this. What would happen in the future if only a year after its birth it was already unsettling the village? *Perhaps it had been a bad idea to let it live.* However, the time to reconsider was well past. The white man had the *zeru zeru*, and the situation had to be resolved as quickly as possible.

That same evening, Kondo, Jackob, and Sefu met at Zuberi's home.

Sefu was furious. "Who took the *zeru zeru* to the white man?" he demanded in a booming voice.

"I was at home having lunch with my wife and baby," Jackob replied, "and next thing I know, the *embulamaro* is in my boss's arms. Believe me, I am as much in the dark about what happened as you. The *wazungu* said nothing more than it was a young woman who presented them with your daughter."

"Avoid offending me and my clan. *It* is not my daughter! I don't care where that creature stays as long as it's not in the hands of that man. My mother is desperate. It should be returned to her today, and it will be the white man who does it." He slammed a rice bowl onto the table. "I want to forget this whole damned story," he yelled.

Kondo and Zuberi left to determine the verdict.

In the witch doctor's laboratory, Kondo watched Zuberi light some candles to alleviate the darkness. Then Zuberi closed the door with a heavy deadbolt and retreated to the back of the space. A number of objects were set in a corner and thick spiderwebs hung from the ceiling. Zuberi shifted some things on the long wooden table, and a hairy spider jumped into a crack in the wall to hide.

"Open the window," said Kondo. "There is still light."

Zuberi pulled him close. "I have valuable objects to show you. It is best to keep it shut." He was pushing aside pieces of worn and worried fabric, glass bottles of various colors, and piles of amulets. Kondo watched Zuberi in the weak light of the candles. Zuberi rolled up a red carpet to reveal a worm-eaten wooden chest that was bolted shut with a modern lock.

"In here are the amulets and ritual ornaments from my innumerable ancestors," said the witch doctor as he inserted a key into the padlock. "They go back to the time when Ukerewe emerged from the water of the lake. My lineage spoke directly to the primordial spirits. These most powerful totems and jujus will remain at rest until the day I need them."

Kondo stepped forward to examine the contents of the chest: pendants, headdresses, fabric panels. *What does this have to do with the* zeru zeru? Kondo asked himself, looking suspiciously at the village shaman.

Zuberi closed the lid of the chest and moved closer to Kondo. "*It* survived the trial of the beasts, the Spirits of the Lake pronounced themselves in its favor, and now it has a name—though sanctified by that charlatan Mosi," said the healer with a flash of irony in his voice. "We can let the *zeru zeru* live on the island until the time comes."

"Like the objects inside the chest?" asked Kondo.

"Yes, like the magic inside this chest." Zuberi flashed a knowing look at the village chief as though they were speaking in their own clandestine language.

"I would have thought you'd be happy it was in the white people's hands. It's a good way to be rid of it," Kondo said. "You must promise me that you will not harm the *zeru zeru*."

Zuberi shook his head. "The time will come when it will be useful. Besides, Sefu is adamant. He wants his mother to have it," he added.

"We have to respect Sefu's will. We must remain vigilant and protect the *embulamaro* so it's not stolen a second time," Kondo said.

"Amulets made from *zeru zeru* bodies are the strongest of all," mumbled Zuberi under his breath. "Yes, we must protect it until the right moment."

JACKOB AND SEFU were waiting in Zuberi's house proper for the two elders to, once again, decide the fate of the *zeru zeru*. Sefu had calmed down and was staring at the fire. Both men jumped when the door opened. The witch doctor and the head of the village walked with slow steps into the room where Jackob and Sefu sat.

"Sefu is right," said Kondo to Jackob. "Go to your *mzungu*[9] and tell him

---

[9] White man in Swahili.

that the *zeru zeru* must remain in the community into which it was born. It must be returned to Nkamba."

Jackob reached into his pocket. "Mr. Charles gave me these." He held out the bills. "To make amends."

"They are for Sefu," said Kondo. "He is the one who has been offended, and reparation should go to him."

Sefu pressed his palm on the smooth blue plastic surface of the table. *How can I accept payment for the disgrace of being the presumed father of a white shadow?* he asked himself. He would take the money, though it wasn't adequate compensation for the humiliating event.

He spied Zuberi who appeared spellbound by the bills. Sefu had no notion that Zuberi envisioned being handed an even greater stack of bills, one day, thanks to the *zeru zeru*.

13.

Jackob drove at a slow pace toward White House. The tropical night had rolled a shaker of dice to disseminate a sky full of stars, and an orange moon hung between the interlaced branches of mango trees like a nugget pendant worn around Heaven's neck. The mission had gone well. Mrs. Fielding's proposal coincided with Sefu's interests. His boss would be pleased, and the ugly event would conclude without consequences.

White House appeared in the distance, illuminated by torches in the garden. Jackob pondered the building's magnificence: it was truly worthy of a king. He found Charles sitting on the veranda in a seagrass rush chair, immersed in the newspaper.

"How are you, sir?"

Charles wavered. He seemed tired, and his eyes were puffy and red. "Have you resolved the matter?"

Jackob took on a solemn air. "Tomorrow morning you can bring the child to her family as your wife wishes. I was able to convince them to take her back and to have you present at the transaction. It was difficult sir, but I did it."

"Thank you, my friend. Thank you." Charles rose from the chair and patted Jackob on the back.

Jackob's employer was stingy with compliments. "My friend." Those two words were balm for his soul. He would have wagged his tail if he had had one. Just then, Sarah appeared on the threshold. She was wearing a light robe that grazed the floor, her hair was down, and she was massaging the back of her neck. She looked radiant. She sat in a green canvas armchair and joined the men. "So?" she asked Jackob.

"The village chief has decided, madam. The *zeru zeru* must be returned to her family tomorrow. He has conceded that you and your husband may bring her to them, though only if that is what you prefer."

Sarah hung her head, pinching the skin between her eyes, and stood up. "Tonight you'll sleep alone, Charles. I'll stay in the room with the child."

Charles exhaled and watched her walk away with decisive steps, her robe fluttering in the dim evening light.

"Go ahead, Jackob. It's been a long day for you too."

His assistant hesitated, shifting his weight from one leg to the other. "There is one last thing, sir."

"What is it?" Charles asked with alarm.

"I should like to suggest that you and your wife pay a visit to the healer to thank him for his interest in this matter."

For Jackob, this would flaunt his connection to the wealthy and famous white man and would provide an occasion to augment his prestige in the village. Besides, a visit to Zuberi would be an extra guarantee for the child: the life of an *embulamaro* was precarious, and Jackob wanted to keep problems in the future from arising between Mr. and Mrs. Fielding. He anticipated at every turn what was best for his boss.

"Impossible," said Charles. "I want nothing more to do with this baby, and, in any case, Sarah would refuse. She is English." He paused and then added, "She has always avoided relations with those types of people."

Jackob shrugged off the insult as he so often had to do when dealing with whites. "Zuberi is very influential in the village. If you secure his favor, the child will walk on streets free of mud. Just as your wife wants," insisted Jackob. "Furthermore," he added with fervor, "he is the most prestigious shaman. His skills as a fortune-teller are well known throughout the island. His friendship and influence could bring you good luck in business."

"Ah, really? My business is thriving without magic. In any case, I'll go if it will help protect the child and, especially, if it keeps our paths from ever again crossing with the child's." He added in a low voice, "Seeing her is bad for Sarah."

Jackob thought of how radiant Mrs. Fielding had looked. He said, "I will accompany you to his home myself. Until morning, sir."

"Wait. Sarah mustn't know of our conversation. Tomorrow, suggest visiting Zuberi on the spur of the moment, if you get what I mean."

"Of course, sir. As you wish. Good night."

CHARLES REMAINED ALONE on the veranda. That mysterious feeling of regret, that strange sense of guilt toward his wife, welled up in him. And, yet, he had given her everything a woman could desire: houses, trips, money, Italian clothes, and his love. Perhaps most importantly, he had given her his respect. He thought of his mother. He couldn't imagine having Sarah look at him in the way his mother had looked at his father the mornings after Finley had spent a night on the town: his mother's eyes flat with disappointment, the expression of a dog whose joy had been beaten out of it by its master. He would avoid inflicting such pain on Sarah. He would always be true to her.

Sarah was lucky to have him as her husband. The day he proposed marriage was when her good luck commenced.

Ah, women, he thought. *Capricious and moody like the weather but such delicious beings!* It would be difficult, maybe impossible for him to live without Sarah—her practicality, her integrity. She was his island of goodness and happiness, a safe haven from which to depart in the morning and return at night, a place for him to be restored. Charles knew how angry Sarah would be if he suggested they visit the witch doctor. She abhorred superstition and religion. She had insisted they be married in a civil ceremony, even though that wasn't his preference. "God does not exist, Charles," she'd said. "There's nothing up there. Each person constructs their own destiny with the help of others on Earth." He had conceded to her wishes, though doing so went against his better judgment. His Christian faith was mercurial, but he bet on playing it safe rather than risk antagonizing some omnipotence. *In the end, who can affirm God's existence one way or the other?*

Charles had heard of shamans' nonpareil powers—how the strongest of them communicate directly with the ancient spirits—and he couldn't help but envision how such a man might help him with the business decision he had been obsessing about. He would have to convince Sarah, make her understand that taking a short detour to visit the healer was in the child's best interest. *Too difficult to explain the truth*, thought Charles as he yawned. *Much better a small innocent lie.*

He folded the newspaper and went into the house. Just before falling asleep, Jackob's words returned to him: *His friendship and influence could bring you good luck in business. When in doubt, best not to displease anyone*, he reminded himself, a lesson he took from his father. It was preferable to have gods *and* spirits on his side. He laughed to himself. He lay on his back, enjoying the cool silk bed sheets. As sleep came and carried him away, he was thinking how he needed all the help he could get for his new endeavor.

14.

Sarah climbed the stairs, bearing an invisible heavy weight. *How many empty rooms*, she thought as she dragged herself along the corridor. The door to the room where the baby lay was ajar. Adimu slept in the queen-sized bed near the window. Sarah had surrounded her with pillows to keep her safe from the edges of the mattress and had unknotted the insect net.

In the afternoon, once she'd succeeded in calming the child, she spoon-fed Adimu *ugali* and creamed chicken prepared by the cook. "Good girl," Sarah had cooed, kissing her with each bite eaten and caressing her golden hair.

She sat on a chair next to the bed and drew the insect net aside. She watched the baby's pink eyelids quiver as she dreamed. Sarah looked at the chubby legs, her rounded, fleshy feet and felt her heart take a dive. She remained like that, absorbed, until her back ached. She considered lying next to the child to sleep with her and immediately decided against it. She would watch over her until the morning. She would stay present, vigilant, ready to protect her. She could see that the child was well cared for and that made her feel tenderness toward her caregiver. The baby whimpered in her sleep, and a memory emerged, one that had been hiding in the corridor of Sarah's mind since the mystery woman had left Adimu in her husband's lap.

It was the last time she'd seen him. Her father. She was eating cereal when he lopped down the stairs. He sat beside her in the kitchen and asked her to plunk herself on his lap. She refused, though hugged him, and he hugged her so tight that it scared her. He kissed her forehead and told her he loved her and to get ready for school.

He was found with a rope around his neck, she had been told when she was quite a bit older. She couldn't help but feel that if she had said something different, if she had sat on his lap, he might not have done it. Because he took his own life, there was no priest at the memorial—just Sarah, her mother, and an aunt who she hadn't known, a big sister to a father she adored. Her mother explained that the memorial was a way to say goodbye to him, though she anticipated his return. Sarah thought about the months that followed. Her classmates' comments. The looks from people on the street, the silence into which her mother had withdrawn, her nocturnal tears. She remembered the meaning of the words that, until then, she had ignored—"sin," "godless." *Suicide.* The shameful word, that was overheard between sobs during a conversation between her mother and aunt. That was the day she understood she would never see her father again. *That* word would torment her for the rest of her life. It would be ever-present, lying in ambush like a guard dog, ferocious, ready to wake up and bite at any moment. She was certain that if she had been by his side and did what he had asked, her father would have desisted from his purpose. She had refused to protect him.

Protecting the child would be her redemption. She looked at her engagement ring, its three carats catching the subdued light. She thought about what that stone signified for her. Not the aesthetic or material value but its promise of endless love. Nevertheless, she would give away even *that* symbol if it meant keeping the child with her. Her heart jumped at the thought.

She heard her husband open and close the tap in the bathroom. She resisted the temptation to speak with him about the yearning she was drowning in. In England, Charles had seemed anxious to have her as a part of his world. Strong. Determined to protect her. Where was that Charles who she had married only five years earlier? It was almost as though a twin had taken her loving husband's place. Almost as though the Charles she had married removed a mask and was showing his true fearful, feckless, angry face. Adimu gurgled and coughed several times. Sarah leaned over to make sure the child was well and caressed her cheek.

15.

News of Adimu's kidnapping spread as quickly through Murutanga as the barking of dogs on a quiet night. When Juma heard of it, she lifted her face and opened her palms toward the heavens. But then regret took hold of her, and she quickly crossed her arms over her chest. Sefu's first wife, Afua, was visiting her sister who'd given birth in a village on the mainland, and she had taken their children. Juma took her rival's absence to mean this was the right moment to speak with Sefu. They were still husband and wife and, despite his denial, the *zeru zeru* was their offspring. Juma felt she needed—and had the right—to express her opinion.

In the evening, she washed and dressed with care. She rubbed coconut oil on her soft belly; on her breasts, which were still firm and high like they had been before the birth; and on her strong thighs. She braided her hair and put on the beaded bracelets her husband had given her as a wedding gift. She glanced at her photo of Sefu that she had set on a stool. A NGO worker had taken it of Sefu beside a flourishing crop of corn, beads of sweat gathered on his forehead. He had been proud of that photograph, as was she. Every night, since he'd left, Juma lit a candle in front of that picture of her husband. Illuminated by the soft light, his face kept her company during her solitary hours and kept alive her hope that the Spirits of the Lake would lead him back to her. Drawing on her remaining courage, she went to visit his other home.

When approaching his hut, she held her breath. Her heart raced. She heard a woman talking with her husband. *Could Afua have returned?* she wondered. Leaning into the front door, Juma recognized the woman's voice. She rested against a tree trunk and exhaled. She imagined that her husband's cousin Yunis must have come to find out about the kidnapping. Juma would hide among the bushes, close enough to hear while out of sight until her best friend departed.

THE MORNING AFTER the dark-eyed woman had left Adimu with the Fieldings, she returned home, upset, and told her husband her version of what had happened in the forest. He advised her to confide in Sefu that very day. And so it was that husband and wife went to visit and explain.

"I took the *embulamaro*. I wanted to abandon it in the forest as an offering to the Spirits. I did it out of friendship, cousin Sefu," she said. She inhaled deeply as if she had come up from the depths of the lake for air. "I wanted to relieve you of your burden."

Only Yunis knew the truth. What happened in the forest was still fresh in her mind: the temptation to escape from the island with the baby. She remembered Adimu's tiny lips latched onto her sterile breast. How she had wished her breasts swelled with milk to nourish the creature! She'd been trapped like a bird in a snare and coerced into desiring the child's well-being. "Baby girl, not *zeru zeru*," she had whispered to the child, rubbing her nose on the infant's tiny one. Her joy had been so immense at the thought of Adimu safe with the white couple that it surely could not have been demonical, could it have been? Demons generate hate and evil. The sensations that had sheathed her body had been good and loving; they were maternal feelings. The woman had always hoped she'd experience the feelings of a mother: now she had. She shuddered and put her arms around her body in shame. She banished her memories into the depths of her being, deeper and deeper where they could remain buried forever. She lifted her head and stared into her cousin's eyes, pretending to express disdain for the baby.

"I hate the *zeru zeru* as much as I am disgusted by what I have done and the pain I've caused through my recklessness, dear cousin. I beg you to forgive me," she said, dropping to her knees before Sefu's rigid gaze.

"I believe you, cousin," he said to the young woman. He expressed to her that her experience in the forest was additional proof of the maleficence of the *zeru zeru*, that it was best for him, for their clan, to have the fiend removed from their lives.

"I forgive you, Yunis. You acted for the good of the clan. I hope you are aware of the *zeru zeru's* power and that you will, from now on, behave as I do and not deign it with a glance."

JUMA LISTENED TO her friend confess, shivering as she pressed herself against the bark of the tree. The tremor began in her belly and radiated out to the ends of her limbs. Why did Yunis act without first coming to her? Had Juma really become so insignificant? Invisible, that's what she was.

She would be better off dead by her own hand. Her legs tired from holding herself up, and she crumpled to the ground.

Hearing Sefu's deep voice startled her.

"Why to the white man?" Sefu demanded. "Don't you realize this dishonors me? Taking the *zeru zeru* to him suggests that he is the real father."

"That was not my intention," Yunis stressed. "The evil creature took charge of me while we were in the forest and guided my steps. Its magic made me go to the *wasungu*. The white shadow possessed me."

Juma heard her husband's and Yunis's words as though they came from afar. She lay curled up on the earth, her knees tight between her arms, tears chilling her face. The orange moon in the sky was vanishing behind a massive cloud front.

Juma finally stood up and dried her tears. She thought she would spit out Nkamba's secret, scorching Sefu with the truth that he was not only a father but also a brother of a *zeru zeru*. Unbeknownst to her, the hem of her dress caught in the bushes, and when she stepped out of the shrubbery without taking care, the fabric gave way and tore. She opened the door of Sefu's hut.

As soon as he saw Juma, Sefu raised his right hand, as if to keep her from entering with the sole force of his open palm, as though she were an evil spirit or a *zeru zeru*. Nothing of the initial impetus that had propelled her to go to her husband remained. A paralyzing fear grabbed hold of her shoulders. From the doorway, Juma did not see her friend's husband hidden in the room's darkness. She shifted her eyes from Sefu to Yunis, their faces illuminated by the light of the flickering fire. She sensed an intimacy between them that she had not been aware of. A flash of jealousy rose in her throat, and heat emanated from her skin.

"Why do you believe her and not me? After what she's done, is she more deserving of your forgiveness?" shouted Juma. Her voice splintered the silence like a glass vase shattering into a thousand pieces on a tile floor.

Sefu shifted on his chair. "Go home, Juma. This business will be resolved within my clan."

Juma was struck dumb. *Inside his clan.* She realized with a chill that she was no longer part of his life. Juma said nothing to her husband. She had lost the will to speak to him of his dead sister. She focused her eyes on Yunis, the sister who had betrayed her, who was now forever dead to her. Juma turned on her heels and disappeared into the night without closing the door. Her husband's avowal weighed on her like a hundred bundles of wood tied to her back. She continued on her way, shuffling her feet along the ground, occasionally stepping on the ragged piece of torn fabric that dragged on the earth, her shoulders curved by the heavy weight of disdain. The village was asleep, and she was alone.

16.

The following morning, Nkamba was in front of her hut, beating grain to make *chapati*[10]. She had spent the night wandering the forest, searching for her granddaughter. At sunrise, when her body felt as though she had plowed a field as large as the entire village, she went home and sat silently on a mat outside the door, watching the darkness dissipate. If necessary, she would walk the island to find her *mjukuu*, she told herself, and she turned her energy to preparing food to take with her as she continued her search. She'd never forgive herself for allowing the child to vanish. As she passed her arm across her forehead to whisk away sweat, she squinted to focus her vision. Strangers were coming. A white couple walking with Jackob, the woman holding a child in her arms. Her child!

"Adimu!" she shouted. Dropping the glass bottle she'd been using to roll out the wheat dough, her hands still white with flour, she rushed forward. She touched the baby's cheeks and pulled her away from the woman, leaving a long streak of powder on Sarah's tanned forearm. The two women glared at each other, eye to eye, though Sarah was so much taller than the wizened elder. Without uttering a word, Nkamba turned and ran inside the house with the baby, slamming the door behind her.

Sarah hesitated, bewildered by the woman's reaction and especially by her ancient appearance. "Charles, is *that* the mother? She's not the woman who brought us the baby."

"Local women look older than they are," he replied.

Jackob jumped in. "Nkamba is the child's family," he told them. Then he suggested he accompany them to Zuberi's home to guarantee the baby's safety.

"Who's Zuberi?" asked Sarah.

"He interceded with the child's family and has taken her under his

---

[10] A sort of unleavened bread eaten commonly throughout Tanzania.

protection," said Jackob. "He is our most famous healer and the spiritual leader of Ukerewe."

"It's for the child's well-being, my dear," interjected her husband. "We need to be certain that she is safe, and that must be done through Zuberi."

Sarah's own happiness hinged on the baby's welfare. Her initial response to this man, this "Zuberi," was negative. She imagined that if he hadn't gotten involved, Charles may have been convinced to adopt the baby. *Charles would have warmed to the idea eventually*, Sarah thought. Sarah's aversion to all types of superstitions was on high alert. Nevertheless, despite her irritation with the old woman who snatched the baby without even a thank-you and the "spiritual leader" who was supposedly looking out for the child's best interests (*then how did someone kidnap her?*), she conceded that she was being selfish, and it was best for the baby to grow up among her own people. She had to put the child's well-being before her maternal instincts. As for Charles, after he recovered from his initial—and despicable—shock at being given a strange baby, his concern for the child had endeared him to her.

"All right, let's go see him," she exhaled, linking her hand in her husband's. "For the baby's sake."

THE HEALER'S LEGS were trembling. He was so excited. He knew who Charles was: the famous mine owner and one of the richest men in the region. Zuberi had never entertained a white visitor and sensed his destiny as preeminent shaman to be so close he could lick it.

He took Charles's hand and observed the woman. He tilted his head forward to study her better. Her curly blond hair framed her tan face, and a glow of health and confidence flowed from her. *A rivulet in which swims much life*, thought Zuberi. *I must be careful with this one.* He had heard that European women reign over the men.

Charles he knew how to handle.

"While my daughter prepares some tea, it would be an honor to show you where I do my work," the witch doctor said. "Serve it in our best clay cups," he muttered to his teenage girl.

"Yes, *Baba*," she replied before scurrying away.

Zuberi's daughter opened the door of her father's private area for the guests to enter. Sarah stiffened as she crossed the threshold of Zuberi's workroom. A row of cock feet hung from a string on the wall, and a great quantity of dried bird, rodent, and other animal heads were stacked on a table. A series of ceramic, glass, and plastic jars containing a variety of teeth, dried unidentifiable animals, and roots and leaves lined a long, rough-hewn shelf.

"I'll wait here," said Sarah, paralyzed on the doorstep, battling a wave of nausea. A putrid, dusty odor hung in the air, and in the faint light of the workroom, Zuberi's wrinkled face and mangy thinning hair made him appear demonic.

"The lady prefers to stay outside?" Zuberi asked, looking to Charles for an explanation of his wife's reticence.

"Oh, no," Charles responded in a hurry. "She's simply not feeling well."

Sarah attempted a weak smile to confirm her husband's excuse.

"The tea is ready, father." Zuberi's daughter set the tray on a table in the sitting room, then stood demurely to one side, her hands clasped in front of her.

To Sarah's great relief, the men moved into the adjacent sitting room, not the workroom with the desiccated animals.

Zuberi invited Charles and Sarah to sit down for tea.

"Thank you, but we really don't want to disturb you." Charles shook his head as he tried to refuse courteously. "We've only come to thank you for your help and to be sure the child will be taken care of."

"Please, sit down. I insist." Zuberi brushed off several chairs while his daughter poured the infusion into chipped cups and stood until the guests sat.

Jackob, who stayed close to Charles, eyed him. Charles was aware that it would be a grave offense to refuse the invitation. He felt his wife's hand squeeze his, and he sat at the table and sipped the infusion. Sarah and Jackob followed and, as he was the host, Zuberi took his seat last.

"You, sir, are a king accompanied by noble spirits. They are invisible to your eyes, but I see that they protect you. I sense you would like to ask me something," he added, taking Charles's hand and holding it between his own hardened palms. Zuberi lowered his eyelids and inhaled. "In your future, I see wealth that is greater than that which you already possess. I see gold nuggets mingled with the soil on which you tread. You are a successful man, and I feel your success," he declared, continuing to hold onto Charles.

Charles was captivated. He recognized that the shaman was reaching into his soul. He thought of the business endeavor—the one his wife was unaware of—that he was in the midst of winding up. Zuberi was predicting his victorious destiny.

Several weeks prior, two government officials responsible for organizing an auction for a tract of land came to Charles's office to propose "a facilitated purchase." They would sell him the mining license before publically announcing the auction. They told him that many other businessmen had expressed considerable interest. In exchange, they'd want a small personal compensation.

"The minister of mining said you are the only one with sufficient means who is in the position to consider this proposal," one of them had said.

Charles leaned forward as the officials pressed on with the sales pitch. The land parcel was adjacent to his most productive mine, and, for a while, ironically, he had been reflecting on how he might purchase it. The necessary soil analyses had not yet been performed, and he wondered if there was enough ore on that tract to bear building another mine. Still, his mine was lucrative, so why wouldn't this other one be? he had asked himself. When he had originally mentioned the idea to his wife—before the officials approached him—she expressed her disapproval. "We're rich enough. More gold and more work. I'd rather we spend time together. Travel. Involve ourselves in conservation work. In philanthropy. Is another gold mine really what we want? Yours is already the most productive in Tanzania," she'd said.

"I need time to consider your proposal," Charles had told the officials.

He stayed awake all night, planning what he might do if he had more money, how just a smidgen extra would forever banish the fear that at any moment he might lose everything—Sarah, White House, his very freedom. He had to decide in a hurry. It was the last mining license that would ever be available in the district, at least for the coming decade. And if he refused the offer, the functionaries would propose the deal to one of his rivals. He knew his interlopers well. They were always looking to outdo him. And they, not he, would get the goodies.

It had been as easy to corrupt officers of the government as to buy off a mother able to feed her children only every other day. The men might purchase a new car or a house made of bricks. A good deed for everyone involved, he had told himself. As for Sarah, once the new mine began to bear fruit, he'd let her know it was theirs—maybe by way of buying her a precious diamond-studded bracelet. His wife might pout for a while, but he knew how to make peace. The bracelet and a nice trip, one deserving of the bride of a king. He contemplated a destination and was surprised he hadn't thought of it before. More than once Sarah had expressed the desire—a silly one in his opinion—to swim with dolphins in the open sea. Well, he would satisfy her, even if he had to go to the trouble of having two or three of them trained to lift her into the air and do flips above her while she floated on her back. Yes, during a sleepless night, Charles decided he would follow his infallible instinct, and with self-constructed wings, he would fly toward the sun. High and ever higher still.

The following morning, he had concluded the deal and was awaiting the ownership and extraction license deeds from the ministry.

"We are here to make certain that the child is safe with her parents," said Sarah to Zuberi.

"The *zeru zeru* lives with the grandmother. Though how can harm come to it if it is under my protection?" he said with a big smile that revealed his blackish gums and several gaps where he was missing teeth.

Sarah was annoyed by the way the man referred to the baby as if she were an object, an "it."

"So the woman who took the child is not her mother?" inquired Sarah, speaking to Charles. Something in that creepy man's voice made her shiver. She hoped her husband would intervene, but, instead, he shrugged his shoulders and turned up his palms, almost as though he was under the healer's power and the two men were combining their energy to subdue her.

"The grandmother asked to care for the granddaughter," said Jackob. "The baby is in good hands."

"If the parents permitted the grandmother to take her, it means they don't want her," insisted Sarah, although she perceived the baby was adored by its guardian and that the elder must be dedicating her remaining days to the baby's care.

Charles drummed his fingers on his thigh. "My dear, is it so strange that in Africa a child lives with its grandparent? It happens all the time in Europe."

"Listen to your husband," said the shaman. "A man who is chosen—as is your husband—is immune from errors."

"Chosen?" A flash of interest appeared on Charles's face.

Sarah noticed it immediately. *So now this psychopath thinks my marriage was arranged and Charles was selected for me?* she wondered.

"Yes…chosen for success," confirmed Zuberi.

Sarah wanted to scream. She despised the unctuous man like a poisonous snake—*he's worse even than Jackob*—and she detested her husband in that moment as well. *How can he listen to such stupidity? What insecurities lurk inside Charles that he attracts sycophants?* she wondered. She stood up brusquely, rocking the wobbly plastic table as well as her half-full cup of tea.

"We're going. Come along, Charles," she said, barely controlling her irritation.

On the way back to White House, Sarah was silent, looking out the car window at the chaotic lushness of the landscape. The bumpy road rocked the vehicle, increasing the nausea that lingered from that Zuberi's reeking lair. As Charles drove, he turned, from time to time, to look at his wife as though he was trying to get a bead on her.

"I hope the words of that imposter have not emboldened you to go forward with your crazy idea of buying a second mine," she said in a flat voice.

"Of course not, dear." Charles chuckled. "I don't need fortune-tellers to know I'm doing the right thing." Although Sarah heard the veiled confession that he had already purchased the mine, she slipped into denial.

She looked directly at her husband. "We've given back what we really need, the child, and we have way too much of the rest. Please stay away from that risky prospect. It will turn sour. I know it, darling."

"Ahhh, don't say that! You'll bring bad luck!" Charles's expression darkened. He braked the car on the roadside and quickly opened the door.

"What are you doing?" She saw her husband thrust his hand in his pocket.

"I'm looking for wood to knock on," he said with forced lightness. "To counter your unlucky words," he teased, grabbing a dry branch that was lying by the side of the road.

"You always want to joke." Sarah sighed and turned her head.

Charles got back in the car and kissed his wife on the lips. "Stop pouting," he whispered, hugging her.

Sarah mumbled and wrinkled up her face. "You know these things bother me," she said, freeing herself from her husband's arms.

"What things?"

"Silly superstitions."

Charles pretended to give no importance to what Sarah said. He started the car and drove off quickly. "Let's take the boat and have lunch on the lake," he suggested. "Would you like that?"

A hen darted across the road.

"Look out!" shouted Sarah.

Charles ignored his wife, keeping the car on its path, and hit the animal. A split-second later, around a curve of the road, a child on a bicycle appeared, coming in the opposite direction.

Charles slammed on the brakes. The car stopped, wrapped in a cloud of yellowish dust.

"Are you all right?" Charles turned to his wife.

"Oh, Charles," Sarah gasped, "if you'd listened to me, you would have hit that child." She hugged him, sobbing.

Her husband pulled her close and smoothed her hair. "Never avoid an animal on the road if it means going into the other lane," he instructed, like an elementary school teacher. "Especially not in Africa!" Charles shook his head.

She continued to sob, clinging to her husband.

He lifted Sarah's face and dried her cheeks with the cuff of his shirt. "Dearest, why all these tears? It was only a hen."

Sarah couldn't stop thinking about the baby that the old woman had ripped from her arms. *Sarah* was the one—not the baby—who was starving for love, for motherhood. It was time to look reality in the face: she felt alone and abandoned. She felt empty inside, as though an enormous desert with heat, phantasms, and skeletons suffused her inner-landscape. Could she have insisted that she and Charles keep the baby? Let the grandmother visit whenever? No, her husband had a hard part that couldn't be mined; he wouldn't have given in. And then there were the superstitions. *How could he abide by them? He pretended not to, but—*

It dawned on Sarah at that moment that she was adhering to a life that wasn't hers, ruled by laws she didn't know. She was in Africa. And although she had been living under its sun and stars for six years, she was a foreigner. She was *the other*. That horrid man, the witch doctor, had been right. She needed to trust her husband who was thoroughly a part of the uncanny continent that she was beginning to cherish. The episode with the hen was proof. If she had been driving, she would have saved the chicken and killed the boy. Another wave of tears threatened to surge, but she managed to hold them back. She looked at her husband. "I'm sorry, dear, I was afraid. I'm better now. Let's stop at the house to freshen up and then go out on the boat."

THREE DAYS LATER, Charles received a phone call from the ministry of mining. The minister himself was on the line, expressing his fervent congratulations. The deal was closed. By the afternoon, Charles had the papers in hand. Charles would tell Sarah about the acquisition in due time, when she was ready to admit that he was right to have bought it, just as she admitted he was right to run over the hen. Zuberi's grin with black gums flashed in Charles's mind.

MONTHS OF INTENSE work followed. Charles gave instructions to build offices and a dining hall and to hire personnel. He planned to erect dormitories for workers who came from villages far away. *Philanthropy,* Charles thought. *Sarah, what I'm doing is my type of philanthropy.*

No one in that part of the country had ever heard of a mine owner investing in his employees' lodging. Charles stood out from the rest of the renowned entrepreneurs. Hundreds of men came for interviews, hoping to obtain a position.

Those from the villages around Mwanza considered Charles a good spirit fallen from the sky. He had burned his wings when flying close to the sun and had tumbled to Earth to live as a man. Fathers told the story to their children. Men, grouped together under the stars in the evening, spoke of the legend and bet on who among them would be hired by the great, benevolent Mr. Fielding.

17.

It had taken most of the savings she had accumulated over the two rainy seasons since Adimu's birth, but Nkamba had finally been able to buy the biggest umbrella she could find on Ukerewe to protect her grandchild from the sun. Adimu's curiosity would often lead her beyond the shade of the umbrella, so Nkamba would weave palm leaves to create a larger shelter for her.

The grandmother saw how the sun blistered and bloodied her baby's flesh. "Don't you move from that shade!" she warned the child, shaking her bony finger, though Adimu rarely listened.

As Adimu grew, she investigated everything that her small world had to offer—a flower, an insect, a seed or leaf carried by the wind and left at her feet. A large part of her days were spent playing alone while Nkamba worked the clan's small fields, supervising her granddaughter from afar.

"*Jua*[11]."

"What did you say?" called Nkamba, turning quickly toward Adimu.

"*Jua, jua, jua*," repeated Adimu. It was her very first word. For many months after that, everything was *jua*: food, the chickens, the yellow earth in the yard, and even the cockroaches that squirmed on the floor of the hut.

Nkamba wondered if Adimu's language skills were stunted because of her isolation. She never, though, questioned for a moment whether the child started speaking at such a late age or whether her vocabulary was limited because of her intelligence. Nkamba had raised a son and a number of Sefu's cousins, and none of them matched Adimu's innate brilliance. As far as Nkamba was concerned, Adimu was *jua*.

ON SUNDAYS, DURING Father Andrew's Mass in the shade of the baobab in the center of the village, the elderly grandmother settled Adimu inside the trunk of the great tree where she was protected from the sun. Wrapped

---

[11] Sun in Swahili.

in the dim, benevolent light, Adimu never tired of touching the baobab's porous bark, her small hands brushing over the wood, tickling the great tree that sheltered her. Her eyes could not bear the bright rays of the sun, and for this reason, she often squinted. In the dry season, when the tropical sun glared violently, her face became a single wrinkle. With it scrunched up, she appeared to be looking about suspiciously. Sometimes Adimu liked to view the world through the green glass of a bottle her grandmother gave her to play with. She held it up to her eyes and turned it slowly, observing with surprise as objects changed shape through the movement of her hand.

Often one or more children would slip away from the group of adults who were listening to the sermon and tease Adimu. They pulled her thin hair or pinched her skin, intrigued by its bright pink color under their touch. She cried in protest only when their insistence caused pain. Otherwise she interpreted their provocations as a game. Sometimes, at the end of Mass, her arms and legs were covered with small pink spots.

Father Andrew noticed that Nkamba left her grandchild in the tree trunk during the service. He conjectured it was due to a lack of faith or, even worse, from the elderly woman's desire to keep the creature away from God. One Sunday, after having made small talk, he asked her, "Why do you hide her inside the tree rather than keep her among us in the arms of God?"

"My *mjukuu* is big now. She is in her third rainy season," the woman replied, stopping her gaze at the religious man's chest as if she wanted to talk to his heart. "Her presence could annoy the others, and we have enough problems."

Father Andrew took her hands in his. "Adimu is baptized," he said, to reassure her. "She is one of Christ's lambs, like all the others. The color of a person's skin is unimportant to Him, and He will be offended if you leave your grandchild outside the place where we listen to His voice."

Six rainy seasons had come and gone since the birth of Adimu, and she was with her grandmother at one of the tiny grocery stores of Murutanga where Nkamba was bartering products from her field for small quantities of sugar, salt, and palm oil. The grocery was a white-plaster structure with a tin roof on which a giant satellite dish was secured. Plastic buckets of various sizes and colors were stacked outside—orange, blue, green, brown, yellow. On the four aisles of shelving were stocked basics that were grown by nearby farmers, fresh loaves of bread baked by neighbors, and a limited supply of household sundries. The local tailors had fabrics available, and there was a freezer filled with King Cone ice cream and Fruit Pastilles ice pops. Nkamba preferred to trade with neighbors for her basic goods and not bring Adimu to the busy street in Murutanga, but sometimes she was forced to visit a store.

While her grandmother negotiated with the owner, Adimu noticed a child who was smaller than she, the shopkeeper's son. He was sitting in front of a mirror by the door, playing with a green bottle. Adimu drew near. She wanted to show him how interesting the world is when seen through glass.

"Can I have it for a moment?" asked Adimu, taking the bottle from the boy's hands. "There's a game I played when I was little."

Adimu concentrated on the bottle, rotating it, admiring its smooth surface. She loved to touch objects. Her eyesight was weak, and her fingertips acted as a second pair of eyes—the smoother the texture, the greater her pleasure. She wondered why her skin—thickened by the sun where it was exposed—wasn't smooth and cool like the bottle. And, above all, why her skin wasn't black like the little boy's.

The boy was mesmerized by Adimu's pale white arm. After what seemed like enough time to walk to the lake from the village, he shifted his eyes to his own dark skin. He gazed at the mirror to take in how he and the ghost girl looked side by side, and then, moving as close to her flesh as possible, he studied the details of her features. Finally, driven by curiosity, he touched her knuckles with his fingers. Adimu pulled away, disturbed by the intimate contact.

At that moment, Adimu, for no reason at all, looked over her shoulder and there, in one of the grocery store aisles, was a woman, white as flour with hair as light as hers, a halo around her face. The blue eyes of Adimu locked onto the blue eyes of the strange lady.

Adimu returned to the present when she heard the little boy ask his mother, "Why is she white?"

White: it was the first time Adimu had heard that word referred to her.

Adimu dropped the glass bottle and left the shop, running under a nearby shade tree just outside the door of the grocery. She had learned important rules from her grandma: always play where she could be seen, never talk with an adult without permission, don't get into a car or on a boat or walk with strangers, not even if they offer sweets. For this reason, Adimu kept her eyes glued on the shop door, though she wanted to run away, embarrassed to be "white" like the figment lady in the aisle.

"Never call out for help if you are in trouble. Instead, shout that someone is stealing cattle. Don't trust the people you know, and never trust strangers. They can jump out from behind bushes and take you away." This was Nkamba's litany that she repeated to Adimu daily.

SARAH HAD RECENTLY received a letter from a college friend, inquiring about her life in Africa. "What is the village like? The people, the food, the stores?" her friend had asked. Sarah was embarrassed to admit that she had not explored most of the mysterious island of Ukerewe. She had lived in Africa for eleven years and roamed freely around mainland Tanzania, but when at White House, she remained within the perimeter of her grounds. She'd spent her time being a homemaker. Recently she had gotten obsessed with floral design, had been making exotic bouquets using native flowers and vegetation.

Every once in a blue moon, she'd think of the baby who stole her heart all those years ago, with her chubby thighs and breathy coo.

That morning, when Adamma, the cook, told Sarah she was going to the grocery in Murutanga to pick up a few things for dinner, Sarah said she was coming along.

What a fortuitous trip to town! When browsing an aisle of the grocery, Sarah saw *her* baby "all grown up," playing with a much younger boy. Could it have been *that* many years since she watched her sleep through much of the night? *She must be nearly five,* Sarah thought. *And the love I felt then was real. I still love her.* At that very moment, as these words formed in Sarah's mind, Adimu looked up at her, and time stopped for Sarah. She was sure the child recognized her, though how could that be? She was barely a year old when her grandmother snatched her from her arms. She started toward Adimu and witnessed a quick exchange between the girl and boy, which resulted in the girl running out the door.

Sarah glimpsed the grandmother—more ragged and tired looking, if possible, than she appeared those years ago—speaking with a young woman in traditional dress and a hijab on her head. Sarah dared to approach the old woman who had been so hostile, as though she had been the one who kidnapped the girl and not the one who cared for her overnight. *Might she remember me?* Sarah wondered. And then she laughed to herself that of course she would. How many white women did the grandma have such direct dealings with? Not many, Sarah surmised.

Sarah asked Adamma to translate for her. "Tell her I want to buy her granddaughter an ice cream."

Nkamba shook her head and smiled. Adamma told Sarah that Nkamba said that she, herself, would hand the sweet to Adimu, that she couldn't allow her granddaughter to take treats from strangers, and she hoped Sarah would understand.

Although the word "stranger" felt like a sharp slap across her face, not a term that applied to *her*, the grandmother's protectiveness was endearing. Sarah bought the ice cream cone and handed it to the old woman.

She watched Nkamba leave the store and, moving to the doorway, saw the old woman give the King Cone to Adimu. Adimu glanced into the store at Sarah. Sarah was sure Adimu understood. *What a bright little girl*, she thought.

THAT EVENING, ADIMU asked her grandmother who "strangers" were. She understood they were a threat but didn't know how she'd recognize them. What about the shopkeeper's son? *Was he a stranger?* What about the ice-cream lady with the blue eyes?

Her grandma had called it "ice cream" and said she should eat it before it melted. Adimu had never tasted anything so light and cool. When she nipped at it, her teeth ached. Then she saved the rest of it in its wrapper. She held it up to her cheek and delighted in its radiating chill, the opposite of the sun. She held it against her arms and legs. She decided she would save it to cool her off the following day, and when her *bibi* wasn't looking, she hid it in her pocket and snuck it under her mat before falling asleep.

The next morning, she pulled out the cone from under her pallet, but the ice cream had vanished. Adimu wanted to cry, though thought better of it. She would have to tell her grandma what had happened and that she hadn't eaten it immediately as she had been instructed. She thought, perhaps, one day she'd find the white lady and ask her for another.

"*Strangers* are people that you don't know," replied her grandmother.

"If I know *who* someone is but I've never spoken to them are they still a stranger?"

"Absolutely."

"What about the shaman and village chief? Are they strangers? Should I go with them if they call me?"

Nkamba wasn't sure what to say. Her granddaughter had caught her off guard. "If they call you and I'm there too, you can go," she said curtly. "When I'm dead and you are big, you can decide for yourself."

Adimu was enjoying asking her *bibi* questions. There was one she had wanted to ask for a while though wasn't sure if it was a bad question that would make her grandma sad. She heard other children use the word "parents" when they talked about the adults who sometimes hugged them and sometimes shouted at them. Just like her *bibi* did.

"Do I have parents, *bibi*?"

"Yes, you have. I will show them to you, but keep your distance. Parents behave in different ways and some can be bad, just as some children can be bad."

One afternoon when they were getting water from the stream, Nkamba pointed to Juma. "That is your mother, Juma." Several days later, she said to her granddaughter, "The man who is waving his arms is your father, Sefu."

THAT DRY SEASON, Adimu began school, and that was when she saw her father again. After the lessons, her classmates rushed to play in the field next to Sefu's land, and while the other children ran after a ball made of rags, she watched from the shade of a mango tree as the adult—her father—walked along a canal on the opposite side of the road.

Since Sefu kept from looking her way, Adimu was convinced that she was, indeed, that thing others called her: *zeru zeru*. A phantom.

Adimu invented a game. Every afternoon when school got out, she followed her classmates to the field where they played, and she waited for Sefu to pass. She wanted proof that he saw her, that she wasn't a phantom, a nobody. One day, she stored all her courage in her stomach and sat on the side of the road where he customarily walked.

Though the sun beat down on her relentlessly, she waited until she saw a figure in the distance. Her heart jumped in her chest. Her father was coming! She told herself if she held her breath until he was only a step away, he would see her and say hello.

She inhaled. With her cheeks puffed out, she remained still. But Sefu walked past without even a glance. Adimu exhaled noisily. She must have made a mistake. She would try again the next day, and the day after that, and the one after that, until the day that Sefu saw her. Her grandmother saw her and so did the children at school. And the white lady with the gold halo hair definitely saw her and bought her the cold sweet. Sooner or later, she would become visible to her father.

On an afternoon when the single-minded sun baked the yellowish earth, Adimu began to hold her breath as soon as she saw her father's outline appear on the horizon. The light was so intense that her eyes confused the line of the sky with the edge of the land, and her father seemed suspended in a vortex of dazzling ether. When he reached her, she let out her breath in one mouthful, and Sefu flinched. It was an almost imperceptible movement of his head, but for Adimu, it was enough. He had heard her!

Adimu didn't tell Nkamba about her game and continued playing it. After several weeks, she tried something even more daring.

Her grandmother had told her she was big enough to graze the goats after school. She was proud her *bibi* trusted her with something so important. Yet she was saddened that the grazing place was far from her father's land…unless she took the goats to graze on the path where he walked.

And that was exactly what she did.

First, Adimu took the little herd of three to the clearing where there was plenty of fresh grass and let them attack the green leaves on the spiny bushes that grew there along the shady side. Right before she knew her father would appear, she led them to the opposite side of the road, firmly holding the tether. Anyone who passed would be forced to slow down and step over the taut ropes.

Sefu appeared in the distance among the heat waves that rose from the ground and the clouds of midge flies that hung midair. Adimu stepped onto the path, pulling two goats along with her; she would pretend she was pushing them out of the way. She wanted to see her father up close; that way, she could look at his every wrinkle. And he could look at her small nose and full lips. She wanted to be seen. She wanted to be touched. When he approached, she was overtaken by an overwhelming shyness and lowered her eyes. Sefu hesitated; Adimu's gaze wavered on the goats' small hooves. She saw her father's enormous feet and the giant shadow of an arm that rose slowly over her head. She squeezed her eyes shut, waiting to be struck, though struck with joy because if her father punished her, it meant he saw her.

Sefu put a hand on the nape of Adimu's neck and with a slight amount of pressure, pushed her to one side. The contact lasted only a moment. He stepped over the ropes of the tethered goats and continued on without saying a word.

Adimu watched him move away from her, waves of happiness rising in her throat. She smiled. She wasn't transparent; she wasn't a phantom! She leaned over the back of one of the animals, resting her cheek on its warm dusty fur, and watched the man become smaller and smaller until he mixed with the light and disappeared, swallowed up by the web of leaves and branches.

The moment Sefu walked through the door of his hut, he looked at his face in the mirror by the window. On his jaw, he placed the palm of the hand that touched his daughter. For a moment, he thought he saw Juma's face reflected beside his. He turned around with a jerk and saw he was alone. Sighing, he shook his head and went back to looking at himself in the mirror. With the razor, he shaved off the shadow of beard on his chin.

PART TWO

18.

A veil of clouds dulled the sky. Kondo was waiting at the pier for the ferry from Mwanza to arrive. His son, Ramadani, was returning to Ukerewe, not to attend a wedding or an elder clan-member's funeral, not even for a school holiday. Ramadani was coming to stay for good, to fulfill his duty as the village chief's firstborn son. It was time for Kondo to prepare his son for his destiny. Kondo was old, and in recent years, fatigue had taken hold of him for longer and longer periods of time; it was important to train his son before the Spirits of the Lake separated him from the land. He had patiently waited for the boy to complete secondary school. The wait was over.

As the ferry glided across the lake, Ramadani saw Ukerewe through the waving flag on the prow. He was filled with joy at the thought of seeing his family and friends. And yet, as the island drew nearer, he felt his chest clench. His instincts told him that he wasn't born to be village chief and spend the rest of his life on the island. He wanted to become a veterinarian; however, his destiny had been charted at the time of his birth. To refuse the position he was born into would break his father's heart and would mean being cast out of the clan.

Kondo saw Ramadani disembark and tears sprung forth, caught in the wrinkles of his weatherworn face. He wiped away the moisture in a hurry and smiled at the young man who approached. When his son was near enough to look into his eyes, Kondo noticed that a shadow of anxiety darkened them.

"Well, son, are you still illiterate?" he joked.

"I've learned to read and write, if that's what you're asking, and in the sand no less!" Ramadani laughed and embraced his father.

On the trip to his ancestral home, Ramadani looked out the car window. The familiar landscape streamed past through the dust that was raised by the vehicle's wheels and set in motion by the wind: trees, paths, small groups of huts, women carrying jugs of water or returning from the fields with baskets of vegetables balanced on their heads, running children. Kondo was quiet until Nkamba appeared on the side of a path, walking hand in hand with Adimu. Kondo slowed where the road narrowed, and Ramadani had plenty of time to observe the girl. He knew who she was, and a memory from boarding school in Mwanza passed through his thoughts. Adimu squinted in the direction of the village chief in his car with an older boy by his side.

"She is still here," Kondo sighed. "It has been seven rainy seasons since her birth. One of the most delicate problems I shall be leaving you."

"Who?" asked Ramadani, distracted.

"The *zeru zeru*, son!"

WHEN THEY ARRIVED home the entire clan, friends, and neighbors waited to celebrate the return of the village chief's son. Among the many faces that greeted Ramadani from across the room was Zuberi. His presence annoyed the young man, and Ramadani turned his eyes away. Though many rainy seasons had passed, he remembered well when the witch doctor killed a rabbit to prepare a potion to cure his typhoid fever. Ramadani had begged his father to prohibit Zuberi from sacrificing the little animal. His prayers went unheard. As soon as the adults left him alone, he had vomited all traces of the potion from his body. He got better all the same a few days later. The memory of his furry playmate, magnified by his recollection of the revolting taste of the liquid Zuberi forced in his mouth, was so vivid that he shuddered.

Zuberi attempted to approach the boy, but Ramadani turned to talk with the first person at hand.

Many people brought gifts. His mother, assisted by his sisters and other women of the clan, prepared a bountiful feast—grilled tilapia and meat stews, onion and tomato salad, and *isombe*[12]. People peppered him with questions, congratulations, and advice. Everyone wanted to ask him something or praise his father for being an outstanding chief, wishing him equal success when the time was right. The village girls, hopeful that one of them would be his bride, danced for him, their wrist and ankle bracelets jingling. With reluctance, Ramadani accepted being the center of attention and did his best to appear happy and appreciative. However, so as not to

---

[12] A dish made of cassava leaves.

yield to feelings of despair, he repeated to himself that nothing had been decided. Kondo was still alive and, for the moment, he was free.

The guests did not leave until late. When Ramadani finally withdrew to his room, he opened the big suitcase he had brought from Mwanza and pulled out books and magazines on zoology and ethology and natural science manuals. He set the volumes on his palm-leaf mat and, on his knees, contemplated the creased covers and touched them lovingly.

Kondo and his wife stood outside their son's doorway. Ramadani's mother turned to her husband, who gestured to leave them alone.

The father slowly entered the son's room. "There are many animals on the island," said Kondo, moving closer and resting a hand on the young man's shoulder. "And they can all be yours!"

The father knew his son's passion without fully understanding it. He could fulfill his duty as leader while filling the courtyard with animals, if that's what he wanted.

"Yes, father."

After his father left the room, Ramadani rummaged among the heap of magazines that he had spread out on the floor and chose an issue of *National Geographic*. By the light of a kerosene lamp, he leafed through the magazine, looking at photos he had seen many times but which never ceased to amaze him. He thought of Adimu. He knew she squinted when she saw him because, besides lacking pigmentation in her flesh, she lacked it in her eyes, that albinism affects the eye structure and optic nerve. She reminded him of his classmate Josephat. He was just like her with his coppery blond hair and pale white skin. Ramadani remembered his own discomfort when he discovered Josephat's desk was next to his, his certainty that his soccer team would lose their matches with Josephat in the lineup, his fear of using the silverware in the dining hall that Josephat might have eaten with. He closed the magazine and sighed. Here he was, back on Ukerewe. Forever. The hope he'd harbored during the party disappeared when faced with the reality—he was no longer free; who was he kidding? He was finished with school, and he would live on the island and do what was expected of him. On Ukerewe. Forever. *Forever,* he repeated to himself.

19.

The doors of the white jeep swung open, and a man and a woman stepped out. They were doctors from a humanitarian organization and traveled from village to village to examine and vaccinate the children on the island. News of the vaccination campaign had spread among the population of Ukerewe, and Nkamba and her granddaughter were waiting with many others under the great baobab.

Adimu was immediately drawn to the woman doctor. It was the second time she had ever seen a person who looked like her. White. She thought of the stranger who bought her the ice cream cone. This one, the doctor, was tall with blond hair that was straight, rather than curly, like hers.

The two doctors set up the small field clinic. The children watched, transfixed, as the white tent started to take shape and strange objects were extracted from the back of the jeep that the children gathered around. When they realized they would have to go inside of what seemed like a mysterious gaping cave—the "tent"—they whined and clung to the multicolored fabrics their mothers wore while the women tried to comfort them. Many of them had never met a *mzungu*. But Adimu had. And the one she had met had given her a treat, was a nice lady. So, unlike the other children, Adimu released her grandmother's hand and went straight toward the doctor, her eyes glued to the woman's skin. She put her own arm next to the doctor's leg—they were the same color. The doctor drank from a plastic water bottle and handed it to one of the waiting children by the jeep and said, "Share it with the others." Adimu touched the woman's thigh and discovered the doctor and her grandmother had the same consistency. The doctor turned, squatted and said, "Hello there!" as she gave a gentle pinch to Adimu's cheek.

Adimu shyly smoothed her dress. When the woman patted her head, Adimu hugged her legs and gazed up. "*Zeru zeru*?" she said, seeking eye contact with Nkamba.

The mothers nearby giggled, hearing the child refer to the foreign woman by that term. Adimu tried to laugh as they did.

"She is not *zeru zeru*. She is normal," Nkamba said with reproach, taking hold of Adimu's arm and pulling her away, clearly embarrassed by her granddaughter's inappropriate words.

Adimu didn't understand why her grandmother was angry. The woman was white, like her.

The grandmother apologized to the physician for Adimu's naughtiness. Challenging her *bibi*'s authority, Adimu hid in the vehicle. Nkamba tried to make Adimu get out of the jeep, but the girl stubbornly ignored her. Adimu planted her feet and snorted, resisting her grandmother's attempts to pull her out. Only when the woman doctor called her did Adimu jump from the car and run toward the tent. Nkamba followed her, walking as quickly as she could.

It was particularly warm inside the tent. The doctor wiped her forehead with a handkerchief, took a syringe from a box, removed the cap, and gave it to Adimu. "Look, you have the needle, so it can't hurt you," she said in perfect Swahili. "Now, look at me."

"It can't hurt me. I have the needle," she repeated to her grandmother, as if to reassure her. Adimu noticed the woman's lips, which were thinner than hers, and wondered if their thinness made her not *zeru zeru*. Adimu was so intent on gazing at the woman doctor that she didn't notice the injection.

After the vaccination, the doctor measured her, weighed her, checked her throat, and looked in her eyes. The woman helped her take off her shirt and touched her stomach and lower abdomen. Adimu watched with rapt attention as the doctor's hands touched her body. On the parts hidden from the sun, her skin was just like the woman's. When the examination was finished, the doctor told her to go and sit inside the jeep. "I'd like to talk with your guardian about adult things," she said with an affectionate tone.

Once they were alone, the doctor asked, "*Mama*[13], who is the girl?"

"My granddaughter."

"Do you know that your granddaughter is albino? Do you know what it means to be albino?"

"I do not know what it means for you, but I know exactly what it means for us."

The doctor described in simple terms the scientific origin of Adimu's

---

[13] Polite address for an older woman in Swahili.

difference, dwelling on how to prevent illnesses that she was particularly susceptible to. She gave Nkamba some tubes of total-block sunscreen, explaining that it was important for Adimu to always wear a hat, a long-sleeved shirt, and long pants rather than traditional attire. "Your grand-child is normal," she added, looking straight at the older woman.

Nkamba lowered her eyes.

The doctor continued. "Albinos are considered supernatural beings only in small villages like this one." She explained that a normal life was possible and that there were a surprisingly high number of cases of albinism in Tanzania, the highest anywhere in the world.

Nkamba was silent. She tapped one cracked finger on the tube of sun-screen in her hand.

The doctor shook her head. "Every difference, whatever it may be, is valuable. It enriches. An antidote against banality." She had her doubts that the elderly grandmother fully understood the meaning of her words. She hoped at least some part of what she said would reach the woman. "In Tanzania there are protected communities where children with albinism can get an education, have friends, and escape persecution," she said fi-nally, handing Nkamba a piece of paper with a phone number. She took Nkamba's hands in her own when she said, "Here's the telephone number of a community in Tanga."

Nkamba looked at the doctor's white hands holding hers. The doctor had long, slender fingers and a thick circle of silver around her third finger. Nkamba took the paper, got up, and thanked the white woman several times. She considered telling the doctor about her first child. She had always wanted to ask someone who seemed to have the answers if it were possible that her daughter had returned through Adimu. She hesitated for a moment, lifting her gaze no higher than the foreign woman's belly and then said goodbye with a quick duck of her head.

While the adults had been talking, Adimu did not wait in the car as she was told to do. Instead, she wandered around outside the tent. She wanted one final look at the white woman, and she hoped she would come out and caress her as she had done before. Then, bored of waiting, she went close to the tent just in time to hear the doctor say, "In Dar es Salaam, albinos like your granddaughter lead normal lives." *Albinos. Dar es Salaam.* She repeated these words to herself a hundred times, determined to remember. *Normal.*

THAT NIGHT, AFTER her grandmother had extinguished the kerosene lamp, Adimu remained awake, her eyes open, searching the darkness.

"*Bibi*, how can I become like her?"

"Like who?"

"Like the woman doctor."

"You have to study very hard."

Adimu wiggled on her mat.

Nkamba sensed her granddaughter's thoughts. "You are not white in the same way as the doctor. You are black. Your white skin is a mistake. It should be dark like mine," she tried to explain.

"Am I white or am I black? Or am I something different?"

The elderly grandmother used the silence to better concentrate. She tried to remember the doctor's words from that morning, but they didn't come. She moved her mouth and lips as if to speak, hoping that would help. Something kept her from talking with her granddaughter as she would have liked. She didn't want Adimu to feel too loved or too understood. Nkamba wanted Adimu to grow up strong, without needing approval from anyone. It was her only chance of surviving after Nkamba was gone. Of this, she was sure. Who would love the girl after she died? She sensed her granddaughter's anxiety, and it broke her heart. Although she wanted to hold her close, she held back.

The girl turned over on her mat, unable to sleep. *Am I really a mistake?* she asked herself. She thought of how the children drank from the white woman's water bottle, though they refused to have contact with her things. *The woman doctor helps people and makes them better. That's why she's respected. I want to help people and be respected,* Adimu thought. After studying very hard and leaving the island like Kondo's son, she would return as a doctor and earn the respect of the entire village.

"*Bibi*?"

"What now, child?"

"Will you tell me a story?" Adimu asked, cuddling up next to Nkamba.

"Do you promise if I do that you'll go to sleep?"

"I promise."

"I'll tell you a new one," said her grandmother. "In a village at the foot of Kilimanjaro…"

Adimu curled on her side, her right hand resting lightly on Nkamba's arm. The folktale told of an old widow who longed to have children and how the Great Spirit of the Mountain answered her prayers by offering her Kikete, a boy who didn't like to work, and Kikete's many brothers.

"The old woman called him lazy and other names and, because of that, the Great Spirit of the Mountain took him from her. The widow begged the Great Spirit to return Kikete to her, that she didn't mean the things she said, but the Great Spirit was angry and Kikete and his brothers disappeared forever, and the old woman lived the rest of her life alone with no one to help her." Nkamba looked at her granddaughter through the veil of darkness. There was a full moon, and thin bands of silver light filtered through cracks in the door and the peepholes that had been bored into the walls.

"*Bibi*, why was Kikete lazy?"

"Because the Great Spirit hadn't created him to work but rather to look after his brothers."

Adimu thought for a few seconds and then sat up. "You won't do to me what the old woman in the story did, will you?" she asked.

"No, don't worry. I know how much my Kikete is worth," she replied, hugging Adimu. "Now go to sleep."

A few minutes later, Adimu was dreaming in her grandmother's arms while Nkamba remained awake. The doctor had written the phone number of the community in Tanga on a piece of paper. What if she lost the paper or it fell in the fire? Gently she slipped her arms from around Adimu, turned on the lamp and, using a knife, carved the numbers on the wall, copying the marks she saw on the creased paper. And in the morning, she'd bury the paper in the earth to keep it safe.

The ferry ticket to cross the lake was more than she could afford, and she knew Sefu would not help with the costs. The best she could do was save as much money as possible. At least enough for Adimu to reach Tanga. That way when she died, Adimu would be able to leave the island; Adimu might be safe. She turned off the lamp and lay down, waiting for sleep to come. Her eyes remained open, and her heart was restless. She searched for the woman doctor's words, the explanation for Adimu's difference. Her mind felt blurred—as soon as she had collected her thoughts, she found she was right back where she'd started. However, she had not forgotten the doctor's advice and was proud of herself for having always sensed how damaging the sun was to Adimu's fair skin.

Nkamba's thoughts drifted to a few days before when she'd taken Adimu to have her head shaved, as was the custom for children. She didn't have a razor and even if she did, her trembling hands would have been useless. The women in the village competed fiercely to be chosen to shave the *zeru zeru*: her golden hair was a desirable reward. When woven into fishing nets, it brought better catches.

Nkamba and Adimu had gone to Siti, Arafa's daughter. There were many mothers with their children in front of her hut, waiting their turn. As soon as Siti saw Sefu's mother and the *zeru zeru,* she quickly finished shaving the adolescent who was sitting on the stool and beckoned Adimu. Siti laid down a large blue tarp—she didn't want a single blond strand to be carried away by the wind or to fall on the ground and be lost. Adimu hated having her head shaved and looked to her grandmother for reassurance, then scrutinized the drop cloth as if she were afraid of falling inside it, as if it were a deep well that would trap her and she'd never climb out of it. She reluctantly sat on the wobbly stool. The sun's rays sliced through tree fronds like sharp swords, and the child's skin—bare and irritated from each stroke of the razor blade—took on a violet hue.

"Wait a moment," said the grandmother to the young woman. "My *mjukuu* is tired. I'd like her to have a drink."

Siti hid her frustration behind a forced smile and went into the house. She came out a moment later with a glass of tea and a saucer of sugar. Nkamba dove her fingers into the sugar to take as much as her fingers could hold.

When the haircut was finished, Adimu got up and Arafa's daughter hurried to wrap up the blue cloth where the hair lay like gold threads.

"Stop!" said Nkamba, approaching Siti. "Those are mine." She grabbed the edge of the drop cloth with the same force she held the scythe during the harvest.

"Give me the hair or pay me for the time I've wasted on the *zeru zeru,*" shrieked the woman without letting go.

"I will pay you for the blade," Nkamba retorted, yanking the cloth so sharply that the young woman released her grip. Adimu's grandmother counted out the money and left it on the stool and then took Adimu's hand, the blue cloth tucked under her arm. She marched among the huts, looking for a blazing fire but found only a few embers that had nearly gone out. She thought of another solution. She went to a latrine, pushed aside the palm leaf that covered the hole, and let the hair fall.

Nkamba returned to Siti's house and tossed the cloth at her feet as if she were sloshing out a bucket of water. She left with quick steps, pulling Adimu behind her while the spectators, waiting in line for their children's turn, murmured and sneered.

"You could have stolen less sugar!" Arafa's daughter had shouted after them.

That night, Nkamba turned on her mat in the hut to look at her sleeping granddaughter. Unfortunately, she didn't have a hat for Adimu. If she let the child's hair grow, her scalp would be protected and no one would attempt to keep her extraordinary hair. With that, Nkamba fell asleep.

20.

Every day that Adimu took the goats to graze, she learned you can love animals with the same intensity that you love people. She studied the temperament of each beast and used that knowledge to make her task easier, whispering words of encouragement to the more docile animals and scolding the arrogant ones. The little herd took the place of longed-for companionship. Once she ran into Ramadani while the goats were grazing. Observing how gentle Adimu was with her herd, he smiled at her. She smiled back. *If only he was closer to my age*, she thought, *maybe I'd have a human friend.*

Although initially she continued to wait with her herd for her father along the canal, he no longer walked that route and, after several weeks of praying that he'd come, she had given up, preferring to take the goats to the clearing where the grazing was better. Adimu figured her father had stopped going to the fields, but Sefu had been taking another path to get there. *Better the long way home than running the risk of meeting the* zeru zeru, he considered.

Adimu's need for contact with others was continually frustrated, sometimes by the reality of her life and other times by her grandmother's words.

"You are different," Nkamba had said. "Only a white girl like you can be your friend. You should appreciate what you have rather than think about what you don't have."

Adimu would sometimes misinterpret her grandmother's sternness for a lack of affection. She was too young to understand that love comes in many shapes and often hides behind masks that make it unrecognizable, nor could she know that love, even though it runs deep, does not offer an antidote to undo mistakes. Nkamba did her job the best she could, and she believed her job was to toughen up her granddaughter.

Once, when Adimu had been particularly angry over her lot in life, she demanded to know how she could possibly appreciate what she had when she had nothing. To teach her a lesson, Nkamba made her go an entire day without drinking water. In the evening, after having begged her grandmother for just one sip, Adimu had understood what Nkamba meant. She would need to accept that the goats were her only friends, at least until another white girl like herself came along to keep her company.

Adimu learned quickly to barter what she had for what she desired and, since there was nothing she craved more than friends, sometimes she exchanged a tuft of her hair for the chance to play with the other children. The lucky boys and girls would run home with their treasure, certain to make their fathers happy.

Nkamba became aware of the price her granddaughter paid to receive the slightest bit of attention from her classmates, and her anger was such that she threatened to take her back to Siti to have her head shaved if she didn't stop selling herself. Adimu cried so hard that her eyes grew puffy and red like ripe apricots. Nkamba, however, was not heartless and tried to think of alternative ways the child might amuse herself in isolation so she wouldn't have to stoop to buying playmates.

"You can draw on the walls of the hut," she told Adimu that same evening. She gave her a little awl. "Use your imagination; engrave whatever you have in mind," she suggested. "The only thing you have to do is stay away from *that* place." Nkamba pointed to where the phone number of the protected community was engraved.

Adimu loved the idea and, in her free time, she decorated the walls from top to bottom, filling them with the things she desired: a little girl just like her, a house with windows, and a television. She outlined the shapes and added colors with her imagination. One afternoon, Adimu accidentally decorated the place where the telephone number was engraved, drawing over the last two digits. In place of the numbers were now the eyes of an imaginary friend.

Nkamba thumped her fists on her chest when she saw her granddaughter's only means of escape from her hellish existence on Ukerewe had been erased. So upset was she that she forgot she had buried the paper the doctor had given her in the earth to keep it safe so that her dream for Adimu might grow like healthy seeds that sprout into plants. She careful recopied the numbers of the community in Tanga that remained etched on the wall onto a small piece of paper that Adimu had lying around. Since Nkamba was not able to read, she spent a long time replicating the shapes from the wall just so. And then she hurried to the shop where there was a public phone. The shop owner saw the fragile woman running at a good clip for someone so old, clasping in her grimy hand a scrap of paper.

"The last two symbols are missing," she wailed. "How can I call?"

The owner didn't have an answer and asked her son for advice.

"No problem," he said as soon as the situation was explained. "You can find the right number by dialing ninety-nine times."

"Do you mean make ninety-nine phone calls?"

"Yes," said the boy. "But you might get lucky and find the number you're looking for before the ninety-ninth call," he sniggered.

Nkamba's feet stirred up clouds of dust that swirled around the hem of her dress as she walked home. She had never been lucky. Ninety-nine phone calls meant, as the youth had explained, the number of your fingers ten times. Who had enough money for that? She told herself she was stupid not to have committed the six symbols to memory. They had been right before her eyes for so long. How could she have been so careless? As hard as she tried, the numbers remained hidden in the meanders of her memory.

AFTER SOME TIME, Nkamba found several pieces of chalk for Adimu. Finally her objects had a color apart from the dull brown of the walls and the bright, earthy colors of her imagination. As the walls were completely covered with her drawings, each time she wanted to carve a new figure, she had to erase what was underneath with a damp rag and wait for the mud wall to dry.

"I'm tired of drawing everything with my same color," said Adimu one evening.

"As long as white plaster is what they put on the outside of public buildings on this island, it will be the only color you have to play with, and you should feel lucky to have it," Nkamba scolded. "These two colors," she added, pointing to the mud brown wall and the white chalk, "are, and will always be, the only colors in your life."

One rainy afternoon, Adimu carved a group of people onto the wall. She wanted to sketch the most beautiful drawing ever. She started with her grandmother and herself and then outlined her father, tall with the enormous feet she remembered from that day when he'd put a hand on her neck. She drew children—lots of them, all the same size and with their arms extended. She drew the woman doctor and the lady who bought her ice cream, and she left a place for herself in the center. When she finished the drawing, she laid her palms over the children and imagined walking hand in hand with them. Making believe, in this way, became her favorite game. She was always the leader of the group. She and her friends went to school together, to the lake together, and they ran after a *real* ball, not one made of rags. They were always hand in hand. Up high, next to the ceiling beam, Adimu drew the sun and colored it with chalk.

"It has to be white," she explained to her grandmother, "because the yellow sun in the sky burns my skin."

21.

Sarah spent the afternoon in Dar es Salaam. Her thirteenth wedding anniversary was in three days, and she was food shopping. No restaurants and no cooks—she was giving the kitchen staff the evening off. She, by herself, would lay out the special dinner in the garden at White House. Pâté and Cornish pasties as appetizer, followed by lamb pie and mashed potatoes, roast beef with horseradish sauce, and finally a rich assortment of desserts. A real English meal. Charles was an imposing man, but he was always too busy to bother with such an unproductive activity as eating. Perhaps confronted with the traditional dishes from his country of origin, his appetite would increase, Sarah reasoned, and her husband would appreciate the gesture of a meal prepared just for him.

Her shoes felt tight, and her back ached when she boarded the evening flight for Mwanza, her suitcase heavy with tins and cartons imported from Europe. As the plane was taking off, she admitted to herself that she had overestimated—she'd bought enough food to feed the two of them as well as the entire staff of White House. She watched the lights of Dar es Salaam fade, swallowed by the night and altitude. What if her husband had made last-minute appointments? If so, her plans to spend time alone with him would be ruined. They had fallen into the habit of spending all their "together time" with friends. Sarah thought about the word "friends." Could they define the people they saw regularly as such? Dinners, lunches, receptions, benefits—when they "socialized," they did little more than finalize business transactions. What hypocrisy!

She'd done her best to integrate with the foreign community of Mwanza. She had dedicated time to afternoon activities for students at the British school, participated in organizing cultural events, and even enrolled in an advanced Swahili course, which she began after running into Adimu and her grandmother at the grocery, the only hobby she had derived satisfaction from. She liked speaking with her husband in a foreign language that was so familiar to him. However, it had been difficult to meet anyone with whom she could establish a real friendship. Most of the English women in Mwanza were descendants of wealthy colonists or spouses of businessmen, like her husband, who concerned themselves with being trophy wives. For a short time, she had volunteered at an orphanage that was managed by an Anglo-American couple in the suburbs of Mwanza. Although she felt more vital when helping the orphaned children than she had ever felt in her life, after six weeks, she'd quit...with regret. Charles disapproved of volunteer work—"Work should be paid" was his refrain—though he wouldn't have pressured her to resign. She quit because it had aroused those feelings of long ago, ones she didn't like. Helping the orphans brought her back to that time in her life when adopting Adimu seemed like a possibility and then that terrifying moment when Charles said *never* and turned into a stranger.

One evening in Mwanza while they were having dinner, Sarah had succeeded in putting her finger on her anxiety. Her thoughts traveled to the children at the orphanage who needed everything, and she was hit by the insight that injustice prevails over fairness. She would have liked to speak about her feelings with Charles, even if she knew his response: "That's the way the world goes," he'd say. Then would come his comforting smile, a tender caress, and he'd hand her money to give to the needy.

She'd stirred the trifle in her dessert dish and observed how the drops of sherry mixed with the cream. Money could resolve the most pressing needs but not the objective reality. That was when she understood: If she continued volunteering at the orphanage, Charles *would* become a stranger. It wouldn't be a passing feeling. Their paths would separate forever. She could not imagine living without her husband; she had built her life around him. She was his shadow. How could she go forward without the man who provided her the protection and love she desperately needed?

After having raided the supermarkets in Dar es Salaam and before taking the plane back to Mwanza, Sarah had visited a shop that sold things for children. She liked to stop in whenever she had the chance. The tiny clothes reminded her of the ones her mother had sewn for her dolls when she was a girl, and she was enchanted by the wooden toys and carillons. On that particular day, she bought an electronic music box. It played various tunes depending on which button you pushed. Sarah walked up to a beggar child on a street corner and gave him the box.

He turned it around in his hands without knowing how to play with it, and Sarah—clumsy and caught unprepared by his reaction—laid her hand on her chest and ran away, feeling stupid. Africa continued to set before her a world she couldn't penetrate. Whatever she did seemed to be inappropriate. Though she had, by then, accepted she was looking at reality through an out-of-focus lens, her sense of impotence and uselessness sometimes stung her like a thorn pushed deep into her heart.

On the day of her wedding anniversary, she prepared the dishes well in advance. When she heard Charles arrive home, she made a quick check in the mirror in the entry hall of her updo and pink lip-gloss and rushed out into the yard to welcome him. She was as excited as a schoolgirl. She had put on a new dress and arranged her hair with care, and the table was shiny with candles and fresh flowers that she took great pains to arrange, creating a splash of color on the lawn.

"Happy anniversary, dear. Come, sit down." She greeted him with a kiss.

Charles stopped in front of the table, a large roll of papers under his arm. "I want to show you something."

"I've cooked dinner for you all by myself," she cooed, stroking his cheek. "Let's eat, and then you can show me."

Charles set the roll on a chair and began to move the silverware and dishes onto the serving cart next to the table.

"What are you doing?" Sarah asked.

"It can't wait. It's too important."

Charles cleared off the table and unrolled the papers until they covered the linen tablecloth. The delicate cutwork embroidery vanished under the thick, grayish paper. A sharp odor of ammonia drowned out the aroma of the food.

"Come close and look," he said, putting on arm around her waist.

All sorts of lines intersected to form something similar to a large building.

"What is it, Charles?" she asked, annoyed.

"Look closer."

Sarah had little desire to play guessing games. She worked long and hard to organize and prepare dinner, and her husband—for the umpteenth time—was placing work before her and their marriage. She said nothing, though, and directed her empty and disappointed gaze at the paper. *Whatever it is, it can go to hell*, she thought.

Charles announced with pomp, "The Fielding Health Center of Ukerewe."

"A clinic with our name. On Ukerewe?"

"That's right," he replied enthusiastically. "What do you think? Where should we put the benefactor's plaque?"

Sarah's only thought was of where she'd like to put the piece of gray paper that was eclipsing her lovely spread.

"What are we talking about?" Her question was cold.

"About the hospital I'm building here on Ukerewe with my name, or rather, *our* surname on it," he said. "That way, if we need a doctor when we're on the island, we'll know where to find a qualified one. Without even waiting our turn." He laughed. "So, where should we put the signage?"

Sarah sighed. "Charles, I'm having a hard time understanding you. Why do you want to build a clinic on Ukerewe when there's already one here? Where's the need for that?"

"The one that's here is outdated and falling down."

"Well then, improve it, refurbish it. For heaven's sake, with the money it will cost to build a new one, you could make the existing hospital the most efficient in the entire country!" Sarah was exasperated. Mostly she wanted her husband to notice how perfectly silky was her pâté, how the candles were the exact hue of those that lit up the reception room on their wedding day, how her skin glistened from a Parisian lotion she bought in Dar es Salaam.

"Darling," Charles said slowly. "I've, of course, considered that. The point is if I want to have my name on it, I have to build it from scratch."

Sarah shifted her eyes away from her husband and to the bone china piled on the cart.

"Do you know any other man in Tanzania who has a hospital with his name on it?" asked Charles playfully.

Sarah stood up.

"Where are you going?"

She waved away his question while Charles continued to study the blueprints.

Sarah said, "At least make sure there are wards for women and children."

Charles was busy lifting his fork to his mouth.

"Look at me, Charles. This is important."

Her husband turned his face toward her, but she could tell his attention was elsewhere.

"If you absolutely must build your hospital, promise me you won't forget the women and children. Please. And AIDS."

"Why all this interest? Do you really think it's necessary?"

"Of course I do. It should specialize in women and children's health, and infectious diseases. Don't you know that in this part of the country, young women most often die from complications of childbirth, that the infant mortality rate is among the highest in the world, and that those sick with AIDS nearly outnumber those sick with malaria?"

Charles poured a glass of wine for himself and took a sip. "I know that. I may be European but I'm also African. Don't forget I was born here. I know about my continent's problems better than you. How is it that *you* know about infectious diseases?"

Sarah sat down next to him. "Haven't you ever noticed the vehicle parked in Murutanga with the hand-painted red cross?"

"Yes, it's an ambulance."

Sarah chuckled. "An ambulance? No, it's a mobile testing-lab for AIDS, Charles!"

"Oh, come on. I can't believe that."

"It's true, ask Jackob. You'll see, he'll tell you. He's already confirmed it for me."

"So," he said as he leaned back in his chair, "are you telling me there's an AIDS problem on this island? It's so isolated. I never would have guessed."

"Of course there is. Ukerewe *is* part of Africa."

"Hmm." Charles looked left and right before whispering in Sarah's ear. "Okay, I promise to add women's and children's services at the hospital. As for the AIDS testing, I want our employees here at White House to have it. Including Jackob. You never know."

22.

When Charles first saw his company's financial statement, he thought he was having problems with his eyes. Something was wrong. According to the business plan for the new mine, it should have started to turn a profit after five years. But not only wasn't it bringing in money, the profits from the first mine were being absorbed by the excavation costs of the second. *Surely this trend will turn around soon*, thought Charles.

He spent a sleepless night, shifting positions from the force of the hands of worry while the hands of anxiety massaged his thoughts. Nevertheless, a voice in his head chanted that his financial setback was only a small detour on the path of a great industrialist who was destined to hold a place in history. After all, he had a lucky charm. He admired how it glittered under the small lamp with the green silk shade. He imagined looking at himself from below: imposing, outlined against the sky, white like a statue. A marble statue—Carrara marble, certainly not plaster. He poked at his thighs to make certain they hadn't yet turned to stone.

A hospital with my name on it, he thought. *What a grand idea. Hundreds of people saved, thanks to me. Their eternal gratitude will be mine. No, I can't abandon the project. Every problem has its own perfect solution, no need to panic.*

THE ISLANDERS SHARED Mr. Fielding's worries about the future.

"For seasons now, we have been pulling empty fishing nets onto our boats," said a disgruntled fisherman while he mended the boat's already often-patched cotton sail.

"Not even reducing the mesh has worked," said another, who was gazing at the lake, thinking about the good old days when fishermen gathered on the dock with cold beers in hand after long periods spent in the water, trying to outdo each other with the number of fish they'd caught.

"When I was a small boy and fished with my father, there were hundreds of kinds of fish. The Spirits of the Lake graced us then. Now there are only Nile perch and tilapia."

"I say all those kinds of fish are still here, only they've learned how to stay out of the nets! They've outsmarted us," shouted an old fisherman who, together with some of the others, was trying out a new method that saved on the cost of fuel. He extended a large net from the beach to his boat that was anchored at a distance. Weights held down the net. From his boat, he pulled the gill net parallel to the shore for about a hundred yards. Then two fishermen pulled the net onto the beach to form a crescent moon in the water to catch the few small fish.

A woman, intent on washing clothes, watched the fish flop silver on the beach. She picked one up by its tail. "They're not even good for soup. The bigger ones end up at the market in Mwanza, and we have to feed our children with the bones."

FROM THE DAY he had accompanied the Fieldings to Zuberi, Jackob enjoyed—as he'd hoped— greater prestige among the villagers, and, in particular, in the eyes of the healer. One morning, the young man went to Zuberi to tell him of his employer's new, incredible undertaking.

"It will be a modern hospital where the best doctors in the country will work," he declared, his eyes bright with pride. "Mr. Fielding has already made contact with the central government that will run it, and soon construction will begin."

Though Zuberi pretended to be happy about the news, his mind quickly went to work on a solution to what he considered an insidious threat. An efficient hospital would mean he'd lose patients, and this was to be avoided. Jackob went on to jabber about the usual villagers while Zuberi was so engrossed in his cogitations that he heard only half of the gossip. Not even the news that Jackob would soon have a second child attracted his attention.

The witch doctor was aware he could not directly block a man as powerful as Charles Fielding and, surely, he shouldn't voice his dissent. Jackob was like a dog when it came to his master: he would run to the white man with the news in his mouth, hoping for a bone and a pat on his head.

After the two men said their goodbyes, Zuberi shouted out, "Jackob, wait. Tell the *mzungu* that I'll favor his project with a good luck gift. I'll make the first brick myself."

Jackob trotted back. "I'm sure Mr. Fielding will appreciate your gesture," he said, squeezing Zuberi's hands as a sign of gratitude.

Zuberi locked himself in his workroom. He needed to find the most potent curse for the foreigner's project. The evil spell could be worked into a brick, and from there it would propagate through the foundation of the building and impede its completion. The shaman went to the old wooden chest. It had remained closed since that evening, years before, when he'd shown it to Kondo. He pushed aside the objects stacked on top of it and threw the heavy red carpet that covered it onto the floor. A cloud of dust rose and a multitude of spiders crawled in every direction. Zuberi panted as he dug through the amulets and venerated ornaments inside the chest. Jane watched him with curiosity from her perch on a shelf.

If only one of his ancestors would appear and give him the solution! Such magic had never transpired for him, though he had been told stories of a great-great uncle who often received visitations. This hospital could compromise his position, forever. It could ruin everything. The official medicine of doctors carried the same seed of doom as Father Andrew's God. *Both were invented by* wazungu *to pilfer the soul of my people and plunder the wealth of my land*, Zuberi thought. *And, most importantly, they threaten me. I am Zuberi, the infallible shaman and healer who soon will have unending trust and respect. Everyone must turn to me for help.*

As Zuberi lined up various ingredients and considered the most efficient formula to enhance the spell, a clap of thunder came from the sky. Jane pricked her ears and lifted her upper lip to reveal her sharp canine and then ran to hide under the table. The rainy season was beginning, the eighth one since their *zeru zeru* was born. Zuberi picked up Jane and held her while he watched the lightning crackle through the window. Mosi and the white man were like water during the first rains of the season—they slid over the dry, clayey earth without soaking in. They did not worry him. He was the good rain—the water that, little by little, worked its way into the deepest cracks of the earth to make the soil fertile. It was about time to put to use his lucky omen that the Spirits of the Lake saved for his advantage.

JACKOB'S WIFE GAVE birth to a healthy boy. The young father was in seventh heaven. So many years had passed with only a daughter to show for their time together. Could a greater joy exist? Jackob embraced his wife who was still sore from the birth. As he held her tight in his arms, he begged her to grant him a wish that he had harbored for many years. He wanted to call his firstborn son after his employer.

"You know how much a name influences the destiny of a man, and I want to give my child an important name," he said to her. "Have you ever met a more extraordinary person than Mr. Fielding? We'll call our son

'Charles.' For the benefit of the clan, he can be known as 'Amri,'" Jackob added.

"Why must our son have two names? If that's what you want, we'll call him 'Charles' only."

"Mr. Fielding would be offended if he knew the son of a simple man like me had been given his name."

His wife looked at Jackob, unable to understand how such a thing could offend someone.

"He will be Charles at home, and everyone else will call him Amri," concluded Jackob, taking advantage of his wife's hesitation.

To herself she thought, *No, we will call him Charles.*

23.

From the day her grandmother had told her that only a white girl could be her friend, Adimu dreamed of a playmate with pale skin. She thought about her so often that she was able to describe her features in detail. Going to school one morning, Adimu saw a doll on the ground, and it was her same color. She it picked it up. It was dirty and had a hole in place of an eye, and it was missing one arm. A tuft of blond hair, caked with mud, hung on one side. Its dress was little more than a scrap of fabric. Adimu examined every detail of the doll that had fallen into a state of disrepair, and, in a fit of compassion, she hugged it to her chest. It had been abandoned. Now it would be hers, and she would call it "Adimu," just like her. Along the road to school, she found a place to hide her treasure, behind a bush that was before the clearing where the other students crowded.

In the evening she showed her grandmother what she had found. "Look, *Bibi*," she said. "I found a white girl, just like me! I hid her so no one will take her."

Nkamba laughed. "In that sorry state, you don't need to worry about anyone stealing her from you," she said. "Tomorrow we will go to the lake to wash her."

"Will you make her a dress?" asked Adimu, trying to pass her fingers through the doll's muddy hair. It was a real toy, and the best surrogate friend she could imagine.

Adimu had no idea that before too long the opportunity she had always dreamed of would present itself, that she would have a best friend who was a live girl and just like her. The chain of events leading up to that miraculous meeting began one afternoon during that rainy season. The roads had been reduced to slurry, but that did not stop a dozen children from gathering near the village mill at a secondary path that linked the forest to the main road, beyond which extended the cultivated fields. The children stood alongside bags full of cassava and maize that waited to be ground. They had seen Adimu lingering and, as always, they ignored her.

Adimu was playing alone, bouncing a ball of rags against the wall and then running to catch it on the fly before it fell. The sky was heavy with clouds, and there was a slight breeze.

"*Zeru zeru!*" a voice rang out.

She turned and squinted. The wad of rags bounced near, landing in a puddle of water and mud.

"*Zeru zeru!*"

The voice came from the forest's cavern of darkness. A branch snapped, and shapes moved among the thick vegetation. She felt like prey, an extra sense she had developed that was deeply ingrained in Adimu by her grandmother. The little girl was in danger. She should run away, yell that someone was stealing the herd as Nkamba had taught her. Instead Adimu's vision darkened, and she remained paralyzed as if waiting for destiny to decide her fate for her, the way a stalked and mortally wounded animal resigns itself to the inevitable.

One boy, Antony, understood what was happening. He ran to Adimu, hooked her arm and shoved her toward the storeroom of the mill, pushing her behind a pile of sacks. The other children were still. They looked toward the forest. They were paralyzed too. Three tall men emerged from the vegetation and ran in the direction of the building. One of them had a long scar that crossed his entire face, transforming his mouth into a grimace. The men, armed with heavy sticks and machetes, searched the area.

The tallest of the men entered the storeroom and kicked the sacks, hitting them with his club. Threadbare canvas tore, and piles of grain poured out. Adimu felt the blows land on the bags. She felt the booming move closer and closer. Though her back ached under the weight of the sack that hid her, she remained immobile—her head between her knees, eyes closed, breath locked in her chest. Her life was hanging by a thread, and her only thought was of Antony's hands. He had touched her! Without being afraid and without her having to give him anything in return. He had saved her.

One of the men was so close to where Adimu had curled up that she thought he had found her. She willed her body to be still, including her pounding heart, although it raced even faster. The man continued on. After long minutes of searching, the three of them approached the children who were standing near the wall where Adimu's ball of rags was lying. The smallest children were crying. Antony was the only one who looked straight at the men, keeping his gaze from wandering toward Adimu's hiding place.

"Where did it go?" shouted the stockiest of the three. He was sweating and puffing as if he were standing under the scorching sun, even though the air was cool.

"I don't know, mister. We were just playing among ourselves," replied Antony, his voice steady.

"Damn," said the man with the disfigured face. "The evil thing must have vanished."

The men circled the mill again like hungry hyenas that smell blood and death in the air. As quickly as they had appeared, they disappeared.

"Keep playing as if nothing happened," Antony whispered to the children, and he, too, continued with their game, shooting sidelong glances at the bags of grain to be sure Adimu stayed hidden. When he was certain the strangers were far away, he went to the storeroom.

"*Mzungu*, you can come out now. They're gone."

Adimu knew it might be a trap. She had disobeyed her grandmother by going off to play with the children, and she had been unable to react as she knew she was supposed to. She would be dead if the men took her. Her grandmother would be alone. She thought of Kikete and how he was lazy so he could care for his brothers, and she knew that her job was to take care of her *bibi*.

Antony kicked the sack. "I said, come out, *zeru zeru*!" He climbed onto the big, rough bags and moved them one by one. Adimu was still crouched with her head between her legs, and Antony had to tug at her to get her to emerge. Her face was frozen in its frightened expression. The sky was still cloudy, a strip of blue peeking out between the gray.

Adimu expected to see the bad men jump out from the bushes or from behind a tree. Cautiously, her face contracted into a half smile and tears dampened her cheeks. She didn't try to speak until the lump in her throat disappeared.

"Thank you for saving my life," she finally said to Antony. She looked at the other children who had scattered around her. "Thank you," she said again. They seemed as perplexed as she was and did not reply.

"We're taking the boat to go fishing," said Antony. "Do you want to come?"

She could hardly believe her ears. If someone had invited her only an hour before, she would have refused without a moment's thought. She had not forgotten Nkamba's warnings. But after Antony saved her life and the other children helped him, her defenses were weakened. However, she hesitated all the same.

"Come on, *zeru zeru*. If we wanted to hurt you, we would have given you up!" urged Antony.

That was true. They protected me, thought Adimu.

Only a few of the children went. On the way to the lake, they spoke among themselves, ignoring her. Adimu kept up alongside the group. Her prayer was slowly coming true. When they got to the boat, the children sat at the back and she sat in the prow, like Antony told her.

Adimu did not know how to swim, and she told herself not to look down into the dark water as the boat moved away from the shore. Best to look at the sky where her joy came from. *Even if no one says a word to me, I am here with them. One day they'll understand I'm not dangerous. I'll be their friend*, she thought to herself. She watched the water on the lake form whitecaps; the air was damp and there was a breeze. It would soon start raining.

When they returned to the shore, Adimu got out of the boat and, with a wave of her hand, she said goodbye to her companions in adventure. She did not give much importance to the fact that no one replied, and while Antony tied up the boat, she skipped away, anxious to tell her grandmother.

When Adimu was almost home, she realized how late it was and quickened her pace. Her grandmother would surely be worried. Adimu found her *bibi* behind their hut, preparing supper.

"Where have you been? I was worried!"

"*Bibi*, you'll never believe it! Today Antony and the other children protected me from three strangers, and then I went in the boat with them. We went fishing. And they told me they had never gone so far from the shore," she said all in one breath.

Nkamba felt an icy shiver run along her spine.

Adimu's face clouded. "Why do you look sad?"

Three strangers: Nkamba's worst fear. A band of *zeru zeru* hunters. Rich and powerful scoundrels paid those killers to obtain *embulamaro*, dead or alive, to make amulets and potions. Then the village children took her out on the lake in their boat, and Adimu thought it was a gesture of friendship, but it was the exact opposite: Adimu was in danger. Adimu was growing up, and her *bibi* could no longer protect her. The time had come to contact the community in Tanga. She remembered that she had buried the special piece of paper the lady doctor had given her and immediately trudged to the old tree where it lay in wait to be dug up. She prayed to the Spirits of the Lake that the last two symbols were readable.

24.

At the end of Mass on the following Sunday, Father Andrew stretched out his arms, a newspaper in his hand, as he approached Nkamba and Adimu.

"Nkamba, let us sit here," he said, making room under the tent that protected him during the service. "I would like to read you an article. Actually, Adimu, why don't you try to read it?" He gave her the newspaper.

"It's better if you do it," she replied, lowering her head.

"Don't be shy! You must be good at reading by now," encouraged Father Andrew.

"I'm not very good at reading aloud," said Adimu in a small voice.

"She doesn't see well, Father, and the teacher sits her at the back of the classroom."

"Go ahead and try," urged the priest.

"Her teacher doesn't understand on purpose," grumbled Nkamba.

"Albino...Woman...Appointed...as...Member of the Parliament." Adimu sounded out the title of the article and then handed the newspaper back to the priest who continued to read it aloud. The article told about an albino woman who had become a lawyer and had been nominated by Tanzanian President Kikwete to be a member of parliament.

"She is a national politician," he told the elderly woman who listened with her mouth agape. Adimu paid little attention. She wanted to go look for her new friends.

While she was sitting with Father Andrew, Nkamba's gaze fell on a mangy goat not far from where they sat. The poor beast, little more than skin and bones, pulled itself along the side of the road with its front legs, escorted by vultures that hopped about, each one making space for itself by flapping its broad wings. Nkamba heard the squawking of the birds of prey that circled above, convinced each bleat would be the goat's last. She saw a vulture land, pushing its way among the others with the patience of one waiting for the certain end, death.

"Nkamba, do you understand what it means?" Father Andrew asked, pulling her away from her thoughts.

"Yes, of course I understand. Are you sure it's true?" The news came from a world she had never imagined existed.

"How can you doubt it? It's written in the newspaper!" he replied. "Adimu, have you understood what you just read? A white woman, like you, has become an important person." Adimu was distracted, still busy looking around for the other children.

Nkamba was tempted to tell the priest about what had happened at the mill and about how she wanted to send her granddaughter to the protected community in Tanga, but she held back. She would have to first speak with Kondo and, with his help, convince Sefu. When she had dug the paper out of the earth, it had been damp and black ink had run into its creases, just as she imagined might happen when the doctor first handed her the telephone number. She was pretty sure that the figures could no longer be read, that the last two certainly were too smudged. And she hadn't saved enough money to make the ninety-nine phone calls or even pay for the ferry. It was unthinkable to ask Father Andrew for money before speaking with the head of the village and her son, especially because the priest belonged to a different clan. The following day she would go to Kondo. Kondo knew how to read. Maybe she was wrong about the smeared ink.

EARLY THE NEXT morning, Nkamba thanked the village chief many times for having assured the necessary protection for Adimu over the years and then told him about what had happened at the mill. She was worried that the thugs would return to hunt down her granddaughter. With her head bowed, she confessed that she wanted to send Adimu away from the island and explained to Kondo that the white doctor had given her the phone number for a children's community in Tanga. She handed Kondo the creased piece of paper with the smeared numbers written in the white doctor's writing. She told Kondo that she scratched the first four symbols on her wall, but the child accidently wiped off the last two. Sefu had the money to send her, and in Tanga, Adimu would no longer be a bother to the community. She begged the village chief to intercede. She begged him to read the numbers from the tattered paper, and if they were illegible, as she feared, to find the complete telephone number so her granddaughter might be safe before she joined Kheri, who, she pointed out, was Kondo's clan-brother. She even reminded Kondo of the daughter she sacrificed for the good of the clan. Nkamba pulled out all the stops—Kondo *had* to help her.

The village chief didn't seem like himself. He showed little interest in her heartfelt words and sent her away in a hurry, saying he needed time to think about it. He violently rubbed the piece of paper Nkamba had handed him and said the ink was blotched, the numbers couldn't be read, and he'd speak with Sefu if and when the opportunity arose. Nkamba saw he was distracted and wanted her out of his home. She saw an inexpressive look in his eyes. Her old friend. The one who was so happy when she and Kheri married and whom she cried to daily after her husband's time in the village ended. Nkamba left Kondo's house more apprehensive than when she entered. *What can Kondo's behavior mean? Might some misfortune be visiting him?*

As soon as Kondo nudged Nkamba from his home, he hurried to a drawer in his main room to retrieve a green notebook and scrawled the six numbers into it from Nkamba's paper, tossing the paper in the desk drawer. *This children's community could free Sefu from his disgrace. I'll have to find out about it,* he told himself. And *what about Ramadani? Maybe this place can help him too. Or maybe there's a simpler solution…*

Nkamba was prepared to send Adimu away without Sefu's or anyone else's permission, even though she was aware she'd be banished from the village. She would do whatever was needed to save enough money for that ferry. Although, at first, she had taken in her granddaughter to repay her debt for abandoning her own daughter, Adimu had become the daughter she always dreamed of having, a unique and precious soul. The face of the infant she had abandoned in the forest visited the old woman's memory, and tears of anger streaked her face. She dried them in a hurry and marched off toward the fields.

25.

Ramadani had been with a group of boys when a medical van with a red cross came to Ukerewe. Most of his friends were reluctant to have their blood drawn. "I don't trust those doctors," said one of the boys. "People take blood from cows to drink," said another. His friends had never left the island for their education as he had, and Ramadani felt he should act as an example, so he said he would take the test. Actually, it was curiosity more than a sense of duty that drove him to do it. Living on Ukerewe bored him to death. He desired to learn new things and was frustrated by how time seemed to have stopped in his village. Days passed without variation. The sun and rain beat down on the island, following their natural cycles. Nothing ever changed.

In what little free time he had—Kondo was incessantly teaching him how to be village chief—Ramadani wandered in search of animal specimens to study. By the light of a candle—to keep his parents in the dark—he studied the manuals he brought from the city. During the day, he welcomed every opportunity to put what he read into practice. Sometimes, early in the morning, he would stand on the dock where the ferries from Mwanza landed in hopes of meeting at least one newcomer he could practice his English on. He yearned for contact with anyone from a different world.

Ramadani had climbed the three unsteady steps into the health clinic on wheels and ducked his head under the low entrance. One of the two nurses closed the door and had him sit while the other asked personal, embarrassing questions. *They've just met me*, thought the young man, *how can they speak to me about such things?* Nevertheless, he left nothing out, except for a few sporadic lies that were necessary to maintain his dignity. After their interrogation, they asked him to extend his arm for the blood sample. He concentrated on following the needle into his vein, though after a moment, he averted his eyes. The sight of his own blood made him lightheaded.

"Come back tomorrow for the results, and try to convince your friends and family to have the test. It's free. We'll be here this week, and we'll return in a month," said the nurse as she deftly placed a Band-Aid on the skin puncture.

"I have to come back tomorrow?" Ramadani would have preferred never to enter the mobile clinic again. His head was still spinning.

"Yes, if you want to know the results of the test."

The next day, Ramadani did return to the clinic, and he was handed a sealed envelope. He folded it and put it in his pocket.

At home, he sat down with a copy of *National Geographic* while he was waiting for lunch to be ready.

"Did you pick up your test results?" his father asked.

"Of course. I told you, I was brave enough to do it."

"AIDS, another disgrace brought to us by the whites!" Kondo said, shaking his head.

"Here." Ramadani handed his father the envelope and returned to his reading.

Kondo tore open the envelope. He held it close to his face. Then he frowned. "Positive?" he said.

"What did you expect?" his wife said on her way out the front door to get more wood for the cooking fire.

"Yeah, did you think I'd be one of those dead-men walking?" Ramadani said, turning the pages of the magazine.

"Positive," repeated Kondo. "How is it possible?" He collapsed onto a chair.

Ramadani stopped reading and looked at his father. "Why this face?" he asked. "Positive is... positive. A positive result."

Kondo shook his head. He struggled to his feet and approached his son. "I've seen the same result for other men of the clan. In the beginning, like you, I thought it meant something good. But 'positive' means you have AIDS. Damn white men and the day they set foot on this soil. I pray the Spirits of the Lake curse them for eternity!"

"You're wrong, *Baba*. It's a positive result. Positive is a good thing," said the boy, taking the letter from his father's hand.

Kondo wrapped his arm around Ramadani's shoulder and pulled him close. "Don't worry, we'll find a way for you to get better. You'll be all right."

Get better? thought the boy. *I'm sick with AIDS? Whose fault is that? How did that happen?*

"No one must know," muttered his father.

"What mustn't they know?" asked Ramadani's mother, tousling her son's hair.

"Nothing important," her husband replied.

"Well, instead of standing there talking secrets, could you stoke the fire? Otherwise today we'll have nothing to eat but your words."

YUNIS'S LIFE HAD become hell since that Sunday, seven years before when she'd snatched Adimu. Her lies to Sefu tormented her, but even more tormenting was that the children she desired had yet to come. Yunis, the-woman-without-children: that was how she was known among the villagers. Every time she met a female relative or friend, she would be offered prodigious advice and remedies. Yunis knew few who shared her pain. Instead, the women of her clan showed interest because in the face of her disgrace they had good reason to consider themselves fortunate.

She avoided going out as much as possible. In part, to minimize the risk of meeting Juma, though she had heard that Juma rarely left her home and cared for her sick, elderly father. The few times that they had run into one another, when their eyes met, Juma lowered her head and changed course. The pain that Yunis caused Juma tore up her heart.

Fortunately, Yunis's husband was against taking a second wife. And one advantage to her condition was that she and her husband had a very active sex life as they were continually trying to conceive—except, of course, during her monthly period. Perhaps, if it hadn't been for the pressure of others, they would have been happy without children. Unfortunately, becoming parents was an inescapable duty within the community. She felt terrible each month when she looked into her husband's eyes and announced that her period had come. She loved him, and she would have done anything to give him what she imagined he desired most in the world.

Days turned into months and months into rainy seasons, and Yunis became convinced that, since it hadn't happened, children were not going to brighten their future. Her anguish distorted her thoughts, which stole her sleep and serenity.

However, that she was barren and aging had given her time to reflect on the responsibilities of conceiving life. She had gained the understanding that children do not exist as pillars for one's old age, nor do they belong to their parents as was generally believed on the island. *A child is his- or herself from the moment of its birth and has the right to choose the life he or she prefers*, Yunis decided after nights of anguish. Instead of thinking about motherhood as the most natural thing for a woman, she began to sense that a child might also be a limitation. Maternity was no longer a desire but had transformed into a requirement created by the laws of others.

CHARLES HAD BEEN thinking a lot, too, and he was tired of wasting his time. Two hours to reach Ukerewe from Mwanza by boat on the weekend was absurd. He saw a sixty-five-foot-long and three thousand horsepower speedboat in a catalog and ordered it: the jewel would take him to the island in only twenty minutes. Charles would have to wait nine months for the boat to arrive, like a pregnant mother, after making a down payment consisting of a series of zeros and no decimal points. The modifications he had requested, including bronze paint with iridescent gold tones, required customizing.

The second mine's lack of productivity and the cost of building the clinic—which by then, the entire community was aware of—had reduced his liquid assets to an all-time low. To pay his workers and keep his good reputation, Charles dipped into his reserves.

Only Sarah and Jackob knew about the speedboat, and Charles could create a credible excuse to postpone buying it without setting off any bells about his cash-flow troubles. Charles phoned the shipyard and, alluding to financial obligations, said that despite himself, he would have to forgo the acquisition. *Only for now*, he explained. The boat-maker insisted that the down payment remain in their hands: he could apply it to another vessel as soon as he was ready for a purchase. Charles posed no opposition. No one must harbor suspicions about his economic difficulties. In any case, it would be resolved soon.

"In a few months I'll buy an even bigger one," he boasted to Jackob. "Unfortunately I have the tax assessor breathing down my neck, and I can't wear a scarf right now." This was his way of saying he couldn't corrupt anyone at the moment and that his financial difficulties were caused only by taxes due.

Charles was far from lighthearted and tranquil as he tried to appear to Jackob. Sacrificing the boat shook the podium on which he performed as a public figure. He had an urgent need to find a solution to his financial worries and to preserve his identity. He obsessed over his behemoth problem.

SIMPLE—ZUBERI'S FAVORITE WORD. It was his response when someone came to him with a problem that called for supernatural power. Whether it was a request for help from fishermen or from Yunis: *Simple*. He knew exactly what to do. For each of their problems, there was a solution. He had earned credibility, thanks to the skill of his father and ancestors. He knew how to set every person's mind at ease.

Even Kondo needed his services. At the height of his anguish, the old man went to see Zuberi about Ramadani's illness. Kondo hoped for a potion to heal the boy, just like when his son was little and had been saved from that fever. The witch doctor clutched Kondo's hands and offered him words of hope. He would heal Ramadani.

Zuberi felt inferior to his predecessors. Anecdotes circulated about each of their extraordinary talent, anecdotes that had been handed down by word of mouth from generation to generation. He had not yet achieved anything so grandiose that warranted commemoration. Not one of his amulets was stored in the great wooden chest. What would people say about him once he lived on the other side? He desperately needed to perform an act that would benefit the entire community and be passed down as lore.

Zuberi's fear increased as the hospital project moved forward. Construction of the building was now far along, and soon it would be operative. The evil spell had failed, which further undermined Zuberi's faith in himself. It wouldn't be long before villagers visited the modern hospital for their potions. Thus, Zuberi's worries grew, sunset after sunset. Fortunately, however, he still had one card up his sleeve, though it was top secret due to its risk. If the authorities were to hear about it, he would be sent to prison. He had to move with extreme caution, and his negotiations had to remain between him, his clients, and Jane. Only at the right moment could he make their amulets and potions. Zuberi imagined the lake filling with fish—all types, like how it used to be. He saw Yunis giving birth to one child after another. He envisioned Ramadani cured of the illness that was destroying his father's equanimity. The problem was how to find the money necessary to buy the universal remedy, the panacea that would assure his place in history. Not so simple. "Where can I find this amount of money?" he asked Jane. "It will take time…but the moment to rejoice *will* arrive!" Zuberi's laugh rose up from the depth of his chest.

26.

Charles awoke and weighed himself. He'd lost two pounds in three days. At first he thought the scale was broken. He checked again three days later. This time, five pounds under his last weight. For years his numbers remained consistent: six foot two, one hundred ninety-eight pounds. Now he was at one hundred ninety-three. A week later when at the couturier, his tailor asked, "Are you sure you've lost *only* five pounds?"

His weight loss was unequivocal, just like the insomnia that tortured him. Charles's sleep routine had been as consistent as his weight. He'd fall asleep within the first minutes of lying down. If he read, he'd do it sitting up so he wouldn't wake in the middle of the night with the book on his chest like a roof over his heart. As soon as he would lie down, he'd sniff the clean scents of the pillowcase and Sarah's hair and then stretched out a foot or arm to touch his wife's body. To his dismay, for several weeks, his routine had been disrupted. Insomnia and weight loss were feasting with one another.

Charles began to embrace the African conviction that there's a link between physical stature and power.

"It's even stronger in Tanzania than in Zimbabwe," commented Jackob. "Sir, you have the good fortune of being tall like a Masai. However, if I may say so, you are as thin as…" Jackob had difficulty finding a suitable and, in his mind, inoffensive simile.

"As what?" insisted Charles. He dragged his assistant into the kitchen so his wife wouldn't overhear them.

"As… no offense, sir…as a beggar," he said, lowering his voice.

"Well, yes, you're right. I can't think of any small, thin African leader." Fat was synonymous with affluence. And now—with his temporary financial setback—was no time to lose weight.

"If you gain some weight, sir, you will put to shame any African man. In part because you are white, in part because of your size."

Jackob excused himself from the kitchen, and Charles immediately began foraging for any rich food in sight that he could grab. To the cook, Adamma, who was chopping up some vegetables, he growled, "I want fatty meat tonight, and it should be black and hard as a bar of chocolate!"

"I am sorry, sir, but…"

"And what is this?" continued Charles, pointing at the uncooked perch. "You know the sight of raw fish makes me nauseous." He swiftly dumped the contents of the plate into the trash. "Even the odor drives away my appetite." The plate clattered in the sink before he walked out of the room.

Charles had difficulty gaining weight since he didn't like desserts because he believed they made him sleepy, and he rarely drank beer as it was, in his opinion, "an indigestible worker's drink." He had to find a solution that would cause the needle on the scale to shift toward the right, to rise like the price of gold at the start of a war.

He decided to contact a famous dietician in Nairobi and made an appointment in his Dar es Salaam office. After the examination, the doctor said, "Sir, you are in perfect health. As a physician, I strongly discourage you from gaining weight."

"I need a high-calorie diet," Charles said in a firm voice.

As always, Charles got what he wanted: a dietary regime that included two thousand calories beyond what was necessary as well as an excessive amount of protein to increase his muscle mass. He doubled the quantities that the doctor suggested. Eating became another occupation.

Charles finished every morsel of the lunch that was served in his office. He ate alone and, as if he wanted to prove his pleasure in ingurgitating his food, he used his hands to eat more quickly—after having first locked the door. *No one must see me stuff myself like a Negro*, he thought. He chewed with his mouth open, letting the condiments drip from his chin. Sometimes he'd eat in front of a mirror so he could watch the food be torn to shreds by his teeth. He drew pleasure from seeing oil coating his food, sugar whitening the top of sweets, and melting butter soaking thick slices of toasted bread. He began to detest water since it added no calories. Beer, which he previously shunned, became a trusted ally. Light foods were for hypochondriacs; whole grain products were for the poor. Vegetables— which took up space in the stomach better devoted to other foods that were richer in nutrients—were for the idle and squanderers. He kept dried fruit in his Rolls Royce and munched on it constantly, supplemented by candies and other sweets.

The diet produced the desired results in six weeks. The scale showed a twelve-pound gain. That wasn't enough, though, to set his mind at ease. He wanted to weigh so much that he flattened the world under the unbearable poundage of his existence.

THAT MONDAY, CHARLES and Sarah had been invited to a dinner and reception organized by the Territory and Mining Ministry, a lead-in to a meeting the following day. The most important businessmen in Tanzania would be there. The minister had organized the prestigious event, offering lodging and dinner at the most luxurious hotel in Dar es Salaam.

During the party, Sarah noticed Charles was biting his lip, a rare habit of his but one that had become more common since the rise of his caloric intake and his frenzied eating. She saw him look around and—when he thought no one was watching—lift the tablecloth to touch the tabletop. He was trying to knock on wood. She laughed to herself and, moving closer to Charles, smiled, although a faint, insidious worry pervaded her. "What's wrong, dear?"

"What do you *think* is wrong?" he responded. "Haven't you heard what people have been saying about my business? They're going to bring me bad luck, that's what's wrong."

Sarah was taken aback. She didn't believe her husband truly had financial woes and imagined what was troubling him was the imminent opening of the Ukerewe clinic, which had taken only a year to build. *He's fabricating financial problems*, she figured, *as a way of distracting himself*. She thought the widening of his waist was a byproduct of the same anxiety. She hugged him and whispered comforting words.

Charles stiffened in his wife's arms and thrust his hand into his pants' pocket. "Damn, I left my lucky charm in the hotel room!"

Sarah fought a wave of irritation, mitigated by tenderness. "You could send Jackob to get it, love." She remembered, not that long ago, when Charles still possessed the dignity to hide his silly superstitions from her.

"How can I do that?" sputtered Charles. "I would have to give him the pass code…You know I use the same number for all my combinations."

Sarah laughed, trying to lighten the mood, and said she'd get the gold nugget for him.

He was annoyed by how patronizing she was being. "*You* have your lucky charm with you," he nearly shouted. "You wouldn't be so calm if you'd left yours in the room."

"What are you talking about?"

Charles grabbed her hand. The Asscher-cut diamond ring glittered under the lights.

Sarah looked into the eyes of her husband, but they were not the eyes of the man she knew. Charles's swollen face was oily, and his flesh smelled of fat. Before her stood the stranger, the weak one who had visited her a handful of times in the past. "You think this is my lucky charm?" she asked, her temper rising. "This is a symbol of my most beautiful memory." Her husband's fingers squeezed her wrist with force. She pulled her arm away and saw a red welt label her as *his*.

"Of course it's your lucky charm! Your luck began the day I slipped the ring on your finger. Since then, you've had every luxury you've ever dreamed of."

Stillness passed between them, and the air seemed to gulp.

"What in the world are you saying?" Two tears dropped onto the collar of her black dress.

Charles inhaled the thick air and glanced around the ballroom to be certain no one was watching them. "I'm sorry, Sarah. I'm going through a difficult period."

"Do you really think I've been by your side all these years for your money? You're the one who always wants more. I'm the one who begged you not to buy the second mine, but you clearly have such a low regard of my opinion that you went ahead and bought it without consulting me. Charles, darling, I want *you*," sniffled Sarah, dabbing at her eyes with a piece of cloth she took from her purse, "not your cursed money."

Charles embraced her.

She slipped out of her husband's arms and commanded him not to touch her. Her look of disappointment was one he had seen on his mother's face.

Sarah scowled at her engagement ring. "As soon as we return to Mwanza, I'm putting this in the safe. I'm not going to wear it until I'm convinced that you know I care nothing for your money."

27.

Construction of the clinic was completed on time. Zuberi's evil spell had failed.

From Jackob's perspective—not aware of the healer's malevolence—the witch doctor's powers were confirmed. The magic amulet placed in the first brick used in the clinic's foundation brought the project to realization.

Charles, who was amazed that the clinic was opening on schedule—considering the government's red tape—agreed with Jackob that Zuberi's benevolence and supernatural powers were responsible for the success.

The soothsayer thought about a plausible excuse he could give to avoid participating in the grand opening. Jackob had expressed to Zuberi that Mr. Fielding recognized the shaman's role in the achievement, and Zuberi wanted to take advantage of being placed in a position of power by a white man. At the same time, attending the ceremony would encourage the villagers to make use of the facility, and he would lose customers. Zuberi thought about how to handle the awkward predicament and finally decided he would stay at the ceremony only long enough to greet the white man. Then he would leave quietly, without being noticed by many.

Sarah had gone to Ukerewe a few days before her husband arrived so she could be on hand for the preparations. The clinic sat midway between White House and the village, and the ceremony was planned for Saturday. Local and regional authorities, inhabitants of the island, the management team of her husband's mines, Mwanza expats, and members of high society would be in attendance. The program included traditional dances and a buffet dinner. Sarah had arranged for a famous Italian chef from a restaurant in Mwanza to prepare the buffet of foreign dishes as a special treat for the local people.

On the night before the inauguration, Charles had difficulty falling asleep. He'd spent the entire afternoon and evening correcting and re-reading his speech. Stretched out on the bed in the dead of the night, he watched the mosquito net wave in the breeze, drifting off only occasionally until sunrise flooded the room. The sun dug its nails into his eyes and laid its heat on his body, forcing him to get up. In Tanzania sunrise is not like in England. Neither pinkish aurora nor muted rays ease out the night. Instead, a ball of fire rises quickly and close to the earth, embossing the sky with daybreak.

CHARLES WANTED TO hurry to the clinic to thank Sarah for arranging the food and entertainment, kiss her, show her how much he needed her. And he wanted her to read his speech and tell him how brilliant he was. Though he realized he was behaving like a child, he couldn't help himself. With his financial reserves diminished, his confidence and spirit were fading.

He hugged her the moment he arrived at the clinic, noting the anxious mask she wore.

"Do people here really believe that a man with AIDS will be cured by having sexual relations with a woman with albinism?" Sarah asked immediately upon seeing him.

Charles's desire to be near his wife vanished. "How should I know?" he replied. "How are the preparations going?" he asked, attempting to direct the conversation to the important matter at hand.

"From the moment the doctor mentioned it, I've been thinking how absurd it is. And dangerous." She paused. "Can you believe he was laughing when he told me?"

"We're in Africa, dear," said Charles with nonchalance. "Can you please read my speech? I want your opinion."

Charles couldn't understand why his wife wasn't giving him her undivided attention. Instead, she appeared as surprised by her husband's indifference to such inconceivable depravity as she was by the doctor's. She took the speech he handed her and skimmed it.

"It's perfect," Sarah said quickly, flashing a smile. As she returned the paper to Charles, she noticed her bare left hand. She was still surprised when she saw no ring on her finger, and was even more surprised by the new feeling of freedom and of self-empowerment that her gesture of dissent had resulted in.

Charles hugged her. If he had stopped for a moment to look at her, he would have noticed that, rather than a smile, she wore a grimace to hide the confusion and sense of oppression she felt from his indifference to human life.

NKAMBA'S SMILE WAS not much different when her granddaughter told her about the comments made by her stepsisters, Sefu's daughters from his first wife.

"*Bibi*, my sisters told me I have to stay home this evening because I'm too young. They were teasing me, weren't they? I know my classmates are going to the party so they must be too young as well! Not to mention that one of my stepsisters is younger than me."

Nkamba knew her other granddaughters didn't want to be seen with Adimu. "You're right. They don't want you there out of envy," she said, satisfied that she found a way to make Adimu feel proud when Sefu's other daughters were being petty and cruel. "The day you were born everyone, including your father, thought you might be the daughter of the *mzungu*— his name is Mr. Fielding—and many people still think it. Your sisters don't want you to be the center of attention." Nkamba went on to suggest Adimu stay home, that there would be lots of people at the party, even more than at the market, and she reminded her treasure that neither of them liked crowds. Adimu shut out her grandmother and receded into her own world the moment her *bibi* let on that everyone thought she was the white man's daughter.

If people think so, then maybe I am. I am white, not black like the other children, she said to herself. *And the black man, Sefu, who* Bibi *said is my father, doesn't act like my father.*

Nkamba's words gave Adimu one more reason to go to the party, though she was well aware that her grandmother wouldn't be there to protect her. Her *bibi* preferred her fields, her animals, and her hut, and she knew she was just as unwanted at community gatherings as her granddaughter.

Adimu thought it would be easy to recognize the white man at the party. She was convinced the two of them would be the only white ones there.

WHEN SHE ARRIVED at the clinic event, she was shocked to find many *wazungu* and immediately panicked, fearful she might not be able to pick out Mr. Fielding. Her initial disappointment, however, was followed by joy. She was not, as usual, the only white person present, and all eyes were not on her.

As Adimu wandered among the crowds, she was reminded of Sunday Mass when everyone had the chance to show off their finery. She was ashamed of her blue dress, nearly worn-out, and her everyday sandals. She kept her eyes down, lifting them only occasionally to look around.

Her stepsisters and their scowls were at the party, and Adimu stayed away from them. Her stepsisters' and stepbrother's eyes were like big hands that pushed her toward the exit, nearly too strong for her to resist, and she had to force herself not to run.

However, Adimu had two excellent reasons to stay: she was driven to meet her rumored white father, and she enjoyed eating dessert, which she heard would be served. The islanders had been talking for days about the special foods that would be at the party. "Italian" was the word they used.

Adimu walked alongside a man with very light skin and curly hair and carefully observed him. His hair was black, not blond like hers; if he were the one, her real father, how could they look so different? she asked herself. Her poor vision hindered her from comparing their features. She did her best, though, to methodically study the face of each white man at the party, looking for a similar feature, some detail that would prove their relationship.

Adimu had just reached the buffet table when Charles was about to unveil the signage bearing his family name. She heard "Fielding" announced on the loudspeaker, the name her grandmother had said the *mzungu* went by. Adimu froze, torn between good things to eat piled high on a long table and a burning curiosity to see the man's face. She would eat later.

She wiggled her way between the groups of people until she found a place by the door of the clinic that allowed her to see the podium. Mr. Fielding wore a white suit. He was a hefty giant. Adimu wanted to get closer to see if their facial features were similar, but a local boy, who was a little bigger than her, spitefully kept her hidden and would not let her move. She relied on her most developed sense: her hearing.

The voice of the man at the podium was deep, not oppressive, and he left the end sounds of his words suspended in the room's echo as if he were holding a musical note.

When his speech was finished, people poured toward the refreshments. She was surrounded by comments, laughter, and exclamations. Groups of youngsters joked and played, trying to be the first at the buffet. Adimu heard Antony's voice but wasn't able to locate him in the confusion of sounds. She would have liked for the crowd to thin out before returning to the sweets table, but her hunger and curiosity got the best of her, and she pushed on into the crowd.

Waiters came and went with trays of food like she'd never before seen. She studied the consistency of the pasta, the shape of the pizza, the colors of the cakes—chocolate, pastry crème, whipped cream. She was so enthralled by the spectacle that she didn't notice the pair of eyes that were glued on her.

Sarah hadn't seen the girl since the day in the grocery, three years earlier. Completing the invisible triangle, Charles, unobserved, was watching his wife. He saw a sparkle in Sarah's eyes as she stared at the girl, whom he recognized as Adimu. *That is her Asscher-cut diamond,* he thought, *her blue faceted eyes.* He could sense the thoughts and desires piling up in Sarah's mind.

Adimu decided she would start with the desserts. She looked at them for a long time so she could memorize their shapes and could sketch them on the walls of the hut. Having committed the bounty to memory, she resolved to serve herself, but it proved more difficult than expected. She was afraid of spilling the food on the table and having someone yell at her. She noticed that many of the other villagers were having difficulty serving themselves too; like her, they were used to eating with their hands and were clumsy with the utensils. While she thought about how to solve the problem, she felt a hand brush against her shoulder. She startled, expecting that the hand was there to push her away, but the touch transformed into a caress.

With a friendly smile, Sarah asked Adimu in Swahili what she wanted to taste. Adimu immediately recognized her as the ice cream stranger. *What luck! She must be a dessert divinity.*

Shy at first but then with determination, Adimu pointed to the dessert she had spied earlier. She thanked the woman for serving, and quickly ran away with her plate to find a quiet place to eat alone.

Outside the reception hall, in the direction of the garden, Adimu sat on the ground, next to a bush. She set the fork beside her and lightly touched the dark top of the unusual dessert. A thin layer of cocoa powder dusted her fingers. She tasted it with the tip of her tongue. It was slightly bitter. She poked at it and discovered that under the dusting of chocolate was a layer of light, fluffy cream, and below that was another dark layer that was moist and porous. She stuck her tongue into the hole she'd made with her finger. Nothing so good had ever been victim of her taste buds.

Adimu ate quickly, licking her fingers and lips. She ate half of her dessert and saved the rest for her grandmother. Then she set the plate aside, next to the fork, closed her eyes, and thought about how lucky she was. She was at a party, no one had sent her away, and the white woman from the grocery had even served her. She reflected that only another person like herself could be so kind to her, like the woman doctor who had examined her when she was little. She thought, *Bibi is right. Only a girl like me will ever be my friend.* She looked at her plate, at the slice of dessert for her *bibi,* the dark powder mixed with the delicious white cream. With her finger, she cleaned off the edge of the plate. Then she licked a little of the cacao and closed her eyes. The extraordinary sweetness filled her mouth; the temptation was stronger than her good intentions. Greedily she ate the rest of it and cleaned the plate as if she were cleansing her conscience. She would go inside and get another portion for her grandmother. Maybe she would run into the woman who had helped her.

Adimu stood up and, while she straightened the pleats of her dress, she heard a man's voice, the same deep one with the hovering end-sounds. It was Mr. Fielding, she was sure of it. Peeking around the corner of the building, she saw him, in his white suit, talking on the phone in a language she didn't know. He seemed upset and walked back and forth, waving one arm in the air. He was headed in her direction. Adimu couldn't decide whether to run or to risk it all and look him in the face. Then she froze where she was. The man walked past her, engrossed in his conversation, and didn't seem to notice her. As he pulled his hand from his pocket, a small shiny object slipped out of it and fell onto the lawn.

Charles walked away, and Adimu ran to where the object fell. With the tall grass and her uncertain vision, she had to get down on her knees to find it. She detected a sparkle and picked it up: a yellow stone hanging from a chain of the same color. It looked like a rock with a tail. It glistened, and it was easy for her to see the light that licked it. Now she had an excuse to get near the man who might be her true father! She thought how lucky this shiny thing was, and forgot about the cake for Nkamba. The only task of any importance was to find Mr. Fielding and give him back the stone. She saw a white spot in the distance. She brought the image into focus and went straight in its direction.

Charles noticed the girl approaching him and ducked behind three very large men. Ten minutes later, while he was talking with one of the minister's assistants, he noticed the girl again, lurking. Wants money, like all the others, he was sure. *It has to be that Adimu. Maybe she was told what happened between us all those years ago.* He excused himself and hurried off in another direction.

Adimu tried for a third time to approach Mr. Fielding and was now certain that he was intentionally avoiding her. She had learned early on to interpret body language; indeed, it was the most accurate form of dialogue she knew. However, she wasn't ready to give up. She figured that maybe he thought he was her father, too, and it made him shy. Just like it made her. So she worked her way through the crowd until she found herself to his right, as close to him as three goats. Summoning her shaky confidence, she looked at him. They didn't seem to share any physical traits, except for the color of their skin.

Charles, who was sweating, was speaking with a woman wrapped in a lemon yellow dress. He kept his eyes on the white woman in yellow, his large hands flagging at his sides. Adimu observed his fingers, and she thought they looked like her own. Charles abruptly took the woman by the elbow and led her away, turning his back to Adimu who stayed behind, swallowed by the crowd. *He cannot be my father,* she thought. *Otherwise he would have spoken to me.*

Disappointed, she began to leave the clinic without getting more cake, though unexpectedly found herself, again, next to Mr. Fielding, who was chatting with a different white woman. Adimu recognized her voice—she was the one who had helped her get the piece of cake and bought her the ice cream at the grocery. *Maybe I can give the stone to the dessert lady and ask her to return it to Mr. Fielding,* Adimu considered.

Adimu waited until the adults stopped talking and Charles walked away. She approached the white woman with long, wavy blond hair, took the woman's hand, and placed the strange stone in her palm. "The man you were speaking with dropped this. I tried to give it back to him, but I'm invisible to many people. Can you give it to him?"

Sarah held Adimu's hand and squeezed it tight. "Thank you very much, Adimu. My name is Sarah."

"Adimu is what my *bibi* calls me. How did you know?"

"I'll give it to him." Sarah bent down and kissed Adimu on both cheeks. "He's my husband. Come along, let's get some cake."

Neither more dessert nor holding the hand of the wife of the most famous white man on the island could have brought greater joy than receiving two kisses. No one before had ever dared such an expression of affection. Few had ever even touched her. Sarah handed Adimu a plate with two slices of cake on it. Adimu thanked her with a smile that went from ear to ear. Her *bibi* was right—she was the center of attention!

She left the reception hall carrying her gift of cake close to her chest. Adimu passed the other villagers with her head held high, ignoring the looks and whispers of disapproval.

AT HOME, CHARLES was on the veranda enjoying the evening air as his wife came close and sat on his lap.

"What a lovely evening. I'm proud of you and sorry I doubted the clinic," she said, passing her fingers through his hair.

Charles sighed, letting himself relax under her gentle, caring touch.

"Do you remember that baby with albinism that was put in your arms shortly after we came to the island? She was at the inauguration."

"Yes, I know. I saw her. She was following me," he replied defensively.

"Indeed! She told me that it had been impossible to get close to you. She wanted to give you this." Sarah let the nugget swing in front of her husband's eyes.

"Oh, my lucky charm!" he exclaimed, touching his empty pocket. "I thought she wanted money."

"Maybe you should lower your guard, dear. Not everyone is interested in your money. There are people who care about you for other reasons," Sarah said as she kissed the back of his neck and rubbed her ringless finger against his cheek.

"My dear, I know how these things go. People get close to you with the excuse of friendship, and then they end up demanding that you help them."

"Who are you talking about?" she asked, pulling back from Charles.

"People. In general."

Sarah sighed and lifted her palms. "What can I do with you?" she said softly. "You're obsessive. First your fixation about your weight, then insomnia, and now you believe the world is conspiring against you. I think it's time to take a vacation. We could go for two or three weeks to England. A change of scenery would do you good."

Charles shook his head. "It's out of the question. I have too many commitments right now." After regarding his wife's dissatisfaction, he added, as a concession, "Maybe...sometime in the future, mind you...I can take you to the savannah to see the gnus and zebras. Would that please you?"

Sarah poured a glass of lemonade for herself from the pitcher on the table next to her husband's armchair. She drank thirstily.

"What would please me is to invite the girl to lunch. We should thank her for returning the thing you value most," she said, thumping the empty glass on the table. "And to apologize for your indifference when she tried to return it to you." The crystal jingled. The sky was veiled, the stars hidden.

Charles caught his wife's irony. "It's useless for me to try and change your mind. I'll have Jackob contact her," he promised, electing then and there to forget to mention it to his assistant.

28.

With a giant platter of crustaceans in front of him, which he washed down with gold champagne, Mr. Fielding opened his heart to Jackob. He was going through a period of bad luck, he admitted.

"There could be an evil eye," Jackob suggested.

Charles barely heard his assistant. The second mine was not turning a profit, and from a break-even budget, the company was operating at a loss. Selling it, though, would be a sign of weakness, and everyone knew that predators prefer prey that is vulnerable, either due to the malice of man or the cruelty of nature. "There must be more gold on that land, more than decorated the courts of Egyptian pharaohs. But how to bring it to the surface?"

Jackob listened in silence. When Charles paused, his head bowed over his plate, Jackob proposed an idea. "There is a solution, and it's right here on the island. Zuberi. People go to Zuberi in times of need. Maybe it's different in Europe, but here in Tanzania, no one is immune to the magic that rules over everything, and Zuberi can turn it to your favor. That's how it is in Africa," Jackob reminded Charles. "He comes from generations of powerful healers. Do you remember the brick he donated for the clinic? It was because of the spell he had worked into it that the building was completed on time. Even though it was funded by you, when does a government project ever open on schedule?"

Charles seemed vaguely interested. *That's how it is in Africa*, Jackob had said. How many times had Charles himself said those same words?

That night, Charles had a nightmare. He dreamed he'd caught a lethal virus that would kill him in the space of several months. The incurable virus was called "misfortune."

Charles bolted awake, blinking in the darkness. He listened to Sarah's light breath next to him. He wanted to wake her but decided against it. If she knew the extent of his financial troubles, she would leave him, or she would suggest he sell the business. It was easy for her to proclaim disinterest in his money so long as she lived under the fanciest roof and was driven in a Rolls Royce. Initially Charles felt stung when his wife had announced she was removing his ancestral ring from her finger. He had never considered she would be able to live without *her* lucky charm. Once he became used to the idea, though, he believed it was for the best, that there was no place safer for the precious gem than in their safe. It wasn't as though she had thrown the ring away. He was certain if he had no designer clothes to offer her, she would be gone. He was sure of it, even if she wasn't. *Sometimes those closest to you know you better than you know yourself,* he thought.

His heartbeat accelerated, and air stumbled through his tightened windpipe. He struggled to get out of bed and down the stairs—the fresh fat around his waist made moving more difficult—and he flung open the door to step out onto the veranda.

He felt a little better in the fresh air. He collapsed into an armchair and sucked oxygen into his lungs as questions raced through his mind. *I know how things work in Africa, don't I? Is the blood that flows through my veins that of my ancestors or the blood of this land? God Almighty, where is this misfortune coming from?*

The white man's science had failed him. Geologists had said there was a low concentration of gold in the soil at the new site. And African wisdom had been of little help. The diviners kept wandering over the tract of land without even the slightest pull on their wands. There was only one option left. He would go to Zuberi.

He would ask Jackob to make an appointment for the weekend and would sneak off without Sarah knowing.

Charles jumped when he heard rustling from a bush near the parapet of the veranda. He sharpened his vision and saw two shining eyes. He remained still, his muscles tense. *Has evil finally arrived?* he wondered. The pair of golden irises sprang out from the vegetation. Charles braced himself. A small, fluffy stray dog trotted toward the garden.

Sarah liked to keep the gate open at night, something about feeling unconfined. He would order the guards to close it starting that day. *Who knows what might wander in?* For once, his wife would have to obey him.

Zuberi was waiting for them in the yard and stepped forward when they arrived. "Welcome to my home," he said, extending his arm toward the door and displaying a radiant smile.

Inside the room, two villagers, who were sitting on the ground, looked at Charles with fear, hiding their faces in their hands when he greeted them.

"Patients persecuted by evil spirits. Their minds are disturbed," explained Zuberi.

Charles took small steps, his attention focused on those sitting on the earthen floor.

"Modern medicine has been unable to help them. Their family members beg me to send away the evil that has taken over their minds," the healer continued.

Jackob, noticing Charles's unnatural silence, interrupted Zuberi. "I need a cure for a headache. Also, Mr. Fielding suffers from insomnia. Could you prepare a potion for him as well?"

Zuberi studied Charles's eyes. "You will see, I will free you from the bad that is troubling you," he assured him. "I act on the cause, not only the symptoms. I heal your soul, I take away the curse, and I strengthen the body."

Though Charles wanted to laugh at the man's words, there was something magnetic about him, and he felt an odd impulse to trust him.

"I am the twentieth generation of healers in my family," the shaman said, making large gestures with his hands. He stopped, suddenly, and leaned closer to Charles. "Trees grew tall while my masterful father guided me."

Zuberi led the way to the main room in the house and invited his guests to sit. He called his daughter to serve the tea.

Jackob explained Charles's situation, the bad luck that had been following him and the second mine's poor profits. "My boss needs help."

The witch doctor could barely contain his enthusiasm. The white man must have been sent by the benevolent spirit of one of his ancestors. He took Charles's hands in his and closed his eyes, inhaling deeply. For minutes he was lost in meditation.

"Simple. There is a very strong curse from one of your business rivals," announced Zuberi. He got up and fetched a large roll of paper that was propped in a corner behind a table. His daughter entered with the tea, threw a glance at the white man, and left in silence. The soothsayer drank greedily and invited his guests to do the same. Then he cleared the table and unrolled the scroll, weighing down the corners of the paper with black stones. Crumpled and yellowed at the edges, the scroll revealed the outline of a human body with red Xs covering various segments of it. Zuberi observed his guests' reactions. Charles's lips faintly lifted at the corners. Zuberi was not certain how to read the white man's conflicting signals, though he knew white men respected confidence. So with half of the *zeru zeru* already requisitioned by his village clientele—sex organs, left foot, eyes, etc.—he would aggressively persuade Charles to place his order. Without the white man, Zuberi's dream wasn't financially feasible.

"Simple," repeated Zuberi, "there is nothing more simple than resolving problems like this one, for me that is. The limb of an *embulamaro*, that's what you need. The right arm, to be exact. It will point to the vein of gold in the earth." The witch doctor continued. "Simple to amputate it. A stick is slid under the limb, and then a clean stroke of a machete to cut it off. To prevent the *isope*[14] from dying so it won't vanish, kerosene is poured on the wound. Your destiny is in the arm of an albino."

Charles was unprepared for *that* solution. His eyes narrowed. "What sort of albino animal are you speaking about? A chimpanzee?"

"Perhaps I have not explained myself well." Zuberi assumed a serious air. "I am speaking of a *zeru zeru*, that which you Westerners perceive as a person but isn't."

Charles limited himself to a nervous grin, tilting back his head, wanting to distance himself from the tangle of sensations that were taking shape in his stomach. "I'll think about it and let you know," he stammered. The ground burned under his feet. Adimu popped into his thoughts. She, of all people, was the one who had returned his good luck charm. *What could it mean?* He erased her from his mind.

At the door, as Zuberi was concluding his salutations, he remembered Jackob's requests. He asked the men to wait and went back into his workshop. He opened a table drawer and searched until he found a package containing two painkillers and a tranquillizer. He ground the pills in separate mortars, added some dry root extracts, and prepared two paper envelopes—one for Jackob and the other for Mr. Fielding. He gave them the remedies and waited on the threshold for the car to pull away. Standing straight as a tree trunk, he waved when Charles turned to look back at him. If Mr. Fielding accepted his proposal, he would be able to save the inhabitants of Ukerewe from their troubles and take his place in history. Only the white man's wealth could put into action such a costly endeavor.

Once the witch doctor was out of sight, Charles asked, "How could he propose such a thing?"

Jackob let his employer vent his outrage. Finally the assistant said, "That's how it is in Africa. Remember, sir, we are not in Europe."

The words echoed in Charles's mind over the following days. The more

---

[14] Another word in Swahili to indicate a person with albinism.

time he spent in the company of his financial worries, the louder were Jackob's words. Exasperated by insomnia, he took the powdered remedy Zuberi had given him and slept through the night. When he awoke mid-morning the following day, he felt rested and fortified. As he stood in the bathroom, looking at the envelope of powder, he had to admit to himself that the natural remedy had really worked as well as, if not better than, regular medicine.

While Charles filled his stomach with a mound of chicken and fried potatoes for lunch, he thought about the terrible consequences that financial failure would have. *I'll have to work in someone else's employ at the bottom of the ladder, eking out a living like a common man. A tiny apartment in the suburbs, barely enough money for rent, food, and gas for my used Toyota. And I will be alone because Sarah—I don't care what she says—will leave me.* The thought of it was unbearable, humiliating.

Although Charles was enthusiastic about the sleeping remedy, he avoided taking it again. The only tranquillizer that interested him was money. If the arm of an albino was the solution to finding his gold, he would procure an arm without killing anyone. *There's always a solution, even for the most difficult problem*, he said to himself. Combing his mind for it, though, produced continued sleeplessness. *A person can live without an arm. How much money is one arm worth?* His next thought caused him to sit up in bed.

So I need the arm of an albino? Fine. No one has to be mutilated on my behalf. Simple, he said to himself, and he smiled for having used Zuberi's expression. Maybe he was becoming a great shaman himself. *If the limb comes from a cadaver…it no longer is needed*, he thought and laughed. The perfect solution. Charles's conscience would be clean, and he'd regain his financial stability.

"No tricks. The *zeru zeru* must be a cadaver…from the start," he said when he explained his idea to Jackob. "The price is irrelevant so long as my conditions are met."

29.

Adimu asked her *bibi* if Mr. Fielding was her real father. Had she been abandoned by the *mzungu*? If she were the daughter of Sefu and the woman called Juma, why were they one color and she another? And why hadn't they raised her?

Nkamba answered: "These things are difficult to understand." The old woman felt her husband by her side, trying to help her explain it to their granddaughter.

It was sunset and Adimu, passing near the baobab at the center of the village, saw a crowd of people waiting in the clearing. During the previous days, she had overheard pieces of conversations between adults and had seen posters announcing the arrival of an important person. Curious, she joined the gathering.

Musamaali Nangoli had been born under a mango tree in Uganda on a rainy day during the time of the coffee harvest. When he had lived for eleven rainy seasons, after he had called for the knife[15], he began asking many questions, too many for the white men who had taken over the land of his ancestors. They told him his God was wrong, as were his clothes and his primitive ways. They sent him to a missionary school, forced him to become Christian and to abandon his name: Musamaali Busima Gidagui Nawodya Nangoli. He was baptized as Peter. He grew up convinced he was a British citizen, but soon, when the first hairs under his arms and on his face appeared, he understood that he was born, and would die, African. He began traveling far and wide, searching for the lost history of Africa, and he had much to say to the people of his land. Africans in many countries knew him. The islanders considered his visit to Ukerewe a great honor.

Adimu held her hand above her eyes like a visor; she had never seen so many people. They were everywhere—on the roofs of houses, on top of the few cars, on the yellow dirt, even in the trees. Besides the inhabitants

---

[15] To be circumcised.

of Murutanga, everyone on the entire island had come to hear the African brother.

After a long wait, Nangoli arrived among a jubilation of shouts and applause. He arrived, standing in the back of a pickup, surrounded by his collaborators who were chanting his name. The truck was followed by droves of young people who were dancing and cheering. Nangoli walked toward the stage, men clearing a way through the horde for him. Villagers pushed through the crush of bodies to touch him or shake his hand. He walked with his head high and a bearing that suggested he was carrying heavy bags of grain in his big hands. In response to the exultant cries, he raised his hands over his head and clasped them together, making eye contact with as many people as he could.

"Africa for Africans!" he shouted from the stage while the euphoric crowd cheered and applauded. *If only he would use the microphone to announce that I'm normal and they don't need to fear me!* thought Adimu.

"Our African culture is in danger of extinction for the fault of the *mzungu*," he said to a new explosion of cheers.

Adimu lurched. *Did he really say that?* She was white, too, and people sometimes called her *mzungu*. Her instinct told her to run, that danger lurked, but she was caught in the crowd, and it pressed against her from every angle.

"Culture is the language spoken by people in a place. It is the way individuals behave, relate to one another, dress, pray to God, take care of each other. No culture is superior to another. Some cultures may appear strange or unusual to the people who do not belong to them, but if they are observed in their context, they are not strange at all. This was the error made by the white visitors when they arrived in Africa. They judged what they saw with their criteria, which are different from ours. They looked at us from a European point of view, and the habits and customs they did not understand were labeled primitive and were destroyed. Current problems in Africa can be traced to the forced introduction of white culture."

The crowd jostled, cheered, murmured, and moved as one giant pulsating body. Even their eyes seemed fused into one single gaze. The man on the podium fascinated everyone.

Adimu wanted to be transparent, to be a true *zeru zeru*. She crouched as low as she could, close to the dusty ground, and continued to listen to the words of the African stranger ride the wind.

"White culture and African civilization are opposites. Unfortunately, more often it is hell that the white man has brought to our land. You, white man, can take a man out of Africa, but you cannot take Africa out of the man!"

Adimu's embarrassment grew. Had people like her, men with *her* same color, caused all the bad things in the world? She looked at her bare arms and legs. She pulled on the hem of her dress, trying to cover as much of her skin as possible, tucking it under her feet so the wind wouldn't lift it up. She bent her head forward, hiding it between her knees.

"Before whites came, we did not pay taxes, there was no crime, no inflation, no unemployment. Men did not hit their wives; they did not divorce. Then whites came and said they would improve us, and our past flew away. Our ancient African societies were organized and sophisticated. Transgressors were rehabilitated and there was forgiveness. Sharing was important and practiced at every level of society. No one ate if there was not enough food for all. The needs of the individual were the needs of the entire community. An offense to the single was considered an offense against the collective. Marriages between members of various tribes were encouraged as a way to create strong ties. Every parent acted as mother and father for all the children of the village. The well-being of the community was the priority until that wretched day when whites arrived." [16]

Adimu was overcome by guilt. Her people had done bad things to Africans, and now she had to pay for their bad deeds.

She thought of a film she'd secretly seen some months before at the traveling cinema. She hadn't had money for a ticket, so she hid in the bushes. It told the story of an African man who lived in a country with many whites. There were lots of yellow cars and tall buildings made of glass and iron. The audience had whistled when the young black man was mistreated and taunted by the *wazungu*. *Finally*, she thought, as she watched the movie, *a black person was insulted in the same way she had been by her neighbors!* She felt a certain satisfaction in seeing her fellow villagers disapprove of the way the black man was treated by the white man. However, it was a movie, and her grandmother had told her that movies were invented stories. The important man before her, who was talking to the crowd, was real.

She crept backward until she found cover in some bushes. From there she ran home as fast as she could, glancing fearfully over her shoulder.

Her grandmother was sitting outside the door in a rare moment of

---

[16] Nangoli's speech as taken from the book *No More Lies About Africa* by Chief Musamaali Nangoli, A. H. Publisher, USA, pgs 47-57.

repose. As soon as Adimu caught her breath, she told her *bibi* what had happened. Nkamba listened with a sad face. What could she do with this child who was always looking for answers. She felt ignorant for not being able to comfort Adimu, for her inability to explain the reason for diversity. "Don't worry. The whites he was speaking about are from outside. You were born here, even if you have their same color."

30.

Zuberi called for each of them to come into his workshop, one at a time. He had to act with great care so as not to raise suspicions. Soon he would be crowned the savior of his community. His time had come; the legend of Zuberi was beginning.

"Simple. Nothing is simpler. If you have malaria, you drink a potion prepared from these herbs and those roots. If you have a curse—this particular type of curse—you need an *embulamaro*. That is the only solution. With a white shadow, your problem is resolved; without one, there is little I can do."

He omitted divulging, however, that his mercenaries would hunt down a dead *zeru zeru*—a minor detail he would mention later, if necessary. For now, he needed to build trust among his clients and concentrate on how to distribute the *embulamaro*.

"For you, fishermen—the hair, legs, and one arm to weave into your nets to attract big fish; some fish will even have gold in their bellies. And I will make amulets from limbs to be worn around the neck or waist."

Speaking with Yunis's husband, he explained, "Your wife needs a potion made from the genitals and breasts of the *nobody*[17]."

An *isope* was very expensive, as the villagers knew. "How much will it cost?" asked the fishermen. Zuberi had been waiting for that question. He had prepared his answer the night before. Now that the white man was involved, he could propose a number and arrangement that would suit everyone, especially Zuberi.

"I ask only for a symbolic amount, not market value. In addition to your personal contributions—as recognition of the value of my work—you will donate a small part of your catch. And, as our people are great storytellers, and the Spirits of the Lake value our stories, tell those in your clan of

---

[17] This English word is used locally to indicate in a derogatory manner a person with albinism.

how my magic healed your sorrows and bettered our community." Finally, Zuberi would get the recognition he craved.

"Why should we pay for something we already have in our village? We could use the limbs of our *zeru zeru*, and it would cost us nothing," said one of the older men, turning his head toward Nkamba's house.

"Do you not remember? The Spirits of the Lake chose life for our *mzungu*. She has another purpose. We must respect the Spirits' wishes."

Zuberi had to honor the agreement he'd made years before with the head of the village: Only when necessary and in common accord could he and Kondo decide a different fate for Adimu. And there was the promise he'd made to Mr. Fielding too—a cadaver, he had said. How could he disappoint the white man who was paying for the lion's share of the hunt?

RAMADANI HAD NOT wanted to visit that loathsome shaman, but he eventually relented to appease his father. Now he and Kondo sat in Zuberi's dusty laboratory.

"The remedy—the only one that works—is contact between the two sexes," Zuberi declared, looking at Kondo.

"Why an *embulamaro*?" the young man asked.

Ignoring the question, Zuberi continued; his eyes still on Kondo. "Ramadani, when I am sure of the hunters' trustworthiness, you can join the group. As the future village chief, you mustn't take unnecessary risks."

Zuberi had to conceal from Kondo that his *zeru zeru* headhunters were after a cadaver. For the young man's problem, he would devise another solution—*perhaps that will be how we'll use our* zeru zeru, Zuberi considered. Kondo had demanded that Ramadani participate in the *embulamaro* hunt as a way of making certain the *nobody* was female. And, Zuberi imagined, Kondo wanted his son to be whispered about as being vigorous, bold, and courageous. At any rate, Zuberi managed to stave off the cadaver problem for the time being.

THE SILHOUETTE OF the body that was drawn on the scroll was covered with red pencil marks. Only Zuberi could make sense of the intricate lines and *X*s that connected anatomical parts to the name of the client who needed it. Occasionally he modified his notes, depending on if an illness lessened or worsened. Erasing and rewriting, and talking to himself. Jane watched him, bored, and though she tried to get his attention by taking the pencil from his hand, Zuberi was too focused to shoo her away. The *zeru zeru* represented his passport to prominence, in addition to being the solution to the village's problems. This was one of the rare occasions when a white man, like Charles, was useful in Africa. *Ten thousand U.S. dollars. And for a corpse.* "The *isope*," he said to Jane, "will return part of what his ancestors took from us."

Once all the *zeru zeru*'s body parts were assigned to various villagers, Zuberi traveled to the border of the mainland, near Congo, where his brother managed illegal trafficking of goods and people destined for the country's markets.

Asani received Zuberi with the splendor worthy of a clan leader. It had been some years since they had last seen each other, and it was pleasant sharing their plans for the future. Asani was younger than Zuberi, and his fourth child had recently been born. Fortunately he had married a woman from an influential clan, and his business was growing more profitable by the day. There was always someone with cash ready to pay a good price for rare and illegal goods, not only for a *zeru zeru*, the price of which had risen dramatically in recent years. "Demand has increased, and the government calls for strict penalties. There just aren't that many audacious enough to risk going to prison," said Zuberi's brother.

It took more time than Zuberi expected to form the group of head-hunters. Each man had to meet precise requirements: enough hunger and anger to block out reason; poverty and ignorance; previous experience; and an ability with weapons. The head of the group was an ideal candidate. He was twenty-five years old, raised with no natural parents, and recruited by force at the age of seven.

While he had been chasing a ball of rags along the beach, a group of mercenaries kidnapped him. The soldiers fed him and kept him alive, which was enough to make him grateful. He was told his name was Thomas. Thomas, and nothing else. FLPC[18] was burned into the skin on his back, branding him for the militia group to which he now belonged. If he tried to look back, those four letters were there to remind him of who owned his body. He'd been assigned to a group of young men from villages in the Democratic Republic of the Congo. His commander was twenty years old. Thomas respected him, obeyed all his orders, and his dedication was rewarded with food and beatings. For Thomas's ninth birthday, he received an entire pack of cigarettes and a Kalashnikov. "You're a man now. It's time for you to learn the value of life in a war," the leader told him after Thomas fired the automatic rifle at his first banana tree.

---

[18] Patriotic Force for the Liberation of the Congo.

White men fascinated Thomas, even if he rarely saw them, perhaps *because* he rarely saw them. He knew white mercenaries had taught his commander to use weapons; they were the ones who made the decisions. He observed the white Gods from a distance and lowered his eyes when he felt they were watching him. That's what he'd been ordered to do by his commander. Look down. He was an inferior, a fact that he accepted. He was content to have food, cigarettes, and to feel part of a group, a surrogate for the family. That was enough. Thomas looked at his black skin and tried to calculate how much more superior to him were the white leaders. White was the color of power, of wealth. No one rose above the white men. He tried to stay out of the sun to become more like them. Once, while his commander and his woman were having sex, Thomas found a tube of cream on a windowsill that his commander's girlfriend used to lighten her skin. He stole it. He put the cream on his skin while he was on guard, hidden among the brush. He rubbed it sparingly on his arms, face, and neck and saw his skin fade until he imagined himself white.

He thought of his commander's words: "Our weapons come from Europe and America. They are perfect. Here in Africa we only know how to make machetes."

One evening, while he was on lookout, camouflaged by a tree branch, the tube slipped from his hand and landed on the head of a comrade who was sitting below him. So loud was his comrade's taunt that it attracted the attention of the commander. Since it was nighttime, Thomas's punishment was postponed until the soldiers were awake to witness it. At sunrise the group went into the forest.

"*Wazungu* are not examples to imitate. They are thieves who have stolen everything, even our sleep. From them we learn how to use weapons so that one day we'll destroy them by their own means," bellowed his superior.

Thomas didn't understand why his commander obeyed the whites if he hated them. An impertinent observation escaped from his lips. "Your girlfriend uses lightening cream."

"She's a woman, little more than an object!" shouted the leader, waving a stick. "You are a man, one of my soldiers!"

The commander's stick slammed against Thomas's legs so forcefully that he fell to the ground. The man hit him again. And again. "Why?" asked Thomas. The more Thomas asked why, the less he understood what was wrong with wanting to look like his betters and the more lashes he received for rejecting his race, his color. He held back tears when the pain kept him from breathing, even when he lost control of his body and felt his pants become warm and wet. Thomas was stronger than he had thought, and through clenched teeth, he repeated that he was a man. A soldier.

Only once had Thomas cried, many years later while he was running away, running from a white mercenary.

That boss had picked up a silvery fish and threw it at Thomas.

"Smell it," the man growled.

Thomas obeyed.

"Where does it stink?"

Thomas looked at another soldier he was with, unsure of how to answer. His eyes deviated to the blade of the white man's knife that was kissing the thick neck of his commander.

Moments stretched into minutes.

"I said, tell me where it stinks!" repeated the man, his pale blue eyes narrowing till they seemed like two crevices at the top of Kilimanjaro.

"All of it stinks," Thomas replied without breathing, fearful he'd give the wrong answer.

The white man forced a laugh, tore the fish out of Thomas's hands, and beheaded it with one clean swipe. "No, nigger," he said, "fish always stink from the head!"

Thomas and the other child soldiers stared at each other, their eyes bulging. None of them could decipher what the man meant.

The white man picked up the headless fish and held it high so all could see. "Now it doesn't stink anymore," he'd shouted. He stepped close to Thomas and put a gun in his hand.

"Shoot him, kill him," he'd urged, kicking Thomas's commander, the white man's voice not much more than a whisper. The gun pointed at the leader, kneeling on the ground.

Thomas's eyes were drawn to the prisoner's nape. It was covered with dirt and sweat and smeared with blood. His gaze lowered and locked on the rope that bound his commander's hands behind his back.

Thomas ran for an entire night. He ran far from his commander's body that lay lifeless in the forest. Nevertheless, Thomas had been the one who'd stayed to hold his leader when he was in agony. The others had escaped. Thomas had wrapped the body in his arms, tried to stop the death spasms, continuing to ask himself, *Why? Why?* Thomas had endured the pain of triumphant loss, had even endured the pain from the machete that chopped off his index finger. As he ran and ran under the sharp-edged moon, he repeated to himself what the white man had said shortly before shooting his commander: "A fish stinks from its head."

Thomas's commander was the closest thing he had to a father. And now the boy was alone, anger buried in a dark corner of his mind.

Thomas had reached the age of twenty-five believing the words "life" and "death" described the same condition. He desired a happy life and, at the same time, wanted to die. Life and death—the hands on a clock that would sometimes meet, were part of the same mechanism. Each one setting the tempo for the other.

Thomas's thirst for vendetta had not a precise target, therefore, he vented his pain against all potential obstacles. He was trained to obey and would carry out any barbarous act. He had nothing to lose. He had stopped asking why. For these reasons, he was the perfect group leader to hunt for a *zeru zeru*.

To Thomas, Zuberi said, "You will have to be very careful. You risk going to prison if you are caught, though it is more likely you'll become rich. And an *isope* will bring you luck. Keep these things in mind. You'll see, it will be easy to do, simple, just find a cadaver, a *ngazu*[19] that's already dead."

---

[19] A person with albinism.

31.

Although Adimu had been invited back out in the boat with Antony, no friendship was born from the excursions. She'd sit in the bow, alone. The children evaded her with their eyes and words. To keep herself from feeling sad, she'd look at the lake and imagine she was sailing with someone just like her. During one of the outings, she saw a glass bottle without a cap floating in the blue, carried by the waves. Water had filled it halfway, and it seemed to be sinking. The bottle was like her, at the mercy of a force too great to fight against. She wanted to be caught by a fisherman named Charles and put on display on a table in a big room, or maybe placed in a refrigerator to hold milk for a newborn.

ADIMU HAD DEVELOPED a ferocious hatred for her own skin. Sometimes she snuck behind her hut to dirty her arms, to make them darker. But the yellowish dust that stuck to her clothes only made Nkamba angry. One afternoon on her way home from school, Adimu saw some men handling a thick dark liquid. They were spreading it on the ground with the help of machinery. Curious, she moved closer, though still out of sight, and noticed that the black substance stained their arms and clothes. *The worksite will be abandoned at sunset, and I can come back*, she told herself. And in fact, when she returned later, she found the barrel from which the men had taken the liquid, and she peered over the edge. It was half full. When she poked her finger into it, the oily substance swallowed her finger completely, and when she pulled it out, she discovered that the color remained on her skin. *It'll stay black forever*, she thought as she flapped her arms excitedly like a little bird inside a pool of clean water. The temptation to fill a bottle with the liquid was irresistible. *Who will ever notice such a small quantity missing from the barrel?* Adimu searched around until she found an empty plastic bottle lying in a bush. She filled it with the liquid and went home with her treasure hidden under her dress. During the night, she fantasized about the permanent stain and how it would make her like the other children.

The next day when school got out, she went home to gather clothes and utensils that needed washing, as was her routine, and hid the bottle in one of the pots. At the beach, the shore was full of women washing clothes and dishes, children who were playing around them, and some fishermen who anxiously hauled in their nets with the hope of a catch. Adimu set her bundle down next to some bushes, and she waited. In the distance, a motorboat glided along on the glittering water.

Suddenly, a child shrieked with joy. He had captured a fish in his hands. The silvery oval reflected the sun like a mirror, and the child gleefully ran with it, followed by his friends. As he ran, he tripped in front of Adimu, and the fish slipped out of his hands, falling at her feet. The group stopped, not knowing what to do with a fish that was so close to the *mzungu*. Adimu swiftly picked it up and, laughing, started to run. The children chased her across the warm sand that was white and soft, like powdered sugar. "How dare you play with us? You haven't given us any of your hair!" shouted one of the boys.

Adimu became afraid and, knowing that she couldn't hold her advantage for long, tossed the fish on the ground. She hung her head from the insults that had been thrown at her and ran to the bush where she had left her things. Behind the vegetation, she pulled off her dress so she was only wearing her underwear. She opened the bottle and poured the dark liquid onto her body, rubbing it all over. First her arms and chest, legs and feet, and then her back. Finally she applied it to her face. She had to hold her breath because of its disgusting smell. She hoped that, with time, the sickening odor would go away. Completely covered by the black fluid, Adimu stepped out from behind the bush and ran after the other children. Frightened, they ran away. The mothers called to their children while the fishermen watched the scene, the nets slipping from the hands. "Who the hell is that?"

"It's me, Adimu!" she cried.

The people recognized the voice and stopped to stare. She was blacker than they were and oily from the petroleum that made her shine in the sun. The women began to laugh, holding their bellies, and the children, caught up in the merriment of the adults, jumped around her.

"I'm like you! Black like all of you!" she shouted, happy to be the center of attention.

The children moved close to touch her and discovered that their palms became black and stained. "She painted herself!" exclaimed a frail boy whose eyes were half closed from some kind of infection. The bigger children studied her before they grasped what she had done. It was only dye. One boy dove into the lake, rolled in the white sand and jumped in front of Adimu, chanting, "You're not like us, you're not like us!"

The adults laughed. Adimu was disheartened. Her joy had lasted such a short time! The boy who had captured the fish walked up to her and said she'd have to be punished for having stolen it from him. "I only wanted to play," she protested, pushing her fists against her sticky thighs. No one listened to her. Instead, the children dragged her off by the arm and made her get in a boat. They touched her—something they never did—as though her black color made her a little like them, even if they would have sworn the opposite. Some of the children were afraid when they saw their palms were slimy and stained. She sat under the blaze of her worst enemy, the sun, as the boat traveled out into the water.

Over the years, Adimu had become increasing intolerant of her *bibi*'s advice about avoiding the sun. She didn't care about getting burned or spending sleepless nights due to the pain. All she wanted was not to feel different. All she ever wanted was to be part of a group of kids. However, that afternoon she wanted to be anywhere else but in the middle of the lake, stared at and taunted by the entire village.

After a while, her skin began to burn, even though it was partially covered in tar. She untied her hair, and her great coppery mass covered her shoulders. She crossed her arms over her bare, blackened chest and changed positions frequently to alleviate her discomfort. She thought of her grandmother as a way to help her gather courage, but it made her even sadder. Her grandmother was right: everyone was against her, all of them enemies.

SARAH WAS RECLINING on a striped deck chair in the motorboat that was gliding on the gentle waves, sipping iced tea with lemon. She was worried about Charles and his health. He was increasingly anxious and distant. And fat. He used to be handsome. She thought of how the weight would tax his heart. What was happening to him? Deep in her thoughts, she hadn't noticed the small fishing boat drifting on the lake, not far from their large motorboat, until she heard voices. One child had caught a big fish and others on the shore were shouting, excited. Sarah saw a black figure with blond hair glinting in the sun. She stepped into her boat's cabin to get binoculars and called to her husband to come out on deck with her. When she lifted the binoculars to her eyes, she was sure.

For a moment, she and her husband were a team, both outraged by the cruel children in the run-down fishing boat. Before their skippers maneuvered closer to the girl, Sarah dove into the water and, when she came up for air, called Adimu's name.

It's the dessert woman! Adimu thought. She stared at Sarah, astonished. "Jump," shouted Sarah. "I'll catch you!"

Adimu, who couldn't swim, was terrified. The other children didn't understand why the foreign woman was so interested in their *zeru zeru.* Sarah held onto the edge of the fishing boat and caught Adimu's arm. Adimu heard the jeering of the children. *It would be better to die now*, she thought, *rather than keep living this way.* She let herself fall into the water and Sarah, with the help of her husband and the skippers, who had come closer with their boat, pulled her aboard.

They took Adimu to the Fielding clinic. She was meticulously washed and treated where her thin skin had burned. "Go find the grandmother and bring her here," Charles told Jackob.

The old woman did not say a word during the trip in the car. She sat rigid with her gaze straight in front of her, Jackob's attempts at conversation in vain.

Jackob and Nkamba arrived at the clinic in the late afternoon. Sarah tried in every way to convince Nkamba that her granddaughter should stay overnight for observation as the doctor advised. The grandmother was unyielding.

"With time, they will understand," said Nkamba, referring to the inhabitants of the village. "My girl is not evil. For now, I am the only one who loves an *embulamaro.*"

"Your granddaughter could have died today," exclaimed Sarah. "And tonight she may be very sick."

"I thank you for your help. It is the price my granddaughter must pay for being in this community. She will come home with me."

Sarah understood why, years earlier, the old woman had grabbed the baby out of her arms and swiftly fled.

Nkamba sat in the waiting room while Adimu rested. The grandmother's dark, wrinkled hands contrasted with the light-colored chair. Her bright traditional dress was the only accent of color in the antiseptic environment.

Though Sarah felt a rush of anger, she had to accept the old woman's decision. She gave Nkamba the medicines the doctor prescribed and walked her into the hospital room to help her awaken Adimu. The grandmother tried to lift the girl but she was too heavy, and Nkamba was forced to ask a nurse for help.

Sarah watched them leave, the curved, frail body transporting Adimu, who was almost her size, and the child leaning on her shoulder.

When Sarah returned home, she told Charles that she would wait no longer to have Adimu over for lunch. She felt a connection with the child and was driven to atone for the hard-hearted children who rejected the little girl.

As a child, Sarah's classmates shunned her once the rumor got around that her father had committed suicide. She knew how it felt to grow up without friends. Now destiny kept on placing her in the path of this unfortunate child. Sarah had always believed, from the time of her very first introduction to Adimu, that if Charles changed his mind about adopting a child, it would be easy to decide who to welcome into their home. Wasn't this how a person became a parent? The parent was chosen by the child, not the other way around. Sarah felt Adimu had chosen her and Charles.

Charles agreed to have the girl to lunch, though only because he was ashamed he hadn't had Jackob invite her earlier when he first said he would. When Sarah mentioned sharing a meal with Adimu, a fleeting sense of regret for having visited Zuberi returned.

During the night, Charles was overcome by guilt. Not weeks after he had agreed to the witch doctor's remedy, an albino girl would be eating his food at his table. The whole thing seemed grotesque. He had an impulse to weep. And it shocked him. *If even the slightest hint of what I've done reaches Sarah, it will be my end. Mine, ours, the end of the Fieldings.* He dissolved a dose of Zuberi's sleep aid in a glass of water, and his body began to relax. He fell asleep with the bedside lamp on and his hands beneath his head.

During the night, Adimu broke out in a high fever. Her body had been poisoned by the tar and singed by the sun. Nkamba kneeled next to the wall, facing the phone number for the protected community as if it were an altar. She prayed throughout the night. Outside it was as dark as the thickest forest, and far away a dog howled.

For two days, Adimu was at the mercy of the fever and suffered from violent delirium. Nkamba was about to lose all hope when Jackob knocked on the door.

"This is from Mr. Fielding," he said.

The elderly woman took the fine paper envelope. "I can't read."

"Give it to me. I'll read it." Jackob opened the white envelope with quick fingers like a curious child. "The Fieldings are pleased to invite Adimu to lunch on the last Sunday of the month."

Adimu heard Jackob's voice from inside the hut and managed to say, "They wrote that it would give them pleasure to invite me to lunch?"

"Yes," replied Jackob.

"*Bibi*, did you hear?" she said after Jackob had left. "Please, give me all the medicines we have. I have to be well enough to go." Someone in the world was interested in her!

Nkamba was equally surprised by the invitation. At the hospital, she had noticed, though, that the wife did appear to genuinely care. She had observed the white woman's liquid eyes fixed on Adimu as she slept on the European-type bed. To deny Adimu this opportunity would mean stealing from her one of the few rare joys she might ever have.

"I have to get better, *Bibi*," she said, drinking the mango juice that Nkamba prepared for her every evening.

On the Sunday morning, Nkamba accompanied Adimu to within a few yards of the gate to White House.

"Have them take you home," she instructed before letting go of Adimu's hand.

Adimu turned to wave at her grandmother. Nkamba remained there, watching her until she could no longer see her shape against the background of the Fielding's immense house.

32.

Though Adimu felt ashamed to be wearing the same dress she'd worn to the inauguration of the clinic, not having proper shoes to wear felt even worse. *Will Mr. Fielding accept me with these old things on?* she worried. *If he's my real father, he will,* she decided.

The Fieldings were on the veranda sipping chilled white wine when Adimu and Nkamba approached White House. Sarah saw the girl and her grandmother walking hand in hand and watched Adimu continue alone through the gate. Sarah met her with a cookie and a wide smile. Adimu wanted two kisses, like on the evening of the party, but didn't have the courage to ask. When seated at the glass lawn table, Adimu found it difficult to hold the gaze of the two adults so she focused on a button on her dress and rolled it between her thumb and index finger. Every object around her seemed enchanted. The paradise that surrounded her was spine-tingling and bedazzling, and her hunger to ingest its every miracle soon eclipsed her timidity. The pure white tablecloth, the blossoming strange-shaped garden, the glittering silverware, the mouthwatering food smells. Her head, though, was full of insecurities, and thus she swung her foot under her chair. *How do I use the utensils? How much should I eat? And what if I need to pee?*

Sarah had spent much time considering how to help Adimu feel at ease and decided that having the food presliced and served in small portions would reduce her anxiety.

"Your hair is so beautiful," Sarah said, as she stroked Adimu's long tresses. Adimu hoped she would never stop.

Adimu felt so buoyant, so safe, that she ignored Mr. Fielding's unwillingness to look at her. After he shook her hand when she'd arrived, he ate in silence.

Though Charles wanted to please Sarah, he was careful not to feed her false hope. Not that girl, or any other, would be their daughter.

As lunch progressed, Adimu became more audacious and peered lovingly at the man as often as she could. She scrunched up her face so she could see him as clearly as possible, though when her blue eyes caught his black ones, she lowered her gaze. She interpreted his glances as a sign of interest. It didn't go unnoticed by Adimu that three times in a row, they both requested seconds of the same food. *We like the same things*, she thought. Looking at him, she was convinced their eyes, mouth, and even their nose shared the same shapes. If she were polite and good—as her *bibi* taught her to be—maybe Mr. and Mrs. Fielding would care for her just a little. It was something she could hope for. The man was shyer than the woman, she realized. Maybe he hadn't gotten around to telling his wife his secret. *That Juma is his other wife. That I am his daughter.*

Dessert was a rarity for Adimu, and when the lightest, sweetest dessert she had ever had was set before her, generously sliced, she was over the moon. It was the same manna that was served at the clinic party. *Is it possible that Mrs. Fielding remembers how I loved it, and she chose it just for me?* A second big dish of the delicious dessert was laid out for her when she finished her first helping.

The delicate flavors of the tiramisu filled her senses, and she imagined how different her life would be if she really were a Fielding. *After lunch, I would go to my bedroom where there would be real toys, even a whole doll. I would eat delicious food every day, and my* bibi *wouldn't have to toil in the fields from sunrise to sunset.* At that moment, Adimu couldn't imagine there was any bad in the world.

After his initial irritation, a strange attraction pulled Charles toward the child. He found he could not behave indifferently to her. Charles served himself an enormous helping of tiramisu, piling the creamy sweetness onto his plate. Adimu giggled when she saw her maybe-*baba* was as fond of the creaminess as she and took the same portion she would have taken if she hadn't been served. Charles dug in a spoon and lifted it, dripping, to his mouth. He turned and saw Adimu smiling at him with joy. He tasted the delicacy with the tip of his tongue. And she did too. For several moments he left the spoon in his mouth as he thought, *I said to them I wanted a dead albino, under no circumstance one that was alive.* He set down the heaping spoonful of cream and ladyfingers on his plate. After his attack of conscience passed, he quickly shoved it into his mouth. Adimu was certain both she and her maybe-*baba* were sharing exactly the same thoughts as the heavenly food swam down to their tummies.

After lunch, Charles pulled out Adimu's chair for her and noticed several golden hairs clinging to it. He looked around, hesitating, and as soon as Sarah and the girl left the veranda to stroll between the flowerbeds, he twisted them around his finger and slipped them into his pants pocket beside his gold nugget. Everything would work out, he told himself. *She returned my lucky charm. She is good-luck gold.*

That evening, lying in bed, a high wall of barbed wire divided Sarah and Charles. When Sarah heard her husband's even breathing—a sign he was asleep—she turned on her side and let her tears dampen her pillow. She wrote a note to herself to get Adimu a pair of eyeglasses.

SLEEP ELUDED ADIMU as well. After rifling through her mind for every clue that might prove that her father was Mr. Fielding and then interrogating her grandmother with a series of trick questions, she finally lay, exhausted, on her mat. Why was her *bibi* so vague about the *mzungu*? she asked herself. Adimu would make it her goal to get a father and a mother, natural or adoptive. In the end, what does it matter?

33.

One day, during her tenth rainy season, Adimu cleaned her sandals in a basin when she got home from school. With the arrival of storms, not one inhabitant on Ukerewe could walk without his feet shrouded in mud.

The school itself, made of mud bricks and stones and a corrugated metal roof, shivered with deafening clatter when water poured from Heaven. It seemed that a bothersome spirit was throwing wet pebbles from the sky.

And in the dry season, there was dust—it got everywhere, burned eyes and slid between teeth.

The single schoolroom could barely hold the desks, the mud walls threatening to burst out the children. So scant was the space that the students had to flatten themselves against one another to slip into their seats. Adimu was relegated to the last desk at the back of the room. Since no one wanted to sit near her, she had more space than the others.

After talking with the woman doctor who vaccinated Adimu, Nkamba had been emboldened and had approached the teacher about Adimu's eye problem and how it was affecting her studies. The teacher, a mature woman who was excessively proud of her job, had listened to the older woman's request with contempt.

"I have been teaching for forty years, and I know better than you what my pupils need." The result of the conversation was that Adimu remained in the last row. The teacher explained that the little girl was an irritation and needed to be kept away from the other students so she wouldn't distract them. So all these years later, though she was a hard-working and smart student, her inability to see the blackboard prevented her from being successful in her studies.

Adimu's favorite subjects were English and Swahili. She also enjoyed geometry. While studying parallel lines, she considered how she fell under the same mathematical law: she and happiness were two lines that would never meet, not even if they traveled high up into the sky.

Since she couldn't read the blackboard, she often had to guess at the answers, which always earned reproach from the teacher.

"If a shepherd has a hundred sheep, the one lamb that remains behind will be eaten by hyenas," the teacher said as she neared Adimu's desk, looking her straight in the eyes. "At least have the intelligence to keep quiet if you don't know the correct response."

It didn't take Adimu long to stop calling out answers for fear of being eaten by hyenas. And she raised her hand only if she needed further explanation. The teacher generally ignored the white arm in the air—the girl was just seeking attention, she was sure.

The afternoon of the last day of school, Adimu discovered she didn't pass and wouldn't be advanced a grade. Though she had been afraid she was going to be left back, she had hoped with all her heart for a miracle, but as usual, no miracle materialized.

The day she found out that she failed, she entered her hut with her head down. Nkamba was at the table, chatting with Adimu's stepbrother. When Adimu walked into her home, her *kaka*[20] didn't ask how she was. He tilted his head in response to Adimu's "*Karibu*[21]."

When he stepped out of the hut to go to the latrine, Adimu asked her grandmother what they were discussing. Nkamba hesitated, which frightened Adimu. She leaned her body against her grandmother's leg, like she did when she was little. She was afraid one of her parents had died or maybe one of her siblings, notwithstanding that her stepsisters were never nice to her; they represented hope that one day her family might love her. She was overjoyed when she learned her brother had come to announce his marriage.

"*Bibi*, do you think I can get a new dress?" she asked, excited, jumping in circles around the old woman. Adimu had begun to daydream about boys, of one day getting married, being carried away from her hateful village by a man who cherished and protected her. *Maybe Antony?* Attending the wedding offered a chance for the villagers to see her in a new way.

"I'm happy you're getting married!" she exclaimed when her brother came back inside. "I can't wait to see you dressed for the ceremony and to meet your wife." Maybe Adimu might be an aunt to their children! *Maybe a godmother?*

He fixed a dark look on her. "You're not coming."

---

[20] Brother in Swahili.
[21] Welcome in Swahili.

Adimu stiffened and, stretching her neck forward, asked, "Why not?"

Her grandmother said nothing, staring down at her bony hands. She lifted her eyes and looked for a long moment at her granddaughter, whose eyes were darting from one adult to the other.

"Why not?" she repeated even louder.

"You're not invited," said her brother.

Adimu felt a quiver through her chest and neck. Her blood had turned into ice water.

"Why am I not invited? *Bibi* told me you are my brother even if you live in another house."

"You know why. You would harm my reputation and my clan's."

Adimu hiccupped out tears to Nkamba. "How can my brother behave this way when my friends are beginning to understand that I'm not a danger? Sometimes, you know, they take me out in their boats," she said to the young man.

Nkamba covered her face to hide her embarrassment. Her grandson let escape a sarcastic smile.

"Why are you smiling, brother? I'm telling you the truth. I have gone out on the lake with my friends many times. I sit on the bow. Antony likes me." Her voice trembled, and her lower lip shook. She was determined to hold back her tears.

"I'm smiling at your stupidity," said the young man. "You think you're there out of friendship? You want to know the real reason they take you with them? Then you'll get it through your thick *embulamaro* head that everyone in the village thinks of you in exactly the same way. Me, your father, your mother, and your sisters, all the boys and girls in your class. Especially Antony. They take you fishing because if the boat turns over, you're their float. Their blow-up life jacket. Even little kids know that a *zeru zeru* doesn't sink. Now do you understand?"

In that instant, any snippet of confidence or hope that Adimu had was swept away like dust from the floor. And on the foundation, below, was the horrible truth. She was a *nobody,* and that's all she'd ever be. She ran outside and threw herself on her grandfather's burial place, crying for him to hold her.

After some minutes, Nkamba came to her and laid her cracked hand on her granddaughter's back.

"Is it true, *Bibi*?"

She nodded. "It is."

"Why did you keep it from me? Why?" Her words were broken by her sobs. "Why didn't you tell me they were using me? I've been held back at school, my brother considers me invisible... What have I done to deserve this?" She tried to stifle her sobs in the folds of Nkamba's dress. She held onto her grandmother with such force that Nkamba's arm stung.

"You have not done anything, my child," she murmured, cradling Adimu against her gaunt chest. "Be patient, things will change. Things always change," she added.

Adimu clung to her grandmother like a wounded puppy, unable to control her whimpering. As night fell, Adimu finally calmed down, her gentle tears wiped away by her grandmother's fingers. Nkamba knew how to cure her pain. She knew that suffering is sometimes like a rainstorm: it doesn't stop until all the drops have fallen from the clouds. The only remedy was to wait for her granddaughter's emotional wound to stop bleeding. She waited in silence until Adimu, with a final shuddering sigh, stopped crying.

"Everything occurs in its own time, my child," said Nkamba, rocking the girl. "Listen to this story about the San tribe, and you will understand. The San tribe lived in a distant time, when the sun was a man who lived among them..."

Adimu held still, except for her fingers that twirled a long blade of grass.

Nkamba told the story of the sun man who let his warm rays wash over the plants and animals or deprived them of light when he slept. "Finally, one day, the tribes people told him, 'Sun man, it is time for you to shine above us. Travel in the sky, dry our rice, and protect us from the cold.' And that's what he did."[22]

"*Bibi*," said Adimu, rising from Nkamba's lap, "why have you told me this story? Everyone loved the sun man. Instead, I'm not loved by anyone. Except by you."

The old woman's face was veiled with melancholy. "The sun man could not rise into the sky before his time," she said, opening the door to their hut, encouraging Adimu with a tilt of her head to go inside. "Your time will come to shine bright, just like him. You must be patient."

The next morning, when Adimu awoke with the first rays of sun that filtered through the roof thatches, she listened to her grandmother's raucous breathing and touched the old woman's rough palm. Nkamba roused with a start. "What's wrong?"

"Do you remember the woman doctor who vaccinated me?"

---

[22] Traditional legend from South Africa.

Nkamba nodded in the dim room.

"The only way I can change my life is to become like her. I'll never succeed at the village school. I must leave the island to attend a school that will teach me and return home only when I've learned how to help my clan. Once I can heal children and adults, I will be respected. Then I will be seen," she said. "*Bibi*, please, find the lost numbers for the community in Tanga that will protect me. I'll work by your side in the fields so we can save more money."

34.

Nkamba could postpone it no longer. The following evening, accompanied by the light of a crescent moon, she walked to Kondo's home. On her way to the chief's hut, she prayed that the problem haunting Kondo when she had last approached him had been solved and her request would, this time, receive more attention.

The village chief was sitting near a small fire in front of his hut, a big black dog lying at his feet. As Nkamba closed in, the animal pricked its ears and lifted its head, though it did not move any other part of its body.

Kondo looked at Nkamba before returning his attention to the fire.

"I'm asking you to get me the telephone number of the protected community in Tanga," she said with a firm voice. She refused Kondo's invitation to sit and remained standing next to the fire, eyeing him.

"Even if I'm able to get you the number, what will you do with it if your son gives you neither permission nor money?" he asked.

"Sefu does not care about my granddaughter. He will let her go."

Kondo made a clicking sound with his tongue. Where had the timorous, respectful woman he knew gone? He stood up and so did the dog, Kondo's shadow, shaking the dust from its coat.

"I will let you know," Kondo said, turning his back to her and entering his house.

Nkamba stood still, rigid.

The weak glow that came from inside the mud hut faded when Kondo closed the door behind him. Nkamba waited outside by the fire, rubbing her hands over her arms. Standing in the light of the moon and stars, she pictured herself forcing her way into the village chief's home and demanding her request be met. They had once been friends. Didn't he remember? Didn't that matter? Kheri and he were of the same clan!

Nkamba padded home, prodded by the thought of Adimu alone and unprotected. She loathed herself for not having the courage to demand he give her the number, and she detested Kondo for making her beg.

IN A ROOM adjacent to his bedroom, Kondo opened the only drawer of the peeling cabinet and rummaged around for a green notebook. He turned the pages, yellowed at the edges, until he found what he was looking for. He returned the book to the drawer.

He had formed a plan to save his son—his foremost concern since Ramadani's positive AIDS test result—but in order for it to work, Adimu *had* to stay on the island. At least for a while longer. He knew Zuberi was self-obsessed, and he wasn't going to trust him with his son's life. And Zuberi still hadn't agreed to allow Ramadani to join the headhunters.

Ramadani watched his father from the doorway. When the old woman arrived, he had been behind the house, observing two small owls he'd never before seen or read about. On hearing the tense conversation, unusual for his father, he edged his way to the corner of the house to listen to the elders.

When Kondo returned to the main room, Ramadani crept into his father's private study to look in the green notebook. On the third page, written in large shaky letters, he saw a phone number. Next to it was written "Community in Tanga." He was sure it was the number Nkamba was looking for. Ramadani could not understand why his father refused to help Adimu's grandmother, why he refused to help the sweet child who was so gentle and dependable with goats.

UPON RETURNING HOME, Nkamba found her granddaughter utterly absorbed in the newspaper she was reading by the light of the kerosene lamp. The girl was sitting beside the wall on which the numbers were engraved, and she was bent over the ink on paper. The broken telephone number, illuminated by the glow of the lamp, was one more condemnation that bore down on the child, the grandmother thought. Adimu looked up. Nkamba was disappointed by her visit with Kondo. The old woman glanced at the mattress in the corner. "Turn off the light. It's time to sleep."

That night, Nkamba tossed and turned, beset by a deafening anger. Her hard work in the fields had been insufficient, not enough for the ferry ticket, not enough for the ten-times-her-fingers' worth of phone calls. Not enough for the trip from Mwanza to Tanga. The distance that separated the two cities was immeasurable. The cost of a bus ticket would eat up all her resources. *Why am I being denied what I need to save my child?* she wondered. It is a simple request.

Ramadani shared Nkamba's thoughts. If one phone number could lift the painful burden from the poor woman, why displease her? Shielded by the deep sleep that pervaded the home, the young man snuck out of his room by candlelight. In the darkness, the cabinet in the study took on a human shape. He opened the drawer and copied the number onto a slip of paper. For a fistful of seconds, Ramadani thought about how he was acting against his father's wishes. He froze when he heard a creak and then realized it was only a woodworm. He put the notebook back in the drawer, exactly as he had found it, and returned to bed.

The next day, when the sun was high in the sky, Ramadani slinked toward Nkamba's hut. At that hour, he conjectured, neither grandmother nor girl would be at home—the former in the fields, the latter grazing the animals. He stood before the closed door and, after making sure he wasn't seen, he pushed the slip of paper through a hole that had been bored into the mud walls of the hut. *If you live, so do I*, he thought, as the phone number disappeared into the brown peephole.

THE SOIL WAS harder and the hoe heavier—at least that was how it seemed to Nkamba. She returned home, exhausted from work, dragging her tools, the hem of her traditional dress dirtied and ragged. Opening the door to her hut, she saw a piece of white paper on the beaten-earth floor.

It must be Adimu's, she thought. Only after picking it up and putting it on the stool did she recognize the symbols. She went to the wall with the paper in her hand and, with her trembling earth-stained fingers, she compared the marks written in pen with those carved into the hardened mud. They were identical! Except for the last two missing ones that appeared on the paper. Nkamba brought her hands together and held them close to her chest as she did when attending Mass. She tilted her head upward, and her eyes traveled beyond the thatched roof. The phone number had fallen like a ripe fruit from the mango tree whose roots were nourished by the spirit of her husband. It is a miracle that can only have come from Kheri, she thought. *He must have talked with Father Andrew's God and the Spirits of the Lake. Adimu can go far from this wretched place. Her prayers will no longer bounce off the ceiling of this prison of a hut and fall to the ground like guano. They will be heard and answered.*

Nkamba blocked her sheet-metal door with a wooden pole and unearthed her savings. She took only a few coins and, as though she had just awakened from a restful sleep, walked briskly out of the hut.

MANY WERE WAITING in line to use the public phone. Nkamba waited her turn, squeezing the coins in the palm of her hand. From time to time, she squatted to rest her legs. When it was finally her turn, she gripped the receiver in her dusty hand and dialed. A woman's voice answered after a few rings.

"Hello, my name is Nkamba from Ukerewe. My granddaughter is a *zeru zeru*, and I'm calling so she'll be safe in your protected community," she said in one breath.

"Who gave you our number?" asked the woman.

"The vaccine doctor. The white lady doctor."

"Who does the girl live with?"

"Me. Her parents rejected her. She is an outcast among her clan and in the village. She is in danger. Please. She is a very good little girl. Help her. Take her."

"Wait a moment, please," said the voice on the other end of the line. After a pause, the woman spoke again. "There is a place available for your granddaughter."

Nkamba was unable to hold back the heavy wave of tears that soaked her cheeks, streaked her neck. A relief she hadn't known in years pervaded her. "My granddaughter can come? When?"

"In a week. Next Wednesday a white man and a woman from Dodoma will be waiting for her at the Mwanza port where the ferry from Ukerewe docks. Their names are Roman and Martha. They will accompany your granddaughter to Tanga."

Nkamba hung up the phone, kissed the slip of paper, and lifted her eyes toward Heaven and Kheri. This was more than she had hoped. And enough money would be left for Adimu to return to the island at least once to visit. She walked home feeling twenty years younger.

THE RECEPTIONIST AT the Tanga office held on to the shiny black receiver. She was thinking. She went outside of the administrative building for the protective community and walked to a stand of trees where she wouldn't be heard. She took out her cell phone, looking around to double check that none of her do-good colleagues could overhear.

A man with a raspy voice picked up the phone and greeted her.

"Get ready," the receptionist whispered. "Next Wednesday a white female fish will drop into the net. She lives with an old grandma. No one on Ukerewe cares about her. She's easy prey."

PART THREE

35.

Zuberi informed his headhunters—Thomas, Amani, Akili, and Aki—of a *zeru zeru* that had died at the hospital in Mwanza. Skin cancer. The four young men trailed the body from the infirmary to its village of origin, hoping to seize the cadaver at some point during the trip. As an opportunity didn't present itself, they waited for its burial. In the depth of night, they located the grave in the cemetery and started to dig. While they worked, the wooden cross bearing the name of the deceased began to lean and then to lay on the soft earth. They continued digging downward without incident until both the shovel and hoe bounced off the ground.

"Stones," said Amani, the youngest.

"Keep digging. Hurry!" ordered Thomas, who was getting jumpy.

They persevered and scratched and pried and gouged. They hadn't hit a layer of stone but rather a layer of cement. The family of the deceased had covered the coffin with concrete to prevent theft of the body. Aki, who tended to be the most skittish of the hunters, swore. Thomas forced himself to be calm—getting angry would only make them lose precious time. "Let's look somewhere else," he said.

"We could kill a *mzungu*, cut off his head, bury it in the forest, and pass off the remaining parts as an *isope*," suggested Akili, who was known as the resourceful one.

"Are you crazy?" said Thomas. "If we kill a tourist, we'll have the police after us. And don't even think about *doing in* a white African. You want to spend the rest of your life in prison and waste the good luck we were promised?"

"If we could get our hands on a living *zeru zeru*," interjected Amani, "nothing could stop us from killing it and saying it was already dead."

"True," Thomas agreed.

The next day, Zuberi called Thomas to say an albino girl had been killed in Shinyanga. "Only its legs have been nabbed; it could work for us," said the witch doctor. His priority was getting the arm for Mr. Fielding, and with the upper body available, he could satisfy most of his other clients.

The group arrived in the village after the funeral had concluded. Neither in the cemetery nor in the vicinity of the family's house were there signs of a recent burial. They camped at the edge of the forest, near the hut where the target had lived with its grandparents.

"Sooner or later they'll visit the grave. Then we'll follow them," said Thomas.

The elderly couple remained inside their home for two days. The four young men searched all around the area for the grave. Eventually they noticed two Westerners with cameras enter the hut and exit.

The next day, Thomas got a call from Zuberi.

"You're wasting your time," grumbled the shaman. "The newspaper ran an article about an old man in Shinyanga who buried his granddaughter under his bed so her grave wouldn't be desecrated. And there's too much attention from the press to kill the old bastard."

"Understood. We'll keep hunting."

Thomas's companions were beginning to show signs of impatience. They had been told this would be a quick job. Instead, many months had gone by with nothing to show for it.

"We're not getting paid enough," complained one.

"Yeah, you said it would be easy," said another.

"Let's cross the border and go to Burundi for a *zeru zeru*," suggested Akili.

"Too risky," the leader said. "If we get caught here, Zuberi will pay off the police or a judge. In Burundi, we're not protected. We have to find the *isope* in Tanzania."

"At least let's ask for more money!" said Amani.

Thomas slapped the boy so hard he lost his balance. "I make the decisions," he barked. "We'll complete our mission and—if I feel like it—I'll get more money. And if I'm real nice, I'll pass some of it on to you. Now, get up and go look for wood for the fire. I'm hungry," he concluded, lighting a cigarette.

ANOTHER RAINY SEASON had ended. The clouds left space for ample stretches of clear sky and the island was a dense splash of vivid green floating in the lake. Zuberi had collected the initial payments from his clients without telling them the whole truth about what they'd be getting for their nominal "donations." It was time to let them know the whole story.

"The largest contributor—the one who's made it possible for you to receive your part of the *zeru zeru* for well under market value—is against a fresh kill. So if the part I need for your potion has already been taken, you're out of luck."

"No way," said Yunis's husband. "My wife and I are dreaming of having many, many children."

The fishermen especially protested. "Tell us who set such ridiculous conditions. Our future is at stake!"

"Do I ever mention names? When you come to me, you're assured anonymity," said Zuberi, sticking out his chin and directing his eyes at the genitals of the man who spoke.

The inhabitants of Ukerewe had invested their hopes and many of them their small savings.

One old fisherman, who paid special attention to the Gospel at Mass, dreamed not of a miraculous multiplication of bread and fish. In *his* dream, the stones on the bottom of the lake turned into enormous fish that—like pieces of iron to a magnet—were drawn to the fishing net. When one of the fish squirmed in the boat and fell back into the water, he was thrilled— thrilled to have a smidgen of room, so full was his boat with fish.

After Zuberi's confession, many of the villagers were feeling discouraged. Everyone knew *zeru zerus* vanish when they're dead. And even if the hunters were lucky enough to find a dead *embulamaro* before it vanished, it wouldn't be as potent as one freshly killed. Skepticism began to spread and persist like a bad odor that hangs in the air long after the cause for the stench has evanesced.

"Who will guarantee that the body's an *isope*?" was asked again and again.

No one in the community was more upset than Kondo. He needed a live one for Ramadani. Thankfully he had an alternate plan. Now he understood why Zuberi wouldn't allow Ramadani to travel with the head-hunters. The shaman was swindling Kondo. *He said he wanted to make sure the future village chief was safe—ha. Safe from the truth!* thought Kondo. Sometimes he was dumbfounded by Zuberi. Always the showman shaman. When he challenged Zuberi on his trickery, the healer responded by saying, "I have only just now discovered this. Do you think I would betray you?"

Yes, Kondo thought, *absolutely.* "I have to think of my son and my clan. What good is a dead body for us? You are the one who said the *only* hope for Ramadani is sexual relations with an *embulamaro*!" Kondo's words came out in short gasps.

Though Zuberi had never heard the village chief so upset, in a flash he intuited how to respond. "Don't you remember our promise? Adimu."

"What does *that* have to do with *this*?"

If Zuberi had been less driven by his hunger for glory and power, he would have caught the look of embarrassment in his interlocutor's eyes. Kondo rarely lied. Lying—even to save his son's life—made him uncomfortable. But conspiring with the witch doctor was something he could not do.

"Nothing, of course," responded the healer, quickly lowering his gaze so he'd appear deferential.

"Nothing will happen to Adimu. Do you hear me?" Kondo's voice was shaking as he yelled, as though he was speaking not only to Zuberi but also to a dark side of himself. "I remember our pact well." Then lowering his voice, Kondo continued. "Working from a dead *zeru zeru* must be the doing of the *mzungu*. I have heard whispers about the frequency with which Jackob comes to see you."

The witch doctor, caught red-handed, lowered his eyes again. "I will find a solution for your son. Don't worry."

Kondo stood up, and in three steps was at the door. Thankfully he was prepared for these unexpected complications, though he'd have to wait to put his plan into action.

36.

As soon as Nkama told Adimu the miraculous news, the girl started to pack her bag even though her departure was a week away. The dream, cultivated throughout so many rainy seasons, was about to become reality. Her two dresses, her pieces of newspaper, her comb, and the few undergarments she owned were folded and placed inside a single plastic bag.

Adimu asked her *bibi* to tell her again and again what the white doctor had told her about the community in Tanga, but Nkamba remembered very little, so to satisfy her dear girl, she began making up small details, harmless stories about how neat the bedrooms would be where the girls sleep, how the nearby mango tree produces especially ripe fruit. Adimu and her grandmother enjoyed chatting about how happy Adimu was going to be in Tanga.

On her last days on the island, Adimu spent every instant fantasizing about her future far from Ukerewe. Her excitement about a new life abounded; not even the thought of leaving her beloved grandmother could sadden her.

The night before the big trip, Adimu and Nkamba slept lightly. Adimu moved about as if she were skipping in her sleep while a recently recurring pain in Nkamba's arm disturbed her. *It's from the extra work I've been doing in the field*, she told herself.

At sunrise Adimu gazed at the white doll she had named after herself and decided to leave it with her *bibi* for company. She felt pity for the broken toy. Though in recent years she had rarely played with it, she associated it with herself and knew it would need their grandmother's love to remain safe on the island. Melancholy gave way to unexpected joy as she imagined all the love that would shine on her in her new community. She pictured herself in a circle with other girls who were just like her. Her future would cancel out her past, *the way soap rubs off mango stains on a dress*, she thought. Adimu said farewell to the saddest part of herself when she left the doll behind.

She skipped out of the hut, laughing beside her grandmother.

Nkamba was happy *and* sorrowful. Since the morning, she had laid the newborn on the earth before the animal pen, she had worried that someone, something, would harm the child, steal her, mutilate her, even rape her. For ten rainy seasons, Nkamba had slept with one eye open. For ten rainy seasons, Nkamba had dedicated her life to raising her grand-daughter, preparing Adimu to be strong and brave and capable of fending for herself. Now she could fully rest, finally rest, as an old woman should. Still, knowing her *mjukuu* would be across the lake where she could not reach her made her eyes grow moist, and her hand cradled her belly. Adimu had given Nkamba's life purpose, and now the old woman's job was done.

Nkamba no longer worried that the clan might discover where she was sending Adimu. It was in Sefu's interest that the girl disappear. She was certain that her son would consider Adimu's absence a liberation. She would tell him herself when she got back in the evening.

Nkamba could barely keep pace with Adimu as they headed toward the dock. She did her best to partake in the girl's excitement, though she couldn't help but feel a shadow of sadness in her heart. Her granddaughter's smiling face glowed with a light that remained invisible to an outsider's eyes but was well known to her: hope.

As soon as she stepped on the ferry, Adimu stomped her feet on the wooden planks. She needed to prove to herself—through sound and sensa-tion—that she really was, in flesh and bone, leaving this hostile world, never to be among the cruel again. She looked at the shadow of her body rippling on the water; it was black, as she wanted her skin to be. For once, she was a passenger, not the lifesaver. Grandmother and grandchild held hands.

Nkamba felt dizzy. A sharp pain traveled up her arm. She freed her hand from Adimu's and went below to rest on a wooden bench.

After nearly three hours on the deck, watching the island of Ukerewe shrink and fade until it disappeared behind her, Adimu ran downstairs to find her grandmother.

"We're there, *Bibi*, wake up. We're in Mwanza!" Adimu urged eagerly.

Nkamba heard her granddaughter's voice approach her from far away. She wanted to turn toward her, but her body wouldn't respond. Adimu shook her grandmother and, seeing she wasn't waking up, the girl sat on the wooden bench beside her *bibi* and lifted the elder's head, resting it on her thighs. Her grandmother opened her eyes. Adimu saw her reflection in Nkamba's ebony pupils.

Nkamba spoke to her with one thread of her voice. "Soon I will go away forever."

"What do you mean, *Bibi*?" asked Adimu. The sight of her exhausted grandmother was surreal. She'd always been tireless and robust, like a centuries-old tree filled with ancient sap.

"Listen to me, dear: two things I wish from you."

Nkamba reached out to dry Adimu's tears. With her strength failing, she set her hand lightly on her granddaughter's cheek.

"Study, promise me. And bury me next to your grandfather, under the mango…" Nkamba's words stopped midsentence.

"*Bibi, Bibi*." Adimu shook the elder with both hands and, when there was no response, lovingly touched Nkamba's dark wrinkled cheek with a quivering hand. She understood she'd gone. Where Adimu could not go. Her grandmother's final wishes were a ringing in her ears like a funeral bell. *Promise me, bury me. Promise me, bury me. Promise me, bury me.*

Adimu held her grandmother's cold, rigid hand against her face, cradling the bony fingers until the captain of the boat approached.

"Are you getting off or not?"

Adimu hesitated only for a moment. If she left now, she could not satisfy both of Nkamba's requests. The love she felt for her grandmother was greater than the bitterness she felt toward her relatives and the others on the island. "I will take my *bibi* home," she told the captain. To herself, she thought, *I am the only one who can escort her on her final voyage. Me. No one else.* She thought of Kikete.

On the way back across the lake, Adimu convinced herself—and accepted the conviction—that with her grandmother gone, it would be impossible to leave the island. Like a young branch, once the roots of the tree have been severed, she was unable to stretch skyward. She had never considered she was leaving Nkamba in the days before her departure. It wasn't "leaving" when she was certain they would see each other again. Now the spark that lit Adimu's flame of hope was dead, along with her *bibi*, her true mother.

THE WHITE MAN and the black woman waiting on the dock watched as the ferry left with the girl still on board. The man threw his cigarette on the ground, grinding the butt in the dirt with the tip of his shoe. "I'll have to deal with this matter in another way," he said. "I've already committed her."

"We'll get her in a few days," suggested the woman.

"Out of the question," the man declared. "One minute she's on her way to the community and then she's kidnapped? Too easy to trace. We can't risk it."

The woman nodded. "I'll keep an eye on her."

MANY OF NKAMBA'S peers as well as members of her clan came to the funeral. Nkamba's body had been placed in a coffin, and she was carried the short distance to where her husband rested under the mango tree. Women from the clan danced behind the small procession.

"We wish you light feet for the rest of your journey, Nkamba," shouted Adimu's older stepsister as she moved her body in rhythm with the others.

Adimu escorted her grandmother, her hand resting on the rough wood, the skin of her palm insensitive to the splinters. Not a single person, including the elderly, dared challenge Adimu's decision to participate in the funeral.

Family members gathered on either side of the grave as the coffin was lowered into the earth. Father Andrew stood at the foot of the box, Adimu at the head. She stared at the coffin that held her *bibi*, wanting to climb inside it.

"Now, Nkamba, you are closer to God," said Father Andrew.

"Now she is closer to the Spirits of the Lake," added an elderly member of Nkamba's clan in a gravelly voice.

"Don't bring trouble to the living, Nkamba," admonished an old woman.

The only thought in Adimu's mind was that her *bibi* was too far away, incredibly far away. She was the one across the lake. And she would stay there for as long as Adimu lived. The handful of dirt Adimu collected in her fist from the freshly dug pile was still cool. She squeezed it, ready to throw it at anyone who uttered stupid words that would ruin it for her beloved *bibi*, who would get in the way of her leaving this world in peace.

None of her family offered her a word of comfort. At the end of the funeral, people gathered in front of Nkamba's hut to eat the meal offered by Sefu to honor his departed mother. Adimu didn't participate; she had no desire to eat. She sat at the edge of the open grave, her feet dangling over the side, her eyes fixed on the coffin. Food will taste different from now on, she told herself. *Bibi* worked the flour, used the fire, peeled the fruit, and prepared the meals in her own way. *All I have are my memories of you to keep me going,* Bibi, *and I don't know if they'll be enough.*

37.

Adimu was forced by her stepsisters and sister-in-law to take on most of their domestic work in exchange for occupying the only home she'd ever known, which she now lived in alone. She washed laundry and dishes at the lake, collected firewood, got water from the well, cleaned the latrine, and took Nkamba's and her stepsisters' and sister-in-law's goats to graze. Nothing from her previous life—with the exception of thoughts of her *bibi* and taking out Nkamba's goats—was part of Adimu's present life. She remembered when Nkamba made her spend a day without water to develop gratitude. Now her life was without water. She desired *everything* that she once had, or didn't have, because her *bibi* had been included in it.

JACKOB TOLD CHARLES and Sarah about Adimu while the couple was eating lunch.

"She was leaving the island to go study when her grandmother died. Let's pay for her education," said Sarah, pushing some rosy tomatoes around on a white and blue china plate.

"Absolutely not," replied Charles. "If we go so far as to maintain the girl, our quiet life will be over. Throngs of needy people, each one with compelling reasons to receive our help, will inundate our house. It will be enough to give Adimu some encouragement. For example…" Charles paused and his eyes swept the room. On his right was a bookcase stuffed with novels, some nonfiction, an old set of encyclopedias, picture books about animals and, on the bottom shelf, a collection of videocassettes. The words "Woody Allen" were on the spine of several of the videos and a line from a movie came to mind—"I read in self-defense," Charles said, right before he had what he considered a brainstorm. "We'll give her a set of encyclopedias!"

"Encyclopedias?" repeated Sarah. "A typical gesture of a Westerner who wants to assuage his conscience with a useless gift." She thought of the time, years ago now, when she handed the little beggar boy a music box and how it had baffled him.

"Why would it be useless?" Charles asked, annoyed.

"If you gave a pair of high-heeled Prada shoes to an African woman, she wouldn't be able to walk in them," blurted Sarah.

"Enough with the preaching, dear."

"You're not as European as you think. You're African, a privileged white African who insists on considering himself European by virtue of his ancestors. You've been trying to foil my every attempt at changing things by using the same few words." Sarah's rage at her husband surprised and excited her.

"Which are?"

"'That's how it is in Africa,'" she muttered. "Who, if not privileged people, like us, can contribute to improving the condition of thousands of people?" she asked angrily. "If humans left things as they've always been, we would still be in the Stone Age. We can make a difference. You just have to believe," she said, reaching across the table to touch her husband's hand, wanting to connect with him, if only physically.

"The encyclopedia is the most I can do for now. I'm sure the village school doesn't have one," he added, shaking his head. "Adimu would be the only one on the island to possess such a precious object! It would help her, even on a social level, because students would want to consult it. You'll see how happy it makes her."

"If you think so," Sarah sighed. "And by the way, give her glasses so she's able to read the damn books."

"Is she nearsighted? Of course I'll give her a pair. Otherwise, the encyclopedia would be like giving her a brand-new car without tires." He chuckled at his own joke.

"I WANTED YOU to see what a nice gift we're giving Adimu before Jackob takes them to her," said Charles, tapping his hand on the set of encyclopedias that sat on a table in the foyer of White House.

"Let's personalize it with a dedication signed by both of us," Sarah pleaded.

"Oh, all right. What do you think of 'All the best, Charles and Sarah'?"

"What a jumble of formality," said Sarah with a half frown. She opened the first volume and quickly wrote, "For Adimu, we wish you all the best. We care deeply about you, like a daughter. Charles and Sarah."

"Why did you write that? You need to take out the 'We care deeply about you, like a daughter' part."

"Too late, it's done. Those words will mean more to her than the entire encyclopedia. Her grandmother just died. The poor girl feels all alone. Adimu is no ninny. She'll understand that we want to show her affection so that she doesn't feel alone," concluded Sarah.

Wanting to have the last word, without Sarah knowing, Charles told Jackob to tear out the first pages of the volume before delivering the books to the girl.

That evening, at his home, Charles's assistant extracted the pages, according to his understanding of his boss's instructions. With surgical precision, he eliminated all the pages for the letter *A* until after the definition of the word "albinism." He believed that his employer did not want the *zeru zeru* to read the meaning of her condition, and each volume opened with a dictionary. *He said, tear out the first pages.* And that's what Jackob did.

Jackob drove to the hut where the girl lived, the volumes spread over the back seat of his car.

"A gift for me, from the Fieldings? Are you sure?" Adimu asked. After carrying the volumes inside, she set them carefully on a plastic sheet as if they were precious puppies. Then she latched the door and opened the first of the series. She read the dedication. She read it a second time. And she read it again and again as if the words were a secret promise from the Fieldings that she would one day be their daughter. Beaming, she turned to the beginning of the book to look in the dictionary part of the encyclopedia for the word "albino" and, not finding it, she thought about the order of letters in the alphabet, turning the pages back and forth, starting from the beginning, starting from the back, and flipping the pages in reverse more quickly. The first word that appeared in the volume was "allegory." Where had the other words gone, the ones that came before? "Abandon," "affection," "adoption," "adequate," "accident," "abuse," "abnormal." Her disappointment lasted only a few moments as she realized there were lots of other words to read and lots of things to learn. *What difference does it make if there are a few words missing, ones I already know anyway? But that one word—the Word—why?*

Night came and Adimu fell asleep curled up with the books on her pallet. The first volume—the one with the dedication—was her pillow.

SARAH WAS RIGHT about the dedication. Adimu read the dedication so frequently that the words became a mantra. The treasured gift quickly became a substitute for the figures she'd drawn on the walls of the hut. With Nkamba gone, she no longer had time to redraw them; she was busy all day in the service of her sisters and sister-in-law and reading the encyclopedia.

The books became her friends. She covered them every night, fearing the humidity could harm them, and she uncovered them at sunrise. "Good morning!" She greeted them with a smile. The light blue fabric bindings were like a piece of the sky inside her hut, and they had her grandmother's spirit.

The eyeglasses the Fieldings gave her were an incredible discovery. Her world took on different shapes and colors when she wore them. The contours of leaves were sharp, not smudges of greens; whitecaps on the lake were shapely; flowers and fruits were not indistinct splotches but shimmering luscious shades; the sky and the earth met in a precise point on the horizon; and the clouds, what fanciful characters they were! Adimu was afraid of using up the glasses, terrified that the lenses might wear out like the sole of a sandal, so she saved them for only when they were indispensable.

It did not take long for Adimu to grasp the value of the encyclopedia. Through these magical books, she would be able to fulfill her promise to Bibi and get an education. The books were her shield against brutality, and her symbol of hope. She carried a volume with her wherever she went. Before long, Adimu noticed villagers staring at her, not because of the color of her skin but because of the precious book in her arms.

While she scrubbed laundry, a book lay open next to the basin. She did her best to read when working, drying the page with her elbow if water splashed on it. Then she'd continue where she'd left off. At home she read too. The stack of encyclopedias was the tree upon which her knowledge grew.

Before she had glasses, she'd put her face next to her reading material and closed one eye to bring the words into focus, which made her lift her upper lip. With her glasses, her smile was no longer a grimace but an expression of satisfaction.

Every morning, she took the animals to graze. Nkamba's goats stayed close, but the animals that belonged to her stepsisters and sister-in-law, the ones that hadn't been trained by her, often ran away, scampering into cultivated fields. Eventually, Adimu discovered she could tie each animal to a bush to form a semicircle, and she'd sit in the shade between the animals with her open book on her crossed legs. After glancing at the herd occasionally to make sure none of the animals had gotten away, she'd resume her reading.

38.

Another rainy season—Adimu's eleventh—abandoned the land and its people to the relentless sun. Although Adimu rarely had time to attend school, on that day she awoke before sunrise to graze the goats. She would be at school and on time: it was the day of the class photo. A most special day. Adimu didn't have a picture of herself and badly wanted one.

The teacher told the students to form three rows. Adimu's classmates kept pushing her aside as she tried to stand near them, insulting and laughing at her. The teacher lamely reprimanded the boys and girls. She couldn't force them to make room for an *isope*. She knew that she, herself, wouldn't have. "You can be in the photo next year," the teacher sighed. "Just wait."

On the way home, Adimu thought about how she was always expected to postpone her dreams. "In the future, people will accept you." That's what Nkamba had said; in the future she would become a doctor; in the future she would be in the photo.

That evening she concentrated on the last volume of the encyclopedia, the Swahili/English/French dictionary. There, she found the word "albino." It was the same in English and nearly identical in French, "albinos." She liked pronouncing words in other languages and imagined the faces of those who might use them. For hours she flew on the wings of foreign words, fantasizing about distant worlds until she fell asleep, the book open to the translation for the word "future." Nkamba came to her in a dream that night, her rough hands overflowing with ripe mangoes, and Adimu taught her the new words she'd learned from the dictionary while stroking *Bibi's* dear skinny, wrinkled arms.

AFTER NKAMBA'S DEATH, Adimu had stopped going to Mass. Father Andrew remembered a conversation he had had with the old woman about how to integrate Adimu into village life, and he remembered Nkamba's reaction.

"On this island, my *mjukuu* has learned to live with very little," the old woman had said. "Only far from Ukerewe can she have a normal life. Have you forgotten the way your people think? When you're here on the few Sundays a month, the faithful wear their best clothes, eat their best food, and rest at home with their families—like Christians. The other days, they obey the ancient laws of the Spirits of the Lake."

The religious man lifted his shoulders. Despite Nkamba's love for the child, she held the same prejudices as the rest of the community. However, now that she had passed on to a better life, Father Andrew believed it was time for him to help Adimu the way he thought best. He spoke to his elderly father who was against the idea. Mosi decided to move forward with his plan all the same. His God demanded that he do good, care for the meek. If Adimu played a vital role during Mass, a strong, clear message would be heard that she was accepted and loved by the Creator.

Adimu held reverential fear of the priest and did what he requested, even though she thought better of it. Thus, one oppressively hot Sunday, she became the first female altar boy in the history of Ukerewe. She clumsily and bashfully carried out each task under the shocked eyes of the parishioners. Adimu helped Father Andrew with his vestments, she turned the pages of the Bible, she handed him the wine, and held the bronze tray under the chins of the few who came forward to receive Communion. No one outwardly displayed their aversion to Adimu's direct contact with the Father and, therefore, with God, but the following Sunday fewer people attended the service. Father Andrew appeared not to notice. As weeks passed, the decline in the number of congregants seemed unstoppable and impossible to ignore.

One Sunday, Father Andrew found the shade of the baobab so crowded it barely covered the participants. His enthusiasm lasted only as long as a deep breath. At the end of Mass, after the blessing, a group of men approached.

"Why let a *zeru zeru* help when there are other more-deserving children?" demanded a young father.

"Because it is what God wishes."

"The Spirits of the Lake tell us of their wishes in other ways," responded the man.

Adimu tried to make herself as small as possible as she hid behind Father Andrew. She wanted to disappear.

"The word of the Lord is the one and only," said the priest, looking straight at the man.

"Your God and our Spirits are not so different," said the man. "They hold power over everything. Sometimes it's best to listen to your God, sometimes to the Spirits. Often they are both right. But about the *zeru zeru*, the Spirits of the Lake are right. It has always been so, and it will continue to be so."

Adimu drew even closer to the priest's tunic. He put his arm around her shoulders as he said, "God is the only one who decides the destiny of a person."

"You're wrong," said an old fisherman who stepped away from the crowd. "We decide whether we listen to a suggestion from your God or the demands of our Spirits. The Spirits of the Lake have been here for much longer than your God." He gestured to the group to go.

Father Andrew was alone with Adimu in the empty space under the great tree. "You'll see, they'll understand."

Adimu nodded, though kept her eyes lowered. The midmorning sun bore down ferociously.

THOMAS AND HIS companions unearthed the body of an albino man who had died some days before. "Good thing we found it before it vanished. Maybe the weight of the dirt on top of the grave kept it imprisoned." The four hunters waited impatiently for the moon to set before delivering the body wrapped in a plastic sheet to Zuberi.

IN HIS WORKSHOP, the gaslight discharged a blue glow, and the skin, where it was not putrid, seemed even paler than it was. Zuberi examined it like a mother gazes at her newborn. His eyes were ecstatic, and he fantasized about the future. "The miraculous talismans I am about to prepare will change my people's destiny. And mine too," he said to Jane as he lifted the monkey, "especially mine."

Mr. Fielding was the first client to be informed of the cadaver, and an appointment at the mine was scheduled for the following night.

On the day that the *zeru zeru* ritual was to take place, Charles had to remind himself repeatedly to stay calm. In the middle of the afternoon he called Sarah to let her know he would be out all evening for work. Of course he wasn't lying, though he was ashamed to imagine what she'd think if she ever found out what he was doing.

THE HEALER TOOK the last ferry to Mwanza. He watched his island float on the sunset like a giant cloud as he glided away from it, and then he sat down on a wooden bench, taciturn, staring at the bow of the vessel. None of the passengers thought much of him being on board, nor did they pay attention to the burlap sack he carried over his shoulder, not even to its rotten odor.

Charles, Zuberi, and Jackob met at the mine shortly before midnight. The three men huddled in a circle. The witch doctor rummaged in the sack and pulled out an object wrapped in plastic. He untied the string that held the plastic in place. A white arm. The left one.

Charles looked away, struggling to hold back an urge to vomit. Sweat dripped from his corpulent body. Zuberi walked across the tract of land holding the human arm. "I brought this left one because the other was in a bad state," he explained. He counted thirty paces exactly, which took him to the center of a flat area, and he began to chant in the local dialect. Charles did not understand the words. As his eyes centered on the witch doctor, his disgust was shattering him from the inside out. With every ounce of energy focused on controlling his repulsion, he lost track of the ceremonial rite that was being conducted by the shaman.

Zuberi continued to chant, shuffling his feet and shaking his body. He turned three times and tossed the amputated arm into the air. It landed nearby. *Thud.* It mimicked the sound of a bird of prey that struck the earth after being shot out of the night sky.

"Come!" ordered the witch doctor. Charles and Jackob rushed to his side. Under the light of the full moon, the limb resembled a broken tree branch. It pointed southeast.

"We've already dug in that direction!" Jackob cried.

Charles looked at the moon to find comfort in its cool light. He had been thinking what Jackob had said.

Zuberi kept calm. He studied the two men, his lips spreading into a broad smile. "It must be buried here. In time, the gold will rise." Then he added quickly, "If it doesn't, it's because this arm came from a cadaver. The rite is meant to be performed with an arm from a living *embulamaro*, the right arm. Not the left. It might be necessary to repeat the ritual."

By THE TIME he arrived home, Charles was tormented by an insidious desperation. Unable to sleep, he sat on the red leather sofa and turned on the television. He leaned forward to take off his shoes. His feet were swollen, heavy, and his excess fat slowed his every movement. He flopped against the back of the sofa, gasping for air. He was drowning in a swamp of emotions. Then, a sudden awareness ejected him from the slimy waters in which he had been trapped. He, Charles Fielding, the great entrepreneur, would live. With new determination, he bent forward to stand tall. It was precisely during complex situations, he realized, such as the one with which he was struggling, that protagonists throughout history had found their tenacity. His trust in himself began to bloat.

THE FISHERMEN OF Murutanga suspected the body had belonged to a white foreigner. "Who can guarantee these limbs and organs came from an *embulamaro*?" asked one.

"The radio transmission test will prove it to you," said the healer. He'd conduct the fail-safe test if that's what the fishermen wanted, though he was taken aback by their cynicism, that they'd demand proof from their healer. His great ancestors, he was sure, had never been doubted like this.

Zuberi remembered the time he had launched the first motorboat purchased by the fishermen's consortium. It had taken the fishermen years to save up enough money to purchase the boat. He had stood in the center of the boat, carefully balanced with his long staff in hand, next to the captain who would start the engine. The captain pulled the cord again and again, each time with increasing strength, and then he'd pause to catch his breath and try again. Five, ten times. The community, gathered on the dock, offered all sorts of hypotheses about why the boat wouldn't start. "It's a humid day." "The motor was built for saltwater." "It refuses to start because there are no fish in the lake."

Zuberi called on the Spirits, he stretched out his arms, he searched the sky, but the motor refused to show signs of life.

A little boy asked his father, "What kind of fuel does it take? Is it the same that cars on the road use?" His father told him to shut up with a slap and the others laughed. They boy furrowed his brow.

Zuberi tapped his staff to stop the buzzing of voices and to attract attention. A reverberation rippled from the concave bottom of the boat out into the water.

"The Spirits of the Lake have spoken through the boy," Zuberi declared. "The solution has been revealed. Have you not understood?" In a charitable tone, he asked, "Where is the gas tank?" The fishermen searched inside the boat without success. Finally, Zuberi pointed his staff toward the beach. The bright red tank had been left on the white sand.

"If it weren't for my guidance, you would drown on the shore," said Zuberi.

The people agreed. It was true: Zuberi was their guide. Did they still think of him as their guide? he wondered.

In the evening, after he prepared the amulets and potions, Zuberi turned on the transistor radio in his workroom while the fishermen crowded in the small space. The station that played was known for its good reception. Zuberi picked up one of the amulets, holding it next to the antenna. The reception became fuzzy, fading into static.

"Such strong interference can only be generated by a *ngazu*," admitted an old fisherman.

"Now you have proof. These are from a recently dead *embulamaro*, caught before it was able to vanish," Zuberi announced.

39.

A year had passed since Zuberi performed rites, spells, and potions with the *zeru zeru* limbs and organs. Yet the fishermen's nets remained empty. Yunis and her husband—although they coupled as often as two rabbits in a small cage—were unable to conceive.

Zuberi was horrified that all his efforts came to naught. He imagined the lineage of ancestors eyeing him from the lake, appalled by his failure and the damage it did to the reputation of the twenty generations that came before him.

Kondo publicly expressed his disappointment that Zuberi had settled for a cadaver, which fed the flame of discontent on the island. Before the cadaver debacle, Zuberi's power in the community had reached an all-time high, and Kondo was pleased that he was able to shrink the witch doctor down to size.

Although Kondo enjoyed shaming the shaman for his shoddy work, it was essential that the spiritual and civil systems of the community coexist, that neither prevail over the other.

The fishermen demanded that the witch doctor give back their money. Yunis's husband agreed with the fishermen.

The witch doctor refused. "I have fulfilled our agreements and have used the 'symbolic' amount you gave me to pay the headhunters."

Zuberi's humiliation ballooned, and he approached Jackob about his dilemma. Charles's assistant assured him that, though Mr. Fielding would not expressly authorize hunting down a living *embulamaro*, neither would he refuse to pay the price if the desired outcome was achieved. Indeed, his employer also had not attained the results he wanted.

The owner of Charles Fielding Gold Limited had given orders to dig deeper in the direction that had been determined by the midnight ritual. The enormous quantity of soil had been sifted and washed, and all that was found was dust, dirt, and stones. Mr. Fielding poured more resources into the project until there were three times as many miners working as there would normally be on a plot of that size. The geologists assayed the extracted material and each time reported it contained insignificant amounts of gold. Debts grew day after day, supplier after supplier. Charles was increasingly worried and irascible. He had paid a great sum for the *zeru zeru*. However, he was determined to reach his goal and would do whatever it took. "Even if it means digging to the center of the Earth!" he bellowed, leaning over a trench several yards deep.

Jackob was concerned about Mr. Fielding's health. He was regularly short of breath, bathed in sweat, and with the added weight, he was having a hard time walking. If the fate of Charles Fielding Gold Limited did not improve soon, Jackob, himself, could lose his position and prestige. And with two children and a third on the way, he could not allow anything to undermine his social and economic position. *I will help Mr. Fielding make the right choice*, thought Jackob. *I'll earn his eternal favor and gratitude. As a white African, his heart is conflicted, and he's unable to admit what he truly wants to do.*

THOMAS WAS, AGAIN, the man for the job, the witch doctor was sure. Kondo threatened Zuberi. He said if Ramadani wasn't allowed to join the new hunt for the *embulamaro*, he would turn the villagers against him. Zuberi agreed, feigning enthusiasm, though it no longer mattered to him either way.

That evening, when Kondo and his family sat around the fire, the village chief told his wife and daughters that he wanted a moment alone with Ramadani.

The young man listened to his father without conveying emotion. Neither the news that his father arranged for him to join the headhunters nor Kondo's plan for Adimu if the headhunting scheme didn't work aroused a visible reaction. Kondo interpreted his son's response as excessive humility.

He left Ramadani in front of the fire and went outside for a walk. Before stepping over the threshold, he turned to look at his grown son. Kondo's first child had been born when the village chief was Ramadani's age. The young man was sitting cross-legged, his shoulders slightly hunched, his neck still slender like that of an adolescent. For a moment, the energetic child who used to jump on the chief's lap appeared before him. A wave of affection overwhelmed him, and he yearned to embrace his son, but he desisted, and after a few moments, he stepped into the darkness. The forest rustled and murmured, and Kondo heard encouraging words whispered in his ear.

THE FOLLOWING MORNING, Ramadani agreed to join the headhunters. With a half-smile the son thanked his father. "Can you give me handcuffs, a flashlight, and a knife? They're for the hunt."

"Handcuffs, like the ones the police use?" his father asked, tilting his head.

Ramadani nodded.

"Where can I get those? Only the police have them."

"Father, I'm sure you can get a pair."

Kondo accompanied his son to the Mwanza ferry where Ramadani would meet Thomas and his gang. Ramadani hung his head as he walked. He attributed the youth's moodiness to his fear of spending time with lowlifes, and Kondo held back from hounding him. Once the ferry was no more than a white spot on the horizon, Kondo put the finishing touches on his plan to save his son's life and the future of his clan. His son was too passive and sullen to find his own *zeru zeru*, the father thought.

40.

The Fieldings were having dinner in the garden of their Ukerewe residence. The air was warm that Sunday evening. Husband and wife seemed to have accepted each other's shortcomings and resigned themselves to the fact that even the best unions cannot be all sunshine and no shadow. *But why such protracted quiet?* Sarah wondered. Only the occasional tinkling of their silverware broke the silence of the meal. *Could Charles and I be growing apart? Ridiculous,* she told herself.

Charles, for his part, couldn't let his wife see his shame, his fast-approaching poverty, or his secret collaboration with the village witch doctor. Their silence spread out like an invisible sheet over the garden, hiding his desire to obtain another arm of an albino and her desire to mother the child with albinism. It was a spell that no magic could break.

"I've asked the cook to prepare fish next weekend," said Sarah.

"Ah, I forgot to tell you…next Saturday I have to be in Mwanza," replied Charles. "I have a meeting with a client at the office. Do you want to stay there with me?"

Sarah shook her head. "No, I have an important engagement here in Ukerewe next week."

"Oh really? What is it?" asked Charles as he sunk his silver spoon into the mango dessert in front of him.

"You'll be in Mwanza. It's nothing you need to concern yourself with," she answered brusquely. "I'm going upstairs to read," she announced as she stood.

Charles stayed at the table to finish his dessert. Then, when he was sure none of the domestic staff was watching, he cleaned every trace of cream in the serving dish with his finger, wiped his hands on the white cotton tablecloth embroidered with his initials, and stood up to join Sarah. He'd forgotten to tell her about a going-away party for a financier who was heading back to Switzerland.

He went up the stairs, calling her name, but got no response. He followed the long corridor on the first floor that led to their bedroom when he heard rustling in one of the guest bedrooms, a room no one ever entered. The door was ajar, and a slender beam of light cut across the floor.

"Sarah, dear, are you in here?" Pushing the door open, he saw his wife quickly close a cupboard. Charles stepped into the room. Sarah looked down.

"What's going on?" he asked. "What are you hiding?"

His wife moved aside as he reached out to open the cupboard door. The shelves overflowed with dolls, many of them still wrapped in plastic. "You collect dolls, and you're ashamed of it?"

Sarah was silent. Charles opened another cupboard and found a rack of girls' clothes. He touched the fabrics, the lace-trimmed hems, noticing they were all about the same size. "They're for Adimu, aren't they?" he asked in a whisper.

"Not only," she replied impatiently. "For your employees' children too."

"My employees have sons as well," remarked Charles. "I don't see anything in here for them."

Sarah took one step back and crossed her arms over her chest. For once, her husband had figured her out. Yes, the dolls and every single dress had been bought for Adimu, but she had never given them to the child for fear of displeasing her husband.

She paused and rested her left hand over her mouth, fingers spread slightly like a metal grate in a gutter, holding back debris. She had followed Charles to the end of the world because only he made her feel loved and protected. But memories of her father had begun to torment her again and shadowy doubts about their marriage swirled in her head like smoke wafting above a fire. She desperately needed the security that marriage offered. *Hold on to him, Sarah*, she told herself. *You did the right thing in choosing him as your life companion. Faced with the same choice, you'd choose him again.* Yet every night, she dreamed of being a mother. That her husband would never allow her dream to come true broke her heart.

She thought she saw a shadow of tenderness in Charles's blue eyes. Clasping her hands together, she said, "Can we invite her to lunch, and I'll give her one of these gifts? A birthday present. She's probably never celebrated a birthday. I'm sure she has no idea when it is."

Charles hugged his wife. "I'll stay here with you next weekend."

Sarah felt a release of tension across her forehead that radiated down toward her neck and chest. She hadn't expected Charles would neglect business to have lunch with Adimu. She couldn't have guessed Charles's conscience was in a knot of anguish. The image of that amputated arm glowing in the moonlight haunted him. It was his nightmare while he slept and his obsession while awake.

INSTEAD OF HAVING Jackob act as messenger, Sarah and Charles decided to surprise Adimu at her home. But when they arrived, she was not there. They waited, attracting the attention of curious neighbors and passersby. Finally, they saw her returning home with a basket of woven palm leaves balanced on her head.

"We'd like you to come for lunch. We'd like to have a party for you, for your birthday," said Sarah.

Adimu had the feeling she had been mistaken for someone else and looked over her shoulder. *Why?* she wondered. *How do they know it's my birthday when I don't know when I was born?* She looked down and slid her foot sideways in the dust. "I don't think I can come. I have to do my stepsisters' laundry. I've only come home to get the dirty clothes."

"We've got a washing machine and a woman who will take care of it while we have lunch," offered Charles.

Sarah looked at him, eyebrows raised.

After a pause, Adimu nodded in agreement. "But how do you know it's my birthday?" she finally was able to ask.

Sarah cupped her cheek and said, "We want to celebrate your life, sweetheart."

Once the laundry was taken to the Fieldings' home, the three of them drove to the port where the adults had organized an excursion on the lake with lunch aboard their boat and a short stop in Mwanza.

As the boat pulled away from the dock, Sarah gave in to her excitement. She beamed, holding out a gift-wrapped box.

For a split second, Adimu stared at the present. Then a twinkle came to her eyes, and a smile crept over her face. She opened it with a quivering hand, careful not to ruin the pretty wrapping. "Two new dresses!" she exclaimed. She slipped into the cabin to try on the dresses, paying careful attention not to detach the colorful tags decorating each collar.

Back on deck, Adimu twirled in her aqua green frock and let Sarah comb her hair. Charles watched them, forcing himself to remain detached. He still saw Adimu as a potential threat to his freedom. He had to admit, though, that neither his wife nor the girl put pressure on him to change the present arrangement. Things were under control, he told himself. He relaxed. His eyes glistened.

I'm sure he's my father, he must be, thought Adimu. *Otherwise why would he be taking me out to celebrate my birthday? That's what fathers do.* Adimu often caught him looking at her. He'd hand her a handkerchief at just the right moment. He even touched her head.

Looking at Adimu, Charles couldn't help but think of his unproductive gold mine. The amputated limb burned in his mind. He contemplated Adimu's thin white arms covered with fine blond fuzz, and his heart contracted with bitter tenderness. The fine bones of those delicate, pale arms would break with a single chop of a machete. He was ashamed of his thoughts and, to distract himself, he looked at her face. She looked older than her twelve years, he thought sadly.

Adimu gorged herself on the lighthearted day as though it was the dessert Sarah had scooped onto a plate for her and avoided thinking about returning home that evening to her sad routine. She spoke freely about her life, unaware that it heightened the two adults' sense of impotence, as though they were in part responsible for her misadventures.

When she told them about how her classmates had pushed her out of the class photo, Charles was astonished. "You've never had your picture taken?"

Adimu's expression clouded. *Why is he so surprised?* she wondered. Not even her grandmother had.

At the end of the day, when they returned to White House, Charles brought a camera into the garden, set it up with a self-timer, and ran to sit next to Adimu and Sarah before the shutter clicked. After disappearing in the house for a short time, he returned, bearing three copies of the photo. "One for each of us," he said. Adimu looked at herself between the adults and turned her head. She was the whitest of the three and wondered how she could be whiter than her father. However, having a picture of herself—and together with the Fieldings!—made her feel so alive that she didn't care about how ugly she looked. She thanked them both and decided that, from that moment on, she would keep the photo with her always.

CHARLES PUT HIS copy of the photograph in a frame and positioned it on the desk in his Mwanza office. *Looking at it makes me smile,* he said to himself. That afternoon, with his Sarah and Adimu, was one of the loveliest he had spent in a while. His money worries evaporated when he looked into the eyes of "his two girls." Might they be his two girls? he wondered. *No...No...*Charles was sure Sarah would abandon him if all he had to offer her were the privations of life. And how could he support a child when he could no longer support his wife?

He couldn't, and he blamed it on his good-luck charm. *You...you...you pledged to be my one true friend*, he thought, holding up his golden nugget, twirling it to catch the light. *I've counted on you*, he murmured, *to stay by Sarah's side during her shopping sprees and to surround me with wealth wherever I go and to give me confidence—and, now, you have abandoned me. Why?*

Impulsively he dropped the nugget into the wastebasket with a plunk. Charles sat at his desk and opened the newspaper. He read the headlines on the front page and then turned to the business section. Suddenly he jumped to his feet and lunged at the basket, rummaging inside, then frantically dumping its contents onto the floor. A greasy napkin and chicken bones from his lunch, along with wads of paper, spilled onto the Oriental carpet. With the toe of his shoe, he poked at the garbage until he found his charm. Lovingly, he picked it up, cleaned it on his pant leg, squeezed it, and tucked it safely back into his pocket. He turned the framed photograph face down on his desk.

One hot and humid afternoon not long after that, Charles turned off the air conditioner in his office. He maintained that the best decisions were made under pressure, and few things were as stressful as torrid heat. The telephone rang, making the dense, humid air tremble. "Never demonstrate weakness by not answering the phone" was one of his mottoes and, so, despite his anxiety, he picked up the receiver, half expecting it to be a creditor or a buyer who was complaining about a delayed order.

The voice on the other end of the line took his breath away. It was the director of his primary bank, a devoted businessman who, until a couple of years before, would have missed his daughter's wedding to do Charles a favor. "Your word is no longer a sufficient guarantee for your debts." He spoke in an apologetic and embarrassed manner as if he were informing a neighbor about a fatal accident. "The bank's main office in Geneva is demanding collateral to cover your loans. I'm sorry, but your only option is a mortgage."

"A mortgage on what?" Charles asked.

"On the first mine," suggested the banker.

"Have I heard you correctly? You're asking me to mortgage my child?!"

Charles proposed other solutions. The bank director did not budge. "If you don't put a mortgage on that mine, you'll have to pay back the money the bank has advanced you and, in essence, declare bankruptcy. I'm sorry,

Mr. Fielding, these orders come from the main office." The banker seemed grieved.

Charles reluctantly agreed to the mortgage. "At least grant me maximum discretion. It would be devastating if this got out."

When Charles hung up the phone, he took a deep breath. He experienced a momentary and inexplicable sense of relief before the deluge of worries returned. His social position was in mortal danger. Sarah and Jackob must be kept in the dark, he said to himself. His wife's silly gesture with her diamond ring was a ploy to gain his trust so he'd open up about his problems, and she'd know the exact moment to jump ship. His assistant would spread the word of his boss's failure and would run away laughing without looking back. His social position was in danger, held at gunpoint, the gun cocked and a quivering finger on the trigger.

ADIMU AND CHARLES were constantly on each other's minds.

He was the father Adimu had always dreamed of. With Mr. Fielding, she'd have family, friends, and an education. And by his side, she'd be the right color. With Mr. Fielding, she was sure that she'd be safe.

Adimu in her hut, Charles in his office—each studied the photo. Charles's in a leather frame, positioned to the right of his computer, Adimu's between the pages as a bookmark of whichever volume she carried with her.

One afternoon, during a now-frequent panic attack, the solution to Charles's lack of liquidity flashed before him. He had been staring at the photo, convinced he was on the brink of losing everything. Then his miraculous insight...he would sacrifice the girl! Only an arm, mind you. *One can live without an arm*, he repeated to himself. The act would be carried out in the least traumatic way possible. Why, he exclaimed aloud, the resolution would benefit her too! They would adopt her, give her a future, permit her to study, and then, one day, she'd be the heir to his immense estate. Sarah would be happy. *This is the solution to all my problems, all three of our problems.*

He rubbed his tired eyes to erase the disagreeable notion and focused again on the image of them sitting together on the veranda, he and Adimu enjoying tiramisu. He was ashamed of his macabre fantasy. *Perhaps I really am losing my mind*, he thought. A sharp stab of affection for the girl in the photo with her adult expression pierced him. And Sarah, more beautiful than ever, seemed younger with Adimu by her side. In the photo, he seemed like the shadow, a white shadow, a phantom, a temporary and fleeting element. With his finger, he traced his wife's outline.

ADIMU RETURNED EARLIER than expected with her stepsisters' laundry and paused longer than usual to look at the photo. With her glasses on, she glanced at the pages beside the bookmark. She read about the word "destiny": *the force that decides events, external to the will of man.* She scanned the letters on the spine of the other volumes until she found the one that contained the *W* for "will." *The ability to act, to reach an objective.* She continued browsing other entries, but those two terms remained in her mind. She could use "will" to modify her "destiny."

For the first time in Adimu's life, she understood it was possible to go after her desires. She would visit the Fieldings, she decided, and surprise them as they had surprised her. Simply the thought of it made her quiver with joy. She turned a blind eye to logistics, what excuse she'd give her stepsisters for her absence and that she didn't know the address. She was filled with happiness. Simple happiness. A happiness that was not long-lived.

41.

Though Kondo hoped his son would find the cure for his illness when he joined the headhunters—*this course of action wouldn't be called "rape" since a zeru zeru is a nobody*—he had a foolproof backup plan, which he had calculated over time. It consisted of Adimu staying in his family home for the shortest period necessary to ensure his son's cure. He would pay for the girl with animals from his herd as though it were a marriage. He didn't want to admit to himself he was glad that Nkamba was not alive to witness this.

Late one evening, Kondo visited Sefu and was invited to sit near the fire with him and his family to share an abundant meal. After their bellies were full, Kondo spoke of why he came, and his request caught Sefu by surprise. If Kondo made such an offer for one of his daughters with Afua, Sefu would never have agreed. "But Adimu is a different matter," he said. Her name felt odd on his tongue, as he had never articulated it, had never accepted she had a name. To send her to the home of the leader of the community provided a modicum of redemption for the shame of having a *zeru zeru* in the family. The agreement was fair: Ramadani would have Adimu as an antidote for his illness, and Sefu would gain more animals for his herd. He accepted the offer.

As Kondo was leaving, he told Sefu to inform Juma's father, who was living with his daughter, of the arrangement. The decision was Sefu's to make, of course, but it was a courtesy owed to the most-senior male of his second wife's clan. Sefu loathed seeing Juma. It did not take him long to rationalize that his visit should be awkward for *her*, not for him, that she was the one who gave birth to the *ngazu*.

Thus, on the morning following his meeting with Kondo, Sefu walked with purpose toward his former home. Juma was kneeling on the ground, and as she stoked the fire, she watched what looked like the shape of her husband take form in the distance. She opened her eyes wider, dropped the stick she was using to stir the coals, and turned to look at the photograph of her beloved. As moments passed, her doubt dissipated. It *was* her husband. And he was about to enter her home!

He crossed the threshold, and his dark eyes fell on his image. The photograph of him taken by the NGO worker was illuminated by the feeble light of a candle. His gaze burned into what he perceived to be a shrine. He inhaled to calm his irritation.

"I have come to speak with your father."

Juma withdrew her gaze from the face of the man she had prayed—for the past twelve years—would walk through her door.

"Welcome, please sit," she said, indicating a mat next to the fire. She moved silently to a corner so the heat would warm Sefu.

The old man, her father, was asleep on a pallet made comfortable by a cushion of chicken feathers. She roused him and helped him sit near Sefu. Then she sat down as well. She intended to stay inside the hut, even though Sefu had made clear he was there to speak with his father-in-law. Whatever had pushed her husband to come under her roof could also offer the opportunity for them to get back together, she figured.

After the ritual salutations between the two men, the reason for Sefu's visit rose to the surface. Juma's presence irritated Sefu, and he kept his eyes far from the shape of her body. With measured words, he listed the advantages that would come from entrusting Adimu to Kondo for a limited period of time. "The two cows will be divided in equal parts between our two clans," Sefu explained. Juma said nothing, seemingly bewitched by the flames that began to gain vigor.

Moments passed before Juma shouted, "Two cows, is that all? We could give it to the white people for more than that!" She threw the stick she'd been holding toward the fire.

"What have the *wazungu* to do with this?" Sefu's voice was as sharp as the look he gave her.

"The white couple seek out the *zeru zeru* every time they come to the island," said Juma meekly. She stood up and moved closer to the fire to retrieve the unburned stick, poking it at the hot coals.

Sefu was both worried and offended. The *wazungu* were rich and powerful. If they wanted, they could take the *zeru zeru* without paying anything. "Ramadani is the best solution. I will give the males of your family one of the two cows," he declared, snatching the stick from Juma's hands and tossing it into the flames.

Juma lowered her eyes. At the door, Sefu stopped, turned, stepped closer to the photo, and blew out the candle flame. He sought his wife's eyes, but Juma's gaze was fixed on the face of her husband in the photograph as he had been, not seeing the man he had become.

JUMA DECIDED TO inform Father Andrew about Kondo's and Sefu's plans. Surely the priest would be opposed to it. She hoped that her idea to draw Adimu and the *wazungu* together would be encouraged. If the *zeru zeru* was no longer around, Sefu would return to her.

When the priest and Juma concluded their conversation at the end of the Sunday service, Father Andrew went straight to Kondo's home with his liturgical vestments still on. Opposition to such exploitation would be a golden opportunity to demonstrate the strength of his God.

"I know what you are planning to do with Adimu," he blurted as he neared the village chief.

Kondo was silent, not so much because the young man was being disrespectful but because of his shame that Mosi knew about the agreement he and Sefu had made, which went against the decision of the Spirits of the Lake. The agreement had been reached as a private accord, and he was concerned that the news would reach his fellow villagers, particularly Zuberi—to whom he had made a personal pledge—before he'd had a chance to tell him about his arrangement with Sefu. "What are you talking about?" he asked, rising from the rock where he had been sitting. He took several steps toward Father Andrew.

The priest said, "I know about the arrangement for Adimu to come live with you, and I know why you have made it. We shall oppose you."

"Who will stop me?" Kondo asked, attempting to force Father Andrew to be more specific, fearing the "we" included Zuberi.

"My God and I."

Kondo laughed. Mosi's God was not one that Kondo feared. "I have not asked for your opinion, but I will listen to you. Come, let us sit and talk."

Father Andrew sat while Kondo went into the house to get some water.

When the chief returned, he handed the priest a glass and said, "Mosi, have faith in me."

The priest set down the glass on the earth. "The reason I'm aware of is a bad one."

"What are you referring to?"

"Your son's illness."

The two men studied each other in silence.

"Does that really seem like a bad reason? Is the life of my son, the future village chief, of such little importance to you?" Kondo's voice resonated.

"The life of Ramadani has the same value as Adimu's or anyone else's," responded the priest, holding Kondo's gaze.

"Have you forgotten that fathers have always decided the future for their daughters? The final decision is up to Sefu, and he has accepted."

"Fathers decide on a daughter's marriage, not on selling her as a remedy for an incurable disease!"

"Perhaps you didn't hear that we have agreed on the bride price,"[23] said Kondo with stubborn certainty, knowing those two words would change the cards on the table.

Father Andrew was perplexed. Juma had forgotten to tell him that detail. "Does this mean they'll marry?"

"Adimu will be protected and accepted by the villagers by living in my house," said Kondo, avoiding a direct answer to the question. He paused for effect and then raised his hands to stop the priest who was about to speak. "What power does God have when only a few people listen to His words?"

The priest's face became inquisitive.

"I have heard that fewer and fewer are attending your Sunday rituals." Kondo waited in silence for his message to produce the desired effect.

"What does this have to do with Adimu?"

"I'm going to propose a pact," said Kondo, ignoring the question. "You approve the arrangement between Adimu and my son, and I will ensure that your meetings under the baobab are attended as they were in the past."

Mosi contemplated his glass of water. His throat was dry. As he sipped the liquid, its freshness had a comforting effect.

"Remember, you owe me. Thanks to my intervention, the *zeru zeru* has a name," Kondo added. "I want what's best for everyone—you and your church, Adimu, my son, and our village."

The priest focused on the positive aspects of the proposal. Adimu would finally be accepted by the community, and she would have a husband, in a way, and a clan to protect her. He envisioned the future and looked into the distance, beyond Kondo's yard, the dusty paths and the straw roofs of the isolated village. In the end, the village chief's words were based on truth. *What exactly had Kondo said? "What power does God have when only a few people listen to his words?" Maybe I have focused too much on the life of one*

---

[23] Payment on the part of the groom's family of an agreed upon number of livestock or money in exchange for the bride. The custom is widespread among many ethnicities in Africa.

individual at the expense of the collective who have, for weeks now, stayed away from the poetry of the most merciful God.

Father Andrew imagined Mass in the shade of the baobab, a crowd celebrating the word of the Lord, shoulder to shoulder like at Thursday market. Adimu would become a kind of wife of the future leader, an honor. Mosi wiped from his mind his initial thought that Kondo would cast out Adimu after a short time, that his "arrangement" would further taint her.

Although the priest's conscience told him he was engaging in a sales transaction, he buried that sensation. To save a myriad of souls lost in pagan beliefs and devoted to a lesser god, to convert them to the truth of the Lord was Father Andrew's one purpose. With Kondo's support, he could reach the objective he had been working toward for years. Father Andrew would convince the entire population of the island of His truth. At the cost of only one life, a sacrifice, like Jesus.

The sun slipped beyond the bluish horizon, and the air cooled. Kondo warmed his hands at the fire.

The crackling of wood brought Father Andrew back to the present. "Will you come to Mass as well?"

"Yes, after Adimu has come to live with Ramadani," answered Kondo.

"Fine. Then you have my approval."

"Do you promise on your God?"

Father Andrew wanted to say that such a promise was impossible, but he understood Kondo needed reassurance.

"I promise," he muttered, looking at an insect that was trying to escape the heat of the fire but was unable to.

"Look at me while you say it."

"I promise," repeated the priest with a contemptuous tone. He crossed himself, as if seeking absolution from a sin just committed.

HER STEPSISTER, WHILE filling the laundry basket with dirty clothes, said to Adimu, "My father wants you to come to our house at dinnertime."

The last time Adimu had seen Sefu was when he ignored her at her grandmother's funeral. The time before that was years earlier, when she had put herself and her goats in his path, when she was a child who drew on walls. The outline of Sefu's giant feet was still visible among the scratches on the hut.

Adimu wondered if Sefu had learned of her friendship with the Fieldings and wanted to apologize for ignoring her. *Maybe he realizes I must be good, and now he wants me too?*

The girl ran to the river, washed herself, rushed home, and put on her aqua green dress. She felt lucky to have such a pretty one. She decided not to eat before her visit because she figured that if Sefu wanted her at his home at the dinner hour, surely he would invite her to join the family at their table. Adimu tried to distract herself by reading until it was time to leave. But every new thought offered a different reason for the unexpected invitation. *Could Nkamba have appeared in his dreams? Or maybe Sefu wants to tell me that Mr. Fielding has admitted to being my real father and has asked to adopt me?* That was what Adimu hoped for the most, though she tried to hold in her hope so she wouldn't be disappointed.

For the first time since her grandmother had died, she thought about the community in Tanga. *What if Sefu wants me to go there? Maybe he wants me to attend school. Maybe he wants me to be a doctor. If that's the case, I'll work harder than my hardest.* Adimu's imagination traveled around the world without a passport, wandering in countries where people lived their lives from one sunrise to another, on vacation and without worries.

It was finally time to go. She told herself that simply being invited to her father's home was a step toward being accepted. She picked up her book, put it under her arm, and closed the door behind her. She paused for a moment to look at the rusted sheet metal as if she were saying goodbye to it and then skipped to the mango tree where her grandparents rested in eternal sleep. She kissed the tree's reddish trunk and caressed the rough bark.

"I'll tell you about it when I get back," she said, looking at the two crosses.

Before the sky darkened, she was at Sefu's home. In the courtyard, her father's first wife and his daughters were tying a pile of twigs into small bundles. They stared at her from head to toe. Adimu suspected they were surprised to see her so well dressed. The almost imperceptible nod of their heads was their way of acknowledging her.

Adimu opened the door to the hut and, hesitating, stretched her head forward. Her father was seated at a square plastic table, upon which there was a plate piled high with pieces of meat. Chicken bones were scattered around the fireplace. There was no evidence of a family dinner taking place. "Come in," Sefu grumbled. He took a bone from the plate and concentrated on gnawing at the meat. Adimu clutched her encyclopedia to her chest with crossed arms, and her eyes dashed around the room to avoid his. He lifted his gaze for an instant, just long enough to verify that before him was Adimu.

"Next rainy season you will marry Ramadani, the son of Kondo. Now you can go, and do not tell anyone," he said as he threw the stripped bone onto the fire.

The heavy volume Adimu had brought with her slipped from her arms and fell on the earthen floor with a thud, raising a small cloud of dust. For a moment she was tempted to beg him to change his mind, but she knew it would be useless. She had been taught to obey any decision made by an adult. Yet how could the man sitting there give her away as a bride to someone she knew only by sight? What would become of her promise to Nkamba?

"You will be his first wife. A great honor for a *zeru zeru*. The marriage will improve the status of our family because of your birth."

Sefu lifted his arm, and Adimu was certain he was preparing to slap her if she protested. She concentrated on keeping her eyes open. If she closed her lids, tears would pour down her cheeks like the rain that leaked through a hole in her roof. She nodded silently and left the hut, maintaining the same composure as when she had entered. As soon as she stepped over the threshold of Sefu's hut, she ran back home, hugging her book against her chest.

I'm going to marry; I'm going to marry him; I'm going to do what Sefu requires, she repeated all the way to her mango tree where she dropped to her knees. She embraced the trunk and cried, imagining her arms wrapped around her *bibi* who she saw as two great branches, reaching down to pick her up and carry her away from the village and from that cruel man. *He cannot be my father,* she thought. *He cannot.*

Adimu turned her head to look in the direction of Kondo's house and then up into the branches of the tree. To Nkamba she said, "I cannot marry a man who wants me for my skin. And if I move to Kondo's house, I will have to leave our goats, to toss aside my dream of becoming a doctor. Surely I won't be allowed to take my encyclopedias. Kondo and his wife and daughters will treat me like an animal. It would be better to die like one than to go there." Adimu felt the strength of the branches of the tree. Nkamba had devoted her life to raising Adimu and to teaching her to think for herself, to see strangers for what they were. That Sefu had arranged a marriage for the *"zeru zeru"* before his older daughter meant only one thing. *I'm no ninny.* Her gaze held tight to the largest branch above her, like the rope she imagined around her neck. Two ripe fruits had fallen from the tree and were lying nearby—*Bibi and Babu*, she thought.

She slumped to the ground and bit into the juicy flesh of one of the mangoes. The succulent pulp was like salve, and its sweetness soothed her sore and inflamed soul by carrying her back to a time when she enjoyed happy days with her *bibi*. She fixed her eyes on her grandmother's grave. She'd given Nkamba her word. *I will become a doctor. It is what I want to do, and it is my duty. I must obey Nkamba and no one else*, she said to herself as she opened the encyclopedia and looked at a photograph of human anatomy in the light of a waning moon. Little did she know that someone else in the village was scratching Xs with a red marker on the right arm of a drawing at that very moment.

42.

Charles and Sarah were leaning against the headboard, absorbed in their bedtime reading. Charles had a copy of *Moby-Dick* open on his chest, which moved up and down as he breathed. He struggled to keep his mind on the book.

The family residence in Harare. The apartment in London. The land in Tanzania, Zimbabwe, South Africa, England, and Italy. None of his holdings existed any longer. At least not for him. An evil magician had laid a black cloth over his assets and whisked them away.

"Think not, is my eleventh commandment," was written on the page before him, but he couldn't stop thinking. *It should have been a right arm and not taken from a cadaver. Next time, I need to make sure none of the magic is frittered away. He'll have to do the severing there at the mine.*

Charles was yanked out of his reverie when Sarah asked, "Darling, did you know that in Africa, people with albinism rarely live to be over thirty?"

"Sorry, what did you say?"

"Forget it," said Sarah as she turned back to her reading.

"No, really."

Sarah lifted a finger for him to wait until she finished the paragraph. "Okay, finished." She set the papers on her thighs "I was saying that according to this article, most Africans with albinism die from skin cancer. Can you imagine? If they're not hunted and killed like animals, malignant tumors will get them."

"I had no idea." Charles set his book aside and pulled himself up higher against the headboard.

"This report by the Tanzanian Albino Society says they rarely live past thirty." Sarah frowned.

What is the value of a life when the person's already condemned to death? Charles asked himself. *The arm of an embulamaro who is terminally ill with cancer, that's what I need!* Charles would send Thomas and his gang of headhunters to a hospital. He'd have them convince the *zeru zeru* to donate the limb in exchange for money. *It's a win-win! I'll be saved, as will my employees since they won't lose their jobs. And the* zeru zeru's *family will have money. A good deed for everyone!*

"I'm going to sleep," said Sarah as she rolled over and turned out the light.

"Hmm? Oh, good night." Charles switched off his own bedside light but remained upright, thinking.

ADIMU WAS WASHING clothes in the lake. She was bent over stones with an open book, the page she was reading in shadow. Abruptly she noticed the outline of the shadow grow bigger. She lifted her eyes and saw a white man and black woman watching her, smiling.

The woman, squatting down, said, "We were told we could find you here. Is your name Adimu?"

"Yes," she said in little more than a whisper, avoiding eye contact with the two adults. She thought of her conversation with her *bibi* about strangers. She knew that since every villager washes clothes in the lake, the strangers might be lying. Though how did they know her name? she wondered.

"My name's Martha, and this is my coworker Roman. We work for an association in Tanga that takes care of children with albinism. In fact, we waited for you at the dock in Mwanza. It was two rainy seasons ago." Martha shook her head and looked at Adimu as though she were sad. "We're here to ask if you want to come with us now."

Finding out that the adults were there for her caused Adimu to stiffen. She continued washing the clothes.

"In our community, young people like you can play and study," said Martha, looking at the book Adimu was reading.

Adimu scrubbed at the fabric less vigorously when she heard that. The woman's words reawakened her hope of keeping her promise to her grandmother. Though she couldn't understand why the strangers would come from the other side of the lake for her. Was it possible that, for them, she was so important? *Are they strangers?* Adimu asked herself.

"Are there girls like me there?" she asked, remembering her beloved *bibi*'s words: "You are different. Only another white girl like you can be your friend."

"Of course!" both the adults said at the same time.

"Really? Are there many?" she asked, setting the wet clothes on a rock.

"About fifty," said the man with an encouraging smile.

"Fifty? Like me?" Adimu stood up.

"Just like you. Some older and some younger," he told her.

Adimu saw herself holding hands with a group of children just like her, all in a big circle, laughing together, like the pictures she drew on the wall, only *real* friends.

The man stepped to the edge of the water where the soapy laundry was piled next to the encyclopedia. He picked up the book. "Can you imagine? We have the exact same book in my office."

Adimu squinted at him so she could see his eyes. "Really?" It had to be a much better school than the one in Murutanga, she thought. And if the children had skin like hers, the teacher would answer Adimu's questions. When the girl thought of being forced to move to Kondo's and to leave her encyclopedias, she smiled at the man and woman who, maybe, were there to offer her a once-in-a-lifetime chance. She wasn't sure.

"Listen, Adimu," said Martha, "we're only on Ukerewe for a few hours. Come back with us to Tanga."

"I don't know if I can right now. My father has promised me to the village chief's son."

"And do you want to marry him?" she asked.

"No. My father decided."

"Well, that's a good reason to come with us," Martha replied sternly.

Yes, it is, thought Adimu.

"You can travel with us, and we'll make sure you're safe," added the man. "But before we get to Tanga, we need to stop to pick up another girl."

"I'll make the trip with a white girl like me?"

The man nodded and patted her head. "A girl with albinism, just like you. She'll be your best friend."

Nothing could have convinced Adimu more than the promise of meeting another girl. *A best friend,* Adimu told herself. More than the anguish of marriage, the promise to Nkamba, or the desire to escape from her prison, she was driven by her desire to not be alone, to be with others just like her. She would no longer be an exception. She could look into the eyes of children who shared her same plight. Adimu took Martha's hand and held it close to her heart.

"If I come with you, can we stop to say hello to the Fieldings when we get to Mwanza? They're my friends."

The strangers exchanged looks and nodded. "Of course. Let's go to the port now. You don't want to stay here on the island forever, do you?"

"I have to go home first."

"No, we have to go now!" Martha urged.

Adimu released Martha's hand as if a hornet were hidden in her palm.

To reassure her, Roman pulled the little girl close. "Go ahead, but be quick. And only bring a few things with you. At the community, we'll give you whatever clothes you need."

In the hut, Adimu set all the volumes of her encyclopedia on the table. She carefully tore out the page with the Fielding's dedication and took the photo of the three of them. Then she put all the books in plastic bags. If it rained enough to flood the house, at least they would stay dry. She gazed at her doll in the corner. *I shouldn't leave her behind like the other time,* she said to herself. *It would be bad luck, and it might bring me back here.* She hugged the Adimu doll and put her in the plastic bag she'd take with her, along with her aqua green dress and the dress with flowers printed on it, the dresses given to her by the Fieldings. She dug up the money her grandmother had left and put it in her panties. There were only a few bills.

She met the couple at the ferry ticket office as they had agreed. When she noticed they were nervous, she felt a stab of anxiety in her stomach. She wondered what awaited her on the other side of the lake. Nothing, though, could be worse than the life she had led up until then. And with marriage in her future, it would only get worse. That very evening she would meet her best friend and see the Fieldings and, who knows, if they saw her leaving with Martha and Roman, they might ask her to stay. Ask her and her best friend. Her new sister.

Adimu sat at the bow of the boat. She didn't glance back at the island she was leaving behind. She concentrated on what was awaiting her.

Roman and Martha asked about her studies and her life. Adimu told them about her grandmother's death on the boat, and the adults touched each other with their elbows.

"It must have been difficult for you," said Roman, caressing her hair.

Adimu saw a flash of light in the man's eyes and felt afraid. The kind touch of his hand and the glint in his blue eyes seemed to belong to two different people. She stared at the horizon to calm herself. Big gray buildings rose from the water in the distance, crowded like stalks of corn. Adimu quickly forgot her fear and wondered how people who lived in houses so close together could go out to walk. There didn't seem to be space for roads. She put on her glasses.

"Have we arrived?" she asked, jumping with excitement.

"Yes," replied Roman. "This is the port of Mwanza."

As the ferry approached, her enthusiasm was dampened by the

upsetting memory of her grandmother's death. Adimu looked at the sky and, though it was as clear and blue as on Ukerewe, the air was stained gray from the smoke and vapor that rose and seeped out of the buildings. She lowered her eyes and, suddenly, as if she were doing something prohibited, something she was ashamed of, she let her doll slip into the water. It floated for several seconds on the surface with its face upward until the foam from the boat's propellers swallowed it. *Much better to end up at the bottom of the lake than stuck on the island,* she thought.

When they reached the parking lot, Roman looked at his watch. "We're terribly late. I'm sorry, Adimu, but there's no time to visit your friends."

"You promised we would go see them as soon as we got here," she found the courage to say. She couldn't understand why the unexpected change of plans. The two adults had been aware of what time the ferry would arrive.

"It took longer to get here than we estimated," replied the man. "We have to go get the other girl in Kigoma. I'll take you to your friends myself next weekend."

Adimu studied Roman's face apprehensively, looking for an expression of betrayal.

"I'm really sorry, sweetie," he apologized, "it's just the way it is. The other girl is more important right now than a visit to friends." He seemed truly sorry. "If you want to go see them, you're free to do so. You can take a taxi to their house, but you have to know we can't wait for you."

The woman nodded.

"I understand," Adimu said with a shrug. *If they want to kidnap me, they wouldn't let me decide what I want to do,* she reasoned. "Can I write the Fieldings a letter? To let them know I'm going to visit soon?"

"Of course you can," said Martha, who found a sheet of paper, a pen, and even an old magazine to write on in the glove box of the car that was waiting for them.

Neither the woman nor the man paid attention to what she was writing, and Adimu interpreted their disinterest as a good sign, which helped eliminate her fears that hadn't totally subsided. *If they have bad intentions, they'll try to see what I'm writing,* she told herself.

THE THREE OF them got out of the car when they pulled in front of the post office to buy an envelope and a stamp. Martha sealed the blue envelope in front of Adimu. "Do you want to get an ice cream while Roman sends the letter?" she asked. "Oh look, we almost forgot! Adimu, you need to put the address on it," she said, taking the envelope back from Roman.

"I don't have the address. But 'Charles Fielding, Mwanza' is enough. Everyone here knows my father," Adimu said with pride.

Roman and Martha exchanged a furtive look. Adimu noticed it and beamed.

The ice cream—dark chocolate and creamy vanilla—tasted delicious. The last time she had some was when Mrs. Fielding bought her a cone at the grocery. The memory was still so fresh in her mind, even though it was a while back, that as soon as the ice cream was handed to her, she crammed it in her mouth, terrified it would melt, become sticky and call out to the black bugs. Adimu liked the sweetness of the frozen cream, though the cold caused her belly to clench and spasm, and she promised herself she'd never eat ice cream again.

After the ice cream, Roman joined her and Martha in the car. Adimu relaxed in the back seat, trying to calm her tummy, anticipating meeting another girl like herself. The two adults and child checked into a secluded hotel that was just outside of the city.

Adimu stayed awake most of the night, replaying anticipated scenes of meeting her best friend for the first time. In each scenario, Adimu felt an immediate sisterly bond. Martha and Roman told her the girl's name was Shida. *Shida, Shida, Shida.* All night she chanted the name like a calming mantra, one with the promise of enchantment.

At dawn they continued driving to Shida's. During the trip, Martha explained things to Adimu. "Shida lives with her grandparents, and you know they'll want to be certain she's going to a good place. So if they ask you, tell them you've lived in the protected community for a year and that you like it."

Nkamba had always told Adimu to tell the truth. But her curiosity about another girl who would be her friend—her first true friend—prevailed, and she agreed to lie for the peace of mind of the girl's grandparents.

When Adimu met Shida she was enthralled. They approached each other slowly, their hands stretched outward to confirm that the other truly existed. After a fleeting moment of disbelief, they smiled at the other timidly, the intense emotion making them awkward.

"Shida, introduce yourself to your new friend," encouraged the grandfather. Shida took Adimu's hand and whispered in the softest voice how happy she was to meet her, as though with Adimu she was certain the two would share a secret language.

Shida was younger than Adimu, about ten years old. Her maternal grandparents had raised her in isolation to protect her. She had never gone to school. In the nearby village, few people were aware that a *zeru zeru* lived in the vicinity—their house was secluded, and they lived off their land and animals. The little girl spent most of her free time listening to a wind-up radio.

Adimu noticed with a sense of longing that her new friend's grandmother behaved differently from Nkamba, who had never been demonstrative. Shida's *bibi* kissed and hugged her often, and her grandfather lived with her, unlike Kheri who had been with the mango tree when Adimu's *bibi* was alive. With a pang of envy, Adimu thought about how she had never had the opportunity to know her grandfather, a good and courageous man who was the protagonist of so many of her grandmother's stories.

The elderly couple observed the girls. Once the children's initial shyness was overcome, Adimu and Shida became inseparable. Their granddaughter's radiant happiness convinced them to let her go with their guests.

"Please stay with us for supper," they said to the two adults.

"Thank you. But we can't. We have a long way to travel," replied Martha.

"Here are the documents to sign for the authorization, and here's a financial contribution so you can come visit your granddaughter," said the white man, handing a one-hundred-dollar bill to the grandfather, along with a stack of printed forms.

The old man looked at the money. He turned it over in his hands several times and showed it to his wife. "Thank you, thank you very much," he said again and again. "I've never seen dollars before."

He scrawled a signature on the papers. He was unable to read but was reassured because, as he said, "Documents guarantee and ink stains, not like words that vanish into thin air."

"You white folks are the hope for this land," he said, his rheumy eyes scanning the forms. "You are the future. Unfortunately, we live in the past. You would never behave like us Africans," he added, looking up. "Why would someone like you come from so far to do us harm? A person only travels that far to do good. Please, take my granddaughter. She deserves a better future than we old farmers can give her."

The grandmother nodded at her husband and dried her cheeks. Letting go of her granddaughter was harder than she had expected.

The car left with the two girls in the back seat. The grandparents stood on the threshold of their hut and watched them drive away. From the car window, they looked like two small plaster statues, hugging each other.

Adimu could hardly contain herself she was so happy, and her hands sought unremitting contact with Shida. That she didn't know where they were headed had become a small detail. With Shida beside her, she was no longer fearful. Shida touched Adimu's hair and ran her fingers along its unusual length. The vehicle raced on as they headed toward the sunset.

.

43.

Adimu's stepsisters noticed her absence the following day when the clean laundry wasn't in its usual place. The complaints reached Juma's ears who, together with Sefu's daughters, went "to the place where Adimu sleeps," as they called it, at sunset. They found the door of the hut closed with a lock. They waited for a while and then continued on to the lake to wash the dishes.

They returned to Nkamba's hut again the next day. The door was still closed, and there was no trace of Adimu, not even a shadow. At sunset of the following day, the youngest stepsister told her father that the *zeru zeru* had vanished. Sefu went to the hut and broke the lock. Inside, everything was tidy, except for a pile of dirty laundry in one corner—garments that belonged to the women of his household.

He paused to look at the books that were wrapped in bags on the plastic table. "This is strange," he said aloud. While the carefully stored volumes implied a willful departure, the dirty laundry suggested a kidnapping. Adimu would never have disobeyed him, of that he was sure. "The lock could have been put on the door by anyone," mumbled Sefu, trying to make sense of the confusing situation. His anger mixed with a strange sensation of privation, like an executioner who, at the last moment, sees the police take away the victim he had been stalking for years. He needed to inform Kondo of the recent developments.

As soon as he heard the news, the village chief called a meeting of his villagers under the great baobab. "Everyone must participate in finding the *isope*," he announced.

The islanders undertook the search, even the villagers who were relieved by the sudden disappearance of the *zeru zeru*. Most of the inhabitants of Murutanga, though, were far from happy. Adimu was their last hope—their guarantee for a future of wealth in case Zuberi's headhunters failed. The villagers had been circling their *zeru zeru* from the moment the Spirits of the Lake gave her to them, waiting for their moment to pounce.

The children participated in the search as though it were a game. They ran through the village shouting the girl's name as loudly as they could. They dashed to their own secret hiding places and ferreted around the school. The fishermen dropped their nets in the water and dredged the lake bottom. The farmers upturned the earth to be certain no body was buried below. The women checked the riverbanks and the lakeshore. The adolescents went into the forest and investigated every cleft and chasm they knew, even the treetops.

Adimu had vanished. Just like a *zeru zeru*!

That afternoon, Juma was at the lake, washing clothes. She rubbed the garments with a piece of white soap and beat them over a smooth stone. She noticed how the other women who were there doing laundry turned their eyes away from her and spoke in low voices. She ignored them and continued washing. *That daughter of mine, that damned* zeru zeru *who ruined my life should be doing this chore,* she thought to herself. Agitated whispers reached her ears in fragments. She had the impression the women were talking about her and her misfortune, injurious words that traveled from one mouth to another, spreading like a contagious virus. The women, the fishermen on the shore, the children who ran naked in the sun, even the branches of the trees and the soft lapping of the waves of the lake seemed to speak ill of her behind her back. As a younger woman, she had had a prosperous business as a tailor, but since birthing a *zeru zeru*, she became a pariah, husbandless, and hid away in extreme poverty. Anger swelled inside her, and her hands continued to move faster and faster, beating the clothes on the rocks with fury. She wrung and kneaded them until the fibers of the threadbare fabrics nearly tore. Sweat ran down her back and between her breasts. *It must have been Sefu who made the* embulamaro *disappear,* she thought, *selling it for money, trading the rotten fruit of our love as he did the day of its birth when he destroyed my pride, my life, and my future. The curse will follow me always.* And the more she thought about the curse of the *zeru zeru,* the more she took out her anger on the clothes until, eventually, her palms were scraped and raw. There was silence around her now. The other women observed her rage until a spatter of soap shot into her eye. Irritation became acute pain when she cupped her hand in the lake and rinsed her face. The soap had tinged the water a bright white that glistened in the glare of the sun, sudsy tentacles reaching across its surface. She wiped her eye dry with the hem of her dress. Then, in a burst of rage, she threw the piece of milk-white soap against the stone that had been her washboard. She saw it bounce off the tip of the rock, sink in the lake, and drift down onto the sandy bottom like a large shell. She grabbed her laundry, hung the clothes as best she could on some bushes, and marched off. One of the women lifted her sarong to wade into the water and recover the piece of soap.

"If she doesn't need it, I'll take it," the woman said lightly, raising a roar of laughter from the others.

From a rock, Yunis surveilled the scene. Her laundry was already rinsed, and rivulets of white foam ran from the stones. She left the clothes she had washed and walked along the path in the direction Juma had taken. Once out of the other women's sight, she started to run to her old friend who she saw through the bushes. She called out Juma's name, but the woman didn't turn around to look at her.

With hurried steps, Yunis got close enough to catch her shoulder. "Please, listen to me."

Juma spun around, her eyes full of disdain. With a jerk, she freed herself and continued on her way, her head down.

Yunis did not give up. "I know how I hurt you by taking away Adimu. Believe me, I was trying to free you, Sefu, and our clan from the curse." Yunis didn't notice the rough terrain as she pled her case. She tripped on roots and stones along the path, intent on having Juma understand. "On that day in the forest, I held her away from my body. But it wasn't long before I realized she was closer to me than I thought." Yunis took a breath. "Then she began to cry. I uncovered her face and saw that she was the same as any other baby. I set her down and touched her, and her flesh was soft like that of other babies I had caressed and cradled. I offered her my breast, and she latched on like any other creature would. I felt like a mother. In that moment—the only time in my life—I felt as if my greatest desire had come true," she said. "The desire to be a mother."

Juma slowed her pace. Shock mixed with anger as she listened to the belated confession. Though she had an impulse to hug the woman, her rancor and suffering caused her to ignore it. She continued to walk, eyes on her feet, Yunis beside her.

"I was telling the truth when I said I had been kidnapped," continued Yunis, "but it wasn't the *zeru zeru* who made me change direction and led me to the white couple. It was the darling baby attached to my breast. She pulled from me the life I could not give her. I could not abandon her, because, in the oddest way, I *had* become her mother. She was the baby I had always wanted...How could I leave her to the Spirits of the Lake to die? What I've just told you is the truth."

Juma could barely hold back her tears. The path had become narrower, and only a few pale bushes dotted the ochre yellow of the ground. Yunis walking next to her, close to her. The silence was broken by the swishing of their dresses and the muffled sound of their sandals on the stony path.

"I can make this confession only to you," said Yunis, stopping abruptly in front of her friend, blocking her way.

Juma stopped and looked into the face before her, for the first time in many years.

"You and I are the same," whispered Yunis. "We each had one daughter, one child, though neither of us had the courage to keep her. That day, in the forest, I thought about leaving the island with Adimu. I lacked the courage. And so I took her where I knew she would be safe." Softly she added, "Far from us."

The sun sank, painting the tops of the sparse trees red. Soon night would fall over the island. Juma stretched a hand across her forehead as if trying to make space for her friendship with the woman standing in front of her. In her heart, though, she did not find a trace of the old affection. Juma turned and, with determined steps, continued on her way home, leaving Yunis behind.

44.

Jackob knew his employer well, better than Mr. Fielding knew himself. Sooner or later his boss would decide he needed a live *and* healthy *zeru zeru*. For Mr. Fielding, all people were goods for sale with bar codes tattooed on their necks from the time of birth.

Zuberi laughed heartily when Jackob told him Mr. Fielding's latest directive. "A terminally ill *embulamaro*! Did he really say that?" He paused and cocked his head to one side. "It does have a certain logic, though the priority is now to find a live *embulamaro* in the shortest time possible. I will give the hunters new instructions this very evening," the witch doctor promised. "I'll suggest they scour the public hospital in Dar es Salaam where patients come from all over the country."

It was, however, only a suggestion, Zuberi told Thomas. "The important thing is to act quick," he said. "By now, I have many, many clients to satisfy."

THE HUNTERS TOOK Zuberi's suggestion and went to Dar es Salaam. Access to the hospital was easy: they divided into two groups and said they were relatives of albino patients, careful to avoid using derogatory terms for *ngazu*, as the witch doctor had reminded them.

Once inside, however, they sensed immediately how difficult it would be to kidnap someone from the ward. The hospital was well supervised by private guards and, during the night, additional support came from the police.

They spent three days observing the hospital. "The white shadows are mixed in with the other patients," a frustrated Thomas told Zuberi over the phone.

"Really?" the witch doctor replied with surprise.

"Yeah, and the ones that are about to die are in rooms where there are always doctors or visitors."

"Oh."

"It's not at all what we expected. We have better chances in villages near the forest where there are places to hide. The city's nothing but concrete and noise."

NOT LONG AFTER, the five young men sat around the fire, their morale expended. The last rays of sun filtered through the forest, kindling the leaves and green branches with a soft glow. The air was thick. They had been on this mission for too long. Thomas was smoking, and Amani gathered wood for the fire. Akili and Aki were polishing their weapons, sprawled among the roots of an enormous acacia tree.

Ramadani, the only unarmed hunter, stared at the flames that licked the twigs. He glanced intermittently at the two men's machetes and listened to them talk about their dreams of a different life—a sheet-metal roof over their heads, plenty of food, a woman who was both wife and good mother, accommodating young lovers, and several sons.

The trip to Dar es Salaam had awakened their awareness of the misery in which they were immersed. The big city had initially frightened and confused them. Now, though, it lured them like a beacon, guiding them away from their dark villages that offered them nothing. They wanted to return to the metropolis with their money from hunting a *nobody* when the mission was finished. A good job, an apartment in a new building, and enough cash to hold their heads high. They would be envied and respected.

Ramadani did not participate in the conversation but, instead, listened to the sounds of the forest. To keep himself from thinking about his future on Ukerewe, he considered the variety of animals moving through the wild, intricate passageways that surrounded him.

His meditation was interrupted by the voice of one of the hunters calling out to Thomas. "Boss, do you want me to sharpen your machete?" asked Akili, testing the blade of his weapon on the trunk of a tree.

"No, I can make my way through the forest just fine as it is," answered Thomas. "And, besides, when the time comes, I have a better weapon," he said, tapping the butt of the pistol tucked in his belt. He took a final toke from his cigarette and tossed the stub into the fire.

Amani added more wood to the flames that were hot and blazing amid them, a pulsing red heart.

"Best thing would be to find a *zeru zeru* near Mwanza," said Thomas calmly, looking through the barrel of his freshly cleaned gun. "Less distance to cover for delivery, fewer risks."

"I know of a holdover place around there that another group uses," said young Amani.

"What do you mean?" Thomas asked.

"A place to let the waters calm after a kidnapping. The group's headed by a *mzungu*. They kidnap *zeru zerus*, keep them there until the families and police stop looking for them. Then they sell them."

Thomas looked at the boy before shoving two bullets in his pistol and, in a single leap, bore down on Amani.

"Why didn't you tell us before?" exclaimed Aki, moving close to his comrade.

Thomas shot his gun into the earth and grabbed Amani by the neck, squeezing so tight the younger man's face changed color. The gun pointed at Amani's chest, Thomas said, "I hope this helps you remember other details that might interest me."

"We're looking for a *zeru zeru* dying from tumors," croaked Amani, "not a young, healthy one. There are only *embulamaro* kids at the holdover place. For politicians and the rich. I didn't think you'd be interested. You said you didn't want to take risks."

Thomas released Amani, and the boy collapsed on the ground, holding his head between his hands. The leader looked at him with disgust, spat at his legs, and took hold of a knife. With long strides, Thomas approached a lamb he had earlier tied to a tree that wasn't far from the fire and took it by one of its back legs. The poor thing bleated desperately as it was dragged backward. It tripped and hit its muzzle on the ground.

Ramadani watched the scene—useless suffering. Torture was not something he could stomach. He wanted to intervene. He would kill the lamb quickly, and they'd eat it. But he knew if he did, Thomas would consider it an affront, and Ramadani would be the next victim of the sadist.

Near the fire, with a decisive gesture, Thomas ran the entire length of the machete blade along the animal's jugular. The lamb collapsed on the ground, bleating soundlessly. Its blood soaked into the soil. Amani shot sidelong glances at the dying lamb, realizing he could come to a similar end. Thomas lifted the dead animal by a hind leg, made a cut near the hock, brought the carcass to his lips, and blew as hard as he could. The animal puffed up slowly like a bagpipe—now it would be easier to skin and gut.

"Tomorrow we'll set out at dawn, and you'll take us to this white man," Thomas said to the boy while he butchered the animal.

"How does the *mzungu* kidnap the *zeru zerus*?" asked Akili.

"He gets the families to trust him and has them sign many papers and gives them fake money," replied Amani. "They don't expect such a thing from a white man. I didn't believe it until my brother told me."

45.

"Promise me you'll leave your cell phone at home, that the only sounds we'll hear will be from the savannah," Sarah said.

"A telephone could be useful in an emergency," Charles replied.

Sarah ignored Charles's tone and took the device from his hands.

He didn't resist.

"You're right." She laughed as she turned off the phone and placed it in the glove box. "We'll use it only if we have to."

"We'll take the other car, not this one," Charles said, pointing to the jeep. "We need a vehicle that's agile."

Sarah took the phone with her as she clambered into the jeep.

After driving only a few yards Charles stepped on the brakes and jumped out of the car.

"Where are you going?" Sarah called.

"I've forgotten something important," he shouted as he trotted toward the house.

Charles returned a few minutes later with a gun.

"What do you need that for?"

"Nothing, I hope," Charles said.

"Darling, we're going to watch gnus and zebras migrate."

"Where there are herbivores, there are predators. Even a buffalo can be dangerous."

Charles set the pistol in the glove box with his cell phone.

Five hours later, they reached the plain. With Sarah's hand in his, Charles let the stress of his body and mind unknot in the limitless space of the Serengeti. He gripped the knob of the gearshift and inhaled. In an instant he felt liberated from the terror of becoming poor, the humiliation of being derided, and the terrible conviction of having to sacrifice an innocent child for his freedom from a disastrous financial situation of his own making. He released Sarah's hand and gently squeezed her thigh just above her knee. He could feel the soft flesh through her pant leg and caressed it.

Sarah concentrated on some dots in the distance and, as the vehicle neared, they took on the shapes of animals. Her expression was full of wonder at the spectacle around her. Though intellectually she knew that the migration was closely connected with survival, witnessing hundreds of gnus and zebras giving birth simultaneously was a celebration of life. How could she ever have imagined herself in the middle of a river of animals that stretched beyond her field of vision? An infinite procession of four-legged grazing animals emerged from a cloud of red dust, behind which the secrets of life and death were hidden. Charles watched his wife, her rapt gaze, and experienced the wonder through her eyes. Her face sparkled from the awe of wild animal behavior, something he had witnessed numerous times as a child. Once again, he appreciated the sum total of his wife, her heart, her mind, and her body, and was overcome with anxiety by the fear of losing her.

Charles and Sarah followed a herd of animals as the sun shifted to the west, each immersed in their own thoughts. As the light began to fade, Charles realized they had migrated far from the main trail. "The GPS isn't receiving signals," he said.

"Oh, really?" Sarah was distracted by the sensation of being in a place with intangible borders, where humans were nothing more than animals like any other, subject to unpredictable laws. She fantasized about her long-standing dream of swimming in the open ocean with Charles, carried by dolphins. Holding on to their fins, they would reach the coast, and then she and her husband would rest on a white sandy beach. She felt closer than ever to the man she loved and safe beside him. She set her hand over her husband's on the gearshift and laced her fingers with his. They traveled for tens of miles to reach a group of red mud huts with straw roofs. Charles drove no faster than a man could trot among the dwellings.

"Let's see if we can find an adult who looks trustworthy and who'll give us directions back to the track we were on," said Charles.

"Why don't we walk?" suggested Sarah.

Charles parked the jeep, and she took his hand as they moved among trees and huts. She had a growing sense that they were being followed by curious and suspicious eyes. Sarah tugged on Charles's hand. "I think I saw Adimu over there."

Though Sarah's comment worried Charles, he reluctantly let her lead him, and, as they neared a brick building that was larger than the others, he, too, thought he'd caught a glimpse of the girl together with another girl like her.

The Fieldings advanced cautiously, as if they were trying to get close to a rare, wild animal, torn between a desire to observe it and the trepidation that if they didn't quickly capture it, it could escape. Unbeknownst to them, they were being kept in sight by two men standing guard not far away. As they rounded the corner of the building, they saw a group of white children of various ages who were playing.

When the children saw the two strangers, they froze. The smallest children ran away. The older ones hesitated, curious.

"Hello. My name's Sarah, and this is my husband, Charles. Don't be afraid. We've lost our way, and we're looking for information." She used her sweetest nonthreatening voice.

"Did you come in that jeep over there?" asked a boy, pointing at their parked vehicle.

"Can you take us for a ride?" an older boy asked.

"Come on, I'll show it to you," Charles offered. As Sarah looked about, she did not see any adults. Following her husband, she led another child by the hand.

The two men who'd been watching the Fieldings burst out of the guard-house and blocked their way.

"Where are you going?" one demanded.

"And you, go back into the dormitories!" the other shouted at the children.

"To my car. We've lost our way, and the children were taking us to you, I imagine," Charles replied mildly.

The guards exchanged looks. "How convenient. You lost your way and ended up at the protected community of Shinyanga," one said sarcastically.

"Ah, that's why there are so many albino children!" exclaimed Sarah.

"Are you implying you didn't know? Why were you heading to your jeep with two of them?" The guard turned to his colleague. "Go check the car."

The man returned with the gun and GPS device, holding them out to his colleague.

"You're imposters," said the older guard. He drew his gun and pointed it at the Fieldings.

Sarah and Charles raised their hands and stepped backward.

"Calm down, we're good people!" said Charles.

The guards made Charles lean against a tree, and they searched him. He turned his head and saw Sarah, her mouth slack. He struggled to get free, but the guard gripped him tightly.

"Stand still!" he ordered.

"Get your hands off me, you filthy Negro!" he shouted in Swahili.

The guard landed a blow behind his knees, and Charles fell to the ground. They handcuffed him with his hands behind his back.

"I'll make you pay for this," shouted Charles. The two men grinned at the sight of a white man on the ground in front of them.

Sarah tried to rush to her husband's defense. One man twisted her arm and handcuffed her. They dragged Sarah and Charles into the building and locked them in different rooms.

Through a small window, Sarah could see the children who pushed and nudged each other to catch sight of her. She noticed how raggedy they looked. When she had read about the protected communities, she had thought they were more agreeable places.

Charles was fuming. *Treating me like a criminal, how dare they*, he thought, pacing to distract himself. *Once they find out who they're dealing with, they'll throw themselves at my feet for mercy!* Revenge was on his mind when the door squeaked open.

"Give me your documents," demanded a guard.

"I'm Charles Fielding. I don't need to carry a Tanzanian ID with me," he replied, glaring down at the man and enunciating his words, although his mouth barely moved. "I am a personal friend of a number of government ministers," he added.

The guard searched him and found Charles's good-luck piece in his pants pocket.

"Hey, give that back, you moron!"

In the meantime, the other guard had come into the room. He studied the nugget.

"Now it's mine! We know you're a killer," he added with a smirk, "and you'll get the punishment you deserve."

"I own two gold mines, you stupid Negroes, and it will be a pleasure to bury you in them as soon as I get out of here," he hissed.

The two men chuckled and left the room where Charles was chained.

WHEN THE TWO guards were alone, one said, "If that *mzungu* had friends in high places, he would be traveling in a luxury car, not an old jeep and without bodyguards." He was excited to have finally captured the most wanted white man in Tanzania. The white man had been kidnapping children with albinism, pretending he was escorting them to a protected community.

"That's for sure. A rich man would be surrounded by photographers and officials if he were coming to a protected community for the right reasons."

Over the phone, the area commander gave clear instructions to his guards: "Keep quiet about the white criminal until I get there tomorrow morning." Having started to hang up the phone, he lifted the receiver back to his ear and asked, "What did you say his name is?"

"Fielding, sir, and he said he owns two gold mines." The guard holding the receiver laughed.

"He's not only a kidnapper and killer, but he's stupid too. He gave you the name of one of the richest *wazungu* in the country…I'll see you tomorrow. Stay alert," advised the commander.

Sarah was worried about her husband. She knew his temper and the trouble it could get him in. She concentrated on how to resolve the terrible misunderstanding in the quickest time possible. She watched the children in the courtyard, and as they whispered to each other, she thought about Adimu. She sensed they were talking about her, and she felt compassion for them, for where they were and for how they lived. *Why wasn't the place surrounded by a fence? Thank goodness there are guards to protect them. And they had intervened promptly to detain us.* All things considered, Sarah believed their behavior was justified. Sarah reminded herself that she and Charles were the intruders, *armed* intruders, and he called them "Negroes."

She felt as if her chest was bound. Each breath was a struggle, and her heart seemed to be fighting the tethers, but, despite the fear that imprisoned her body, she tried to keep her mind clear and to think positive. *As soon as the guards get word from Mwanza of who we are, everything will be fine. At least for us. As for the children, they'll probably have to live here—alone—for many more years to come, some of them, perhaps, forever.* Her eyes stung from tears as she watched the children watch her. She smiled at a group that was brave enough to come close to the window.

Once Charles's anger had died down, he looked around the room he was locked in. He noticed the paint on the walls flaking from the humidity, the plaster peeling off the yellowish walls in the feeble light. A big cockroach crawled along a deep crack in the uneven ceiling. He imagined sharing the small space with other prisoners, inhaling the acrid odor of stinking bodies and rotten teeth. "Hey, I need to go to the bathroom!" he called out repeatedly to his jailers. They pretended not to hear him. Unable to hold his bladder any longer, he wet himself. He had never felt so miserable in his entire life, so impotent and frustrated. So humiliated. If that business about the albino hunt came out, the cadaver arm, his shameful secrets, prison would really be his new home, maybe forever. All the gold in the world wouldn't suffice to get him out of trouble. And he'd never see Sarah again.

Now, in the darkness and locked inside a protected community, breathing in the fetid odor of misery, Charles knew he had no choice but to call off the hunt. It was too risky. *Even if "that's how things are in Africa," I will have to find another solution to my problems.*

At sunrise, the Fieldings were put in a car and taken to the police station in nearby Shinyanga. There, Charles was allowed to make one phone call.

When the regional police chief heard the interior minister ordering him to immediately free the man and woman in custody, he nearly fainted. Mr. Fielding demanded immediate restitution of his good-luck charm. The two guards from the day before were standing before him, curve-shouldered, their gaze fixed on their feet.

"Please, sir, forgive us. We cannot afford to lose our jobs. We have big families, and we were only trying our best to protect those children. There's a white man out there who's responsible for the deaths of many children. We've been trying to apprehend him for years." Beads of sweat framed the older guard's hairline.

"Please, please…" insisted the younger man, clutching Charles's hand. He dropped down on one knee.

Charles was tempted to get the two of them fired but, as always, Sarah appealed to his more lofty conscience: "Dear, they were only doing their job. Better to go home and forget about it."

Sarah shivered when the guard mentioned a white man tricking and kidnapping children. She thought of Adimu and prayed she was home in her mud hut, safe.

"Tell Zuberi the hunt is cancelled," Charles ordered Jackob as soon as he was back in his office. His assistant simply nodded.

That evening after dinner, Jackob left to visit the healer. He would follow his boss's orders. Halfway there, though, he stopped under an acacia tree to take a moment to think. Jackob knew his employer well, and that meant he knew he would change his mind again. Mr. Fielding was confused and, above all, afraid. It was up to him, Jackob, to guide Mr. Fielding in the right direction when his compass was broken; that's what a good assistant does. Even if his employer considered himself African, he was still a *mzungu*. No, he would not say anything to Zuberi. He breathed in deeply and stood up, leaning his hand on the great trunk for support. Jackob could already imagine the benefits that he and his family would obtain from the *zeru zeru*; above all, he envisioned the favors they would receive from his employer who would be full of gratitude. He returned home, humming to himself. The future had great things in store for him, of that he was certain.

PART FOUR

46.

The car stopped in front of an industrial-green metal gate that was flecked with rust. To Shida and Adimu, who clung to one another, it seemed high and wide, insurmountable. They had held hands for most of the trip on the way to what they believed was a protected community, squeezing the fingers of the other whenever each needed comfort. Now, in front of that high wall of iron, they looked into the other's eyes for reassurance. Neither of them had expected the community to have such an imposing gate, just like a prison, and the armed guard standing before it, dressed in ill-fitting clothes, had a machete tucked in his belt. The guard's bulging eyes, red and watery, and his jerky movements set Adimu on edge. Her instincts were on high alert.

The car passed through the gate.

Flocks of children playing on a green lawn; bright flowers; shouting and laughter; new, well-built buildings: there were none of these things. None of what Adimu had imagined when she had thought of the place associated with the telephone number scratched in the mud wall. None of what Nkamba had told her she'd find. Before her was a dusty space. Its quiet was broken only by the scratching and pecking of ten or so mangy hens. *The other children must be in school*, she concluded.

Roman and Martha took the girls to a big room that was empty, save for a few crooked beds piled under a window with opaque panes. "Wait here," Martha told Shida and Adimu. The foam rubber mattresses were filthy, and a couple of them were flattened. The broken window frames and rotted ceiling, from where rainwater had leaked in, confirmed the girls' initial impression: the place had been abandoned for some time. Shida, discouraged, sat on one of the beds.

"They're having us wait in this abandoned dormitory until the lessons are finished. Then we'll join the others," said Adimu, trying to lift her friend's spirits. She was really trying to convince and calm herself too. "Let's go see what it's like outside," she added, making a funny face.

"Martha told us to wait here," whimpered Shida.

"Come on, let's take a look so we can figure out where we are," insisted Adimu, pulling her friend's arm.

Shida resisted, crossing her legs and arms. Adimu smoothed her dress and went out alone. In the courtyard, the sun was ferocious. She peeked around the corner of the building and saw other derelict structures. Scrawny, dried-out plants had grown into gaping cracks in the plaster. Silence. *Where are the other children?* she asked herself. She moved cautiously to look through one of the windows in the lowest building. The pane was broken. Inside she saw no furniture, only filth. No beds, no desks, no chairs. Nothing that suggested the presence of any children of any age.

She hugged the wall and crept toward a small building that seemed to be in better condition. It was painted the same pale green as the entry gate. Adimu stood on her tiptoes so she could peek in the window. She put on her glasses and saw Martha and Roman talking with the guard. In the middle of the room was a desk and behind it a bookcase that held a set of encyclopedias. *The same one the Fieldings gave me! Roman had told me the truth at the lake. What else would those books be for if not for studying?* Adimu thought, trying to convince herself of something she severely doubted. Suddenly, Martha turned to the window, and Adimu ducked down and snuck away. Her heart pounded in her chest.

She checked to make sure she was not being followed and kept close to the perimeter wall. She stopped for a moment, thinking she could hear her grandmother's voice in the darkness of their hut.

"At the end of the ocean there was a great tree..."

It was one of the fables Nkamba used to tell her at bedtime, the story of the monkey and the shark, and Adimu remembered that the shark tried to trick the monkey to eat her. In the end, the monkey was the smarter of the two because she came up with a way to convince the shark to let her go.

Though Adimu realized the only way out of that place was through the metal gate, she wondered if she'd be risking her life if she attempted to escape through it. Instead, like the monkey, she could devise a ploy to escape. Her attention was drawn to a lizard that had worked its way through a crack in the wall. She moved slowly toward it to touch its tail.

The lizard was completely still. Just as Adimu was about to catch it, a shadow much bigger than hers projected onto the concrete wall. Roman was there, smiling. He put his hands on her shoulders as if about to hug her. She posed no resistance and closed her eyes, froze, just like she'd done many rainy seasons before when she was hiding with the bags of grain at the mill. Just like the lizard had a few moments before. Her *bibi* was reminding her to use the tricks of nature to let the Spirits help her.

The man's arms held her against his adult body, a pillar on which her future was leaning. She opened her eyes enough to see the soft cotton of his shirt pierced by the sunlight. She could smell the clean fabric, pleasant like flowers in a field.

"It's against the rules to go out. It's for your own good," said Roman with a reassuring voice. "This is only a waiting place. Soon other children will come. Then we can all go together to the community. Don't worry," he added, patting her head.

Adimu clung to the man. If the adults wanted to hurt us, they already would have, she told herself. *Why doubt what he says? His embrace is like Sarah's. And besides, now I have a true friend to consider. Shida is younger, more afraid and less experienced than I am. She needs my help.*

THE ISLANDERS EXTENDED their search for Adimu beyond the confines of Ukerewe. Residents of Mwanza and other towns along the coast were contacted to find out if they knew of her whereabouts. Few people were convinced that the *zeru zeru* used its supernatural powers to vanish. If it had been able to do so, it would have done it a long time before. Several sailors who worked on the Ukerewe ferry confirmed the presence of an *embulamaro* going to Mwanza.

"It was traveling with a white man and a Tanzanian woman; the *mzungu* paid for the tickets," confirmed the deckhand.

The theory that it was Mr. Fielding was eliminated immediately: The sailors knew him well and swore it was not him. "A foreigner, I said," explained the captain of the boat, raising his voice to dispel any doubt.

At first the most probable supposition was that the two adults were part of an association for the protection of albinos, though the authorities stated that the possibility of a kidnapping could not be excluded. Word was that a foreign white man ran the most active organization in the trafficking of *zeru zerus*.

The Ukerewe police contacted the seven protected communities in the country. None of them had Adimu among their residents. "The associations for the protection of Africans with albinism work in coordination with the families," said the director of the community in Tanga to the commander of the local police station. With that information added to the mix, kidnapping seemed the most likely explanation for Adimu's disappearance. Someone had sold the *zeru zeru*. The inhabitants of Ukerewe began to wonder who among them was the traitor. Suspicion spread like an oil spill in the sea, suffocating friendship and solidarity with its stench and sticky consistency.

After hearing all of this, Kondo and Sefu knocked on the same door—Zuberi's. Each wanted to know where Adimu had gone. Zuberi carried out the same magic ritual for each man, the one that matched up with requests of this type. He slit an adult cock's throat, soaked a rough piece of fabric with its blood, and then sprinkled it with a powder that contained lion teeth and sheep teeth, cat claws, and a bat paw. Sefu was informed his daughter's kidnapping was tied to someone who had changed his mind about Adimu. To Kondo, Zuberi said money was the motive, and a man was earning a heap of it from the disappearance.

Sefu began to harbor doubts about Kondo. Kidnapping the *embulamaro* would have been convenient for the village chief. That way he wouldn't have to pay the agreed upon price, nor would Adimu enter his home and ruin his reputation.

In turn, Kondo suspected Sefu. He imagined he received a better offer for his *zeru zeru* from someone in another village. The *zeru zeru* had been seen with a white man, and Zuberi had spoken of a large sum of money. There had to be a politician involved or a very, very rich *mzungu*.

The inhabitants of Ukerewe chimed in with their opinions about the kidnapper.

"The white shadow is something that belonged to the father, and he could do with it as he wants," said an old farmer as he swept the dirt in front of his wares at the market.

"If it was that shaman, his actions will not be forgiven," said another villager, shaking his hands at the sky.

"How could Zuberi take advantage of our good faith and speculate on our misfortunes?" wondered a cassava farmer, his voice full of resentment.

"Sefu and Zuberi must be earning money behind our backs," grumbled a peanut seller as he toasted nuts over a metal drum.

A group of fishermen held the suspicion that Adimu was in the hands of the most desperate of their trade. In an attempt to collect proof to support their hypothesis, three of them went in the night to check among the nets for amulets made from the remains of an *isope*. They did not find anything to confirm their hunch.

Since the day Adimu disappeared, there was not a single family in the village of Murutanga or the entire island of Ukerewe who, during the evening meal, did not discuss what had happened. People spoke of nothing else. Bad feelings and gossip passed from one mouth to another, poisoning everyone's thoughts.

47.

Mr. Fielding scanned his office at the mine that was producing gold. Within those four walls, his word was law; there, he was all-powerful. It was forbidden for anyone to enter his room unless he was present or they had his permission. The office could be cleaned only in Jackob's or the secretary's presence. The objects that best represented him decorated it. There were testimonials to his financial successes and some items with sentimental value, such as his desk made out of a door that came from South Africa and dated back to the time his great-grandfather had immigrated. It was a thick piece of ebony, carved with an abundance of detail, and was protected by a piece of glass that was polished every day until it shined like a mirror. The wooden panel rested on four taxidermic elephant legs, amputated at knee-level, belonging to a pachyderm shot by his father on one of his many hunting expeditions. The tusks of the last elephant he had killed shortly before hunting was banned in the new state of Zimbabwe decorated the armrests of the desk chair. Towering behind his chair was a photograph of Charles with President de Klerk. The walls held mementos of some of the most significant events in Charles's life—his wedding, the day he received his degree, and his framed diploma from Oxford. Behind his wedding photo, in a frame larger than the others, was a small safe that contained cash, documents, and a .38 caliber pistol.

Charles was on the telephone with a real estate agency in Dar es Salaam, negotiating the sale of his house on Ukerewe. The man on the other end of the line was driving him to lose his patience by insisting on a ridiculous price for a home worthy of a king. In frustration, Charles snapped a pencil in two.

Indeed, the day had begun badly and seemed to be getting worse. Along the road to the mine, he had seen his first and last name written in red paint on a wall, followed by advice that he go fuck himself. It was written in English, which meant the author had wanted to be certain that Charles received the message.

As soon as he had reached the office, Charles gave instructions for the grounds janitor to scrub off the writing on the wall. All the muscles of Charles's face were tight. His chin was contracted and pulled downward as he closed the door to his inner office. He had seen tangible proof of how his reputation had worsened. No longer was he the people's savior, an angel fallen from the sky. He was viewed as an imposter. He was several months behind in paying his employees' salaries and was forced to lay off workers.

He was still on the telephone with the real estate agent when he heard a loud commotion and shouting from the outer office. Among the voices was his secretary's. He put a hand in his pocket to find the key to the safe and with the other he held the phone receiver. All at once, as if pushed by an ocean wave, his office door swung open. The hinges heaved, and a horde poured into the room.

Charles dropped the receiver, petrified. Twenty, thirty, forty people pressed up against him, trampling his precious carpets, pressing their palms onto the immaculate glass of his desk. For ten long seconds, Charles was unable to understand who the mendicants invading his inner sanctum were. He finally recognized several faces and realized they were his employees, miners with their wives and children who had come to demand their salaries. In Swahili, in English, in a multitude of local dialects, each one shouted the same thing: "Pay us! Master, where is our money?"

The women, many of them with babies in slings on their backs, others with newborns at their breasts, shouted more than the men and waved their arms. Some of the bigger children laughed with excitement, others held their fathers' hands and were silent, staring at Mr. Fielding with a fearful expression. One child did not take his eyes off Charles's face, and when their eyes met, it was the adult who lowered his head. In those young pupils that were black as the wings of a crow, Charles saw many questions that he did not know how to answer, questions he didn't want to ask himself.

Very few of the miners had taken off their hardhats. No longer did their boss deserve respect. Too many of them had been fired, underpaid, or didn't have a shilling to buy flour. "We don't belong to you anymore," one older man said.

Charles was sweating and his breath came out in short gasps. With relief, he recognized Jackob's face as he pushed his way through the crowd, encouraging everyone to calm down. Reassured, Charles felt a flash of hilarity. Before him was a jumble of unsightly, colorful people set in the baroque frame of his priceless designer pieces. "Open the window," he whispered to Jackob when his assistant got near enough. The sense of hilarity passed, and what remained was crushing claustrophobia. He loosened his tie and unfastened the first button of his shirt.

Jackob acted as mediator for half an hour. One of the miners, certainly the most courageous, threatened to attack the mine, to occupy it, and confiscate whatever they could extract. "This is our land, not yours!" he shouted at the white man.

With the help of two men from security, Jackob was able to placate the crowd and usher them out. Charles, left alone in his office, was overcome by a sense of despair. He had to find a way to stitch up the gash out of which the mob had spilled.

"Charles, you have to pay them," he said to himself aloud. The scourge of being hated prodded him to admit that his employees were worth much more than the arm of a phantom that was about to die of cancer anyway.

LATER THAT DAY, Sarah saw embarrassment scrawled across the faces of Charles and Jackob as soon as she walked into her husband's office. Charles, who was seated at his desk, was startled when he saw her. Jackob clumsily hid the paper he was holding, covering it with a magazine that was on the desk. Their unfinished conversation hung in the room.

"Were you speaking badly about me?" She smiled, closing the door and stopping midway into the room with her hands clasped in front of her. Charles, having recovered from the initial surprise of her visit, smiled back. Sarah, who was wearing a pair of wide-leg trousers and a tight blouse, looked like a teenager.

"Darling, come in!"

"If you prefer, I can come back later," she said, moving toward the desk to glance at the paper Jackob hid.

"Jackob, tell her what we were discussing," Charles said to his assistant.

Jackob, surprised, looked at Charles for confirmation.

Charles nodded. "Please, Sarah dear, sit down."

"This is a list of the protected communities that have *zeru zerus*," said Jackob with hesitation.

Sarah's mind shot out of the starting gate at a gallop. She thought of the ragged, fearful children who lived at the community in Shinyanga. Sadness, poverty, solitude, neglect, ignorance.

Sarah squinted. "*People* with albinism, not *zeru zerus*, Jackob," she said, setting a hand on his forearm.

Jackob bowed his head, recognizing his error.

"Charles, you're not planning to place Adimu there, are you?" Sarah looked at her wrists. She could still feel the guard's forceful grip that left purplish marks on her delicate skin.

Charles, seeing a mask of melancholy blanketing her face, got up from his chair, went around the desk, and hugged her from behind. As he did, his eye caught sight of a small handprint on the glass tabletop, a remnant the cleaning attendant had missed when he disinfected and polished the furniture. Charles thought of the boy who had stared at him, the one who seemed to be made of stone.

Sarah sighed deeply, and Charles turned to look into her soft eyes. "Do you want to help Adimu?" asked Sarah, who stood, lifting herself onto her toes to nuzzle her face between her husband's neck and shoulder.

"I already am."

"If you really want to help, send her somewhere better than a protected community."

Charles gently pulled away from his wife while resting his hands on her upper arms. "Adimu has disappeared," he said. "It seems she was last seen in the company of a white man. I was asking Jackob to contact the communities to find out if she'd been spotted. The police have already called them but without success. I prefer to check myself."

Charles had hoped the little girl would swiftly and safely be returned to her small mud hut and his wife would never need to find out about her disappearance.

Sarah gasped and tried to free herself from her husband's grip, but Charles didn't let go. He pulled her into an embrace. Her face froze with the exception of her quivering lips.

How many unpleasant emotions can arise in a single day? Charles asked himself.

That morning, before the employees' incursion, the police had been at the entrance to the mine. The two officers knew who he was. "Excuse me, Mr. Fielding?" one of the policemen asked.

"I know Mr. Fielding," responded Charles. "He's here, but he's not here. How's that for an answer?"

The policemen understood that between the lines Charles was saying, conclude your business rapidly and with respect and discretion.

Better to perform their duty close to home than count banana trees and listen to Kalashnikov bullets whizzing through the air on the border of the Congo. Everyone in Mwanza knew the white man in the light suit was one of the most powerful in the country, and they had heard about the stupid mistake their colleagues in Shinyanga had recently made.

"We will disturb you only for a moment, sir," the man said mildly. His partner nodded. "Do you know an albino girl named Adimu who lives on Ukerewe? Have you seen her recently?"

"What's happened to her?" asked Charles.

"She's been missing for three days, sir," the policeman informed him. "She was last seen with a white man and a Tanzanian woman. We are from the Mwanza district headquarters, the missing persons and homicide division."

"I know the girl. Unfortunately, I haven't seen her since she's been reported missing," Charles responded.

The agents thanked him and left quickly. Charles focused on his breathing. The muscles in his stomach were tight as a fist. *I'm looking for an albino too*, he said to himself. *God, I hope I didn't give anything away. What if this is the police's way to keep an eye on me?*

"Is it true that Adimu has disappeared from the island?" Charles asked Jackob right after the employee uprising.

"Yes, sir, into thin air."

"Why didn't you inform me of it?"

"Because…well…" Jackob was trying to come up with a good excuse. "I thought it was just temporary."

Charles went to his desk and sat down. "The visit by the police has got me concerned. This isn't the moment to make waves. Wait a few days, and then tell Zuberi to start the hunt again for a terminally-ill albino."

Jackob was pleased with himself. He had made the right decision about not going to Zuberi. He knew his employer well.

48.

"I'm bored," said Adimu.

"Me too," said Shida tugging on a thread at the hem of her dress.

They had been told to stay inside the dormitory from sunset until early afternoon. "It's for your own safety," Roman and Martha had said. They were allowed to spend a few hours outside in the afternoon, in the presence of the two adults and the guard, so long as they stayed within the walls.

The girls entertained themselves by running after the hens or, when it was too hot, walking hand in hand in the shade along the perimeter wall. The tickling game was Adimu's favorite way to pass the time with her new friend. They touched and explored each other with the curiosity of two small animals that had been kept in isolation. It was fun to roll on the ground, laughing without fear of being rejected or blamed.

"Nothing can ever come between us," promised Shida.

"Nothing, I…I promise," stuttered Adimu, overcome by a sudden wave of emotion.

At least once a day they asked Martha and Roman to confirm that they were going to be placed in the same community, and their affirmative reply guaranteed the girls the necessary dose of daily happiness. Adimu often thought about Charles and Sarah and how much she wanted to see them before she was moved to her new residence. Her request for a meeting with the Fieldings was ignored, and it both demoralized her and added to her increasing sense of anxiety.

One afternoon while Shida was resting, Adimu asked Roman if he had a book she could read. He returned shortly with a thick volume that had many pictures in it. Adimu put on her glasses and began to turn the pages. It was a beautiful book, written in large letters and with magnificent color illustrations. Overcome by the array of stories, she opened to a random page and began to read. After more than an hour, she was sitting in the same position and hadn't noticed Shida had awakened and was looking at her with interest.

"What are you doing?" she asked with a still-sleepy voice.

"I'm reading," replied Adimu, turning a page.

"You look funny with glasses!" Shida laughed. "Do you always have to wear them when you have a book?"

"Yes, whenever I read," she replied with maturity. "Otherwise my eyes hurt."

"What are you reading?" Shida sat down next to Adimu.

"It's a beautiful story about a man who has three children. But his wife dies, and they go to live in the forest."

"And then what happens?"

"He builds a house in a tree for himself and his children. The only way in or out of the house is with a rope ladder. Every day, before he goes to work, he tells his children not to let anyone climb the ladder because witches inhabit the forest. One of his children asks how they can be sure it's him when he asks for the ladder."

"And what does the father say?"

"He says that if they hear someone call out 'Kithengee, Kithengee' they must lower the ladder and let him climb up. One day, however, a witch, who had been watching them for many evenings and heard the password, imitated the voice of their father and kidnapped the children."

Adimu paused to show Shida the illustration. "See?" she said, pointing to the page. "This is the tree, and there is the house."

"What happened to the children?" asked Shida, worried.

"Their father saved them. With the help of the village shaman, he found the witch's hiding place and killed her and freed his children."

Reading the book had raised a doubt that Adimu had never completely put to rest. Could Martha and Roman be imposters, just like the witch in the story?

"We're lucky like the three children," said Shida, distracting Adimu from her thoughts. "We have a big room all for ourselves. We're safe, and soon we'll be in school with many other children who are just like us." She turned the pages of the book, looking for other pictures.

Adimu did not reply. She understood that it was useless, if not cruel, to alarm her friend. She recalled things Shida had told her—about how she'd always slept next to her grandparents, how in the winter, they prepared her sleeping mat near the fire and let her sleep with a goat to keep her warm. Adimu realized Shida had lived without the fear, shame, or the sense of having been abandoned that Adimu had felt since birth.

Now Adimu understood why Nkamba had never praised her too much or had taken her side often. Her *bibi* had wanted her to be clever and independent, to shy away from strangers, and not to count on her clan for her survival. Shida, instead, was naïve and sweet. *I need to protect her now that she doesn't have her grandparents,* Adimu told herself.

"Don't you think that Roman and Martha sometimes tell lies?" Adimu asked.

"My grandparents never told lies."

Adimu decided not to insist. "Do you want to take a walk outside?"

"They told us to stay here," replied Shida, unable to imagine disobeying an adult.

Adimu went to a window. *Better to avoid the door as the adults might be watching it.* She dragged one of the rusty bed frames under the window and climbed onto it so she could reach the handle. It squeaked as she pulled it open.

Shida watched her friend's movements with attention. "Where are you going?"

From the windowsill, Adimu replied, "Outside."

"Wait! Stay here with me!" Shida begged.

"I'll be right back." She jumped down.

Adimu's first thought was to discover where the adults were. She snuck past the office. Through the window, she caught sight of two men and Martha. They were talking and gesturing excitedly. She moved closer to the window, ready to flatten herself against the wall. She had spied on her peers in the village for years and knew how not to be seen.

Roman was sweating, and he had his hands in the pockets of his jacket. He pulled out something flimsy and rectangular and used it to fan his face. Adimu put on her glasses so she could see better. What she saw paralyzed her. The muscles in her face sagged. They were imposters! *Even white people behave dishonestly!* Roman was waving a blue envelope in front of his face, the letter he was supposed to have sent to the Fieldings.

Martha looked at him, lifting her eyebrows. Deep lines formed across her forehead. "I thought you'd thrown that away. Why have you kept it?" she asked.

He hesitated. "As a reminder of just how gullible children are," he said with a mocking smile on his lips. He looked at the envelope and put it back in his pocket.

Adimu moved closer to the wall and heard the man next to Roman say, "We'll do it when the moon is full. We'll start with the girl from Ukerewe. We'll take her into the forest, like the other times."

Adimu recoiled from the window with such force that she fell backward and onto the ground. Her legs extended out in front of her, and she stared at her feet. Her slip-on sandals flew up in the air and landed by her hand. She turned to the gate, her heart beating as loud as rain on a sheet-metal roof. She ran as fast as she could toward it. The iron gate was heavy, and it took all her strength, plus the strength lent to her by her *bibi,* to push it open and run away. Her body sprung forward like a cat's. She paid no attention to the sharp rocks under her bare feet.

Once in the forest, she kept running. And running. And running. She gripped Shida's hand and murmured encouraging words through her choppy breath. She ran, she flew, and she saw the lush branches that would protect them from the shark, like in Nkamba's story. She stopped and gazed up at the vegetation of a tree in front of them. The branches were unreachable. A moment before, the plants had been reassuring. Now they seemed to twist and tangle, and she feared they would trap them in their foliage. She heard what sounded like an animal, a rustling that was moving closer. She squeezed Shida's hand and turned to look at her friend. But Adimu's hand was not clasping Shida's; Adimu's was a tightly closed fist. She was alone.

Adimu returned to her senses. She had run off, abandoning her best friend. She had to go back to bring Shida with her, but if Martha and Roman found out that she escaped, she knew they'd never let her out of their sight. *Oh, Bibi, what should I do?*

She rested on the roots of a tree to catch her breath as she recalled what had happened the day before. She and Shida had been in the courtyard eating. When Adimu had been distracted, the guard dog had devoured the food on her plate. The dog hadn't gotten to Shida's food so Shida offered Adimu hers. *The only other person who would give me the scraps off her plate was Bibi.* How could she leave Shida behind? "'Destiny,' ours will be one and the same, alive or dead," Adimu declared about Shida to her friend the wind.

She could live in a prison so long as she had a person to love, someone who loved her back. Hadn't she been living in a cell built of rays of sunlight until only a few days before? Her jailers had been Prejudice, Superstition, and Ignorance. The time she served was Hate, Contempt, and Estrangement.

She noticed small colorful flowers among the tangled roots. She picked a few. She would pretend to have gone for a walk. She needed to stay calm. It was the only way she'd convince her kidnappers she had no intention of escaping.

An attentive eye spotted Adimu while she was picking violets. He held his gaze on the girl. Akili was hidden and still. He was on patrol. The others were scoping out other areas around this *zeru zeru* hiding place. The young man had considered jumping on and capturing Adimu, but he was afraid. What if the *zeru zeru* put a curse on him? He shifted his weight from one foot to the other, swaying in place, trying to decide what to do. If Thomas found out he had let an opportunity escape, he would kill him on sight. However, if the *isope* vanished, it would end everything. It was wise to wait until one of the others was with him. He would keep his mouth shut. Who would ever know about this lost opportunity? *No one. No one. No one,* he repeated to himself. He was convinced he made the most intelligent decision.

After having collected a sufficient number of violets to justify her absence, Adimu ambled toward the iron gate as though she had been innocently gathering a bouquet. She heard Martha railing against a guard for not having closed the gate with a chain. Adimu felt a tremble radiate out from her knees as she materialized behind the woman.

"It's okay," she said with feigned lightness. "I brought flowers for our room. I didn't go out through the gate; I went through the wall. I can do it, you know," she added, sure to make an impression.

The guard took a step back. Martha dropped her chin and lifted her eyes. Her jaw clenched, like a bull ready to charge.

"Who do you think you're fooling, you stupid girl!" she yelled, slapping Adimu with force.

Roman saw her and jerked Martha's arm before she could strike again. Adimu was silent, her eyes brimming with tears that overflowed and splashed on the ground, and her upper lip lifted and trembled. The man took her by the hand and walked her back to the dormitory.

"You shouldn't leave the compound alone," Roman told her. "I'm going to have to lock the door so you and Shida don't do such a foolish thing again. Martha was terrified that something had happened to you."

Adimu didn't say anything and let Roman take her back to the room where Shida was waiting for her, the book of fables still in her hands. "I'm sorry, I won't go out again," Adimu said to Roman before he closed the door.

Night fell, and as soon as Shida was asleep, Adimu slipped out of bed and climbed onto the windowsill. Through the dirty panes, the sky seemed dusty. She was enchanted by the treetops that were reaching to kiss the moon, which was big and yellow like a ripe peach. It was almost full.

49.

From the day Adimu had disappeared, more and more islanders had attended Sunday Mass. Father Andrew continued to invite the faithful to pray for her return. Her disappearance had served to bring the villagers back under the baobab to seek salvation from Jesus, he thought, alleviating some of his guilt for having sacrificed—yes, *sacrificed*—Adimu.

The inhabitants of Murutanga were consumed with remorse for having permitted the theft of their *zeru zeru* from right under their noses. "Not a theft, a plunder," one of the fishermen had specified. The only hope they'd had to improve their mediocre existence was gone. Really, they felt more treachery than regret. Now another community would have the chance to use Adimu to resolve their problems. If they had known this would happen, they would have already chopped off her limbs.

"The only thing worse than our misfortune is knowing our enemies are profiting from it," said a cassava farmer to the fishermen who were waiting for the wind to pick up.

"Adimu was born on this island, and they've stolen her through trickery."

"It's not right," mumbled a middle-aged man, intent on removing the shells caught in his nets.

"Can you imagine what will happen if the fishermen in Mwanza get hold of the *zeru zeru*?"

"The few fish on this coast will migrate straight into the nets of our neighbors. Thanks to our own stupidity."

YUNIS LAY ON the bed next to her husband, worried about Adimu. When she finally fell asleep, she dreamed of being at the lake with Juma. In the dream, they were both unclothed, pregnant, bathing under the golden light of sunset. Yunis watched as the water rolled off her friend's taut, black rounded belly, under the warm, glowing rays. A sense of peace pervaded her as she thought of her childhood friend. She looked at her own belly and whispered to the creature she felt moving inside her. With cupped hands, she lifted water from the lake and poured it over her breasts and abdomen, feeling it flow toward her groin. She laughed.

She awoke with the sensation of wetness between her legs, and she put her hand where, in her dream, the water had collected. She opened her eyes and leapt from bed at the sight of her dark red blood. She covered the stain with a cloth so her husband would not see it when he awoke, and then she went to wash. The moon was already in the sky, and the night was dark. Yunis shivered in the cool breeze.

She was tired of waiting for Zuberi's longtime promised *zeru zeru*. Plus, she knew Adimu was a real baby, and benefiting from the mutilated breasts and genitals taken from a real woman with albinism repelled her. An aunt of her mother had given her the name of a well-known gynecologist who, once a week, received patients at The Fielding Health Center of Ukerewe.

ONE SUNDAY, FATHER Andrew noticed with surprise that Mrs. Fielding was among the faithful. It was the first time she had come to Mass. He gloated. His mission would get recognition if well-to-do white people began attending his Sunday services. The white woman stood out among his fellow villagers like a poppy at the edge of a field of wheat. The usual congregants didn't take their eyes off her during the Eucharist. Sarah was last in line to receive the consecrated host. When it was her turn, Father Andrew looked into her eyes and smiled, his lips stretched just enough to reveal a thin line of white teeth. He wanted to express to her his appreciation for her support.

Sarah wore a tense expression. Father Andrew held the dish under her chin and the host to her mouth. She kept her lips sealed.

"The body of Christ."

The words seemed to break into pieces against the woman's impervious expression and fall to the ground as dust. Sarah stared at the priest; he looked at her hands. Maybe she wanted to hold the host herself, he wondered. The woman opened her palms and lifted them, showing him a lemon candy. She unwrapped it in front of the shocked priest, put it in her mouth, and returned to her place. At the end of the service, Sarah remained seated and waited for the others to leave. The priest went to her.

"Do you think I offended your God more than you have?" she asked before he could say anything to her. "I had heard people speak highly of you. Instead, I see someone who is poor in feelings and rich in ambitions, like most everyone here," she added, sweeping her arm to indicate the huts in the village as well as the mainland.

Father Andrew's right eyelid began to twitch, and his mouth closed so tight that the skin above his chin puffed out.

"How could you give your consent to the marriage of a child?" Sarah said with a trembling voice. She stood up and walked away, leaving him petrified that she found out.

From the moment, Sarah had heard of Adimu's disappearance, she had been unable to think of anything else and began her firsthand investigation. She had received confidential information from her faithful cook who, for her part, had overheard a conversation between two coworkers at White House. They had spoken of a secret—how Father Andrew had given his consent to the preteen's marriage.

A dark sense of guilt, which grew greater as each day passed, hounded Sarah. Anger and frustration were driving her crazy and, on that Sunday morning, she allowed herself the small satisfaction of morally slapping one of the people she held responsible for having sealed Adimu's fate.

Above all, she was angry with herself. She could have done more for Adimu if she had been braver and more independent of Charles.

Father Andrew tried to rationalize his sin. He asked himself how a white woman could possibly know what was best for his parish. The marriage might have been a small step forward for Adimu, and, in any case, she had disappeared before the exchange with Kondo had taken place. It was useless to torment himself over the opinion of some privileged white woman. *What does she understand?* The important thing was the number of people who attended Mass. Each Sunday more worshippers were praying under the baobab than the week before. His words rang in the souls of his brothers and sisters more strongly than the church bells in the town of Mwanza. His preaching directed his people on their path toward the Lord. What more could he want? Only one thing: Adimu's return.

CHARLES HAD TO be sure that the healer was not involved in the girl's kidnapping—not even indirectly. The visit by the Mwanza police had upset him.

"Don't concern yourself, Mr. Fielding," said Jackob, when his boss approached him. "The police have spoken with everyone who knows Adimu. However, if it makes you feel better, I will speak with Zuberi."

But Jackob didn't. It was not necessary, he assured himself more than once. They were already in agreement about finding a *nobody*, possibly a terminally ill one. Possibly...though not necessarily. Moreover, Jackob was certain the witch doctor wasn't involved in Adimu's disappearance. It was prohibited to decide the fate of a member of the community without authorization from the head of the village and the clan elders—Zuberi wouldn't have taken her without Kondo's consent.

A few hours after the conversation with his employer, Jackob called Charles.

"Sir, you have nothing to worry about. I contacted Zuberi as you requested," Jackob lied. "And, as I thought, he had nothing to do with Adimu's abduction. In fact, I have heard from the director of the protected community in Musoma that she is a guest there. For now, this fact must remain confidential as it seems there was a group of hunters following her, and we wouldn't want to tip them off about her whereabouts."

"Really? Oh, what a relief!" Charles said.

When Jackob hung up, he stared at the telephone. The lie was already weighing on him. The stakes were too high, and he could not afford to make a mistake, nor could he allow Mr. Fielding to be overcome by emotions and lose sight of his interests.

50.

"I'm tired of staying inside," whined Shida.

"I told you, Martha and Roman want to protect us," Adimu replied. "Do you want me to read you a story from our book?" She opened the volume, turning the pages to find a new one.

"No." Shida sighed as she lay down on the mattress where her friend was sitting.

Before the sun set, the moon had become visible, pale, as though it were a distant cloud, full and round like a giant egg. That night, the lock on the dormitory door clicked, and it swung open with a squeak. Adimu had been waiting for them to come for her, watching as the moon, each night, grew a little more swollen. Shida had fallen asleep in her arms, and she awoke when that human contact ceased.

"Shida, dear, we need Adimu's help," cooed Martha. "She will be back before you know it."

The sky had darkened, and the moon was hidden behind the mountains. The room was scarcely lit and seemed haunted. Shida whimpered. Then she began to cry in earnest. She gripped her friend's arms and dug in her heels to keep them from taking Adimu. The guard pushed her, and she hit her head against the wall.

A cloudburst of tears ran down Shida's face; her body froze in fear. When Shida heard the lock turn, only then did she take action. She climbed onto the windowsill and out into the night. Shida ran as fast as she could across the courtyard. She tripped, fell, and got back up. There were footsteps nearby, and she saw the arc of light from a flashlight. Her friend's blond hair glowed in the dimness. Shida rushed to her and clung as tight as she could, yelling and crying as she never before had.

"Please, don't go! I want to stay with you!" she sputtered through her tears.

The guard lost patience. He grabbed Shida's arm and, as he dragged her into the office, she heard Adimu repeat, "I'll be back soon, I'll be back soon." The guard opened a metal cupboard. He tied Shida's wrists with a rope and brought the guard dog near. There was a dish with leftovers from dinner on the floor, and he pushed Shida's hands into the mush. She turned her head, and squeezed her eyes shut. The food was damp and slimy, and he wouldn't let her pull away. The animal's tongue began to lick her fingers.

"See how much the dog likes you?" the guard sneered. "Do you see? Answer me!"

Shida barely nodded, looking at the door. She imagined her grandfather barging into the room to free her. The guard pushed her into the cupboard and locked it.

"If you try to escape from the cabinet, the dog will be waiting for you," he hissed before stomping from the room.

Outside, the adults and Adimu started past the gate and toward the forest, guided by the beam of the flashlight and the full moon that had emerged from behind the trees. Adimu's mind was cluttered with thoughts of Shida, of Nkamba, of Charles and Sarah. She begged Martha, Roman, and the guard not to hurt Shida.

Roman told Adimu that she and Shida would be unharmed. Adimu wanted to believe him. She remembered that any creature touched by God could live or die. Jesus was the one who decided, that was what Father Andrew said during Mass. Well, if He decided that either her new sister or she would die, then He was a killer, she thought.

Adimu would have known they were entering the forest even if she had been blindfolded. The damp, penetrating scent of the dense vegetation reminded her of secret hiding places, muffled sounds, putrefaction, birth, and death. A violent rustling alarmed the adults. The guard gripped his machete. "It's probably an animal."

"Where do you think you're going?" said a voice in the dark.

Roman, Martha, and the guard looked around. From the thick of the forest, where the moonbeams were weak, they saw five young men, three of them brandishing machetes.

Ramadani, who was at the rear, recognized Adimu. The initial surprise gave way to euphoria.

"Who are you?" asked the white man.

Ramadani understood that the foreigner was not afraid.

"Who are *you* to ask questions, *mzungu*?" replied Thomas.

"Let us pass," said Roman, without betraying the slightest emotion.

The five headhunters surrounded the three adults and child. Amani drummed his fingers on the blade of his machete.

"Which of you is the leader?" asked Roman, facing Aki. "You?" he tried, offering a cigarette from the pack he'd pulled out of his shirt pocket.

Aki gave a knowing glance to Thomas. Roman followed his eyes and offered Thomas the pack. "I think *you* are."

Thomas looked at him with disdain. "This is no place for you, *mzungu*. You think you can come here and order us around?" His feet were solidly planted on the bare dirt.

"I'll pay you if you let us pass."

Ramadani stepped forward. "The typical white man. He talks to us like he's in a film. He comes to Africa to take what he wants...You think poor banana-eating black men will accept your leftovers," he said in one breath, hoping to win Thomas's approval. He was fearful that the stranger's offer might be accepted.

Adimu lifted her head. She recognized the voice.

Ramadani scowled at Adimu so she wouldn't let on that she recognized him.

She fixed her eyes at her captor's feet.

"As I said, we're ready to pay. Just name your price," gambled Roman. He felt trickles of sweat along his hairline and lifted his hand slowly to rub them off.

Thomas examined Roman, looking him up and down, and in his white face he saw the faces of the mercenaries who he had once considered divine. His memory of when he'd seen a *mzungu* up-close for the first time visited him. On that day in the forest, the commander was kneeling, wrists tied, head bowed to the ground.

He hadn't been able to pull the trigger. Thomas's commander had been violent, sadistic, but he'd also been like a parent. Thomas had let the gun fall from his hand and lowered his head. The *mzungu* had kicked the side of the boy's face and picked the weapon up off the ground. Slumped forward, swallowing the blood that poured from his lips and gums, Thomas had watched as the man shot three bullets into his commander. He continued to swallow blood and then vomited.

Roman smiled at Thomas, invited him to the compound where he keeps his *zeru zerus*, suggested they might share a meal of fish, that they would come to an agreement since both men had business in those parts.

Thomas, lost in his thoughts, looked at the white man. "What part of a fish stinks?" growled Thomas.

Roman continued to offer the young man incentives as he reached for his wallet.

Thomas's index finger stung. All those years ago, his right hand had been held down on the tree stump and, after the quick chop of the machete, not a sound had escaped from the boy's gaping mouth, nor did a tear slip from his bulging eyes. He had balled his hand into a fist and forced himself to hold in every emotion and sound that was fighting to pour out with his blood. His commander would have been proud of him, if he had been alive. He was proud of himself for not having given into the *mzungu's* intimidation.

"From now on you'll have a good reason not to pull the trigger," the white man had cackled.

"Did you hear what I said?" insisted Roman. "We'll pay you well for our passage through your territory."

The man's voice seemed to have traveled from far away. Thomas stared at him. For an instant, Thomas saw another pair of irises, pale blue. Ice.

"Take the *embulamaro*," Thomas said to Ramadani, ignoring Roman's words. "Do whatever you have to with it before we give it to the boss. We'll handle these three." He flexed his fingers around the butt of his gun and stepped closer to the white man. "The *zeru zeru* is from our land and belongs to our people. Not to whites, not even to black traitors," he concluded, eyeing Martha and the guard.

Ramadani took Adimu by the arm and pulled her toward him.

"Here in front of everybody, I can't. I'm going over there," he said, pointing into the vegetation.

Thomas watched as his comrade tugged at the *zeru zeru.* He noticed she moved in an odd way, as if her legs were imprisoned in blocks of dried mud. She tripped, trying to keep up with Ramadani.

"What are you going to do?" screamed Martha at Thomas.

"Did I give you permission to speak?" he hissed. "I think we'll have some fun with *you* while we're waiting."

The guard tried to run, taking advantage of the moment's distraction, but Amani caught him before he got away. "What do you want me to do with this one?" he asked Thomas with a tilt of his head.

"He can start by digging a hole."

The revenge that Thomas had hoped for—and had fantasized about often—occurred. The white man fell to his knees and begged for mercy. The group leader had not a single drop of pity in his heart. Pleased, but at the same time irritated, he grabbed Roman and pulled him toward a large tree, pointing the gun in his face. He cocked it. Roman flinched. Thomas thought he saw the pale blue irises in the dark and shoved his gun into his belt. He had more interesting plans in mind. "Roll up your sleeve."

The white man's hands were shaking.

Thomas took his machete in his right hand and put his black arm next to Roman's white one. "This is the difference between me and you." Then Thomas lifted Roman's chin with his left hand. "Look at me, *mzungu*." In one effortless jerk, Roman crumpled to the ground, his jugular sliced clean. Thomas watched with satisfaction as the man contorted in agony, his hands on his neck. "Return the blood you have stolen," he said, and he cleaned the blade of the machete on the white man's shirt as he looked at his comrades.

"Bury the black traitor, alive. And cut up the *mzungu*. Hide his head in a tree so the police can't find it. And bury the other pieces so we can claim them later. We'll pass them off as *zeru zeru*. Let's first have some fun with this slut."

RAMADANI BROUGHT ADIMU to a small clearing that was isolated from view by thick vegetation.

The girl looked at him passively. When she had first recognized his voice, she thought she and Shida were safe. Kondo's son was there in the forest to take her back to the village and marry her. Now she believed she had misunderstood. He'd come to kill her.

Before speaking, Ramadani listened to the far-off voices to be certain the others were busy. "Look at me, Adimu." Ramadani said it a second time because her eyes were tightly shut. When she finally opened them, she saw Ramadani's friendly expression.

"Listen to me carefully," he whispered. "I know it's not true. I'll die of AIDS."

Adimu's eyebrows lifted high onto her forehead.

"Run. Run as fast as you can in that direction," he said, pointing. "Don't look back, don't stop for any reason. Run as far as you can."

She did not move. She looked at the face of the man who was to be her husband. *What cruelty is he planning?* she wondered. Ramadani grasped her shoulders and pulled her close. Adimu held her breath, terrified he would force himself on her.

Then he hugged her. "Run away, Adimu, escape," he whispered with his arms wrapped around her narrow shoulders.

The light fabric of her dress was damp where Ramadani had leaned his face against her. *Maybe it isn't a trick, maybe he really is letting me get away*. She sighed. She knew they'd find her sooner or later, if not those men, others. *What difference does it make? I'll die at their hand or someone else's.*

She began to sob. "Where should I go? How can I get away? I'm not normal. I'm sick, a *zeru zeru*, an *embulamaro*. When I die, I'll disappear like a ghost. I might as well get it over with. I'm tired of always running." She paused. "I ran away from you, from our marriage," she added softly, certain that her confession would make him angry.

Ramadani squeezed her shoulders. "I'm condemned to death too. I have an incurable disease. Zuberi says that I have to have relations with a *nobody* in order to get better. That's why I'm here with these thugs. The stories our people tell about *zeru zerus* are myths. You have a different skin color, that's all. I learned about it at school in Mwanza."

Adimu looked at the ground. *It's just another trap*, a voice inside her said.

"Please Adimu, you have to believe me!" Ramadani shook her. "I would have helped any albino escape. Not just you." Ramadani thought of Josephat. "I obeyed my father and joined the headhunters so I could save whoever they were after. I would never hurt an animal so how could I hurt a person?"

Adimu shifted her eyes from his feet to his chest.

"What about the numbers 5-7-1-1-5-3?"

How does he know the first four numbers of the telephone number—and the ones that got erased? she asked herself. She blinked several times.

"I was the one who slipped the paper with the telephone number through the peephole of your hut. To help you get to Tanga, to a real community. There's nothing wrong with you, Adimu, you're albino!"

"What do you mean?"

"You're black, but you have white skin."

"Why?"

"I only know you're not a phantom like people say. So now, please, run away. Go on or they'll kill me too! We'll meet again on Ukerewe, as friends, not as husband and wife. Now go! There's a village in that direction." He pushed her.

"I have to go back...what about my friend?" Her doubts about who and what she was had vanished. Not even Nkamba had told her she was normal. Nkamba's love for her had never succeeded in transmitting the confidence Ramadani had given her in just a few minutes. *I can be a person like everyone else,* she told herself.

"Don't worry about your friend, save yourself!" he insisted, handing her his flashlight.

Adimu turned off the flashlight and snuck into the dark forest. She hid among a mass of branches and roots that reached into the soft, fragrant earth. She covered her arms and face with dirt to hide her color. Then she ran, looking straight ahead, in the direction Ramadani had indicated. She wouldn't, though, run away without Shida.

Ramadani remained in the spot where he spoke with Adimu, letting as much time pass as possible. He undid his pants and let them slide down his thighs. He put the handcuffs he'd brought with him from Ukerewe around his wrists.

"Ramadani? Have you done it?" shouted Thomas from a distance.

He didn't respond.

"Hey, if you still want more, we've got this bitch here," continued Thomas, laughing.

Still no response.

Thomas and Aki found Ramadani in the clearing. He looked confused, his gaze soft, his pants like a pool of water around his ankles.

"What happened? Where's the *zeru zeru*?" asked Thomas, looking at the young man's wrists.

"I dropped my pants and she vanished," he mumbled. "I tried to shout, but she took my voice, and my hands...She went that way." He gestured with his cuffed wrists, opposite from where Adimu had really gone.

"If she vanished, how do you know she went that way?"

"She started to run and then disappeared into thin air," said Ramadani with a sustained blank look on his face.

"Damn!" said Thomas. *It's useless getting upset*, he thought after a moment. *Next time we'll do better. At least I got my revenge on the* mzungu. "Now we know, for sure, a *zeru zeru* can vanish. The next one we find, we'll lock up!"

51.

Adimu waited until she was sure the hunters were long gone before she ran back to the compound.

As she approached it, the guard dog was growling and baying. The iron gate was closed, though not latched. When she opened it, the dog took off and was swallowed up by the forest.

Adimu rushed to the dormitory to fetch her best friend. "Shida! Shida!" she called out as she searched frantically under the beds and in the bathrooms. No one was there.

When Adimu reached Roman's office, she forced open the door, crying out her friend's name. Shida's muffled reply came from inside the metal cupboard.

"Shida, I've come back!" Adimu scanned the room for a heavy object to break the cupboard lock. She saw a large terracotta vase sitting on a table. She picked it up. It was heavier than she would have thought, but what she saw underneath it surprised her even more than its weight. She didn't allow herself to be distracted by the unlikely discovery. She threw the vase at the lock with all her strength. The fired clay broke into pieces that scattered over the floor, and the lock gave way as well. Adimu helped Shida out of the cupboard, and they embraced. Words were unnecessary.

Before they escaped, Adimu needed to get a better look at the book under the vase. It was the first volume of the encyclopedia, the same one she'd received from Charles. The book was stained yellow and warped from moisture. She opened it quickly, looking for the pages that were missing from her own copy. She tore them out and stuffed them in her left pocket. Her right pocket held her glasses and her photo with the Fieldings. The small sum of money she had inherited from her grandmother was still hidden in her underwear. *I have everything we need*, she thought.

THE GIRLS WALKED hand in hand through the forest, hidden in the darkness, a flood of moonlight amid the teardrops of stars. All night, the girls walked in the cool, damp air.

It was shortly before dawn when they found an asphalt road.

"I'm tired," were the first words Shida said.

"I know, Shida, so am I. But the hunters are looking for us. We can't stop yet. It can't be too much farther to the village."

They walked close to the vegetation, close to one another. By the time the sun climbed into the sky, they reached an intersection in which two road signs were posted: one pointed to Mwanza, the other to Dar es Salaam.

They girls looked quizzically at their choices.

"Where do you want to go?" asked Adimu.

"Wherever you want. But I need to rest. Please?" said Shida, her shoulders sagging as she spoke. Adimu could see her friend's exhaustion. Round pouches had formed under Shida's eyes, which were rheumy and unfocused. Adimu's feet, legs, and head all hurt. In the previous weeks, in "prison," the girls had hardly any exercise, and now they were driving their bodies to save them.

They hid among some prickly bushes, and Shida took off her shoes. "Just for a few minutes. I promise I'll get up when you tell me to." As soon as her limbs touched the soft earth, she fell into a deep sleep, and Adimu, mercifully, let her rest. Adimu wanted to close her eyes as well, but if she fell asleep, too, she knew it could cost them dearly.

She needed to decide where they would go, and in a hurry. The less time spent on the road the better. She thought about Roman and Martha and wondered what had come of them. She imagined they had met their destiny. Adimu willed her inner strength to propel her forward so she would one day forge the destiny that Nkamba wanted for her. She took her photograph out of her pocket. How she wished Charles and Sarah were her parents! However, they weren't, and she could not ask them to take care of her and love her forever and ever, as she wanted more than anything in the world. It was one thing to stop by for a visit on her way to the community, and it was another to show up to stay for good. What if they didn't want her? She had Shida with her too.

She thought about the two road signs, wondering which was the safest direction to take. She knew the thugs with Ramadani weren't the only men who hunted albinos. The conversation she had overheard between her grandmother and the white doctor many years before reverberated in her memory. The woman had mentioned Dar es Salaam. She had said that there, children like her—albino children—lived like normal people. She and Shida needed to go to the capital[24]. Her heart, though, continued pushing for Mwanza in hopes of finding the Fieldings. In the heat of her emotional wrenching between heart and mind, Adimu yielded to fatigue.

When the sun was directly overhead, the girls were awakened by a flock of goats intent on grazing on the bushes in which they were hiding. An elderly shepherd was watching them.

"I'm hungry," whispered Shida. Adimu was hungry, too, but had no idea of where to find food. More importantly, though, Adimu was afraid the shepherd might hurt them or, more likely, sell them to someone who would.

[24] The capital of Tanzania is Dodoma, not Dar es Salaam.

52.

Yunis had to go into the examining room, alone, with the doctor and his nurse. She wanted to cry. She imagined what the exams might consist of and what questions the doctor might ask. She felt her neck and face grow warm. The nurse led her behind a light blue screen and asked her to undress. In exchange for her traditional red and yellow cotton garb with a floral pattern stamped on the cloth, the nurse gave Yunis a pale green gown made of nearly transparent fabric that was open behind. She was embarrassed and did not want to come out into the exam room with it on. The nurse tried to encourage her, but Yunis's steps were uncertain, like those of an old woman walking over uneven ground.

With her legs spread open and her feet in cold metal stirrups, the doctor turned on an enormous light and pointed it between her legs. Fat tears began to roll down her cheeks, collecting in the folds of her neck.

The nurse held her hand, and the man put on a latex glove and put it there, where only her husband had seen. He touched her breasts. The doctor squeezed her nipples, asking her if she had secretions. Yunis's mouth opened, though not to speak. How could anything come out of her breasts if she had never nursed a child? she wondered. "No, never," she replied.

He nodded.

She was allowed to dress, and the nurse invited her husband into the room. Yunis knew her husband had never had a medical exam either. The receptionist who had made the appointment explained that he would be seeing a specialist at the same time she was being examined. Yunis wondered if he had gone through a humiliating experience like she had. *Where had their hands touched him?* Yunis kept her eyes down in shame and remained silent.

"From my examination, your reproductive apparatus seems healthy, but we will have to wait for the results of the swab and the blood and urine tests," the gynecologist told them, looking at Yunis. "Your test results, sir, will be ready at the same time."

Yunis and her husband left the clinic. They walked without speaking, each tormented by his and her own thoughts.

A whisper of a breeze revived Yunis. She lifted her head to the sky and breathed. In a few days, she would find out what was wrong with her and if there was treatment for it.

Later that night, after a long and emotionally exhausting day, they got into their bed. Yunis settled herself next to her husband and fell asleep, hugging him from behind.

CHARLES WAS IN his office, defeated by worry. He was unable to summon up the solution to his problems without picturing Adimu. And, yet, he had feelings for the girl; it was useless to deny it. He inserted a small key into the lock on his desk drawer, opened it, and took out a tiny silver box. It contained the strands of Adimu's hair he had collected from the back of her chair the first time she had lunch at White House. He set the sparkling, delicate strands in the palm of his hand and allowed himself to scrutinize them. When he heard a knock at the door, he ignored it. Adimu's hair looked like thin strands of gold. He took a single strand and burned it with a large tabletop lighter. It curled up and disappeared, leaving a smell of singed hair in the room. It was not gold. Rather, it was a hair like that from any human. But he had been well aware of that before he burned it. *Why can't I get this girl out of my head?* he asked himself. *If I help Adimu, I'll make Sarah happy.*

There was a second knock at the door, then a third and with greater insistence. He stood up quickly, but the door opened before he had time to send the visitor away. Two men crossed the threshold. Following on their heels was his secretary, who was trying in vain to precede them.

"Who the hell are you?" demanded Charles.

"Good morning, Mr. Fielding. My name is Robert Marvin, and I am a bailiff for the court of Mwanza," said one of the men as he leafed through documents in a folder. "It is my duty to present you with this sequestration order regarding your property," he continued, extracting several papers from the folder and handing them to Charles.

"Impossible. There must be a mistake." Charles asked his secretary to leave the room.

Mr. Fielding sat at his desk and read the documents. It was a standard foreclosure decree and appeared to have legal validity. He reread the court order. He turned to look at his walls: the photo of him with the president of Tanzania, the one with the mining minister when his mining license was granted, the photos of him on his yacht, the photo of him as a child sitting on a stuffed lion in his father's office, Sarah smiling from a cliff in Cornwall. For a terrible instant, it seemed to him that the memorabilia on his walls were questioning where his life took a wrong turn.

The child who sat on the lion seemed to be shaking his head in shame. Tears were teeming down Charles's cheeks like rain hammering the dry earth after a devastating drought. A moment later Charles said to himself, *By God, get hold of yourself, man! There is only one thing to do.* He told the officials he needed to make two phone calls. They agreed to leave his office. He was, after all, Charles Fielding.

He contacted the minister of mining and the president of the court in Mwanza. A few minutes later, the cell phone of one of the court representatives—who was now sitting in Charles's outer office—rang. The man answered, listened, and nodded. In the meantime, Charles opened his safe and took out some cash. American dollars.

"We're leaving," said the man to his colleague as soon as he put away his phone. He knocked gently on Charles's door, which Charles opened. "Please excuse us, Mr. Fielding, for this unexpected visit. We're very busy and have to go. It will be at least another ten days before we can consider your situation."

"No problem," replied Charles, handing an envelope to each of them, which they took in exchange for a handshake.

Charles sank into an armchair. The faces hanging on his walls went back to being photos. The solution was at hand: *Adimu. She will be a good daughter and a happy girl, even with only one arm. She will be rich beyond her wildest dreams.* His temples pulsed.

He rushed out of the office, told his driver he was taking the car, and jumped behind the steering wheel. He'd reach the protected community in Musoma in the shortest time possible.

Driving at an insane speed, Charles was unable to think of anything other than ending his nightmare. A baby impala stepped into the road and looked at the headlights of the Rolls Royce. There was a dull thud, and the sound awakened Charles from a trance. He stopped, got out of the car, and ran to the body of the animal. It was sprawled on the pavement, mortally wounded. The poor beast was struggling for breath. Blood seeped from its muzzle. *Why did I do this?* he asked himself. *It could have been avoided.* He lifted the little animal's body and set it on the side of the road. He opened the car door and fell to his knees. Charles thought of how Sarah would have cried if she witnessed this pointless death.

He finally arrived at the protected community in Musoma, road-weary and dusty, his eyes red and swollen. He had not expected the director of the community to tell him that Adimu was not and had never been a resident there.

"That's strange," said Charles. He asked the director for the phone numbers for the other communities. Excluding calls to his wife and closest friends, Charles Fielding hadn't placed a call that wasn't for business in years. On that day, he called one community after another. Adimu was not in any of the centers.

On his way back to Mwanza, Charles thought about the impala, Sarah, and Adimu. "What the hell am I doing? Am I losing my mind?" he asked himself aloud and more than once.

53.

When Adimu and Shida finally reached the village, Adimu bought two ears of corn and a small piece of charred chicken, which they tore in half. Then they went to the bus station to get information about transportation to Dar es Salaam.

"You need to go south," a street vendor told them. "Have you got enough money for the ticket?" Adimu nodded. "Go wait over there where those people are," the man explained before he hurried off to sell bags of toasted peanuts through the windows of a bus that was leaving.

The two girls went where the man pointed and hid behind a pyramid of peeled oranges that were ready to be sold in bags of five. They waited for what seemed like an entire afternoon. Finally, the bus appeared on the horizon, a tiny speck in the distance.

They stepped onto the bus after the other people got on. Adimu studied the faces of the passengers, one by one, and only when she was certain they'd be safe did she give her money to the ticket seller. She noticed with regret that she had but a few shillings left.

"How long will it take to reach Dar es Salaam?" she asked the driver.

"Only twelve hours," he chuckled. Deep wrinkles formed at the corners of his eyes.

After the girls took their seats, he winked at his colleague standing beside him. In a cheery voice he said, "Today is a doubly lucky day—not one, but two *embulamaros* on the bus."

Shida fell asleep as soon as the bus took off, bumping its way down the road.

Adimu, who had been sitting forward, her foot swinging beneath the seat, leaned back and began to relax. Finally she could read the pages from the encyclopedia and find out more about that word!

Albinism is a hereditary, congenital condition that manifests in an absence or reduction of the melanin in skin, hair, body hair, and eyes. It is found in all ethnic groups and in all animal species. It is considered to be one of the

*most widely spread genetic disorders in the animal kingdom...The parents
of most children with albinism have normal pigmentation of their skin, hair,
and eyes, conforming to their ethnic group of origin, and they do not have
a family history of albinism... Development and growth in children with
albinism are consonant with their peers. Intellectual development is normal.
Overall health is regular...*

Adimu reread the passage over and over, wanting to be certain to have
understood every sentence. She didn't know the meaning of all the words,
but she gleaned that she was considered neither a phantom nor a beast.
She would never vanish. She did not have the power to cause bad or good
luck. Ramadani had told her the truth. According to science, the blame for
her white skin belonged to her parents, not to her. She had done nothing
wrong, and she hadn't caused harm to others: no curses, no witchcraft, no
shame. She felt her heart skip a beat and then thump faster than usual. *Is
this what happiness feels like? A fluttering inside, almost the same as when
I'm afraid,* she thought. *Sefu and Juma might really be my parents even
though their skin is black, and Mr. Fielding probably isn't my father. I wish
he were, though it's better to know the truth. He could be the best adoptive
parent in the world.*

She looked at Shida sleeping beside her and set her hand delicately on
the back of her head. She wanted to wake her to tell her about the incredible
discovery but decided to let her rest. She passed her fingertips tenderly over
her friend's face and the marks where Shida had been beaten. The skin on
her wrists was red from rope chafe, and she noticed bruises and scratches
on her slender legs. How was she going to take care of this little girl? She
didn't even know how she would take care of herself. She fixed her gaze on
Shida's face. Her pink cheeks were streaked from tears and, although they
had dried, narrow strips of brown dust remained. From the window of the
bus, Adimu saw a woman shouting at a little boy. He'd started to walk into
the road, and she pulled him close to keep him safe. Like a light beaming
in a dark room, Adimu understood that Shida would be in danger if they
stayed together. It was too dangerous—at least until she found a safe place
for them. Her heart broke when she thought of separating from her best
friend. It would be better for Shida, though, Adimu knew, to return to her
grandparents. If only she had thought of that before getting on the bus.
Shida could have gone to Kigoma instead of making the trip home from
Dar es Salaam all by herself. Maybe it was better this way. The long trip taking her friend in the wrong direction would make it harder for the hunters
to find her. Rocked by the movement of the bus, Adimu gave in to sleep.

The vehicle stopped abruptly and Adimu awakened with a start. She realized her head was leaning on her neighbor's legs. She felt her face flush from embarrassment and began to move. The woman set her hand gently on Adimu's shoulder. Then Adimu remembered what she had just read: she was normal. She was a person like everyone else, and there was nothing strange about a normal girl leaning against an adult. She'd seen other girls her age do it. She relaxed, and shortly before falling back asleep, she turned her face toward the woman's belly, reached out her arm and hugged her around the hips. Feeling confident about who she was made it possible to trust a stranger.

The bus driver was tired of staring at the backside of the big truck in front of him. It was slowing him down. His wife and children were waiting for him at home so they could all eat together. He thought about the meat soup simmering in his kitchen, and his mouth started to water. The driver downshifted and pulled out to pass the truck. The motor of the bus strained as it gained speed. Over the crest of a hump in the road, a van appeared, bearing down on the bus at great speed. The driver and his colleague gasped. At the last moment, however, the oncoming vehicle swerved, letting the bus pass. They exhaled.

"I would never have tried passing if we didn't have those two *zeru zerus* on board," said the driver to his colleague. "I knew they'd bring us extra luck."

They finally arrived in Dar es Salaam.

"We have to split up," Adimu told Shida as soon as they stepped off the bus. The five words came out of her mouth hard, flat, and cold.

Shida teetered and shifted her right foot to maintain her balance. Her ears filled not with the chaotic noises of the city bus station but with a high-pitched buzz that numbed her senses.

"Did you hear me?" said Adimu, grasping Shida's shoulders with both hands. "We have to go in two different directions."

Shida's eyes were wide open, unblinking, and she shook her head.

"You have a family that loves you. They're waiting anxiously to know how you are, and if they don't hear from you soon, they'll die from heartbreak."

Shida had never had to choose between the people she loved. The thought of seeing her grandparents, her home, and her goats made her eyes fill with tears of joy, but leaving Adimu would be unbearable. And she was afraid of facing the trip alone, not to mention the night. She sought her friend's hands. "Come with me."

"Don't behave like a little child," said Adimu. "Don't be selfish. Think of your *babu* and *bibi*. You're very lucky to have them. Don't worry, I'll come visit you soon, and then we'll go together to a real community."

At the bus stop for Kigoma, they said goodbye. Adimu paid for her friend's ticket and gave her the rest of the change. Shida got on the bus without looking back and sat in a seat next to the window. She looked down at her feet, and her face appeared rigid.

Adimu waited for Shida to turn and wave. With a weight in her chest, Adimu walked away.

It was in that moment that Shida put her face to the window and saw Adimu's blond hair float among the crowd. She had wanted to call out to her, but a knot in her throat kept her from making a sound. With her eyes, she followed the hair until all she could see was a small white shape, which then disappeared, swallowed up by the colors of the city in motion.

54.

Thomas and the rest of the group searched every inch of the forest. They couldn't find a trace of the *zeru zeru*. They went back to the compound where Adimu had been locked and found the place deserted. They overturned all the rooms in hopes of finding some clue as to where she might be heading. Ramadani took advantage of the situation and left the headhunters. He had enough. He'd redeemed himself by completing his mission: to save the life of an innocent person. In his mind, he was making amends to Josephat by joining the hunters. That he had the chance to free the girl from Ukerewe made his undertaking all the more meaningful.

Thomas was convinced that a curse the *zeru zeru* had put on Ramadani was responsible for his disappearance. The *zeru zeru* they'd found was an especially powerful one, and if they could catch her and bring her in, Thomas could demand top dollar.

The group traveled to the only village in the area—the one Adimu and Shida had passed through. When they got to the town market, they saw a small crowd and several buses preparing to depart. Amani asked if an *embulamaro* had taken a bus, and the peanut seller said that he had seen not one but two *zeru zerus* get on a bus for Dar es Salaam that very morning. Suspecting the man was making fun of them, Thomas asked a woman who was toasting ears of corn the same question, and he got the same answer. They jumped into their car and left immediately.

"We have to be careful. This *zeru zeru* has incredible powers," commented Akili. "It can disappear, make a copy of itself, and make an enemy evaporate into thin air."

Amani nodded, contemplating the road they had in front of them.

ADIMU WANDERED AROUND the bus station. The only time she had been in a city, aside from passing through with Roman and Martha, was her short "birthday" trip to Mwanza with Charles and Sarah. Now it was evening, and the city was bright with a thousand lights shining everywhere.

Buildings, twice as tall as those in Mwanza, ones as high as trees, shaded the paved roads. People walked with their arms full of fabric and plastic bags, worn out suitcases, and screaming children. An indefinable smell mixed with the familiar odors of roasting corn and chicken. *Shida would have been scared to death in a place like this,* Adimu thought. She felt a pang of sadness and yearning at the thought of her friend. A woman whose face was hidden by a black veil bumped into Adimu and kept walking. Three children skipped behind her. Adimu wondered why the woman was shrouded in black from the top of her head to the tip of her toes. *Could she be albino too?*

To keep herself from thinking about her hunger, Adimu focused on the shop windows, which mesmerized her. Displayed in them were things she wouldn't know how to use. She was struck by the objects' shapes, colors, and prices.

She was overcome with awe by the giant dolls in one shop window when it dawned on her that people walked past her without paying any attention. *No one avoids me or stares at me or insults me or spits on the ground. The white woman doctor told the truth: in this city, no one takes notice of the color of a person's skin.* Slowly an unknown sensation took hold of Adimu—it was freedom. She felt light, free from the shackles of a body that had never been accepted by others.

On the opposite side of the street, Adimu saw an adolescent albino boy with a bag over his shoulder. He was wearing shorts and sneakers and a T-shirt of the same green color. Adimu had never considered the possibility that male albino children existed. She had always imagined herself with a friend exactly like her. She realized how shortsighted she'd been.

She crossed the street and followed him from a distance so he wouldn't notice her. He turned into an alleyway that ran along the side of the bus station and from there into a large grassy area. Adimu noticed something extraordinary: all the boys who were gathered there were albinos. They wore green soccer uniforms with black numbers printed on their backs. Their skin was white like hers. She sat down on the sidewalk, her legs trembling from emotion.

The match began, and Adimu watched as the boys laughed and joked, patted each other on the back and argued. She put on her glasses so she could see them better as she watched them play. She cheered for the team with the boy who had involuntarily led her there. She was so happy she forgot she hadn't eaten since the morning. Exhausted as she was, she felt her eyelids grow heavy, little by little. She adjusted her position so she could lean her back against the wall of a building but then became afraid. It was so tall. *What if it collapses on me?* A tree was planted at the center of a dry flowerbed in the sidewalk, and she went to sit under its canopy. *I'll just close my eyes for a moment while the boys play,* she told herself as she got comfortable, *and at the end of the match, I'll make friends with them.* Her drowsiness got the best of her, and soon she was asleep.

Adimu awakened suddenly with someone squeezing her wrist.

"We've got our *zeru zeru!*" shouted a male voice.

She didn't have time to be shocked. She saw a flash of gray sky above her as she was picked up and carried into a car.

Thomas stopped the car just outside the city and called Zuberi to let him know the job was completed. When the witch doctor found out they'd caught a female, he couldn't keep himself from shouting with glee; female breasts and genitals were more desirable than male parts and would be perfect for Yunis. He squeezed Jane with affection and tossed her playfully into the air.

"But how do we keep it from vanishing?" Thomas asked. "And what if it tries to put a curse on us?"

"Trap it inside something that makes it visible," suggested the healer. "For example, a plastic bag would work."

"I could paint it or rub mud on it."

"No, no! Don't do that! The skin and hair must remain untouched. They are worth their weight in gold!"

Thomas got back in the car, bringing with him a big wad of plastic he'd pulled off the top of a pile of garbage. "Akili, wrap the *zeru zeru* inside this. It'll keep it from vanishing," he said as he took his place behind the steering wheel.

Akili wound the plastic around Adimu, leaving only her head and neck exposed as if she were wearing a transparent, synthetic wraparound dress.

"Damn, there's not enough," mumbled the boy. His hands moved quickly as he tried to cover as much of her as he could. Then he took the rosary, looped it on his wrist, and hung it around Adimu's neck. "God will help us. If He can't do it with this devil of a phantom, who else can?"

"God will help me, not you." These were Adimu's first words since she had been pulled into the car.

"What did you say, *ngazu?*" asked Amani, turning to glare at her.

"I said that God will help *me* and not you. *Ngazu* is a word that doesn't mean anything, and you all are ignorant," she replied, enunciating each word. "Do you know what 'albino' means?"

They looked at each other with their mouths shut.

"Read this," said Adimu to Akili, awkwardly working her hand into her pocket to get at the page from the encyclopedia.

He threw a quick glance at the words on the page. To his eyes, she had handed him a piece of paper with rows of black markings on it. He held out the encyclopedia page to Thomas.

The leader of the group would never admit it, but he couldn't read either. He took the paper, crumpled it up, and threw it out the window.

"You don't scare me. I'm normal, like you. The things people say about *zeru zerus* are just stupid legends. I'm even better than you because I know how to read and write, and I'm going to become a doctor," she continued with a new contempt in her voice. She was free, and she would no longer accept being treated like a monster.

"If what you say is true," sneered Aki, "how did you disappear into the forest?"

"Ramadani let me go," she replied.

"Ha! The one whose life was linked to yours let you go? You think we're stupid enough to believe that?" shouted Akili.

"Shut up," growled Thomas.

Oddly, Adimu felt safe. If they had wanted to kill her, she knew she'd already be dead. *Kondo must have ordered they kidnap me and take me back to the village to marry his son, even if Ramadani doesn't want that.*

CHARLES DID NOT want Jackob or Zuberi involved in his plans for Adimu so he asked his driver to take him to a healer in Mwanza to help him find her. He needed information from an African who was skilled in the magical arts. Sitting in front of the old witch doctor, he felt like a child being punished. The man asked him about the evil for which he needed a cure, and Charles confessed his desperate financial situation and opened up about Adimu's kidnapping.

"I-I-I just want to know where she is," Charles said.

"I'm sorry; I cannot help you," the healer replied, shaking his head.

"What do you mean? Aren't you a shaman?"

The old man looked into Charles's eyes. It seemed to Charles that the face before him had been shot through with a bolt of compassion.

"We depend on the will of the Spirits, but we are subject to the hands of men," he said with a sigh. "As is the girl."

"I beg you, tell me where she is."

The healer took the white man's hands in his. His rough palms felt like dry wood, and Charles had a wild impulse to pull them to his lips and kiss them. He could no longer offer sums of money, but he would have borrowed any amount if it meant finding Adimu.

"Sir," said the old man, "I use the fruits of my land to heal the illnesses of my people. I am a traditional healer. I am sorry; I cannot help you."

RAMADANI WAS IN no rush to return to Murutanga. He had not spent time in Mwanza since graduating from school and decided—free from his father's overprotective gaze—to spend a few unscheduled days there to visit with former schoolmates, now married, many with children. He had heard rumors that a few of his friends had continued on to university, which had been Ramadani's dream. But mostly, Ramadani wanted to visit Josephat, and he knew just where to find him. That morning, before taking the ferry back to Ukerewe, Ramadani went to the university where his friend studied. Josephat welcomed him with a hug and asked him about his life.

"There's not much to tell," said Ramadani lowering his eyes, thinking about his time with the desperate headhunters. "What about you?"

"I'm going abroad on a scholarship. After I graduate, I'm going to work with a team of researchers who are studying the HIV virus," replied Josephat.

"Really? Tell me about it."

"There aren't many people here who know the name of the virus that causes AIDS," Josephat said, looking at Ramadani with his light, light eyes. "I want to do my specialization abroad and then come back to help. There's still too much ignorance about this disease." Josephat invited Ramadani to lunch, but he declined.

On the ferry to Ukerewe, Ramadani thought that maybe it wasn't too late for him. He would try to talk with his father, confess that he didn't want to succeed him as the village chief, that he had a calling to study and was willing to make whatever sacrifice necessary to realize his dream. Above all, Ramadani would make an appointment to see a doctor, to find out how much longer he had to live.

After the ferry docked, he went home on foot, not wanting his family to know he had returned to the island. Ukerewe was the same as always, although it seemed something subtle had changed, was irreparably lost.

The sun was setting, and the sky was striped purple. Kondo was happy to see his son safe. He looked at Ramadani, and his oldest seemed to be hiding something, a hunch that Kondo couldn't explain, as if a frosted glass wall had been erected between them.

"My son," he whispered as he opened his arms.

Ramadani stepped forward and pulled his father's body toward his.

"Are you cured?" he asked.

"Yes, I am," Ramadani replied firmly.

The following morning Ramadani made an appointment with an infectious diseases specialist at The Fielding Health Center of Ukerewe.

BEFORE OPENING THE door to the medical suite, Ramadani dried his palms on his pants and then wiped them again. He didn't want to shake hands with the doctor by offering sweaty palms. He was led to an examination room, told to undress, and was examined. After the examination, the doctor asked Ramadani to meet him in his office.

Sitting behind his large metal desk, the doctor read Ramadani's medical file carefully. Looking in his patient's eyes, he said, "You're HIV positive as I believe you know. But do you know what that means?" asked the physician, peering at Ramadani through a pair of metal-framed glasses.

"I have AIDS."

"Not really. You are only HIV positive."

"Yes, I have AIDS," repeated Ramadani.

"I'll be as clear as possible," said the doctor. "Being HIV positive does not mean you have AIDS. You can infect other people by having sexual relations without using a condom or through contact with your blood. For now, though, you do not have the disease."

"Does that mean I'm going to live?"

"You are living now, and you will continue to live a healthy life if you follow the treatment I prescribe for you. This treatment won't cure you, but it will prevent your HIV from turning into AIDS."

"How long do I have to live, doctor?" Ramadani asked, which was his most important question.

"If you take the medicine I prescribe, for the rest of your long life."

55.

Charles leaned his elbows on the table and dropped his head into his hands. His office building was deserted. He wasn't able to bring himself to return home that evening. When the phone rang, he was tempted not to answer it, though after a few rings decided to. *It might be good news,* he thought. And anyway, he did believe in always answering the phone.

"I'm not leaving you because you don't have a shilling," he heard the voice of his wife say, "but because you've been lying to me. And have been for years. That you honestly believe I married you, followed you from one continent to another, that I gave up my dream of having children...all because I wanted your money is proof that you don't know me. And that you don't deserve me."

Charles produced a sigh, the only sound he was capable of making after receiving such a sharp blow to his gut.

"It's over," said Sarah, and she hung up. She had finally looked through her husband's papers, and she'd found the folder that contained the property seizure. She knew everything.

Charles had the sensation that all the air had been sucked out of the room. With difficulty, he stood up and searched his pocket. He found the key and opened the safe. There was very little left inside—no gold, no cash. Only a few documents, and a gun. He looked at the revolver for a long time, keeping himself a stride's distance away. He stared at the barrel, the trigger, the cylinder, the ergonomic grip. His hand reached out as if it had a mind of its own. He counted the number of bullets. *I only need one.*

He returned to his desk, clutching the gun in his hand, and he sat down, setting an elbow on the arm of his chair, the barrel of the gun pointing at the ceiling. Charles inhaled, forcibly lowered his eyelids, and opened his mouth. He focused on the sensation of his wide-open jaws. His lips stretched over his teeth. The hand holding the gun quivered and began to lower. The barrel halted in line with his temple. What would the metal feel like against his skin? he wondered. He imagined the lead boring through his skull. The blood splatter on the wall. *His* blood. His body sprawled on the table. *His* funeral. His wife wearing a lost expression, worse than his mother's. His wife reliving the loss of her father. His desperate creditors. *What do I leave behind? A small clinic with my name on some signage. Is that what I've lived for?*

The sound of the gunshot rang through the air. Charles opened his eyes slowly and touched the ear that had been so close to the barrel of the gun. It was on fire. *Fire.* A runaway train roared in his head. His eyes traveled to the bullet's trajectory. It went through the photo of him with President de Klerk, right through his own chest in the image. He looked around at the other photos in the room. His eyes rested on the two Fielding males who had come before him. Their expressions were full of pride and dignity. He pulled the trigger again and again until the barrel was empty and the pictures riddled.

Charles swiveled in his chair to face the windows. Here he was, sharing a room with death, and it had almost succeeded in soothing him, of convincing him to stop the struggle. It was dark outside, and nothing was discernible beyond the glass, but that didn't frighten him. He had turned his back on death, and the dark of the night held no threat. It, too, was part of life, his new life that would start in that very instant.

Once the gun was back in the safe, he took a cigarette from the case he kept on his desk. "The first after so many years," he muttered to himself.

He held the unlit cigarette in his right hand, rolled it between his fingers. They no longer trembled. *I wanted to protect you, Sarah. I love you, Sarah, Sarah,* he repeated over and over. He thought that he heard his wife's voice. *"You never loved me. You loved your power, your money, your success. You don't know how to love."* Charles opened his wallet and took out the one hundred dollar bill that was inside it. With his eyes fixed on Benjamin Franklin, he set the bill on the table, continuing to roll the cigarette between his fingers—index, middle, thumb. *For my mother, I was a reminder of the man who had ruined her life. For my father, I was an unexpected burden, something that had to be tolerated. Not a son. Just one more accident that occurred along the road. Sarah, I've never been a good husband. But I want to be, more than anything. And I will try to be a good father.*

Charles picked up the lighter on his desk and lit the cigarette. Then he lit a corner of the hundred dollar bill. He spat out the heavy smoke, coughing, and threw the cigarette into the wastebasket with the smoldering money. The flame crackled. He moved the basket to watch the flames grow, spellbound by the fire. He tossed some paper into the wastebasket to help feed the tentacles of the monster. *But love is imperfect, isn't it, Sarah? And the one thing you're wrong about is that I do know how to love.* He would show Sarah that he no longer cared about money. With his foot, he pushed the wastebasket under his desk and let the fire lick at the wood. The flames were climbing up the elephant feet desk legs as he left his office and locked the door. He was killing the monster, burning it. He had been buried in the hardened mud of money, imprisoned for years. And now, suddenly, it rained and, like a lungfish, Charles was coming back to life.

THE FOUR YOUNG men had surveilled in shifts, from sunset till sunrise, convinced the *zeru zeru* was capable of vanishing. The plastic and rosary had worked. "We can't let our guard down on the last night, not even for a second," they had told each other.

Before the sun came up, the phone rang. "Take the *zeru zeru* to the second Fielding gold mine. Everybody knows where it is. Wait for me in the forest nearby," the witch doctor told Thomas. "I'll be there when the sun sets."

As soon as he hung up with Thomas, Zuberi called Jackob. "Let the *mzungu* know."

"Don't worry, I'll take care of it," Jackob assured Zuberi.

"I want the ritual performed in his presence. He must see that the *zeru zeru* is alive," insisted Zuberi.

"I doubt he'll come. He doesn't like to dirty his hands."

Once the arrangement was settled, Jackob stopped to consider his next step. Mr. Fielding had not answered his phone for hours. And Jackob didn't believe he should notify his boss that the ritual was taking place that evening. Lately, Mr. Fielding had been extremely anxious, especially since the Mwanza police had come to see him. He had changed his mind so many times about what kind of *zeru zeru* should be found—dead, alive, with cancer—that he himself probably didn't remember what he last requested. The only important point was that Mr. Fielding had ordered the amputation of the arm of a living *zeru zeru*. Whether it was dying from skin cancer or would be dying from skin cancer in ten years, what difference did it make? He would let his employer know the day after, when it had already been done. *I know my boss better than he knows himself,* Jackob reassured himself.

CHARLES WAS DETERMINED to win back his wife's trust, though he knew words would not be enough to convince her of his radical change. He needed to arrive home with something she could see with her own eyes, touch for herself. Something that would prove to her he was a changed man. Only then would she believe he'd been transformed. He'd bring Adimu to her, the daughter she had wanted for years and that the old Charles had denied her. He had set fire to his kingdom so he could emerge clean and pure, like a tender shoot that escaped a wildfire.

From his car, he called their house and was satisfied when his wife did not answer. *Better to meet her after I've completed the task and a happy Adimu is holding my hand.* He needed cash to find the girl, and he'd sell the jewels that were in his home safe where Sarah's engagement ring was stored. Then they would fly away—the three of them—like a real family. He would fulfill Sarah's long-standing desire to swim with the dolphins, and Adimu would be with them, swimming too.

When Charles arrived home, he went into the bathroom, took off his shirt and tie, and examined his bare chest in the mirror above the sink. He washed with cold water, giving extra attention to his nails, which he cleaned with a brush. He smelled the smoke being scrubbed off his flesh, replaced by wild lavender. In his thoughts, the sound of the running water mixed with the fury of the flames. Charles looked again in the mirror and liked what he saw. "I am alive," he told his image. As he turned away, he remembered to pick up his wedding band. He'd set it on the vanity before washing his hands. He put it back on his left ring finger. *In sickness and in health*, he repeated in his mind, recalling the day he had kissed Sarah when she was dressed in white.

He put on the first clean white shirt he found in the closet, moved the dresser, and opened the wall safe. He saw her jewels, which were inside a blue velvet box, and her engagement ring, which was nestled in a small case padded with white silk. Seeing the gem sparkle in the artificial light reminded him of the last time the ring had seen daylight, in Dar es Salaam.

"As soon as we return to Mwanza, I'm putting this in the safe. I'm not going to wear it until I'm convinced you know I care nothing for your money."

Charles was finally convinced that Sarah loved him, had always loved him. It took the sound of her heart breaking to convince him. He had heard her gasp when she told him she was leaving. It broke Charles's heart that he had broken hers.

"What are you doing here?" asked Sarah, startling him from behind. "I'm serious. I'm done with you."

Charles jumped and faced her, his eyes wide with surprise and his mouth forced into a hopeful smile. He went to her, hugged her hard, and leaned his cheek on her shoulder.

She was cold. Rigid.

"I'm sorry, darling, for the lies I've told you," he whispered, tears welling up in his eyes. "I was trying to protect you. Believe me, there is nothing more important in this world than you, than us. I'm here to surprise you. I know you will understand everything once you see my surprise."

She looked into the empty safe. "Why are you taking the last of my memories?" Her voice was little more than a soft breath.

"If you knew, you'd approve."

"I'm sick of your secrets!" Sarah's lips formed a straight line, and her eyes drilled into him.

"You, Sarah, are my pure gold," said Charles, "and Adimu is what we need. I'm selling your jewelry to put together cash for Adimu."

"You know where she is?" Sarah's face brightened.

Charles shook his head. "No, but I'll find her. If she's been kidnapped, I'll pay the ransom. Then we can live together as a family. It will be quick and easy to adopt her. We'll leave the country."

"Just bring her home." Sarah's anger transformed into a breeze that lifted off her flesh, and she was transported back more than seventeen years when Charles proposed marriage on one knee. Sarah took her engagement ring from its case. The diamond glittered with blue light as she handed it to her husband.

"No darling, not your ring. It's the only…"

"Just do it," she told him. She tried to slip the ring onto his index finger, but it was too small so Charles guided her toward his little finger, where it was only moderately tight. The two lingered momentarily, gazing into each other's eyes, and kissed. Then Sarah pushed Charles to continue on their mission, and he rummaged in the sack that held the jewelry. He pulled out an assortment of pendants and bracelets and pins, and, for a moment, it seemed to him that the gold in his hands turned gray like lead. There was a long blond hair entwined in the links of a necklace. Golden and as fine as filigree. He tried to untangle it and wondered how it had gotten there. It was tightly wound around the chain links. The only way to remove it was to tear it. Charles frowned. He felt a dark presentiment shroud him as if his destiny and Adimu's were linked forever to the yellow metal he held in his hands. It occurred to him that possession of it was a curse, and he felt deep revulsion toward himself and the hunt he had instigated.

Sarah was digging through her underwear drawer, looking for an envelope that contained cash. Charles lovingly watched her thin back that he had embraced so many times. He pitied himself. His eyes shifted to the blank wall. In his imagination, he projected many masks onto his own face: Hitler, Amin Dada, Gheddafi, Mugabe. He squeezed his eyes shut.

Charles tore the hair from the necklace and, for a moment, thought he saw blood stain his hands. Dead flesh. Adimu's arm covered with fine blond hairs, lying on the ground next to the torn hair. He gasped at the image. The bag of jewelry fell from his hand as if it had suddenly become too heavy a burden to bear.

56.

"No. Absolutely not! Any other white shadow but not that one!" shouted Zuberi at Thomas as soon as he saw Adimu inside the car that was parked at the second gold mine.

"You told me to get you a *nobody,* and that's what I've done," said Thomas.

Though Adimu recognized Zuberi and Jackob, the car in which she was captive was too far away for her to hear the conversation between the three men. She figured that, thankfully, Mr. Fielding must have sent his assistant to negotiate a way out of the marriage agreement. A grin stretched across her face, and her hands and feet fidgeted. Even though she liked Ramadani, she had promises to keep to her *bibi.*

"It can't be this *zeru zeru,* the *mzungu* will never pay for her! The entire village will be after us, and Kondo will be first in line," stressed the witch doctor.

"Unless…" interrupted Jackob.

"Unless what?" snapped Zuberi.

"Unless we do more than amputate her arm. Take the parts you need and get rid of the head. No one will ever know. Mr. Fielding isn't coming this evening, and, soon, Sefu will give up the search."

"Do what you want," interjected Thomas, "but either way, we want our money. And a nice bonus for such a powerful one. Now."

Zuberi made his decision on the spot. *No one will know the amulets came from Adimu's body. She disappeared weeks ago.* Jackob's point was well taken.

Then Zuberi grabbed a saw, a machete, a branch stripped of its twigs and leaves, and a small tank of kerosene from his car—his instruments. And next he reached for his most sacred instruments.

Earlier in the evening, before heading to the mine to meet Thomas, Zuberi had unlocked his wooden chest hidden under the red carpet in his workshop and carefully removed two of the most powerful amulets and one totem, bringing them with him to perform this rite. He had been told—as had his father before him—that these were tools the Spirits themselves had passed down to his ancestors. Zuberi had waited his entire life for this moment.

"Let's go," he said as he gathered everything up. He was ready.

CHARLES WAS LEANING on the dresser with both hands.

"What's wrong? Are you all right?" asked Sarah, alarmed.

"Just a pain in my head, dear, nothing to worry about." A pain caused by his sins, he imagined.

I have to stop Zuberi, he said to himself, *and speak with Jackob. I'll take Sarah and Adimu, and we'll move to Zimbabwe to start over.* He forced himself to stay calm so Sarah wouldn't become suspicious of what he had been planning before his great transformation.

"All right, Sarah. I think I've got what I need to find Adimu. I'll keep you posted." Before leaving the room, Charles hugged his wife, then took his lucky nugget out of his pocket and put it in the palm of Sarah's hand.

She made no effort to hide her disdain, pulling her head and shoulders away from the piece of gold on her open palm.

"It belongs in the past," he said, looking her in the eyes. "Do with it as you think fit."

WHEN CHARLES CALLED Jackob, voice mail picked up after the first ring. Then he phoned him at home. Jackob's wife told Mr. Fielding that her husband was out, that she understood he was going to the second mine.

The fear that his "trusted assistant" might be less than trustworthy induced Charles to drive recklessly, tearing through the infernal Mwanza traffic.

What is Jackob doing at the mine on a Sunday? Why did he lie about Adimu being in the protected community?

Night extended its long fingers through the city. A few bright homes and the sporadic streetlights kept the darkness at bay. While waiting for a slow traffic light to change, Charles nibbled on a fingernail and took several deep breaths to calm himself. Surely the sacrifice of the *zeru zeru*—of the albino with cancer—was not taking place on *that* evening. *So much anxiety, and just because Jackob has his phone turned off!* Charles tried to ignore the images of machetes that were dominating his imagination. The traffic light turned green, and Charles sped off.

When he arrived at the grassy clearing of the mine, he parked his Rolls and ran with all his might to the spot where the last ritual that Zuberi performed took place. Despite the cool air, his flesh was damp with sweat and sizable dark circles formed on the armpits of his button-down shirt. Below his feet, Charles felt the forest pulsate and breathe. The man's heart beat faster as he approached the knoll, which was shaped like a witch's hat and set on the head of a tortured body. He needed to get to the other side of it. The sky was aglow with mist, and its dull light collected in the mining holes that had been gouged out of the earth.

THOUGH THE HEADHUNTERS blindfolded Adimu when pulling her from the car, she caught a glimpse of the machete. Her whole body trembled. Someone tore her dress. Her panties were her sole shield. "I'm cold," she said through her tears, trying to warm herself with her crossed arms. She forced herself to visualize Mr. Fielding coming to save her. She willed him there. Then a strong man grabbed her right arm and tied it to what felt like a piece of wood. Her arm was bound straight. She was unable to move it. He held her still, and the rope scratched her delicate skin. It burned. She yelled, and the strong man clutched her with his big hands to keep her from moving. He was hurting her. She thought of her *bibi*. "Stop! Please, let me go! Stop!" she begged. There was no hope of escape. She heard a brief cavernous sound and felt a flash of pain as if Zuberi were pulling her heart out of her chest.

She screamed and screamed again and again. "I don't want to die!"

Adimu lost consciousness.

CRIES OF PAIN and terror tore through the night, and Charles ran toward them. He instinctively held his arms up over his head as if something would strike him from above. As he climbed the slope to reach the spot, he told himself the wild scream must be coming from an animal. Though he knew he was lying to himself. When he reached the plateau, he saw a group of men and rushed toward them. Slipping on the slurry around the excavation pits, mud covered his trousers. Finally he drew near enough to recognize Zuberi who was holding something long in his right hand.

"Stop!" Charles shouted when he got within a few yards of the group.

A white body lay on the ground, drowning in a pool of blood. A small, slender body. Motionless. Next to the muck of a pit lay an aqua dress, the delicate dress that Sarah had presented to the little girl on her pretend birthday. The dress looked like a tangle of wilted leaves. A strong odor of kerosene hung in the air. Charles saw a mass of long blond hair splayed on the ground like a rare bush.

The mine owner threw himself on the ground, lifting Adimu, cradling her on his legs. An image of the young impala he had hit with his car came crashing back. "Adimu!" he shouted, his lips quivering as he turned his head frantically, searching for someone who could help, who could bring her back to life.

Thomas and his companions looked at Charles. The man seemed more like a father crying over his dead daughter than a rich *mzungu* who lacked scruples.

I'm not going to prison, thought Akili.

There's no way I'm going back to jail, thought Aki.

Zuberi considered that perhaps the white man really was the father of the *zeru zeru*. *If he is, there will be trouble, and he'll have to meet the same fate as his daughter.*

Jackob, ashamed of the weak and vulnerable man before him, *not at all the great leader who I took to be my mentor*, would need to muster in himself the strength the situation called for.

CHARLES PLACED THE flaccid Adimu on the ground and, unsteady on his feet, lurched in the direction he'd come from. Thomas blocked his way, the machete gripped threateningly in one hand. Intimidated by the white man's size, he lowered the tip of his weapon to Adimu's exposed neck. Aki and Akili took positions near their comrade.

"Don't touch him!" ordered Jackob. "He's on our side." He added, "He's like this with animals too. Though he eats meat with gusto, don't show him how the animal on his plate was killed or he'll pass out like a girl."

The headhunters laughed.

Charles, whose face had paled to the color of Adimu's skin, took another step in the direction of his car. He would go for help; if there were the slightest chance, he'd make certain that Adimu survived.

Akili attacked Charles from behind, his fist striking Charles's right kidney. As the large man fell to his knees, he caught sight of Thomas over his shoulder, glinting machete still in hand.

"How could you let this happen, Jackob?" Charles spat through clenched teeth, his body swaying.

Jackob set his hand on Charles's shoulder in a fraternal gesture. "Mr. Fielding, we've worked together for years. I knew this was what you wanted in your heart. You've been so worried about your business, and I've been so worried about you. You'll see, everything will go back to how it was. If not better. Your business will fly high like vultures during the great migration of the gnus and zebras. Don't worry, sir. It's only a *zeru zeru*."

Only a zeru zeru. Charles thought of how Adimu looked at him when they shared tiramisu on the veranda. He thought of her chubby legs when she sat on his lap as a newborn.

"Sir, you have trained me to obey you from my first day on the job," Jackob added.

Zuberi watched Jackob and Charles from a slight distance. He had been harboring a doubt from the moment he propelled the arm in the air and it landed on the soil. "Come with me, Mr. Fielding," he said to the large man crumbled in muddy white clothes against the earth. "I must show you something extraordinary," he said, moving closer.

Charles crawled to Adimu and cradled her, again, in his arms, cleaning the dirt from her face with the tail of his shirt. He observed subtle movements of her chest. She was breathing.

"I'll come," Jackob said to Zuberi, looking back at his boss who was preoccupied with the *zeru zeru*.

Jackob and Zuberi walked the short distance and stopped in front of the arm that had been Adimu's. "I've never seen anything like this," Zuberi said in a hushed, anxious voice. He scratched the side of his head and gnawed at the inside of his cheek. The arm was leaning against a large rock, and it was perpendicular to the ground. The hand was pointing straight up toward the sky. "Could it be a message from the Spirits of the Lake?" asked Zuberi. "An arm pointing skyward...difficult to interpret." He sighed.

"Should we finish it off now?" Thomas asked Zuberi, tilting his head at the girl on the ground.

"It is for Mr. Fielding to decide," said Jackob, always the thoughtful employee.

Charles took his eyes from Adimu to glance at the arm pointed toward the starry sky. He imagined it belonging to someone who was buried alive, searching for air by reaching one limb from the earth. He wasn't sure if that tortured soul was his or Adimu's.

"I asked, should we off her or cut her up alive?" insisted Thomas, louder, the skin on his neck covered with reddish splotches.

"Shut up! Leave her alone!" howled Charles.

Adimu opened her eyes. Her gaze traveled up the arms that held her. The first face she saw was Charles's. A weak smile formed on her lips, then disappeared when she saw the other men standing nearby.

"You'll be all right," Charles said, keeping his eyes on her, his hand holding hers. "Forgive me." His voice was muffled.

Adimu lifted her eyebrows, the only part she could move. She pressed her body more tightly against Mr. Fielding's, looking for protection, and hid her face in the bend of his arm. An excruciating pain electrified her. She arched her back, trying to resist the agony. Someone was tearing off another part of her body. She could feel it. Charles held her tighter. "I'm the one who wanted the arm of a *zeru zeru* to find more gold," he stammered. "But I never wanted it to be you. I want to adopt you and love you like a daughter."

Adimu heard the words: "*zeru zeru*," "you," "daughter."

Charles continued to sputter apologies, but she had turned her head, could hear nothing over the electrocuting torment of her body. She felt herself give in, give up—her chest, her neck, her legs. The unbearable pain was diminishing.

"The pocket of my dress, look," Adimu managed to mumble.

Charles took off his jacket, rolled it up, and set her head on the improvised cushion. Once she was as comfortable as he felt he could make her, he seized her discarded dress and fumbled with the fabric, pulling out her glasses, the photo of them together, and a folded piece of paper. He opened it. There was the dedication signed by him and his wife. *For Adimu, we wish you all the best. We care deeply about you, like a daughter.* The mud that had soiled the dress had soaked through to the pocket, and part of it had become damp, stained pulp. He knew Jackob was to have torn up that page from the encyclopedia a long time ago, *but that isn't important now. Nothing but Adimu's life is important.*

With a weak movement of her head, Adimu gestured for him to come closer. Charles leaned down over her so he could hear her.

"Did you do this to me?" she asked, using her last morsel of strength.

She tried to pull her hand from Charles's, but he held onto it and squeezed. Adimu resisted, though Charles wouldn't give up. At last, she closed her hand into a fist and leaned her head back, giving in to the feeling of stupor she had been fighting for some time.

Charles took Sarah's engagement ring from his pocket and worked it onto Adimu's middle finger. He pointed the gem inward toward her palm. She was still but for her weak breath.

57.

Ramadani was in his room, lying on a mat of woven palm leaves. He had returned from a walk in the forest, happy and full of hope. He extended his arm to pick up the copy of *National Geographic*, the one he had read so many times. The pages were folded and yellowed at the edges. He looked at the image of the albino lion cub marching next to the mother along with the rest of the litter. It had not been abandoned to predator birds or hyenas on the savannah but had been fed and protected like any cub. It wasn't even dirtier than the others, despite its white fur. On the next page was an albino gorilla staring at the camera from between forest leaves. The caption explained how the gorilla, Snowflake, had been transferred to a zoo in Barcelona to protect it from poachers. Ramadani envied Josephat—he wanted to go to another part of the world, too, where albinos were protected, not killed. Where life was less cruel. And, above all, less difficult. He looked out the window of his room at the sky and the green trees. Soon a new rainy season would begin, and the vivid blue of the sky would be replaced by gray. The air smelled of blossoming clouds. He set the magazine down, took a book from the stack next to his mat, and leafed through it until he found the photograph he was looking for. He smiled at the image.

Ramadani washed and dressed, putting on the only tie he owned. He took the photo with him as he left the house. He walked through the village, his chest puffed out and his shoulders back. People greeted him with respect and wondered where he was going, so elegantly dressed. When he arrived at the great baobab in the center of the village, where there was a village notice board, he removed two thumbtacks from an old, faded poster and attached his photo instead. Memories of that day at school in Mwanza flooded him. The teacher had asked, "What is the most important and reliable magazine that communicates the wonders of the world?"

"*National Geographic!*" he'd shouted before two other classmates gave the same answer.

The teacher had passed a copy of the magazine around the class and told each of them they were to write a three-thousand-word report about one of the articles. Ramadani was assigned a piece on albino animals. He had tried to hide the article from the boy who had become his desk mate that semester, the boy he initially treated cruelly.

With Josephat at the desk next to his, Ramadani had been forced to face a reality that was different from what he had always known. The article demonstrated that in the natural world, there was no discrimination toward albino animals, and he had begun to question whether his *zeru zeru* classmate really did bring bad luck. He, after all, was on his soccer team and most often the team won. Thinking about that article had been Ramadani's first step toward Josephat. *How can we, humans, be more beastly than wild beasts?* Over time, he and Josephat became friends, and Ramadani discovered they were the same, except for the color of their skin. And he understood that tradition conflicted with evolution. It was difficult to arrive at that realization. *Our eyes look forward; they are not on the back of our heads*, he'd say to himself. He would continue to move forward. To run, if necessary, toward his future, because that was where he wanted to live.

Ramadani stepped away from the bulletin board, looking at the photo of himself embracing Josephat, both smiling in their soccer team uniforms. The image was a little out of focus as if it had come from the distant past. Ramadani knew that it represented his present and, above all, his future. He laughed as he thought about what the villagers and his father would do when they saw the photograph. Their opinions had no impact on the way that he would lead his life, he told himself, as he held out his money to the ticket seller at the ferry dock. "One way, please."

THE DRIVER OF the bus that Adimu and Shida had taken to reach Dar es Salaam was on the road again after a day's rest. That morning, when two albino kids got on board, the driver could hardly believe his eyes. Another pair of *zeru zerus* and so soon after the two girls! These were wearing green soccer uniforms with numbers printed in black on the backs of their shirts. They were talking about a girl they had seen at the soccer field where they played on Saturday evening.

"She was there by herself, watching us. When we left, I wanted to wake her but decided to let her rest," said the bigger of the two boys. "I went back to the field early on Sunday, but she was gone."

The driver looked in his mirror, chuckled to himself, and elbowed the second driver. He started to pass a slower vehicle, certain of his good luck. When he saw a truck coming in the opposite direction, he closed his eyes and never opened them again, nor did most of his passengers. Some days after the accident, the second driver, who survived, recalled the two *zeru zeru* girls who had taken the bus and the two *zeru zeru* boys on the day of the accident. He kept thinking about what had happened, though he never came up with a plausible explanation. The truth was, he didn't even know what question to ask.

YUNIS SAT IN front of the physician.

"The only way for you to become pregnant is to change husbands," the doctor joked. "You're healthy, and there is no impediment to having children. He's the one who cannot."

Yunis's jaw relaxed.

"There is, however, a therapy we can try," said the gynecologist with a reassuring smile. "Most probably, your husband's infertility can be treated. Though I cannot be sure until we've done more tests."

A sheen of calm embellished Yunis, now that she knew she wasn't sterile. *Maybe having children isn't important*, she thought. And if she wanted some, she could ask her sister-in-law for one or two: *she's always saying she has trouble feeding all of hers.* How many times had Yunis's husband suggested that option? It hadn't interested her, but now that she knew she wasn't at fault, she didn't feel the need to get pregnant. *I have spent most of my life miserable, lost my friendship with Juma, and for what?* She remembered Adimu on that distant day in the forest. The baby was made of flesh and bone like all babies, and she'd known it the moment she held the infant in her arms. Her body and heart and gut knew it. She had almost been responsible for the death of two human beings: an innocent baby and an innocent woman. Yunis had been prepared to prey on the breasts and genitals of a soul with albinism. She didn't deserve to have children. With her index finger, she wiped away a tear.

"Let's go straight to Zuberi and withdraw our request. I don't care if he keeps our money!" she said to her husband.

58.

Adimu awoke in the hospital. Three days had passed since her arm had been amputated.

She opened her eyes to find Sarah stroking her hair. Adimu adjusted her gaze to see if others were present. No, she and Mrs. Fielding were alone. Shifting her eyes to the right, to her horror she saw she had not been dreaming. She moved that arm and could feel it. She just couldn't see it. The ring Charles had slipped on the finger of her left hand reminded her of that nightmarish evening. A slow moan issued from her lips. Sarah tried to comfort her.

"Where is he?"

Sarah didn't have the courage to answer the child or ask her to recount her memories. The woman had found the daughter she'd always wanted and had lost the only man she'd ever loved. *I have not behaved much better than Charles*, she told herself. *I've been blind and cowardly*. She had lived her life in denial, refusing to see the full portrait of the man with whom she shared her bed. She chose, rather, to believe that Charles was her paternal superior, a replacement of the father she had never stopped mourning. Now she understood that she couldn't blindly follow another. That overdependence leads to affliction. Now she understood that awareness, acceptance, and courage were the medicine for pain. *Some things are best faced alone.* Charles had been her refuge. Love, though, she finally understood, was not something to hide behind. The innocent girl lying in the hospital bed had paid the price for her learning this lesson.

Sarah stepped out of the room and leaned against the corridor wall. "Oh, God, why did she have to be the one?" she whispered, thinking of the fateful phone call that she received the morning after Adimu's sacrifice. The officer had told her that her husband had been stopped shortly before sunrise by a patrol car. He'd been driving to the Mwanza hospital at an excessive speed and in a state of shock with a wounded albino girl in the car. He had confessed at the police station. "I did it, all alone. It was my macabre fantasy," he had told them.

"The girl?" Sarah had asked the officer, her voice low. "How old is she?"

"Around thirteen. She's in intensive care."

Upon hearing the girl's age, Sarah rushed to the hospital and found the attending doctor. "A popular belief was responsible for saving the girl," he had said.

"What do you mean?" Sarah had asked.

"Common folklore maintains that albinos vanish when killed. The wound was stanched with kerosene so she wouldn't bleed to death. And it's a good thing some man got her here and fast; it saved her life."

A wave of abhorrence crashed over Sarah. Her eyes closed. She slowly lifted her right hand to her forehead, to her diaphragm, left shoulder, and finally, her right shoulder, making the cross she had rejected since her father's death.

It was three days before Adimu could receive visitors. At first, Sarah thought of going to Murutanga to speak with the girl's parents about adopting her. When she reached the port, though, she changed her mind. She wouldn't negotiate with those who had driven out their daughter, nearly to her death. She'd gotten into the Rolls Royce and, when digging through her handbag to find the car key, her fingers felt Charles's lucky nugget. Charles. Her husband. The man who mined for gold and hunted people. She had believed he changed when she gave him her jewels to find Adimu, when he vowed he'd bring her back. She wanted to believe he changed. She wanted to forgive him. After what he did, how could she ever forgive him? But, she considered, the doctor had suggested it was Charles who saved the girl.

Charles had called two days earlier. She'd come home exhausted from waiting all day on an uncomfortable wooden bench to see Adimu, who was still too weak for visitors. Sarah flopped on her cushioned armchair in her living room, staring at the wall. The phone on the side table rang. Her eyes shifted, and she looked at it with panic until it stopped. It began to ring again. Then silence. And more persistent ringing. No voice-mail message. It could only be Charles, she was sure. She set her hand on the receiver, considered whether she had the mettle to lift it to her mouth and have her voice face his, the one who did this to her daughter, the man who stole her dreams. She closed her eyes and let the phone ring. It stopped. Her hand continued to rest on the receiver.

Charles had begged the prison guard and made promises he knew he couldn't keep for permission to call her.

"Five minutes, no more," the guard had agreed.

He had held the receiver to his ear. It rang and rang, no answer. He hung up. Again he placed the coin in the slot, again the phone rang and rang.

Please answer, Charles repeated in his head after he dialed the number at their house in Mwanza for the third time on the grimy telephone hanging on the jail wall.

Again the phone rang and rang. And then he heard, "Hello?"

At the sound of her voice, he began to weep. Words piled up in his throat and got stuck in that small dark place. With the palm of his hand, he covered the receiver so she wouldn't hear, wouldn't know. *She cannot, she must not, I cannot let her hear me cry.* He was about to hang up the phone when a salty stream gushed forth, and he let out a wail that would soften the hardest, most obdurate heart.

Sarah's face was marked by tears. Her body was limp. The phone sat on her lap and was cradled in her hands. She listened to the grief of her husband emanate from the receiver while her soft sobs shredded any resolve she had.

"Mr. Fielding, it's time to go back to your cell," said the guard, his voice subdued.

Charles waved his hand at the man and wiped his tears with the sleeve of his shirt. Leaning his forehead against the wall, he sucked in his pain and spit out, "I love you beyond reason. Let me have nothing else in life but you and Adimu, and I will be the most favored man on this whole Earth." He hung up the phone and slammed his fist against the plaster.

"Did you talk to her?" his cellmate asked when he returned.

Charles curled up on his cot, face to the wall.

THE FOLLOWING MORNING Sarah took the yellow nugget between her fingers and walked to the lake and onto a small wooden pier that extended a few yards. The sky was clear, the sun vibrant. She looked at the depths below her and picked up a flat rock, which she threw. The surface of the lake rippled, making concentric circles. She held her hand out over the water and let the stone on its chain fall between tiny waves. Charles's good-luck charm sank, leaving behind a glittering wake that lasted only an instant before it vanished.

Over the next three days, whenever her husband came to mind, she'd slam the door shut on his image, barricading him in a faraway prison. At night, she dreamed of his grief. One early evening, she dreamed he had finally metamorphosed into a butterfly of a man who could embrace wife and daughter. When she opened her eyes, she remembered she had fallen asleep at the hospital, awaiting a nurse to tell her that Adimu was out of intensive care and ready for visitors. Now, finally, she was looking at the child's gaunt face, wiping away tears.

"Do you know where my best friend, Shida, is?" asked Adimu, sniffling.

"No, sweetie, I don't. But don't worry, we'll find her as soon as you're better," replied Sarah, although she did not yet know who they were talking about.

Adimu looked at her missing right arm. "How can I study and become a doctor?" she asked.

Sarah laid her hand on Adimu's cheek. "Is it your arm that studies and becomes a doctor?"

Adimu looked at the ceiling and after several seconds said, "No, but I need it to write."

"You can use your left hand," said Sarah.

Adimu turned to Sarah and, holding her eyes at chest level, said, "People who use their left hand are bad."

"Who says so?"

"People on Ukerewe."

"Are the people who did bad things to you left-handed?" Sarah raised her eyebrows.

Adimu's eyes darted around the room as she thought about Roman, Martha, Sefu, and the others.

Sarah saw the terrified expression on the little patient's face, hadn't intended to bring Adimu's painful memories to the surface. "I'm left-handed," said Sarah. She picked up her handbag and rummaged inside. "Look." She took a pen with her left hand and wrote in a little notebook.

"Can I see what you've written?"

Sarah showed her the page. In perfect Swahili she had written, "Am I a bad person?"

Adimu's face shone. Then, as if a passing cloud covered the sun, her expression changed. "With only one arm I can't become a doctor," she said.

"Why do you say that?"

"All the doctors I've ever seen have two legs and two arms."

"How many doctors have you seen?" asked Sarah.

"Oh, lots. Two in Murutanga, the doctors at the clinic on Ukerewe..." Adimu's face became somber, "and the doctors here."

"There are millions more people in the world who don't live on Ukerewe, love. People with one arm, like you, are normal, just like everyone else. And like everyone else, you can become whatever you want to be. It's up to you. Do you believe me?"

Adimu puckered her mouth and nodded her head.

"Do you want to become a doctor?"

"Yes. It's the most important thing. I promised my *bibi*."

Sarah turned her head to hide her moist eyes.

"My father, mother, and siblings…Do you have news about them?"

Sarah was silent. She did not want to tell her that none in her family had shown any interest in what had happened. "If you want, from now on I can be your mother," she said, looking into Adimu's eyes.

Adimu looked to the foot of her bed and nodded just a little.

"Is that a yes?"

"Yes," replied Adimu. "And will Mr. Fielding be my father?"

"Do you want him to be?" Sarah asked.

Adimu said nothing and tilted her head. "I always wanted a family. A mother." She took a few deep breaths before continuing, "And father," she said in a softer voice. "And I want to go back to Murutanga and tell my sisters and my brother it's not my fault I'm this color. I'm not a white shadow, and I'm not a phantom, and I'm not even sick. The lady doctor who vaccinated me said so, and Ramadani told me in the forest, and I read it in the encyclopedia too. Don't let me die now. I want to tell everyone I'm normal. And maybe I want Mr. Fielding. I always thought he'd be the perfect father. Would he be?"

Sarah didn't know what to say about Charles. How could she shred Adimu's little hope in human decency and tell her what he'd done?

"I promise you. You're not going to die, and everyone will know that you are a girl just like all the others."

IT WAS SUNDAY, and Ukerewe shone under golden rays of sunlight like a giant emerald rising from the indigo waters of Lake Victoria. Much rain had fallen the previous days, and the villagers awakened to crisp air that painted the island with a vibrant palette. The old people rested outside their huts, the young women did their hair, and the children ran along the road, playing made-up games. The mothers nursed their babies in the shade of lush trees, and the men enjoyed their Sunday rest on mats. The aroma of food wafted from every hut in the village of Murutanga.

Jackob's wife stirred the chicken soup. She believed she was pregnant, though wouldn't mention it to her husband until receiving positive results from the Fielding clinic so as not to raise his hopes. If she was, after the birth, she would follow the woman doctor's recommendations to avoid getting pregnant again. Better to have four children and send them to a good school than bring more into the world without being able to give them an adequate education. The world was changing rapidly, and she understood that. She peeked into the bedroom and saw little Charles, who was combing his hair in front of the mirror. He was wearing his best clothes for Mass. Jackob came in the back door, urging his son to hurry. Otherwise they would be late.

"What did you call me?" asked the boy as his father stepped into the bedroom.

"Your real name, Amri," replied Jackob, smiling.

The boy smiled back, took his father's hand, and they set off down the path.

FATHER FRANCIS HAD been ordained little more than a month earlier and was sent to Ukerewe as Father Andrew's replacement. At the end of his first Mass on the island, he had stepped away from the makeshift altar under the baobab and mingled with the faithful. They gathered around him. Francis opened his arms with his palms turned toward the sky and said, "God is in every human being. The life of a human is worth as much as the life of all humanity[25]. If we offend a person, we insult God."

The worshippers looked at each other. An elderly woman opened her mouth. "Father Francis..."

The priest interrupted the woman with a gesture of his hand. "Think about what I have said. Remain with God, and He will remain with you."

The woman insisted. The priest interrupted her again. "Go in peace." He paused for several seconds while he searched with his eyes among those present. "And let there be peace," he added. He returned to the altar and removed his vestments.

The inhabitants of Ukerewe did not know why Mosi no longer celebrated Mass. When he found out what had happened to Adimu at the mine, he locked himself away for a life of solitude. He sat on an old straw chair,

---

[25] In the original Italian text, the author had written...*life of the community.* However, when His Holiness Pope Francis read this sentence, among others of the book, to lend his voice to the social audiobook project, he read it as...*life of all humanity* and the author decided to adopt his modification.

immobile, in a darkened room without the light of a lantern to dispel the gloom.

SARAH PARKED THE Rolls in front of the brown brick prison. She warned Adimu that inside those cheerless walls, behind the iron bars, they'd find Mr. Fielding. Adimu thought of when she and Shida were captives at the compound in the forest, and she felt a pang of pity for the man. Sarah had told her that Charles confessed to a crime that he hadn't committed, and he'd be out of jail once his lawyer cleared up the misunderstanding. Adimu took note that Sarah hadn't mentioned what crime Mr. Fielding confessed to, nor did she ask. A funny feeling swam around the pit of the girl's stomach, and it wasn't a good funny feeling. There were snakes there, and slime. Something was very wrong; she was unable, though, to bring herself to look it in its face. She supposed what was wrong had to do with Mr. Fielding's mine. Had to do with *that* night. She remembered him cradling her; she remembered he mumbled lots of words, the sounds, in Swahili and English, bursting out of his mouth like thunder and lightning when the dark skies would break open; she remembered the machete. Screams. Crying stars. Milky moon and crisp, crisp bone. Howls and screeching: they might have come from her. They might have come from the night itself. Smells—the warm, wet earth, rusty blood. Kerosene. Popobawa [26]. Senses glued together, and she was unable to pull them apart, to sound them out like something difficult that she tried to read and understand, though try as she might, she couldn't. Her mind and eyes wouldn't let her. The terror of that black fabric of a sky had frayed into fragments.

Sarah helped Adimu out of the Rolls Royce. The woman patted the pleats of the girl's new pink dress. The shiny black shoes squeezed Adimu's toes. She felt she looked pretty, and Sarah looked pretty, too, with her glossy red lips. They were dressed better than if they were going to Mass.

"Ready?" Sarah said, gripping Adimu's hand, and she turned toward the jailhouse.

Adimu dug her heels into the sidewalk. She wasn't sure if she was more scared of the jail or the man inside of it. She thought of her *bibi* and the word "stranger."

Sarah turned back to the little girl and saw her trembling. Adimu scrutinized her shoes to avoid Sarah's gaze. She was ashamed of a deep-seated

---

[26] An evil spirit, a shapeshifter.

fear that she didn't understand. Sarah squatted to be level with Adimu and waited several moments for the girl to look her in the face.

When they were eye to eye, Sarah said, "I understand you're afraid, darling," caressing the girl's cheek. "To tell the truth, I'm a little afraid too. But...I do know that Charles loves you, and he loves me, and I know he would never intentionally do anything to hurt us. And he asked us to visit him before we leave Tanzania, so I believe we should. It will do us both good. And you and I are strong together." Sarah hugged Adimu tightly.

"Your family is here," the prison guard called to Charles as he brought him to the cramped waiting room where Sarah and Adimu were sitting on a wooden bench. Woman and girl heard the guard's words and flinched. Both hearts leaped. Charles's heart leaped too. He had rehearsed for this moment all night, had been made hopeful when Sarah agreed to visit. Now the most important business meeting of his life was here. He thought of how his universal solution to all problems had been reaching into his safe for American dollars. What offer might he make Sarah and Adimu that they wouldn't be able to refuse? he wondered.

Cautiously Charles kissed Sarah's cheek and Adimu's head. He observed the place where the girl's arm was no more, and he began to shed tears the way a tired old tree sheds leaves at the end of its season.

"Thank you for visiting me," he finally managed. "I want you to be happy. Whatever it takes. When I get out of here, if you want, you'll never see me again. But if you'd rather, if you would allow it, I'll dedicate the rest of my days to making you happy."

Charles noticed Sarah reach for Adimu's hand, and Adimu clasped her palm.

He knelt, bringing him face to face with Adimu. He could see her fear.

"I want to send you to a private school in Harare where the three of us will live as a family, if you'll allow that. You'll study like any other girl, and you'll be able to be anything you want when you grow up." Looking up at Sarah, Charles said, "And I will be open and honest about everything in my life, always. And we'll be a family."

As though continuing his vows, Sarah said, "And my eyes will be open. No more living in denial. No more obeying you without question. No more following you as your shadow."

Adimu started crying.

"What's wrong, darling?" both Sarah and Charles asked. They quickly glanced at one another, realizing this was their first moment as parents.

"Something in my stomach is telling me this is bad. What were you doing at the mine?" she asked Mr. Fielding.

Charles and Sarah exchanged another glance, their second as parents. Charles bit his lip, unable to lie.

After some time, Sarah said, "Adimu, *Baba* went to save you, to bring you back to me safe and sound. But he got there too late. We will never forgive ourselves for getting to you late. Now we all must forgive each other. Because that's what families do."

Charles's gaze locked onto his wife's. He wept.

Sarah fell to her knees, and the three of them hugged and cried and trembled and prayed and dreamed that one day this monstrous, lightless nightmare might possibly pass, like ancient fables filled with harm, like the seasons of long, hard rains.

THE END

Honest reviews of this book are necessary for our campaign. We genuinely believe that word-of-mouth is the best tool we have to get this story known and advance the success of this campaign.

We thank you for your support and cooperation!

ABOUT THE AUTHOR

CRISTIANO GENTILI is an author and a civil servant, from the Italian region of Tuscany. He is married and has a child.

Since his graduation, where he obtained a BA in political science, a MAs in humanitarian assistance and a PhD in social science, Cristiano's work has taken him to some of the most challenging locations around the world, often dealing with the after effects of war and natural disasters. He currently works in Ukraine, in the hazardous border area with Russia.

In 2011, he went on a personal fact-finding trip to Tanzania, to assess the living conditions of Africans with albinism. From that experience his goal became to raise awareness of the living conditions of African albinos through the #HelpAfricanAlbinos campaign. His novel, Then She Was Born, is the English translation of his book, originally written in Italian.

Cristiano has met with eleven Nobel Peace Laureates, the Dalai Lama and Pope Francis, who have each read a part of his novel and have leant their considerable support to the campaign.

In the case of Pope Francis, Cristiano was invited to an international symposium on Africa at the Vatican, to speak about Africans with albinism. He stayed in the Pope's residence for four days and had a private meeting with him during that time. As a result, the #HelpAfricanAlbinos campaign is now endorsed by Pope Francis as an universal and interreligious message of peace and brotherhood.

Cristiano's next target is to get celebrities to record video messages, just as the Nobel peace laureates and the Pope did, and spread them on social media to increase awareness of the living conditions of Africans with albinism, the last among all others.

The official campaign website is www.HelpAfricanAlbinos.com/en
#HelpAfricanAlbinos

Printed in Great Britain
by Amazon